DRAKAS!

edited by
S.M. Stirling

DRAKAS!

Copyright © 2000 by S.M. Stirling

A Baen Books Original

Baen Publishing Enterprises
P.O. Box 1403
Riverdale, NY 10471
www.baen.com

ISBN: 0-671-31946-9

Cover art by Stephen Hickman

First printing, November 2000

Distributed by Simon & Schuster
1230 Avenue of the Americas
New York, NY 10020

Production by Windhaven Press: Auburn, NH
Printed in the United States of America

CONTENTS

INTRODUCTION, S.M. Stirling 1

CUSTER UNDER THE BAOBAB, William Sanders 4

HEWN IN PIECES FOR THE LORD, John J. Miller 32

WRITTEN BY THE WIND: A STORY OF THE DRAKA,
Roland J. Green 90

THE TRADESMEN, David Drake 122

THE BIG LIE, Jane Lindskold 142

THE GREATEST DANGER, Lee Allred 182

HOME IS WHERE THE HEART IS, William Barton.... 222

THE LAST WORD, Harry Turtledove 248

A WALK IN THE PARK, Anne Marie Talbott 284

HUNTING THE SNARK, Markus Baur 294

UPON THEIR BACKS, TO BITE 'EM, John Barnes 312

THE PEACEABLE KINGDOM, Severna Park 338

INTRODUCTION

To coin a phrase, the 20th century has been the best of times, and the worst of times; the century when smallpox was abolished and the century when a new word, "genocide," entered the lexicon of politics. It started with the serene confidence of the Edwardian Enlightenment at the end of a century free of great international wars, when reason and progress seemed to be rolling forward on a broad invincible front.

Then it took a wrong turning in the slaughters of Passchendale and Verdun, descended into the abyss of Stalingrad, Nanking, Buchenwald and the Gulag. Even the motor of progress, science, turned out to have some very nasty exhaust. For fifty years we hovered on the brink of annihilation, forced to threaten the survival of civilization, if not humanity, to hold totalitarianism in check.

And then, all at once, things got better...

Anyone who studies history eventually runs across a little jingle that goes:

1

> For want of a nail, the shoe was lost;
> For want of a shoe, the horse was lost;
> For want of a horse, the message was lost;
> For want of the message, the battle was lost;
> For want of the battle, the kingdom was
>   lost—
> And all for the want of a horseshoe nail!

What's more, you come to appreciate the essential truth of it. There are broad, impersonal forces at work in history; if Christopher Columbus had died as a child—most children did, in his age—someone else would have discovered the Atlantic crossing soon enough. Basque fishermen may well have crossed to Newfoundland before him; an English expedition set out to America a few years after; the Portugese blundered into Brazil on their way to India (it makes sense, in sailing-ship terms) a few years after that.

The knowledge was there, and the ships, and the civilization that produced them, a strong hungry people ready to burst out upon the world. And so we live in the world the West Europeans made, built on foundations laid by the empires of sailing ships and muskets.

But oh, how the details would be different if it had not been Columbus, but another man a few years later! And how those changes might have rippled on, growing through the years.

So a thought came to me; suppose everything had turned out as *badly* as possible, these last few centuries. Great changes make possible great good and great evil. The outpouring of the Europeans produced plenty of both.

The great free colonies of North America were perhaps the best, for it was here that the great 18th-century upsurge of popular government began, and here the power that broke the totalitarians was founded. My friend Harry Turtledove has imagined a world in which America broke apart in its Civil War, and no strong *United* States was ready to come to the aid of the beleaguered Allies against the Central European aggressors.

Imagine a change even more fundamental. Perhaps the worst product of the great wave of European expansion, before this century of ours, was the South Atlantic system of slaves and plantations. Eventually it faded away—or was blown away by the cannon of Grant and Sherman, although we still feel the after-effects.

What, though, if a fragment of that system had fallen on fertile ground, and grown? Say that the potential of South Africa, so neglected by its Dutch overlords, had fallen prey to it . . . a base for that deadly seed to grow, unchecked by free neighbors, until it was too strong to stop. An Anti-America, representing all the distilled negatives of Western civilization.

From that thought was born the alternate history of the Domination of the Draka. I've chronicled the rise and transformation of that dystopia in four novels.

But a world can be a playground big enough for more than one imagination to run in. Here are stories others have set in that anti-history, a funhouse mirror held up to our own.

William Sanders is a Cherokee; maybe that has something to do with the sardonic irony in the eye he trains on history. Maybe not; how could anyone doubt all is for the best in the train of events that produced we our glorious selves?

Will has produced science fiction and fantasy stories—many of them alternate history—highly regarded by the critics and by his peers. His novels *Journey to Fusang*, *The Wild Blue and the Gray*, and latest *The Ballad of Billy Badass and the Rose of Turkestan* have shown a wild inventiveness worthy of Jonathan Swift, plus an encyclopedic knowledge of history, and a combination of high literary skill and crazed, gonzo abandon that could only have been born on this continent.

Herein we have a George Armstrong Custer who escapes the arrows of the Sioux, only to find that even in another history and on another continent, some things never change . . .

CUSTER UNDER THE BAOBAB

William Sanders

The baobab tree is one of the world's most remarkable vegetable productions. Its soft, swollen-looking trunk may be as much as twenty or thirty feet in diameter; its grotesquely spindly limbs may reach up to two hundred feet toward the African sky.

Anywhere it grows, the baobab is an impressive sight. On the great dead-flat plain of the Kalahari Desert, where the land stretches empty to the horizon and even a cluster of stunted acacia trees is a major visual event, a lone baobab can dominate the entire landscape.

This particular baobab is of no more than average size, but it is still the biggest thing in view in any direction. Beneath its spreading branches, just now, are four men. Three are dead.

The fourth man sits on the ground, his back against the sagging folds of the baobab's thin bark. A lean, long-limbed, long-faced white man, dressed in dusty brown near-rags barely recognizable as having once been a smart military uniform; thinning yellow hair straggles from beneath the broad-brimmed hat that shades his face. His right hand lies on his lap, next to a heavy revolver.

Centurion George Armstrong Custer, of the Kalahari Mounted Police (former Brevet Major General, United State's Cavalry), licks his dry cracked lips. "Libbie," he says, barely aloud, his words no more than a whisper lost in the whine of the wind through the baobab's branches, "Libbie, is this what it all comes to?"

"I don't know, Custer," the Commandant said, ten days ago. (Wasn't it? Custer realizes he is not sure.) "A man of your rank and experience, leading a minor patrol like this? Pretty silly, isn't it?"

"Possibly, sir." Custer stood at attention before the Commandant's desk, face expressionless, classic West Point from crown to boot soles. Not that these Drakians demanded much in the way of military formality—and the Mounted Police weren't even a military organization, even if they did like to put on airs and give themselves fancy titles of rank—but it was, Custer had found, a subtle but effective way to bully Cohortarch Heimbach.

"I need you here," Heimbach continued. "Things to be done, paperwork piled up. Don't stand like that, Centurion," he added peevishly. "This isn't your American army."

"No, sir," Custer said tonelessly, not shifting a hair, keeping his eyes fixed straight ahead above the Commandant's balding head, exchanging stares with the portrait of Queen Victoria that hung on the mud-brick wall. Cohortarch Heimbach was one of the handful of conservatives who still insisted on the fiction of Drakia's membership in the British Empire.

"Things to be done right here," Heimbach repeated. "Instead you want to ride off chasing Bushmen. Tetrarch Leblanc could use the experience, and he's eager to go."

Custer didn't reply. After a moment Heimbach blew out his breath in a long loud sigh. "Oh, all right—"

He fumbled in his desk drawer and got out a short-stemmed pipe and a pouch of tobacco. "Actually," he said, thumbing tobacco into the bowl, "this *is* a bit more than a normal patrol. Seems our little friends, out there, have gone very much too far this time."

Custer waited silently as he lit up. "Two days ago," Heimbach went on after a moment, blowing clouds of foul-smelling blue smoke, "a bunch of Bushmen raided a cattle ranch in the Ghanzi area. Usual sort of thing—cut a cow out from the herd, killed it and butchered it on the spot, you know."

Custer knew. The Bushmen were constantly bringing trouble on themselves with their addiction to cattle-rustling. Of course, living as they did on the edge of bare subsistence, they must find the scrawny Kaffir cattle irresistible targets.

"This time," the Commandant said grimly, "things got out of hand. The rancher happened to show up as they were cutting up the kill. He shot one of them. The others scattered into the bush—but when the damned fool dismounted, one of them put a poisoned arrow into his back."

"Good God," Custer said involuntarily. "They killed a white man?" That was unheard-of; Bushmen were a nuisance but seldom actively dangerous.

Heimbach was nodding. "And so they have to be taught a lesson. Orders from the top, on this morning's wire."

He pointed the pipe stem at Custer, like a pistol. "Which is why I'm not altogether unhappy to let you take this one, Centurion. Some important people want this done right."

Cohortarch Heimbach got up from his desk and went over and stood looking out the glassless front window. Out on the parade ground, an eight-man lochus stood in a single uneven rank, while a big red-faced NCO inspected their rifles. He didn't look happy. Of course sergeants—decurions, Custer corrected himself, damn these people with their classical pretensions—rarely did. Beyond, past the high barbed-wire fence that ringed the little post, the Kalahari shimmered in the midday sun.

"So I'm giving you your wish," the Commandant said, not looking around. "Take the Second Lochus from Leblanc's tetrarchy—that's Decurion Shaw's lot, he's a good man—and of course Boss and his trackers. Ride up to the ranch, pick up the trail, and go after the culprits. You know what to do when you find them."

"Yes, sir." Custer went wooden-faced again. He did know.

"And, of course," Heimbach added, "the same for any other renegade Bushmen you find."

"Yes, sir." Since no Bushman had any legal status whatever—outside of a few bondservants, mostly raised from captured infants and kept as household novelties by aristocratic Drakia families—they were all in effect "renegades" and subject to out-of-hand disposal on sight. Custer, however, did not point this out.

"After all," Heimbach said, "you do, I believe, have some experience of pursuing and punishing savages."

Custer managed not to wince. "Yes, sir," he said once more, face blank, looking at Queen Victoria, who looked back at him without joy.

❖   ❖   ❖

His face is blank now, under its coating of dust; his long bony features register nothing of the voices within:

"Colonel Custer, was it not your mission to pursue and punish the savages?"

"I learned that their forces were overwhelmingly superior to mine. I saw no reason, sir, to lead my men to certain defeat."

"And on what basis did you make this evaluation?"

"My Crow scouts reconnoitered the Sioux encampment and reported it contained thousands of warriors."

"So on the word of a few ... aborigines, you not only abandoned the offensive but ordered a general withdrawal from the area? Colonel, are you aware that expert witnesses have testified that no Indian band has ever been seen in the numbers you allege, in all the history of the frontier?"

"There were enough of them to defeat General Crook six days earlier, on the Rosebud."

"May I remind you, Colonel, that General Crook is not on trial here—"

And at last the dry sour voice of little Phil Sheridan: "It is the finding of this court that on June 24, 1876, Lieutenant Colonel George Armstrong Custer was guilty of dereliction of duty and of cowardice in the face of the enemy, in that he did fail to attack the hostiles as ordered . . . . "

He hears the voices now without bitterness or chagrin; all the old emotions are gone, leaving only a profound and bottomless fatigue. Too tired for fighting old battles, too tired, he thinks dully, ever to fight again—

"Fight them, Autie." Tom Custer, arguing, urging. "They're railroading you. They've been out to get you ever since you exposed the way they're starving the reservation Indians. Now Sheridan's making you the scapegoat for his botched campaign."

Libbie: "Yes, Autie you've got to fight back, it isn't right, they can't do this—"

But of course they could, that was never in doubt, no army ever let a lieutenant colonel fight his own generals, not even a lieutenant colonel who had once been a general himself.

Well, Libbie was gone now, of a fever the doctors said, but then the medical profession did not recognize a broken heart as a cause of death. And Tom, good faithful Tom, resigning his own commission in protest against his brother's disgrace, only to be gunned down on a Kansas street by a vicious thug named Wyatt Earp, whom he had accurately but unwisely accused of cheating at cards.

His eyes move, now, his gaze dropping to the revolver in his lap: the same big English .45 he carried on that last campaign against the Sioux, a good reliable weapon, faster to fire and load than the standard-issue Army Colt. True, in the end there was no occasion to use it. . . .

Not, at least, on anyone else; there were, to be sure, plenty of times afterward when he found himself considering the ultimate alternative. He wonders why he never did it. Maybe, he thinks, I am a coward after all.

But he might have taken that route, in the end, but for the letter: "Dear Genl Custer, pardon my fammilierty but I fot the Rebs under you & now I read about your trobles & I say it is a H—l of a thing after all you done for our Countrie. You shoud come to Drakia, a White man has a real show hear. They got more gold than Callifornea & dimons to—"

He never found the man who wrote the letter; his inquiries, around the gold-field settlements of eastern Archona, drew only shrugs. At first he sought the man to thank him. Later he thought more in terms of killing the well-meaning fool.

The Dominion of Drakia did indeed possess a wealth of gold and diamonds; but, as new arrivals quickly learned, Drakia was no California. All the major fields were firmly in the hands of big combines, the mines big elaborate affairs, worked by armies of slaves.

(Bondservants, the Drakia insisted on calling them, claiming that slavery was extinct and even illegal now. But that was sheer sophistry; the poor devils were slaves, whatever the official terminology, as much as any character of Harriet Beecher Stowe's.)

There was little room here for the romantic figure of the lone prospector. A few remained in the remoter areas—such as that awful Namib Desert, over on the southwest coast, that made the Kalahari look like the Garden of Eden—but their day was rapidly coming to an end.

And anyway, despite all that silliness in the Black Hills, the truth was that George Custer knew virtually nothing about gold or mining; soldiering was the only trade he had ever studied.

Very well, then, he would soldier here. But that idea too came up short against Drakian reality. The Dominion's legions did indeed contain many former Americans, but almost all were ex-Confederates. A man who had fought on the antislavery side, in what was still regarded here as an Abolitionist war, was regarded with grave suspicion by the Drakian command; and a onetime Yankee officer who had been convicted of cowardice, in a campaign against native savages, simply need not apply.

In the end it was Jeb Stuart, of all people (now Strategos Stuart of the Third Legion; the Drakians had easily recognized at least one genius), who stepped in to help. Still the perfect Southern knight, extending a magnanimous hand to a fallen former adversary:

"I am mortified, sir." It came out "Ah am mo'tifahd, suh," it would take more than a decade or so of Drakian residence to obliterate that Virginia drawl. "Even to make such an offer, to a man of your ability—I hope you will not take offense, General Custer, at my temerity."

"Temerity was always your long suit, General Stuart."

"Why, I appreciate that, sir, coming from a man whose audacity I once had all too good cause to know." Smiling, stroking the ends of the long mustache; most of the American immigrants, Custer included, got rid of their whiskers and long hair in the African heat, but count on Stuart to put style above mere comfort. "But as I was saying, the Mounted Police—"

"They're offering me a job as a policeman?"

"Technically, yes. But then the soldier often has to serve as a policeman. After all, our former duties against the Indians could be considered in the nature of police work, could they not?" Stuart smiled again. "And the Mounted Police are practically a military organization in most respects. True, the men are sometimes a trifle rough, but . . . . "

A trifle rough, yes. That was good. That was another voice he had occasion to remember in the time that followed. As for example on the present operation, during the ride north to pick up the trail of the Bushmen who had killed the Drakian rancher.

Riding along beside the little column, looking over his command, he considered that he had never seen a scruffier lot. All wore at least the major components of the KMP's brown cotton uniform—it was comfortable, after all, and free—but each man had felt free to make his own modifications: shirt sleeves and trouser legs hacked off to taste, shapeless slouch hats substituted for the regulation cap, leather cartridge belts festooned with unauthorized private weaponry. Some wore cowboy-style boots in place of the knee-high issue jackboots; none, whatever their choice of footgear, seemed to have heard of polish.

Well, a man's appearance was a poor indicator of his worth; Custer had seen at close quarters the magnificent fighting qualities of ragged, shoeless Confederate troops, let alone the near-naked warriors of the Plains. But he knew these men, had dealt with most of them personally at one time or another—usually for disciplinary offenses or dereliction of duty—and he was under no illusions. Hardcases, they would have been called on the American frontier; excellent shots and skilled horsemen, to be sure, tough as rhinoceros hide and physically brave to the point of recklessness, but constitutionally incapable of accepting discipline, of playing by any rules but their own.

None of the eight ordinary troopers was native Drakian; all had come here from elsewhere, some dreaming of gold and diamonds, some at odds with the governments of their homelands—like the army, the KMP included a considerable number of unreconstructable American rebels—and, though the subject was not safe to talk about, more than a few running from criminal warrants. Custer had seen their kind drinking and raising hell in the cowtowns of the west—or staring out from WANTED posters, or dangling from the ends of ropes.

Of course there were exceptions. Up at the head of the troop, Decurion Shaw sat upright and impeccably uniformed astride his beloved bay mare. Custer had often wondered what Shaw was doing in the KMP; Drakia born, well educated from his speech, and absolutely steady and reliable, he was wholly out of place here. A broken love affair, perhaps, or family trouble; Custer had never inquired. The KMP had one iron rule, never written down but never broken: *Don't ask.*

Out in front of the column rode another exception: old Luther Boss, onetime elephant hunter (and, some said though not to his face, diamond smuggler.) A civilian on contract to the KMP, Boss didn't bother even going through the motions of looking military; he wore loose flapping shorts, exposing big bony knees, and a bright-patterned *dashiki* shirt such as the blacks wore up along the coast. A huge dirt-brown hat shaded his weathered face. Flanking him, dressed in castoff rags of KMP uniform, his two black trackers Ubi and Jonas sat easily on their tough little Cape ponies.

A dozen men, good God, what a pathetic command for a man who had once led regiments . . . but in this case there was no choice; the few small waterholes of the Kalahari would never support a larger mounted force, not at this time of year. As it was they would be pushing their luck.

The patrol got even smaller next day. As they left the isolated ranch where the cattleman had been killed, Trooper Lange's horse pulled up lame. Custer thought he didn't look terribly disappointed at having to drop out. The others called out various derisive remarks as Lange led his horse slowly back toward the ranch.

"What the hell," one of the troopers remarked as they rode on. "Already lost a man and we ain't even got started. Bad sign."

Custer turned in his saddle. "No," he said with forced joviality, "it's a good sign. Thirteen men, everybody knows that's an unlucky number. Now we're only twelve."

The trooper gave Custer a long stare. "Shit," he said finally. A wiry little man named Pace, he was from Texas and seemed to think that proved something. "How do you add that up? I don't see but ten of us."

Then he glanced forward and made a face. "Oh, you counted them two niggers? Hell, ain't that just like a bluebelly?"

The man riding behind him, a burly North Carolinian named Garvin, laughed out loud. "Jesus Christ, Centuri'n, a nigger ain't a man. Ain't you learned that yet?"

His voice was loud enough to carry to the head of the troop, as Pace's had been, but if Ubi and Jonas understood they gave no sign. Luther Boss, however, looked around and gave both men a glare that would have stripped the hide off a hippo.

"Bluebellies," Pace said, ignoring the old man, and shook his head. "I'll never understand 'em."

The Kalahari is unusual, as deserts go; nothing like the naked wastes of the Sahara or the nearby Namib, and in fact quite a lively place, considering the almost complete lack of surface water for most of the year. The flat sandy plain wears a patchy covering of tall tough grasses, laced with hidden thorny growths; clumps of thornbush and wind-bent acacias dot the landscape, while along the crests of the occasional rocky hills groves of mongongo trees offer shade and edible fruit. Giraffe and various kinds of antelope manage to live there, and jackals and brown hyenas; even, in the slightly wetter north, lions and elephants.

In the rainy season, from around the end of October through the following March, an uninformed observer might not recognize the Kalahari as a desert at all. Herds of animals come to the pans and waterholes, while the grasses and trees turn cheerfully green.

By April the rains have ended; the pans begin to shrink and go dry. Hunting is good, though, because the animals cluster more densely around the remaining sources of water; and the temperature drops, over the next few months, until by June the days are pleasantly cool and the nights downright cold.

Now it was the end of August, and getting hot again, the grasses turned yellow and the pans long since gone dust-dry. The animals had mostly migrated north, toward the Okavango country; there was always a rise in cattle-rustling incidents, this time of year, when the scarcity of game drove the Bushmen to take desperate risks.

Which, Custer reflected as the troop moved westward, was why this patrol had to deliver results; time was running out. A few more weeks and the central Kalahari would be almost impassible for any humans but Bushmen—and even they would be holed up around the few permanent waterholes, traveling as little as possible in the terrible heat—and would stay that way until the late-October rains. Even now, it was hard to imagine how anyone or anything could live in this parched desolation.

Yet life there was. Trooper Caston found that out on the third day, when he went to relieve his bowels next to a clump of thornbush and surprised a black mamba.

"I don't like it," Custer said as they rode away from the crude grave. "We never left our dead behind on the Plains."

"We have no choice," Luther Boss pointed out. "Carry a dead man along, in this heat? Impossible."

"It'll be all right," Decurion Shaw added. "When we get back the Commandant will send out a party to recover the remains."

That was nonsense and they all knew it. All the rocks they had piled on top of the grave had represented nothing more than extra exercise for the men—and for the brown Kalahari hyenas, who would have the body exhumed before it was dark.

"It was so fast," Custer said wonderingly.

Luther Boss grinned, big yellow crooked teeth surrounded by bristling white whiskers. "A mamba's a bad customer," he said. "Just another reason to be careful in this country. You don't get but one mistake."

Two days later they found the Bushman camp.

There was no question of moving into position and making a textbook attack; no one, certainly not white men with horses, could hope to sneak up on Bushmen in their own country. The only possible tactic was to move in fast and strike before the quarry could escape.

Even so, the Bushmen were already scattering as the riders charged, little yellow-brown forms vanishing into the tall yellow-brown grass. The slower ones, the elders and the women who paused to snatch up children, were less lucky.

It was over in a very short time. The troopers swept in, yipping like wild dogs, firing their pistols— the Drakia T-2 rifle was an excellent infantry weapon, but much too long and clumsy for horseback use— or simply riding the Bushmen down. Custer saw a pregnant woman trip and fall in front of Decurion Shaw's horse; her mouth opened as the hooves struck her, but her shriek was lost in the racket. Another woman, running fast despite the baby slung on her back, almost made the cover of the grass, but Pace reined his horse to a stop and held his revolver in both hands and took careful aim and knocked her over with a single shot.

Custer's own sidearm remained unfired, almost forgotten in his hand. He watched the butchery from the shade of a lone acacia tree, paralyzed by unexpected memories, pictures flashing in his mind like a magic-lantern show: the Cheyenne camp on the Washita, the troopers firing and the Indians running out of the teepees and being shot down in the snow while the band played "Garryowen." And the old man, white hair hanging to his shoulders, who had materialized suddenly through the falling snow, eyes full on Custer's face, pointing a long bony finger, calling out something in Cheyenne just before a .45 slug cut him down. . . .

At the time it had been no more than a neat bit of professional work, tactical surprise against a usually clever enemy; but the satisfaction had given way, with time, to—not guilt, no, a soldier could never feel guilt at carrying out his orders, more a weary disgust.

The recollection sickened him, now, as did the pathetic spectacle before him. He shook his head angrily and looked around as Luther Boss came riding up. The scout's big double-barreled rifle rested across his saddle-bow, but Custer knew he hadn't fired it; there would have been no missing the blast of that old cannon.

"Ubi and Jonas went after a couple of the ones who ran," Luther Boss reported.

Custer made no reply. The scout scratched his beard and added, "They say these aren't your culprits. The ones who killed the rancher, the ones we've been following, were Kung. These are Gwi. Southern tribe, don't know why they'd be this far north."

Custer shrugged. "It doesn't matter," he said tiredly. "You know that."

Luther Boss nodded heavily. There was no need to spell it out. A white man had been killed, an example had to be made; there had never been any question of selective action. Anyway, Drakian policy—never officially stated, but universally understood—was that the Bushmen were basically a species of pest, to be eradicated as soon as possible. (Though a few old-school aristocrats, who sometimes enjoyed the sport of hunting them with dogs, had been agitating for the establishment of preserves for Bushmen and other challenging game.)

"We'll bivouac here for the night," Custer went on, "and then tomorrow we'll get on the trail of the others again. How far is it to the next waterhole?"

"Long way," Luther Boss said. "Hell of a ride, in fact—"

Later, no one could figure out where the old man had come from. The grass was too short and thin, all around the acacia tree, to cover even a Bushman's approach. He was just *there*, all of a sudden, standing no more than a dozen feet away: an old Bushman, the oldest Custer had ever seen. He couldn't have stood much over five feet and his nearly naked body was nothing but bones and dried-apricot skin. He was pointing a finger at Custer, calling out a string of tongue-clicking syllables, his voice high and hoarse.

Custer jerked back in his saddle, eyes wide; he almost screamed, but his throat had closed shut.

There was a loud flat *bang* and a quick twisting shock against his right palm. The old man stood still for a moment and then toppled backward, limp before he hit the ground, like some assemblage of dry sticks. Custer looked down in amazement at the smoking revolver that he had not aimed, had not even been conscious of firing, had in fact forgotten he still held.

Decurion Shaw rode up, holding his service pistol muzzle upward. "Sorry, sir," he said to Custer. "Can't think how we let him get past us like that." He looked down at the tiny body and then back at Custer, smiling. "Good shot, Centurion."

Custer made a vague gesture with his left hand. For the moment, he had no words. He had a strange mad thought that if he tried to talk, he would find himself speaking some savage tongue.

They settled in around the waterhole, the troopers tethering and unsaddling the horses, then wandering briefly about the Bushman camp, examining the bodies and commenting on their marksmanship, picking up souvenirs from among the Bushmen's abandoned possessions. One man was fingering a little bow, like something a child would make to play Indians, and a couple of arrows, being very careful with the latter; the slightest scratch from the poisoned tip could be mortal. Another man found a collection of ostrich-egg shells, the Bushmen's water container of choice, in one of the tiny grass huts; the other troopers gathered around, drinking and laughing and filling their canteens.

Ubi and Jonas came out of the bush, grinning, and spoke to Luther Boss.

"They caught a couple of women," the old hunter told Custer. "Had themselves a little entertainment, too, I'd wager."

The trackers looked at each other and then at Custer, still grinning. They were an odd-looking pair; Ubi was tall and long-limbed and very black—Herero, he claimed, with a dash of Zulu and a touch of Hottentot—but Jonas was almost as small as the bodies on the ground, and close to the same color. His mother had been full-blood River Bushman, taken in childhood from her home in the Okavango marshes by Ba-tswana slave raiders and sold to a brothel in Virconium; he had, he admitted cheerfully, no idea who or what his father had been.

Both men had been with Luther Boss for a very long time. Technically they were his bondservants, as much his property as his horse or his rifle. In reality the relationship was obviously more complex, with an easy familiarity that annoyed some white men.

"They say maybe eight people got away," the scout continued. "Maybe nine. They think all men."

Whom, of course, they hadn't pursued too closely in the high grass; why risk a poisoned arrow when there was safer and, as a bonus, rapeable prey to be had?

Custer said, "Decurion, have the men haul these

bodies clear of the area. Take them a good long way out, or the hyenas will be spooking the horses all night."

The waterhole turned out to be a pretty desperate affair, even for the Kalahari in August. The sandy soil was thin here, and next to the Bushmen's camp the rock was fully exposed in a low rough outcrop, which some ancient force had cracked right down the middle. The water was deep at the bottom of the cleft, out of sight and very nearly out of reach.

But Jonas took off all his clothes and wriggled down into the fissure, clutching a gourd dipper taken from a Bushman shelter, while Ubi stood ready to lower the canteens down after him. Custer watched, amazed; it didn't seem possible a human being could fit himself into such a tight space, let alone move about down there.

"Hewers of wood and drawers of water," Decurion Shaw said to Custer, "eh, Centurion?"

The next day's ride was a very long and hard one, just as Luther Boss had predicted. But at the end there was a good waterhole, more accessible than the last, and as the men made camp Ubi and Jonas found fresh Bushman sign.

"They say we'll catch them tomorrow, sure," Boss reported, and Custer let out a grateful sigh. With any luck this business would be over soon; and then back to the post and a sensible settled adjutant's life, never again to trouble Cohortarch Heimbach with requests for patrol duty. . . .

But in the middle of the night he woke to the shouts of men and the screams of horses and a loud dry crackling roar that he recognized even before his eyes opened and saw the licking red-orange glow against the night. "Fire," a man yelled, and another, "Brush fire, God *damn*—" and then Shaw's bellow: "The horses! See to the horses!"

Too late, though, for that; as Custer fought free of the blanket and got to his feet he could see the horses silhouetted against the wavering wall of flame, rearing and pawing the air and lunging against the picket ropes, shrieking in pain and fear. Black shapes of men moved among them, trying to grab them and lead them away, but the beasts were too far gone in the blind brainless panic of their kind, and the fire was already on top of them. First one horse and then another broke free and charged away into the dark; then here they all came in a rumbling rush, while men sprinted to get out of the way.

A horse went by dragging a man, his arm apparently tangled in the broken tether rope; in the flickering light Custer recognized Decurion Shaw, his mouth open in a high agonized yell that died away as the horse dragged him off into the night.

The fire was coming right through camp now, flames leaping up high as a man's head, the dry tall grasses blazing up with almost explosive speed. "To the rock," Custer shouted, but it was an unnecessary command; the men were already scrambling hastily atop the rock outcrop, coughing and cursing and slapping out smoldering patches on their clothes.

Custer hurried after them, grabbing up his gunbelt and his hat and boots. Clambering sockfooted up the steep side of the outcrop, he slipped and almost lost his balance. But then Luther Boss's voice said, "Here," and a big hand pulled him upward, and a moment later he was standing on top of the rock, staring disbelievingly out over the blazing desert. All around the rock the thornbush clumps were starting to catch fire, with a crackling sound like an old man's dry hating laughter.

Later, when the worst of the fire had passed, Custer did a quick headcount. Three men were missing: Trooper Mizell, who had been on sentry duty, and

another man named Butler, and of course Decurion
Shaw.

Butler they found first, next morning, though it was
not easy to identify him. His clothing had been mostly
burned away and his face and body were blackened.
His left leg stuck out at an unnatural angle. "Broken leg," Luther Boss said after a quick examination.
"Probably got run over by a horse, couldn't get clear
in time. Like as not the smoke got him before the
fire did."

Mizell had fallen on a relatively bare patch of earth;
the fire had hardly touched him, except to smudge
his face a little, and to singe the feathers off the tiny
arrow that protruded from the small of his back.

"God-damned murdering little sand monkeys," Pace
said. "It was them set the fire, too, wudn't it?"

"Almost certainly," Luther Boss agreed.

As the sun climbed into the sky they fanned out
across the flat, searching for the horses. It was a
hopeless job; even Ubi and Jonas couldn't find trails
across that charred and still-smoking ground. They
did find Decurion Shaw, half a mile or so from the
waterhole, his right arm almost severed at the wrist.
He had, quite literally, no face left; the flock of
vultures that rose flapping and squawking from the
body, as the other men approached, had finished what
the dragging had begun.

At last Custer ordered a halt to the search. The
horses were long gone and nothing could be gained
by all this wandering about in the sun; they would
need all their strength for the walk back.

Most of their equipment had been lost or ruined
in the fire; they had the scorched and filthy clothes
they wore, and their sidearms, and not much else.
They picked through the smoldering site of their
camp, finding little. Only four rifles remained in
working condition, and not much ammunition for
those.

And only nine men left, Custer thought numbly,
counting of course their fine leader; a third of the
command lost . . . . Even if I had attacked at Little
Bighorn, the Indians could not possibly have inflicted
such losses.

Next day they started back.
It had taken all day to make the journey between
waterholes on horseback. It was very soon obvious
that it would take longer than that to do it on foot.
The going was slow and hard, once they were clear
of the burned area; tough bushes and vines hid
beneath the tall grass, snagging clothes and tearing
skin, and here and there broad patches of soft sand
dragged at their feet, while a steady hot wind stung
their faces and dried their throats and drove dust
particles into eyes and nostrils. Their boots had been
designed for riding, not walking; everyone had blisters by the middle of the first day. And the water was
not really enough, not in that heat; they should have
been carrying two or three canteens apiece but there
were not that many left intact, most having burst in
the fire when their contents boiled.

Ubi and Jonas led the way, backtracking the patrol's
trail from the previous day. Their heads were down
and they muttered to each other. Luther Boss gave
Custer a sardonic grin. "They say this patrol is under
a curse."

"Tell them to be quiet," Custer said irritably.
Thinking: the patrol, or its commander?

They camped that night in a grove of acacias,
nibbling sparingly at what food they had managed to
salvage. In the morning Ubi and Jonas were gone.

"Deserted," Luther Boss said blankly. "I can't
believe they did that. We've been together through
worse than this."

Pace laughed, an ugly hoarse cackle. "What's the

matter, old man, did your faithful darkies take off?"
He shook his head. "Thought they were your God-
damned little brothers, didn't you?"

One of the other troopers, a thin redheaded boy
named Hankins, said, "My pa had all these niggers
on the old home place, back in Virginia. Never
whupped 'em, fed 'em good, he really thought they
loved their ol' massa. Broke his heart when they all
left with the first Yankee column to come through."

The old hunter seemed not to hear. He stared out
over the desert with sad red-rimmed eyes, mutter-
ing to himself, too low for the words to be understood; till at last Custer took his arm and said gently,
"Come on, Luther. You'll have to lead us now."

The second day's march was even harder than the
first. The sun seemed hotter, the bush denser, the
open stretches rockier; that was how it felt, at any
rate, and certainly there was no doubt that the water
situation was much worse—for Ubi and Jonas, they
discovered while breaking camp, had thoughtfully
helped themselves to four of the canteens.

Late in the afternoon they reached the Bushman
campsite and threw themselves on the ground around
the waterhole, only to find that—as Custer had
feared—there was no relief here. The cleft in the rock
was too narrow, the water too far down; none of them
could get within reach. Only Pace and Hankins, the
smallest men in the group, even tried; and Pace gave
up immediately, after getting dangerously stuck.

Hankins, however, refused to quit. "I can do it,"
he cried, wriggling an inch or two downward in the
fissure, lacerating his skin against the rough rock but
paying no mind. He squirmed himself into a new
position, his right arm disappearing into the depths
of the crack. "Just a little fu'ther—"

His eyes went suddenly huge; his mouth opened.
"Oh, shit," he said softly, and then he screamed, and

kept on screaming as they hauled him free. His right hand had already begun to swell.

The scorpions of the Kalahari are not as instantly lethal as the mamba. It took Hankins the rest of the afternoon to die. They piled rocks atop the body, having neither tools nor energy to dig a grave.

"Cursed," Luther Boss said, sitting down next to Custer in the evening, resting his back against an acacia's spindly trunk. He picked up something white from the ground: a fragment of ostrich-egg shell. The troopers had smashed all those they found, the day of the massacre, after draining their contents; you never left anything that might help the survivors go on surviving.

"Africa is cursed," Boss went on in a strange voice. "The whole world is under a curse. A curse called the white man."

"I don't agree." Custer didn't feel like talking, but the old man was obviously distraught. "The black Africans used to kill Bushmen, and each other, even when they had the country to themselves. You know that."

"True." Boss nodded slowly. "Yes, that's true. I was wrong. The name of the curse is mankind."

Just before sunrise Luther Boss shot himself. The noise was tremendous, waking everyone at once. They gathered around, Custer holding a torch from the fire, and stared. The big double rifle hadn't left much of Boss's head.

"Crazy old turd," Garvin said, "what'd he do that for?"

In the gray light of false dawn the four survivors piled a few token rocks atop the body and moved out. The trail was fairly easy to follow at first, but then they lost it in a big patch of soft sand and it was a long hot time before they found it again. By now the sun was high and the water almost gone.

Trooper Evans was a dark, husky, taciturn Welshman

with a record of disciplinary infractions, mostly involving drunkenness; he had soldiered well on this patrol, though, doing his share and never complaining. About midday, as they crossed an open sandy space, he suddenly stopped, turned half around, said, "Christ," and fell unconscious to the ground, his face very pale.

"Heat stroke," Pace said, feeling Evans's wrists and forehead. "Seen it on cattle drives."

"What do we do?" Garvin asked.

"Not a damn thing we can do," Pace said, straightening up. "Pour water on him, only we got no water. Get him in the shade, only there ain't no shade anywhere close. He's a goner."

They loosened Evans's clothing, fanned his face a little with his hat; it made no difference. In less than an hour he was dead.

"We'll have to bury him here," Custer said. "Find rocks—"

"Naw," Pace said flatly. "I ain't toting no more rocks. It's too hot and we got too far to go."

Garvin nodded, folding his arms. Custer said, "I'm giving you men a direct order," and knew immediately he'd made a mistake.

Pace snorted. "You don't pull no more rank on us, bluebelly." His hand dropped to the butt of his revolver. "You want to try us?"

Garvin unslung his rifle from his back. "Yeah," he agreed. "Come ahead. Show us what a big hero you are."

Pace peeled back sun-split lips in a grin. "Like you showed them Injuns, huh? Shit," he said. "You ain't gonna do nothing. Just like that bluebelly captain back home, wanted to take me in and hang me for shooting one of his uppity black nigger soldiers. He didn't have the guts and neither do you. Come on, Roy."

Contemptuously, ostentatiously, Pace turned his back and began walking away, followed after a moment by Garvin. Neither man looked back; and after a moment, stumbling and staggering, Custer followed them.

They came to the baobab just as the sun was going down. "Good a place as any," Pace said. "Let's get a fire going."

"What for?" Garvin asked. "It ain't cold and we sure-God got nothing to cook."

"Yeah, but it'll keep the hyenas away." Pace picked up a fallen branch and broke it over his knee. He had to make three tries; they were all very weak by now. " 'Course they're gonna get us anyway, but I don't want 'em eating on me till I'm dead."

Custer sat on the ground, leaning against the baobab, hearing the voices but paying no attention. It didn't matter now, after all. There was no longer any hope of making it to the next waterhole. Pace was right: they would be lucky if they were dead before the vultures and the hyenas got to them.

They got the fire going just as it got dark. That was when the Bushman appeared.

He came out of the bush, into the circle of fire-light, walking steadily and straight toward them: a skinny little man, naked except for a skimpy hide loincloth. His flat childlike face was without expression; his eyes stared straight ahead.

Garvin said, "Son of a *bitch*," and reached for his rifle.

"Wait," Custer said urgently. "Look what he's got."

In both hands, held out in front of him like an offering, the Bushman held a large white ostrich-egg shell.

"Water," Garvin said, and licked his lips. "Lord God."

Pace got up from the ground and walked forward to meet the Bushman. He took the eggshell very gently from the small hands and hefted it in both of his. "Damn," he said softly. "It's full."

He raised the big eggshell and put his lips to the opening at the top. His whole body seemed to quiver as he took a long, throat-bobbing drink.

"Oh, Jesus, that's good," he said, lowering the eggshell, holding it out to Garvin. "Roy?"

Garvin's hands were shaking. "Careful," Pace warned as the big man raised the eggshell to drink. "You drop that, we're dead."

The Bushman was still standing there, a couple of paces from the fire. He held out one hand, palm upward. Custer said, "He wants to trade. For God's sake give him something."

Pace's face fairly lit up. "Oh, sure—"

Custer had never seen a man draw a gun so fast; Pace's hand barely appeared to move, yet suddenly the long-barreled revolver was in his hand. Custer cried, "*No*," but the sound of the shot drowned out his voice.

"There, sand monkey," Pace said as the Bushman fell to the ground. "Don't say I never gave you nothing."

"You fool," Custer said tiredly. "You evil murderous little swine. He could have gotten us out of this. He could have gotten us home."

"Shit." Pace holstered his pistol. "We're gonna be okay now. That's enough water to make the next hole. Hell," he said, grinning, "you ask us nice, we might even let you have some—"

He stopped. A puzzled look came over his face. "Huh," he said, and rubbed his chin in an odd motion. "Hey, Roy, I feel kinda—"

He took a couple of aimless little steps. "*Uh*," he grunted, and fell face forward into the fire.

"What," Garvin said, and dropped the eggshell. As it shattered on the rocky ground he made a strangled sound in the back of his throat and collapsed amid the white fragments.

Custer watched, unmoving and without any great

interest, as the two men kicked and flopped and writhed and then lay still. On the far side of the fire he could see the dead Bushman's eyes, still open, staring at him. The small round face seemed to be smiling.

Now, as the sun breaks clear of the eastern horizon, Custer looks at the bodies and then up at the circling vultures. He wonders how much longer they will wait. Not much longer, he guesses, and puts his hand over the gun in his lap, which is still warm from firing at the hyenas all night. He is almost out of ammunition. Perhaps he should take Pace's gunbelt, or Garvin's rifle.

He gets to his feet, very slowly, his movements those of a very old man, or perhaps a sleepwalker. He stands for a moment gazing about him, at the empty grass-covered plain and the enormous sky.

"Oh, Libbie," he whispers, hearing now the tiny sound behind him, turning, feeling an almost gentle thumping sensation halfway down his right thigh; looking down, now, entirely without surprise, at the ridiculous little arrow sticking barely an inch into his leg. "Libbie—"

John Miller resides in the arid lands of the southwest, an environment not totally different from the Sudanese deserts of this story. He has written for graphic novels, and some highly inventive stories for the great *Wild Cards* alternate history series.

Herein he tells a tale of the great Christian hero Charles "Chinese" Gordon, an unwitting accomplice of the Draka in a much darker Africa . . .

HEWN IN PIECES
FOR THE LORD

John J. Miller

"It's not the heat, so much," William Hicks said as he took a sip of chilled wine from a delicately-stemmed crystal goblet, "it's the humidity. Bally muggy for a desert."

Hicks had retired as a colonel in the British Army six months earlier, but finding the prospect of living on half-pay unpalatable, had joined the Draka, who were desperate for experienced command officers. Within the last decade and a half the Domination had added vast African territories, but their control over some of these new lands was nominal at best. Hicks, who had never even stepped on African soil before joining the Draka, had immediately been given the rank of strategos, handed a legion of Janissaries, and ordered to pacify the territory once known as the Sudan.

Merarch Kevin Harrison, his chief of staff, mopped his brow and dropped the sodden handkerchief on the camp table. Harrison was an ex-soldier of the Confederacy who'd been a Draka for a decade. He'd spent most of those years in the Sudan and in fact had been a tetrach in the expeditionary force that had brought this hellish country into the Domination. His job now was to provide the newly appointed strategos with the benefit of his local experience.

The officers were sitting in the shade cast by the canvas awning of the command tent, taking afternoon tea as their legion settled into the day's encampment. They were somewhere in the northern Sudanese desert, chasing an army of rebellious natives who had so far proved remarkably elusive.

"Humid, yes sir." Harrison preferred tea to wine, and beer to tea, but when in field camp you do as the strategos does, even if the strategos knew less about deserts than a bloody penguin.

Hicks held his empty goblet up for the Janissary orderly, standing somewhat at attention near the wine bucket, to re-fill. He waved his other hand vaguely at the desert.

"I know the Nile's in full flood, just over there-away's, keeping Fuzzy Wuzzy off our backs, but when the sun goes down the damn mosquitoes are almost as bloodthirsty as the Mahdi's chaps. Haw. Haw."

"Yes, sir." Harrison didn't care for the sweet wine, but the ice, caravaned regularly into camp in straw-wrapped blocks, slipped soothingly down his throat.

"Though I expect the rain will cool things off."

"Rain?" Harrison looked at Hicks as if his superior had suddenly been stupefied by heat stroke. "I don't think it'll rain, sir. It *never* rains this time of year in the Sudan."

"Well, why's it thundering, then?"

"Thundering?"

Harrison frowned, concentrating. He'd been in artillery while in the Confederate Army and he'd paid for that with diminished hearing. After a moment of concentration, he more felt it rather than heard it himself, a low rumble spilling across the empty desert like the droning of countless angry wasps. He jumped to his feet, knocking over the camp chair and spilling chilled wine all over tiffin as a tetrach raced across the bivouac to the command tent, sweating and disheveled, his face red from heat and fear.

"Fuzzy Wuzzys, sir, thousands of them!"

He pointed desperately at the ridge over his shoulder. Cresting it, shimmering in the heat waves rising off the sand were thousands of the black, green, and red battle flags borne by the hairy, half-naked Sudanese tribesmen they called Fuzzy Wuzzys. With the flag bearers came battle drummers, beating a wild rattatatat on their tin drums that sounded like thunder rolling across the desert. With them came spearmen and swordsmen and archers and even some riflemen, rapidly descending by the thousands upon the surprised camp.

"Bloody hell," Hicks said.

I.

Charles George Gordon was tired.

All his life he'd possessed an indefatigable reserve of energy that he could draw on to get him through any situation, but somewhere, somehow, he'd lost it. It had happened recently, right about the time he'd turned fifty and resigned his commission in the British

Army. This evening, he thought, was proving particularly difficult.

Gordon had always disliked social gatherings and public functions, and he'd always been ill at ease in the presence of women. He was therefore doubly uncomfortable at a dinner party with the cream of Alexandrian society where he was surrounded by curious—and bold—Draka women eager to meet him.

Alexander von Shrakenberg was the host. The setting was the dining hall of his Alexandrian manor, the largest, grandest dining hall that Gordon had ever seen. Considering that he'd endured many such affairs in many great homes in many big cities while he'd been in the British army, that was saying a lot.

But, back then, Gordon could afford to be eccentric. He could pick and choose which invitations to accept and which to decline, and actually he'd declined most of them. His relative isolation from society had hurt his career, of course, but he didn't care for the vain-glories of fame.

Much, a sly voice whispered silently in his mind.

Gordon patted his lips with his linen napkin.

Down, Agag, he said silently to his private inner demon. *I would think you'd be very happy with this evening. The pomp, the glamour, the vanity of it will give you much ammunition for our debate . . . later . . .*

Agag slipped away, content, perhaps, to merely observe for awhile, and Gordon was glad to be rid of him, if only for awhile. Agag never completely vanished. He lived in some deep, dark crevice of Gordon's soul, popping out at the most inopportune times, braying like a fame-starved jackass when Gordon most desired to be humble, silent, and Christian. By naming him, by actually engaging him in argument, Gordon refused to accept the fact that Agag was really a part of him. He was a piece hewn apart from Gordon's whole, because the attitude he represented was unChristian.

Gordon relinquished his fish plate to one of the legion of servants who were ferrying food from the manor's vast kitchen in seemingly endless rounds. Gordon liked to eat as much as the next man, but apparently not as much as his host, Alexander von Shrakenberg. Von Shrakenberg was young, not much over thirty, but unlike most of the Draka Gordon had met, was already fleshy. If he kept up this pace of eating and drinking he'd be uncontestedly fat within a very few years. He was also quite jolly for a Draka, full of smiles and had what seemed to be a genuinely hearty laugh. His vast holding on the outskirts of the Egyptian city of Alexandria consisted of cotton fields and associated mills. The manor at the estate's heart was huge and decorated in expensive, luxurious, but, Gordon conceded, quite good taste. Besides his cotton plantation, Von Shrakenberg was also connected with the Alexandria Institute, the foremost scientific conglomerate on the continent. Gordon had to get the Institute's approval if he hoped for his plan come to fruition and The Plan, as he thought of it, was now all he had to live for.

Gordon had had an extremely full and adventurous life. He'd been a career soldier, but one more honored by foreign nations than his own. A field marshall in both the Chinese and Ottoman armies, he'd also fought in the Crimea, produced the first accurate maps of the Danube River and its tributaries, been the Governor-General of the Sudan, surveyed the Holy Lands, and discovered the location of the Garden of Eden.

He'd always had a reputation as an independent eccentric, heedless of conventional wisdom and eager to flout higher authority in the name of justice. Though a devout fundamentalist Christian, he was not a bigot. He believed that every man should be left to worship his own particular god in his own particular way, as long as he worshiped *some* god.

Recently it seemed as if perhaps the controversy that he'd thrived on as a younger man had finally caught up to him. The British Army had no more use for him. Other countries he'd served no longer existed, devoured by the relentless Draka beast. He was tired of the military, anyway. As he'd learned during his tenure as Governor-General of the Sudan, all the blood, sweat, and tears in the world mattered nought when politicians arbitrarily drew lines on maps and instituted policy with eyes solely on their pocketbooks.

After he'd resigned his commission in the British Army, Gordon, recalling conversations he'd had as a young man with de Lesseps, the father of the Suez Canal, decided that his legacy to the world would be what he now thought of as "The Plan," a scheme to dam the Nile River and make it the longest navigable waterway in the world. Since the Draka now owned the Nile like they owned the rest of Africa, Gordon had to plead his case before them. They were good listeners, but tightfisted with both money and authority. Von Shrakenberg was sympathetic to Gordon's Plan, but by no means was he the only Draka whom Gordon had to convince of its feasibility.

To this end Gordon had suffered endless discussion, debate, and formal dinners. This night Gordon's immediate table companions were sisters of Edith von Shrakenberg, his host's wife. Both were young, lean, beautiful, and much too predatory for Gordon's comfort. Katharine, on Gordon's left, was unmarried. Amelia, on his right, was married to the merarch who sat across the table from Gordon, but that didn't prevent her from sending welcoming glances Gordon's way. He did his best to ignore her, but almost dropped his fork when during the peacock pie she put a hand under the table high up on his inner thigh.

Before Gordon could think of a suitable remonstrance, her sister Katharine said suddenly, "You have the clearest, bluest eyes I have ever seen, Strategos

Gordon, and such fine hair and features. We could have beautiful children together."

"Ah, er." He firmly grasped the hand massaging his leg under the table and removed it from his thigh. "Well, er. I am retired from the military," he said stiffly. "Just call me, ah, Charles."

"Charles." Katharine purred like a cat, licking her lips at the taste of his name, the tip of her pink tongue visible behind her even white teeth.

Gordon had the sudden vision of another hand reaching under the table towards his body, and barely suppressed a shiver. He looked urgently about for a means of escape. Fortunately the dinner finally seemed to be on the verge of breaking up, but then he'd be forced to endure—

"Now Katharine, Amelia . . ." Somehow Edith von Shrakenberg had come up unnoticed behind them, pushing her ungainly stomach ahead of her like a tug chivvying a laden barge. She was grossly pregnant, looking as if she would drop the baby at any moment. "We can't monopolize the field marshall's time, I'm afraid."

Gordon got hastily to his feet. He was a short man, not much taller than his pregnant hostess, and much slighter than her in her current state.

"I no longer use military titles," he said, with more than a little relief in his voice. He smiled. "Besides, neither China or the Ottoman Empire hardly exists any more. They've both been swallowed by your Domination."

Edith von Shrakenberg smiled prettily. "Politics." She waved it away. "I have other things on my mind lately. Ooohhh."

"Are you all right, madam?" Gordon took a step towards her, a concerned look on his face.

"Yes, certainly," she smiled again, palely. "The boy has kicked me." She reached out and took Gordon's hand. "Do you wish to feel him?"

She tugged his hand towards her swollen stomach. Gordon said, "No!" a bit more loudly than he'd intended, and pulled away. "No. Er, quite all right, I assure you."

He was terrified that he'd insulted her beyond all bounds, but her expression didn't change.

"Well then, come, Mr. Gordon," she said, "there's something I must show you." She held out her arm.

"Quite." He bowed to his dinner companions, and murmured goodbyes, taking his hostess's arm as she led him away.

"Poor Mr. Gordon," she said, not unsympathetically. They left the immense dining room and walked down a carpeted hallway that was as dark and quiet as the dining room had been colorful and loud. "You must be quite unused to the forthrightness of Draka women."

Gordon inclined his head as she patted his hand. "You are correct, madam."

"Well, that's not unusual for you Englishmen. Or Scotsmen, if you prefer." They had stopped at a door ornately carved from rich, dark wood.

"It is all the same to me, madam."

Gordon frowned as he noticed the distasteful scene which had been hewn into the dark richness of the wood. A man with the classic chiseled Draka features stood in a horse-drawn chariot as it was pulled between ranks of crucified serfs—men and women both. The execution of the carving was as exquisite as the subject matter was repellent. The relief seemed vaguely familiar to Gordon—then he realized that it represented a famous scene in the career of Alexander von Shrakenberg's grandfather, Augustus, who had put down a serf revolt a generation earlier by crucifying five thousand of them—whether they'd been personally involved in the rebellion or not.

Edith took both his hands in hers. "No need to be shy, my dear Mr. Gordon." She leaned forward, conspiratorially. "My sister Katharine has taken quite the fancy to you, and would like to get to know you better."

It was all Gordon could do not to pull away in panic. "Well . . . she is, um, quite an attractive young woman, but . . ."

"No 'buts,' Mr. Gordon. I'll tell her that you'll be expecting her in your room, later tonight."

She frowned at his sudden frozen expression.

"Or, if you'd prefer Amelia . . ."

"It's not a question of *preference*," Gordon began.

"Good." She smiled, cutting him off. She gave him a conspiratorial wink, released his hands, and knocked loudly on the closed door. She went off down the hall, smiling.

"Um—I say—" Gordon choked, and then a deep voice came from within the room.

"Come in."

Gordon made half a step to follow her but stopped, swallowing the blasphemies that attempted to erupt from his throat, and threw open the door. He took an automatic step forward, then stopped again, frankly astounded by the room in which he found himself.

It was von Shrakenberg's study. Alexander was waiting for him behind a great desk along the far wall, smoking a fat cigar. Two of the walls were covered by crammed bookshelves. On the floor and in shelf niches were statues, Roman (or perhaps Greek) and Egyptian. The rugs were thick and beautifully hand woven. Paintings by half a dozen European masters competed for the remaining wall space. And behind von Shrakenberg, behind the glorious desk at which he sat, smiling at the look on Gordon's face, was a set of French windows opening up onto the manor's gardens. And set in the gardens . . .

Gordon took a step forward, staring beyond von Shrakenberg. The Draka's smile widened with true pleasure as he watched the expression on Gordon's face.

"Ah, like my little folly, do you?"

"It's . . . stupendous."

Von Shrakenberg took a contented puff on his aromatic cigar. He stood, turned, and looked out the window with Gordon at the two colossal statues in the center of his garden. They were sandstone giants with time-mutilated faces, sitting sixty feet tall on battered thrones.

"The Colossi of Memnon," Gordon said in a small voice.

"That's right." Von Shrakenberg reached for a carafe of brandy on the corner of his desk, poured a glass of the rich, aromatic liquid and held it out for Gordon, who took it automatically. "Saw 'em, oh, years ago. Just sitting out in the desert. Nobody to appreciate 'em. Well, I had some of my boys bring 'em out here, set 'em up in my garden. They're a bit worn, you know, but I like 'em. Like to look out 'em, drink a little brandy, smoke a nice cigar, and muse on the folly of human existence. Sit down," he gestured at the comfortable-looking chair in front of his desk.

The chair, Gordon found, was comfortable. The brandy was excellent.

Von Shrakenberg regarded Gordon silently for a long moment. As the seconds ticked off Gordon had a sinking feeling that the week he'd spent in Alexandria had been wasted, that von Shrakenberg had gotten him here, alone, to tell him that the Draka had decided not to take up The Plan. But finally, when von Shrakenberg spoke, his words took Gordon by surprise.

"I realize that you're familiar with the Sudan. You spent several years there trying to quell the slave trade and bring a civilized government to the region. And you succeeded better than could be expected."

Gordon inclined his head in recognition of von Shrakenberg's praise. Agag, the demon of pride that so bedeviled him tried to leap up and crow, but he forced him back down before he could put any words into his mouth.

"I'm afraid," Gordon said, humbly, "that whatever good I did faded quickly after I departed."

Von Shrakenberg waved his hand. "Perhaps. But the Sudan is part of the Domination now." He smiled in a friendly, non-Draka way. "At least, we lay claim to it. It's two-thirds desert, one-third swamp, and in actuality not at all controlled by us. It's easy to say that it's ours; it's another thing to *make* it ours."

"Many nations have said that about the Sudan through the millennia."

Von Shrakenberg nodded. "There's this man who calls himself the Mahdi. Have you heard of him?"

Gordon shrugged. "There've been scores of Mahdi's over the years. Islamic fundamentalists calling for overthrow of the current government. This one seems more successful than most. I know that he's managed to unite most of the tribes. No doubt he desires to remove the Draka from the Sudan in the name of Allah."

"No doubt," von Shrakenberg said, "he's succeeded. He and his dervishes have this past week destroyed a Janissary legion eight thousand strong. Completely. Or so it seems."

Gordon sat back in his chair.

"Impressed?" von Shrakenberg asked. "So are we." He eyed Gordon speculatively through a cloud of aromatic cigar smoke. "You can do us a service, Gordon."

"How so?" he asked, but his mind was already harking back to the hellish country where he'd spent two years of his life galloping back and forth on racing camels, trying to bring civilization to a nation that was determined to remain uncivilized.

"You know the area quite well. Undoubtedly, you still have contacts there. Men you can call upon. Perhaps men who know this Mahdi himself, personally. It wouldn't hurt if we knew more about him, perhaps even somehow brought him to our side. After all, we're reasonable men. Men from many nations have become Draka." Von Shrakenberg shrugged. "And the sooner there is peace on the Nile, the sooner you can began to build your dam."

Gordon and von Shrakenberg locked eyes for a long moment.

"And this is the consensus of your people?" Gordon asked.

"It is." Von Shrakenberg paused. "Generally. There are those who favor a more . . . direct . . . solution to the problem of the Mahdi."

"Direct?" Gordon asked.

"Direct. Unmistakable. Brutal. Kill them all and let the valkyries sort them out. Myself, I find such an approach wasteful of resources. But the Security Directorate . . ." Von Shrakenberg shook his head. "They're a newly organized arm of the Domination . . . and ambitious. Be wary of those who wear the black, Gordon. Be wary of everyone, but especially those who wear the black."

Gordon nodded. "I see. What exactly do you suggest?"

Von Shrakenberg leaned forward eagerly. "I have a dirigible waiting in Alexandria. We can have you in Khartoum in a matter of days. Officially the situation has been handed to the Security Directorate, but it'll take time to get their men—and another army—in place, and then time, of course, to pursue their hunt of the Mahdi. If you can get in there quickly, and find a somewhat more diplomatic, shall we say, solution to the problem, I would say that undoubtedly your future would be assured."

"My dam?" Gordon asked.

Von Shrakenberg smiled. "I have the papers here."

He reached into a drawer of his desk, and handed Gordon a sheaf of documents. Gordon, well versed in the bureaucratese of half a dozen nations, read

through it carefully. It was couched in somewhat
cryptic, but ultimately satisfactory language. And it
had already been signed by von Shrakenberg.

"When do I leave for Khartoum?" he asked.

The Draka smiled. "I like a decisive man," he said.
"As I said, I have a dirigible waiting. You can leave
at your convenience."

Gordon stood. The thought of that woman waiting in his room was like a hand of ice clutching his
guts. He couldn't face her. He could not—

"I'll leave now," he said, carefully folding the papers
and putting them in his pocket.

April 23, 1883
Alexandria en route to Khartoum

My Dearest Augusta:

Your loving and humble brother does at times
find himself in the oddest of circumstances in
the oddest places in all of the world. All of
which you know quite well, of course, because
I can go nowhere or do nothing without impart-
ing to you my thoughts, fears, and hopes via
these epistles, which while not of the same great
significance of those letters of the four evange-
lists, at least warm the heart of this poor trav-
eler when he knows his dutiful sister is eager
to hear of him and his humble doings in the
world.

As I write I am, as incredible as it sounds,
some thousands of feet in the air, borne aloft
not by the angelic wings as is the host of Our
Lord, but a great big windbag. No, not a PM,
or even an MP, but an actual balloon some six
hundred feet long filled with air. A Draka
dirigible, called the *Arsinoe*, gliding silently and
gracefully through the aether like an angel of
Our Lord, but driven by propellers turned by

steam turbines and not our prayers. We sail through the air at speeds approaching forty miles an hour, and can keep this up long enough to achieve our journey's end some 1100 miles distant. Imagine, I shall be in Khartoum in less than two days! Remember how long it took me to make this same trip by Nile steamer and camel? More than two months!

I am amazed at the scientific progress the Draka have made in such a short time. They are an amazing people, though, personally I find them repellent. The only likable Draka I have met so far is Alexander von Shrakenberg—and he is morally bankrupt. They are sinners all, though it is my job neither to save them from Hell, or preach to them of Heaven. They will likely all burn forever. Some, like von Shrakenberg, because of mere folly, others because of a deeper, more pervading evil.

But enough of that! I have, dearest Augusta, good news! Von Shrakenberg has agreed to The Plan, and through him I have gotten the backing of the Alexandria Institute as well. The Nile dam will become a reality! The greatest river in the world will be navigable from its source in the Lakes to its mouth in the Mediterranean. This will be a task to consume my energies for many years (If only I can keep Agag properly in check! He is like to swell up and burst into view at any moment, my pride feels so vast!). It will be a fitting capstone to my life and a monument to last down through the centuries.

First though there is a small matter that I must handle for von Shrakenberg in Khartoum.

I hope Mother and the rest of the family are well sheltered in the Hands of Our Lord. Please kiss them for me and give them all my very best wishes. You may write me in Alexandria, but it may take some time for me to actually get your letters. I don't know how long I will be in Khartoum. Perhaps days, perhaps weeks.

The captain of this fabulous vessel has agreed to take this letter with him back to Alexandria and post it from there. I understand that the mail service in Khartoum is unreliable.

Yours in Christ,
Your Humble and Loving Brother,
C.

II.

The dirigible *Arsinoe* arrived at Khartoum, located on a spit of land between the confluence of the Blue and White Niles, at sunset on the second day after leaving Alexandria. Gordon, looking down at the breathtaking view, remembered again the years he had spent there a decade and a half ago, before the Sudan had been ingested by the Domination.

Gordon, fresh from saving China from the Tai-pangs, a sect of fanatic Christian fundamentalists, had been sent by the Sudan's Ottoman masters to Khartoum as Governor-General to bring order out of chaos, ensure the uninterrupted flow of taxes, and suppress the slave trade. Once there he found that chaos was the natural order in a land two-thirds desert and the rest mostly swamp, and also discovered—perhaps most importantly—that without the slave trade there would be very little in the way of taxes to collect and pass up the chain, as human chattel was the most valuable commodity this land produced.

Nonetheless, he'd gone about his job with great

skill and indefatigable energy. He'd built an army and police force. He'd constructed a string of forts to protect the long suffering citizenry from slavers and bandits. He'd broken the backs of the slaving clans. The Turks had thanked him for a job well done, dismissed him, and now discovering the Sudan to cost more to maintain than it was worth, abandoned it. The slavers and bandits returned, and it was business as usual until the Draka swept through the Sudan and closed their iron fist upon it. But, much like the desert sand and swamp ooze which comprised most of this poor country, the Sudan, unsurprisingly, seemed to be trickling through that closed fist.

Familiar, well-remembered sensations engulfed Gordon as he disembarked at the mooring station outside the city's mud-brick walls. The desert heat drenched him like a ferocious wave. The smells, though he was still outside the city proper, slapped him in the face with their intensity: camels, sewage, waste, and the odors emanating from too many people confined in such a small place in so hot a climate.

A Draka centurion approached him as he stood breathing in the still-familiar, strangely-unforgotten sensations. The officer snapped a smart salute.

"Sir. Centurion David Desmond. At your command."

"Ah, yes. Desmond. Von Shrakenbeg told me about you."

Desmond looked to be an ex-American, probably another of those Draka officers who had once soldiered for the Confederacy and had immigrated to the Domination after the Confederacy had capitulated in 1868.

"He did?" He smiled speculatively. Clearly Desmond wanted to ask Gordon exactly *what* von Shrakenberg had said about him, but could find no graceful way to do so. Actually, von Shrakenberg had had very little to say about Desmond. The centurion had been left in command of a small garrison by Hicks when the strategos had gone off into the desert on his ill-fated offensive against the Mahdi. Since no one at all had come back from that disastrous foray, Desmond was the ranking officer in Khartoum and thus in command of the city.

"This way, sir. The merarch has been anxiously awaiting your arrival."

Gordon paused before climbing into the open carriage that Desmond indicated. "Merarch? I was given to understand that you were the commanding officer in Khartoum."

"Ah, yes sir. I was. Merarch Quantrill arrived this morning. His legion is still on the way. He came ahead, up from Archona on a steam dragger."

"Quantrill?" Gordon asked. "William Quantrill the American bushwhacker?"

"Yes, sir."

Gordon had never met Quantrill personally, but the man's reputation preceded him. In fact, he was notorious. Quantrill had also fought for the Confederacy in the American War Between the States, but he really hadn't been much of a soldier. He'd been a raider, a murderer, a thug, and a thief. Most famous for leading the raid on Lawrence, Kansas, that had resulted in the death of every man and boy in the town, he'd picked his battles more for the promise of loot than recognizable military purposes. After emigrating to the Domination Quantrill had preserved his reputation as a vicious, brutal, and ruthless killer during the Domination's rapid expansion over the last fifteen years.

"Is Quantrill in the regular army?" Gordon asked thoughtfully. "Has he been ordered to bring the Mahdi to heel?"

"No," Desmond said. "Well, yes. His orders are to destroy the Mahdi and his savages, but he's not regular army. He's a Merarch in the Security Directorate. As I understand it, the problem of the Mahdi is theirs to solve."

"I see," Gordon said. He looked into the distance.

"He's expecting us," Desmond said after a moment.

"Yes. Quite." Of course, this was turning out to be complicated already. Von Shrakenberg had warned him about the Directorate in general, and, specifically, this Quantrill was an unsavory fellow. Not a real soldier at all. Just a freebooter in uniform.

Gordon looked at Desmond, who was frowning uncertainly.

"Have my luggage brought to headquarters," he said briskly. "I shall be out and about quite a bit, of course, so I'll need just a small room. Nothing luxurious."

"But—"

"I say. May I borrow your carriage?" Gordon looked around. "I don't see many others and I have to get into the city as soon as possible."

"But—"

"That's a good lad." Gordon swung into the forward facing seat of the mule drawn carriage.

"But—"

"Give the merarch my regards. Tell him I'll drop by the garrison soon as I can."

"But—"

He leaned forward. "Driver?"

The black holding the reins turned back to face Gordon.

"Do you know the establishment of Nomikos the Greek?"

The man nodded."Take me there."

"But—"

The black twitched his whip above the head of his mule.

Desmond had time for a final forlorn "But—" as Gordon, waving cheerily, headed towards the mudbrick metropolis of Khartoum.

The city hadn't changed much the years he'd been away. Constructed largely of sun-dried mud bricks that tended to melt together after a few years and a few rainstorms, its slumping buildings were easy to pull down and build over. Thus Khartoum was constantly changing without really changing as every few years a new veneer was put up over the same time-ravaged features.

When Gordon had known Nomikos in years past the Greek merchant had traded in gum and ivory and Kordofan gold, but had never dabbled in the most valuable Sudanese commodity, human flesh. He was knowledgeable, intelligent, and though a merchant he was also an honorable man. And he was in Gordon's debt, he and his caravans twice having been saved from bandits by Gordon's patrols.

Gordon was glad to find him still alive and prosperous, if fatter than ever. Nomikos, too, was apparently glad to see Gordon, if more than a little astonished that the old Pasha had suddenly appeared on his doorstep.

Dubious to the announced identity of his surprise visitor, Nomikos' eyes became as big around as fat Greek olives when he realized that the man waiting outside the gated entrance to his domain was indeed Charles Gordon.

"Gordon Pasha, a thousand forgivenesses." Nomikos would have gone down to his knees, but Gordon gripped his forearms, stopping him. There was no telling if the rotund merchant would have been able to fight his way back up to his feet again. "I never knew you were back in Egypt, let alone shining the light of your greatness upon the streets of this humble city, right even upon the door of my most unworthy abode."

"I've but arrived, old friend, and already I find myself in need of help."

"Come inside, Gordon Pasha, come, and we shall talk of the old days and of current needs."

Gordon sighed, not without a certain resigned acceptance. He knew that he was in for a long night.

The pathway of hospitality was not swiftly trodden in this land. First coffee, drunk in small glasses so laden with sugar that it was a thick syrup. Then food offered on laden trays by Nomikos' curious concubines. Dates and pastries dripping with honey. Sweet, cold melon, and slabs of fish, fresh that day from the Nile, picked free of bones. Cold meats and dried figs.

It was food Gordon had not eaten the like of in more than a decade. Simple and hardy, yet delicious, it was wonderful to feel those tastes again on his tongue.

With the food came talk. Not, at first, talk of today, but of years gone by when Gordon had first come to the Sudan and broken the slavers. He had made the country safer for everyone, especially far-ranging merchants like Nomikos, who well-remembered those days and liked to reminisce about them.

Gradually they worked their way through the years, and Nomikos told of mutual friends and mutual enemies. Who had lived, who had died. Who had prospered, who had disappeared into the dust of a lost caravan. Finally they reached the present day, and Nomikos told Gordon who had joined the Mahdi and who had defied him. And what few of the defiant ones still lived.

Finally Gordon came to tell him what he wanted, and Nomikos's eyes got large as olives again and he spent over a hour trying to dissuade Gordon from his madness. But Gordon only shook his head and finally the Greek nodded in sad agreement.

"It will be your death, Gordon Pasha," Nomikos told him.

Gordon shrugged. "Something will be my death. Long ago I put my life into the hands of my Saviour. He hasn't seen fit to gather me to his bosom yet."

"You haven't changed," Nomikos said, and Gordon nodded. "Very well, then. I will send a man to you at the garrison tomorrow. He's in Khartoum now, otherwise there's no telling when I could ever find him."

"He travels far?"

"He does. Like I did before I had this." Nomikos slapped his big belly resoundingly. "He's a strange one. He will do much for gold. He's the only man I can think of who might do this for you."

"Can I trust him?" Gordon asked.

The Greek shrugged. "As you can any man in Khartoum. Take that for what you know it to be worth. But I do know one thing about him. He is stubborn. You can buy him and he will stay bought. At least, he always has, before."

Gordon nodded, said his farewells and took his leave. His carriage had waited, the driver patiently sitting in the dark, half asleep.

"Headquarters," Gordon said.

Before rousing the mule from his standing slumber, the driver lit the glass-barreled oil lamp hanging from a pole adjacent to his seat.

As the driver awoke the mule with a click of his tongue and a touch of his whip to the animal's flank, Gordon could see in the bright patch of lamplight a series of numbers tattooed on the back of the man's neck.

They were, Gordon knew, serial numbers that the Draka had recently started to tattoo on their serfs, another sign that these so-called serfs were actually slaves. Gordon hated slavers, no matter what their guise, and, patently, the Draka were slavers. Perhaps they were somewhat more benevolent than those he was used to dealing with in the Sudan. Perhaps, somewhat. But that didn't wipe out their sin. And slavery was a sin, though it required careful reading of the Bible to ascertain that. The Bible, though inerrant, wasn't as straightforward as some would have you believe and it took—

A volley of shots, five or six closely spaced together, suddenly rang out, shattering the serenity of both the evening and Gordon's reverie. The lantern exploded, bringing darkness again to the street. The driver reared back, then slowly puddled forward. The mule shied and shrieked. It, along with the lantern and the driver, had probably stopped a couple of bullets.

Gordon acted instantly, almost without thought. He flung himself forward and reached over the driver who was now lying on his side on the high carriage seat. The driver had twisted the reins in his fingers, so Gordon grabbed the man's arms, then slid his hands down upon the driver's wrists. Shouting at the mule, Gordon jerked the lifeless hands still clutching the reins and the beast took off at a run as a second volley sounded.

One bullet whined past Gordon's ear. Others thudded into the carriage. Gordon felt the body of the driver shudder at two more impacts, but the man gave no sign that he felt the additional wounds. Gordon suspected that he was already dead.

The mule, though, was alive and scared. Gordon gave it its head and it ran through the dark streets. He let the beast run where it wanted to, and simply concentrated on keeping the carriage upright. Gordon was in an awkward position, leaning over the body of the driver, using the dead man's hands to keep the frightened animal under control. It took all his strength to keep the carriage upright.

The muscles in his back twitched, anticipating another hail of bullets at any second. He was frightened, certainly, but his mouth was also twisted in a strange smile of exhilaration.

Some one wants to kill me, he thought. I'm still important.

He hadn't felt this good in years.

April 26, 1883
Khartoum

My Dearest Augusta:

I'm writing this short note from my room in the Draka military headquarters, Khartoum, just to inform you that I have arrived safely and all is well.

The dirigible trip was exhilarating. Khartoum, I must say, is something less so. It is the same old drab town with the same old mud-brick buildings and the same old narrow, choked streets that are as difficult as ever to drive even the smallest carriage through.

It's late at night—or rather very early in the morning—and I find myself so excited about the prospects of achieving real success on this mission that I can't sleep.

You'll be happy to know that already I've met some old friends—you may remember I've written about Nomikos the Greek in the past—who will be able to help me with my business here. It was good to just sit and chat of old times with Nomikos. He has prospered, and is even fatter than ever.

The only disagreeable note is that I've discovered that William Quantrill has taken command in the city. I haven't met him yet, but have of course heard of him. He's a most disagreeable chap and may be something of a problem. Nothing, however, with the help of Our Most Benevolent Lord, that I shan't be able to overcome.

Ah well, Dear Sister, time to post this short missive. Hopefully the mail service will get it into your anxious hands sometime before my planned return to England this fall!

Your loving Brother in Christ,
C.

III.

Gordon still couldn't sleep. An assassination attempt could cause insomnia, but it was excitement and a burning need for action that roared through his system like an undeniable drug, not fear.

He wrestled with Agag for a while, pinned the demon down into the dark hole where he dwelled, and finally fell into a light sleep. He awoke at dawn a few hours later, got up, dressed, and wandered through the still-sleeping old Palace. The Palace was the finest, strongest building in Khartoum, so naturally the Draka used it as headquarters, as in fact Gordon himself had done when he had been Governor-General. It hadn't changed much since then—except, of course, it was quieter and much emptier since Hicks had gotten most of his command slaughtered somewhere out in the desert.

He dropped into the officers' mess for breakfast. It was empty. He waited impatiently, for there was nothing else to do. After about an hour a sleepy-eyed orderly wandered in. He snapped to attention at the sight of a frowning Gordon.

"Do the officers habitually breakfast so late?" Gordon asked.

"Habitually? Well, sir, I wouldn't call it a habit, but, lately, well . . ."

"Yes," Gordon nodded briskly. "I can see how the death of nine-tenths of the garrison would make the remainder lazier in their habits."

Wisely, the orderly chose not to reply.

"Please bring me some tea and toast, if that would not be too much trouble at this apparently early hour."

"No, sir, not at all." The orderly saluted, turned, and marched off to the kitchen.

Gordon ate his toast with butter and marmalade, and lingered over his tea. After a while other officers drifted into the mess. They looked at Gordon, and then looked away, whispering among themselves. Gordon knew that he was an anomaly here, and armies, officers particularly, hated anomalies. No doubt the officers knew who he was (Down Agag!). Word of his arrival had no doubt been whispered to ears eager for news, and the story of the attempted assassination had already doubtlessly also made the rounds. They were certainly wondering what he was doing in Khartoum, but apparently they decided to do their wondering at a distance. No one approached Gordon, until Desmond himself wandered in, looking as if he'd gotten considerably less sleep than Gordon had.

"Join me?" Gordon invited.

Desmond started at the sound of Gordon's voice and rubbed his face like a man who had just awoken.

"Yes. Certainly, sir. Thank you, sir." He sat, and Gordon poured him a cup of tea.

"Thank you, sir," Desmond said as Gordon passed the cup to him. "You . . . you are all right, sir?"

"Why shouldn't I be?"

"Well . . . last night. You had some, ah, problems . . ."

The centurion's voice faded away as Gordon shrugged.

"Khartoum, I perceive, can still be a dangerous city."

"Ah, quite. Yes. Indeed. Probably bandits of some sort. Probably."

"The merarch not down for breakfast yet?" Gordon said after a moment of uncomfortable silence. It was more of an observation than a question.

"Uh, no. I believe not. He may be off inspecting . . . something . . ."

"No doubt." Gordon smiled into his tea cup. Given Quantrill's reputation, if he was inspecting anything this time of morning it was probably the inside of a chamber pot because of his excessive drinking of the night before.

"Sir—"

The orderly appeared at their table before Gordon could further probe into Desmond's opinion of his superior officer.

"Someone to see you, sir."

"Who the hell would want to see me at this hour?" Desmond asked irritably.

"Uh, not you, sir, *you*, sir." The orderly looked at Gordon.

"Very well, then," Desmond said, his irritation redoubled. "Send him in."

The orderly shifted his stare to a point somewhere between Gordon and Desmond.

"It's some kind of native, sir."

"You heard the centurion," Gordon said quietly.

"Yes, sir." The orderly marched off, trying not to look scandalized.

He came back a few moments later with a slight, dark-skinned man in neat, clean Arab dress. The whispering among the other officers redoubled as Gordon inclined his head, offering him a seat.

"Thank you, monsieur."

Gordon realized that the man wasn't a native. His English was smoothed by a French accent. His eyes were as sharp as Gordon's, only a slightly darker blue. His hair was black but his thick, drooping mustache was nearly blond. His teeth were in good shape, but stained an unhealthy-looking green.

Gordon immediately recognized him as a *chat* chewer. *Chat* was a mildly narcotic, mildly addictive drug widely utilized in the Sudan, and even more common in Abyssinia, to the east.

"This is Centurion David Desmond," Gordon said to him. "My name is Charles George Gordon."

The man inclined his head to Desmond, and returned a speculative eye to Gordon. "You're not unknown in the Sudan. My name is Arthur Rimbaud."

"Rimbaud," Desmond said, half to himself. He crinkled his brow in concentration, then suddenly snapped his fingers. "Say, you're not that Frenchy poet fellow, are you? Fancy meeting you here. Dressed like that. I mean . . ."

Rimbaud looked at him. "That was another lifetime, monsieur. I am now just a merchant."

"You come highly recommended by a friend," Gordon said. "He said that you are honest and trustworthy."

Rimbaud shrugged. "I try, monsieur. What is it that you wish to purchase?"

Gordon leaned forward. "A meeting," he said, "with the Mahdi."

Desmond looked dismayed, but Rimbaud smiled, a quick flash of stained teeth in a sun-darkened face.

"An expensive item, to be sure. And quite a dangerous one as well."

Gordon stood. "I have money enough. And courage, as well."

Rimbaud smiled his enigmatic smile. "No doubt, monsieur. When do you wish to leave?"

"As soon as possible."

Rimbaud suddenly stood. He seemed to Gordon, even on such slight acquaintance, to be a quick and decisive man. "Then we should leave."

Gordon arose. Desmond looked back and forth between the two of them.

"Right," Gordon said. "I just need to fetch my kit."

"Just a moment," Desmond said. "Shouldn't you . . . I mean, you haven't reported to Merarch Quantrill yet. And . . . there were those . . . difficulties . . . last night. Surely you should inform the merarch—"

Gordon silenced him with the full force of his cold blue eyes. "I'm not a member of your command. Certainly, I shall call upon the merarch at his convenience. When I can."

"He'll be angry," Desmond blurted. "You don't know him. He can get very angry!"

Gordon shrugged, and turned to Rimbaud. "Come, sir."

"Difficulties?" Rimbaud asked as they left the room. "If it is not impertinent, may I enquire about these difficulties?"

"Oh, it was nothing much," Gordon said. "Some one tried to kill me last night."

"I see. Considering the nature of our journey, perhaps you'd better get used to that."

Gordon smiled. "You forget, monsieur. I have been in the Sudan before."

April 27, 1883
Khartoum, en route to El Dueim

My Dearest Augusta:

I write this in the dark on a dhow rocking on the currents of the White Nile, so please forgive my hand if it is not as legible as it usually is.

I found Khartoum little changed. The weather is still hot. The streets are still dusty. The Palace is unimproved. The people are still largely the same. As a whole, the country hasn't prospered in my absence. I say this with all due humility. Oh, some segments of the population have grown wealthier. The slavers are back and are pursuing their filthy trade in the open. The Draka, I am sure, will close them down eventually. Not, I am also sure, out of moral repugnance, but because in the Draka view it should be the state that profits from the bondage of human beings, but they have one or two little matters to take care of before they can turn their attention to such mundane problems as slave traders.

In these matters I shall probably play some small role, though I have had second thoughts about working with the Draka. Some seem to be among the lowest elements of humanity I have ever had the displeasure to run across. Ah well—we are all simple men and imperfect before the Eyes of Our Lord. I shouldn't judge them, for some day like all men they will stand naked before the greatest Judge of all and He will accord them their proper position in all eternity.

By the way—I should be remiss if I didn't mention my traveling companion. I've had to journey to El Dueim, a small hamlet, a mere trading post some 110 miles south of Khartoum, situated on the banks the White Nile. No great air ship to carry me to my destination this time, but a humble dhow, much like those that have sailed the Nile for the past several millennia. (This particular dhow, by the way, is so venerable, leaky, dirty, and smelly that it may have been sailing the Nile, *itself* for the past several millennia.)

My guide, astonishingly, is a Frenchman who has spent some years in the region as an itinerant merchant. His name is Arthur Rimbaud. It seems that as a younger man he was a poet of some note. Actually, I am unfamiliar with his name, but, knowing how poets feel about that sort of thing, have not told him that. I have not prodded him to recite any of his verses, and oddly enough he has not volunteered any. That seems strange, for a poet. Have you ever heard of him?

Your Dear and Loving Brother,
As Always, In Christ,
C.

IV.

El Dueim had a sense of impermanence about it, no doubt because most of it was washed away almost every year by the flooding of the White Nile. The hamlet's structures were flimsy huts of wattle, mud, and reed. The piles and wharves leading up from the banks of the river were ramshackle. Gordon marveled that he and Rimbaud didn't plunge through their rotten planks at their first footstep.

The hamlet, such as it was, was dwarfed by the camp on the surrounding floodplain. Thousands of natives were bivouacked around the small settlement, so confident of their safety that they hadn't built even a token zarada, a barrier of sharp scrub thorn usually built around encampments in the region, to protect themselves.

Gordon was impressed by what he saw. The Mahdi's men were usually called dervishes by outsiders. Dervish, which actually means "poor" in Arabic, was a term more properly applied to a class of Moslem friars who'd taken vows of poverty. Commonly called whirling dervishes, there were actually any number of dervish types—dancing, howling, singing—who sought to achieve mystic union with the divine through the constant repetition of simple physical acts until they fell into a trance. These friars were also fierce fighters, loyal until death, although such authentic dervishes made up only a portion of the Mahdi's army.

"Actually," Rimbaud explained to Gordon as they made their way through the camp, "the Mahdists call themselves 'ansar.' "

" 'Helpers,' " Gordon said. "As the people of Medina who gave aid to Mohammed during his exile called themselves."

Rimbaud nodded. Gordon could distinguish

representatives from numerous Sudanese tribes in the camp. Beside the authentic dervishes, there were Bedj tribesmen from the Red Hills, Arabs of the northern desert, and animist Nuer from the Sudd, the great swamp that constituted the southern third of the territory.

There were thousands of tribesmen, tens of thousands of them. Gordon and his guide had arrived at the camp early in the morning, and breakfast was being cooked over a myriad of campfires. The *ansar* awaited their food, *ful*, or mashed fava beans, a Sudanese staple, with general good patience. If the Mahdi was smart (and he was that, Gordon figured) he fed them regularly. That alone would be enough to keep most of them happy. These men didn't ask for much for their undying loyalty. They were fierce fighters, loyal to the death, but as they passed among them Gordon didn't see many modern weapons.

Most of the *ansar* were armed with the traditional sword and spear. Some carried nothing more lethal than cudgels or hard-wood sticks. A few guns were visible—some ancient Arab-style flintlocks and a couple more rifles of rather outdated European manufacture. These were spoils, no doubt, from recent battles with the Draka.

Rimbaud appeared to be rather well known. No one stopped them. He was challenged, or rather greeted, by a few who seemed to have some authority over the teeming rabble, but some muttered words from him always seemed to suffice for their passage.

"The first stage of the journey is over," Rimbaud said as they made their way through the camp. "Now we must take the road to El Obeid. Though the Mahdi has a tent here, he actually spends most of his time in the city."

Gordon was familiar with El Obeid, which, after Cairo, was the most populous city in Egypt-Sudan. It had naturally fallen to the Draka when they had originally annexed the region. But the Draka had only left a token garrison while making Khartoum their headquarters. They had chosen Khartoum because it was more central to the entire region and also because it was located at the confluence of the Blue and White Niles, thus controlling to some extent all river traffic. It was also more easily defendable than El Obeid.

The hand of the Draka had fallen rather lightly on El Obeid, which was the historic capital of Kordofan, the richest and most important Sudanese province. As such it was also the region's economic center, the heart of the gum, ivory, and slave trade. Other than replacing native economic concerns with their own, the Draka let things go on as they had for centuries. The capture of El Obeid had been the Mahdi's first great victory, as well as the impetus for Hicks's disastrous probe south from Khartoum.

The actual trading post at El Dueim was the best-built building in all of the hamlet, so naturally had been taken as the camp's general headquarters. It stood higher up on the river valley, out of the flood-plain that would be swept clear by the White Nile's yearly floods, and was made of sun-dried brick and timber. Next to it was a corral made of thorn bush that held a score of rather thin and tired-looking horses. Hobbled camels grazed freely on the sparse grass beyond the corral. A dirt road, more of a track really, ran west and south, into the interior to El Obeid.

Half a dozen men lounged around the front porch of the headquarters' building, under the half-fallen ramada that almost sheltered them from the already sweltering sun.

"Sabah il-kheer," Rimbaud said, greeting one or perhaps all with a graceful good morning and a sketchy salaam.

They returned the greeting with various interest

and grace. Rimbaud, it seemed, was a familiar figure accorded a certain, but not excessive, respect.

"My friend and I have business in El Obeid, and need horses . . ." Rimbaud began, but his voice faltered and ran down to nothing as he looked down the road.

Gordon followed his gaze to see a white cloud in the distance, billowing on the early morning breeze. It was too far to see details, but clearly a moderate-sized body of horsemen was approaching the camp.

Rimbaud looked at Gordon and spoke in English. "Perhaps we may be in luck. Perhaps our business comes to us."

Most of the men on the porch stood and joined them as they looked down the trail, shading their eyes to better see the riders. It was not long before the excited call of "Mahdi! Mahdi!" started to rise up in the camp.

"It's him," Rimbaud said after a moment. "I can see his personal flag. The men with him are the *mulazamin*, a picked force drawn from tribal leaders. They are his personal bodyguard."

The news of the Mahdi's approach swept through the camp like fire raining from the heavens. His faithful abandoned their cook pots and merged in a swarming mass where the trail ended before the headquarter building. The horsemen approached at a brisk gallop and, just before Gordon was sure there was going to be a terrible collision, the Mahdi and the fifty or so men of his bodyguard braked abruptly, horses rearing and snorting, flags waving, men cheering and moaning, "Mahdi! Mahdi! Mahdi!" in unison.

The Mahdi leapt down to the ground while the horses of his bodyguard still pranced nervously, excited by the noise and the swarming crowd. Some of the *mulazamin* unlimbered rifles and fired in the air to add to the general din and confusion. These men,

Gordon noted, were all well armed, and their rifles were all of Draka manufacture, which made them the finest in the world. They evidently had gotten the pick of the loot from Hicks's ill-fated expedition.

Gordon could see the Mahdi quite clearly. He was tall, dark skinned, and slim. His eyes were black, his teeth white with a prominent gap between the front uppers. There was a certain air about him, an aura of strength and confidence. His smile energized the crowd as they all reached out to touch his simple white linen jibbeh. His robe was the only one that was pure white. All the other Mahdists who wore robes had variously colored patches sewn onto them, signifying the impure state of their wearers. Only the Mahdi could wear immaculate white, for he was the only man among them without sin.

The Mahdi threw his arms out wide and began to speak. At first his words seemed unremarkable to Gordon. He spoke the usual stuff about Allah and paradise and fighting to the death and victory over the infidel Draka—but his voice was deep, resonant, magical. Men heard that voice and believed him, implicitly and utterly. Men heard that voice, saw his eyes, and loved him, immediately and totally.

Gordon, too, felt it. The Mahdi's charisma was overwhelming. His physical beauty was astounding, but there was a depth to him, an apparent spirituality that Gordon had rarely encountered in the world.

"Quite a figure," Rimbaud said, "is he not, monsieur?"

Gordon took his eyes from the Mahdi who, deep in his oration, laughed wildly one moment, then, recalling the sacrifice of his loyal helpers, wept like a baby. The Sudanese tribesmen, watching their leader cry, bowed their heads and cried with him.

"Yes," Gordon. "Yes. Of course. One would expect such . . . charisma."

Rimbaud spit out a chewed wad of *chat*, took some

fresh leaves from his pouch and tucked them in the fold between his lip and jaw.

"Would one?" he asked quietly, looking at Gordon speculatively.

He knows! Gordon thought to himself. He can feel the . . . attraction I feel. Am I so transparent? How could I let my emotions be so apparent? Perhaps the Frenchman does have a poet's sensitivities, but, still, damn the frog!

The crowd was parting as the Mahdi turned to the headquarters building. The Mahdi suddenly caught sight of Gordon, and stopped, puzzled. Dark eyes looked into blue. A spark of something passed between them, a recognition, perhaps, and Agag came roaring from the hidden cavern in Gordon's soul which was his dark home.

He knows me! Agag said. *Fifteen years has not dimmed the fame of Charles George Gordon even in this dark and ignorant land. He knows who I am!*

Rimbaud was between them, smiling a strange smile. He bowed deeply and greeted the Mahdi, then gestured with both hands to Gordon.

"This is Gordon Pasha," he said in Arabic. "In times past Governor-General of Sudan. He seeks an audience with you."

The Mahdi was young, perhaps thirty. He would have been a boy when Gordon had traversed the Sudan armed only with his riding crop and dagger, a crescent-bladed *jambiyah*, crushing the bandit clans, destroying the slavers, building forts and settlements throughout its desolation. At first, when Rimbaud spoke, there was a blankness on the Mahdi's face and Gordon's heart sunk. Inwardly he raged at his demon, flaying it with bitter words, calling it a fool, a liar, a charlatan.

The Mahdi no more knows me than he knows who the Prime Minister of England is, he told Agag bitterly.

But then the Mahdi's expression changed. Comprehension lit his eyes.

"Of course!" he said. "I remember—when I was a boy you did great things for the people of the Sudan. You broke the injustice of the Turk. But then . . . but then you left."

"I had to," Gordon felt compelled to say. And indeed he had. The most powerful man in Sudan was nothing to the bankers and ministers who really called the tune.

The Mahdi smiled and the effect was dazzling, like the sun to a man who had been locked in a cold, dark dungeon for half a year.

"And well you did—for you have left it for me!"

He laughed again, and all those who heard it laughed with him, just happy that he was happy. And Gordon laughed as well. Lord help me, he thought. He could not help but laugh, too.

"The pleasure is mine, Gordon Pasha," the Mahdi said, "to meet a man of such renown. How may I serve you?"

The Mahdi had that quality about him, Gordon mused, that would make men follow him to Hell— and once there to shield him from the fires with their own bodies. Gordon himself couldn't help but fall under the Mahdi's spell. Had he, he wondered, at this advanced age at last found the man whom he could willingly serve?

"By listening, my lord, to what I've come to say. By thinking, my lord, at what I'm about to offer."

The Mahdi laughed aloud. "That doesn't sound so difficult. Come!" He put his hand lightly on Gordon's shoulder, and rather than repelling him the Mahdi's touch seemed to warm his flesh. "Let us retire to my tent and you can tell me this great thing you have come to say. And I shall listen."

They went together, Rimbaud trailing, and the bodyguards following after them.

April 28, 1883
El Dueim, Camp of the Mahdi

My dearest Augusta:

I fear that I shall burst with pride! Agag, it seems, has finally won our little battle and is in full control of my faculties. But, really, I'm not wasting time worrying about that. Instead, I am happy as I ever could be, glad to know that I am useful in the world again and have succeeded easily where others would very easily have failed.

It will doubtless be some time before I can post this letter, as I am now in the camp of the man known as the Mahdi (which means "The Guided One" in Arabic), the man who was leading the Sudanese rebellion against the Draka. I say "was" advisedly, because I have managed to enlist him to the Draka side. I have gotten him to sign a treaty to join the Domination of the Draka, to accept a place in it for himself and his people, rather than continue an armed rebellion which, I convinced him, would ultimately prove to be useless.

The Mahdi is an intelligent man, as well as handsome, charismatic, and virtuous. I am happy that I was able to bring him together with the Draka. Otherwise I would most certainly witness his utter destruction at the hands of a more numerous and technologically superior foe.

There are, however, certain elements among the Draka who most certainly will not welcome this development, so my job may not be quite done. Soon, though, I am quite convinced that everything will be in order and I shall be able to get on with the task I came to Africa for. In the meantime, pray for me as I certainly do for you and our family every night and day.

Your loving brother,
C.

V.

Gordon and Rimbaud stood together in the hot night on a ramshackle pier overlooking the rushing waters of the White Nile. The breeze off the river lent a touch of coolness to the evening, but the clouds of voracious mosquitoes made Gordon eager for the relative safety of the Mahdi's big white tent.

"Once you reach Khartoum, go by camel," Gordon told the Frenchman. "A steamer would be faster, but it may be more dangerous."

Rimbaud shrugged. "Living is dangerous, monsieur. When we die, then we shall be safe."

Gordon looked at the enigmatic merchant. There was something about the man that inspired trust. Perhaps it was his quiet, almost laconic attitude. Whatever caused it, Gordon hoped that the trust he put in Rimbaud wasn't misplaced.

"All right," he finally said. "I leave it to you. Go the way you feel would be best. But be careful. And deliver this message only to Alexander von Shrakenberg. He has promised to be waiting—with a legion—for word from me at Aswan, at the end of the railroad line. If you don't find him there, you must find him wherever he is, as soon as you can. Oh—and, if you will, as a favor to me, take these letters for my sister and post them at the first opportunity."

Rimbaud accepted both packets, the one containing

a signed copy of the Mahdist treaty, the other containing the letters Gordon had written to his sister Augusta over the last several days. They disappeared into his voluminous, disreputable robes.

"That I will, monsieur." He made as if to go, then paused. "May I offer an observation of my own, monsieur?"

"Certainly," Gordon said, somewhat surprised. Rimbaud had never before made free with advice.

He fixed Gordon with his curious burning gaze. His eyes had clearly seen a lot in life, and this experience shone in them as he addressed Gordon. "The Mahdi is but a man like all of us. Follow him if you will. Love him if you must. But do not worship him. If you do, you will be lost. *Comprendez vous?*"

"Y-yes," Gordon said, a little startled by the man's words. Before he could say more, though, Rimbaud turned, and climbed down into the waiting dhow. Gordon watched him go, contemplating his extraordinary advice. It was almost as if the Frenchman had followed Gordon's own private mental processes, almost as if he could directly interpret the words and looks that had passed between him and the Mahdi. How could Rimbaud know his own unexpressed thoughts and desires?

Not that he could ever really love the Mahdi, in the physical sense. That was surely impossible. It was not natural. It was a sin. True, it was a sin he had carried with him since his thirteenth year when he'd been forced into such a relationship with a teacher at his preparatory school. Not forced in a physical sense, but overwhelmed by an older and more powerful personality, a personality he had loved, had worshiped . . .

Since then Gordon had wished fervently that he was a eunuch so he'd never be tortured by such terrible desires again. He had felt them since, but had never given in. His iron will and determination

had prevented him from again slipping into sin.
But—

Don't even think about it, Gordon told himself.
Don't even think about it. There was much yet he
had to do. There was much to occupy himself with.

He gave a final wave to Rimbaud as the dhow
slipped downstream. Gordon couldn't be sure but it
seemed as if Rimbaud also waved a farewell. After
the dhow faded from sight, he turned away from the
river and went up the rickety pier to the muddy path
beyond.

A faceless tribesman jostled him in the darkness,
and Gordon felt a sharp, bitter sting across his
ribcage. Instantly, without conscious thought, he drew
the jambiyah he always carried at his waist and slashed
outward.

He felt the blade bite flesh and the Arab sprang
back with a curse, his hand flying to his cheek where
Gordon's dagger had slashed him from the corner of
his mouth to the corner of his eye.

There were others on and around the pier, but the
knife work was so fast, so quiet, that they had no time
to react even if they realized what was happening.

Cursing, the Arab crouched low and came in again.
Gordon stood his ground, surprising him. While it had
been some time since Gordon had had blood on his
own hands, his physical courage had never dimmed.
The tribesman lunged, but Gordon blocked most of
the blow's force with a strength that surprised his foe.
The tribesman was even more surprised by the speed
and accuracy of Gordon's counterthrust as it lodged
deep in his throat.

"Damn!" Gordon stepped back, avoiding most of
the spray that geysered from his assailant's throat. The
tribesman fell. "Damn it all, anyway!"

By now those standing nearby knew that something
odd was happening. A crowd quickly gathered around
Gordon, and helped him up the river bank and to

the Mahdi's tent. They rushed him in, calling for a doctor, and laid him on soft cushions in a quiet alcove.

Gordon was breathing heavily, shallowly. He felt hot and cold, sweating and shivering at the same time. He knew his wounds weren't particularly bad, not even the stomach wound, but wondered why they were affecting him so severely.

Then he thought, "Poison," and tried to rise, but couldn't. He tried to call for paper. He wanted to, he had to write to his sister, to tell her . . . tell her . . .

He couldn't remember what he had to tell her. He lay back among the cushions, totally unaware of the chaos which raged around him.

VI.

Gordon woke to darkness.

He was not in a tent, but in a dark room in a building, exactly where, he didn't know. A woman sat by his side, dozing, and as he woke he sat up, and felt the pull of barely-knit flesh across his stomach.

The woman woke at the sound of his involuntary groan. She was young and probably beautiful, though he could hardly tell for the darkness and the veil and robes she wore. In any event, her voice was young and her hands gentle and tender as she lightly touched his chest and urged him back down upon the soft bed.

"Where—" Gordon croaked, his mouth dry and voice rusty from disuse.

The woman made soft noises of disapproval and reached for a carafe beside the bed. She held it to his lips and he eagerly gulped sweet, diluted wine, ignoring the rivulets that dribbled down his chin.

"Where am I?" he tried again. This time his voice worked reasonably well.

"Shh!" The woman said. "Lay back and rest. I shall bring him."

And she was gone before Gordon could stop her.

Gordon sat up as best he could against the fluffy cushions, and looked around. He was obviously in a dark bedchamber. It was night, and warm. Of course. City sounds and smells came from the grilled window, as did some light from a half-full moon. So much for his surroundings. As for himself—he was naked, covered by a sheet damp from his sweat. His chest was half wrapped in bandages where the knife blade had raked his ribcage. Another bandage was wrapped about his stomach where the blade had sunk in an inch or two. He probed carefully, pushing lightly with his forefinger, and winced. It was still sore. But—he was alive and feeling reasonably well if somewhat weak and more than a little disoriented.

"Praise be to Allah!"

The Mahdi stood at the entrance to the room. He gestured to the bodyguards who accompanied him to wait outside and closed the door.

"We thought we had lost you so soon after first knowing you—but praise be to Allah—and your own great strength—that neither the blade nor the poison on it could end your life!"

The Mahdi stopped at the foot of the bed and gazed down on Gordon with his intense, piercing eyes.

"As you yourself did to the man who struck you."

"Who was he?" Gordon asked. He looked back up at the Mahdi. He felt that he should pull the sheet up to cover himself, but for some reason couldn't. The Mahdi moved closer, around the edge of the bed.

He shrugged shoulders clad in an immaculate white robe.

"Who knows? An assassin sent by an old enemy, perhaps. You still have many enemies in this country, Gordon Pasha." The Mahdi sat down on the edge of the bed. Gordon could feel the heat radiating from the body pressing against his upper thigh, covered only by the thin sheet. "A man is measured by the strength of his enemies."

They looked at each other for a long moment. Gordon felt an unaccountable rush of heat flush his entire body.

"Where—where are we?"

"Ah." The Mahdi gestured around them. "My palace in El Obeid. We thought it would be best to bring you here from the camp. Your wounds . . ."

His fine, strong-looking hand reached out slowly, almost as if of its own accord, and touched Gordon's bandaged chest, gently. Gordon flinched at the touch, but did not move away from it.

"You've slept for three days," the Mahdi continued in that same dreamy, far-away voice. The touch became a caress, moving down his chest. Suddenly, the Mahdi sighed and took his hand away. "It's a pity," he finally said. "You no longer have the suppleness, the skin, the softness of a youth. A pity."

"Yes," Gordon said, quietly. He looked away, queerly hurt in a way he couldn't even think about, let alone define.

The Mahdi stood, his voice suddenly brisk, businesslike.

"It's well that you've awakened. We have . . ." he paused, searching for the correct word, " . . . visitors."

"Oh." Gordon still did not look at him, fiercely willing himself not to cry. He didn't know why he wanted to.

"Yes. A Draka legion has surrounded the city."

This was something he could think about. Focus his mind on.

"Who commands it?" he asked in a strong voice.

It couldn't be von Shrakenberg's legion. They couldn't have arrived so quickly from Aswan.

"A merarch named Quantrill. He has asked to meet with me."

Quantrill. Again. Perhaps at last they'd come face-to-face. "I wouldn't much trust him."

The Mahdi smiled. It was heart-breakingly beautiful.

"I don't. It would help if you attended and showed him the documents I have signed."

"Of course," Gordon said. He sat up with hardly any pain. "As you desire."

The Mahdi was already leaving the room, calling for servants to clothe Gordon for the meeting.

May 2, 1883
El Obeid

My Dearest Augusta:
I find myself now in El Obeid, a city (without much to recommend it) in the heart of the Kordofan province of what used to be the Sudan, which is, de facto, the capitol of the Mahdi's little empire.

I confess that I am weary. I had a little accident a couple of days ago, nothing serious, I assure you, and am well recovered even as I write these words. It is not that which causes my weariness.

I scarce know what to say or how to explain it. I am tired of a battle I have fought all my life, a battle thought long won which, actually, I came extremely close to losing. Yet—in the ensuing victory I feel no joy. Only continuing loss.

It is all very confusing. I must pull myself together. I've just come from mediating a face-to-face confrontation between the Mahdi and

Merarch Quantrill of the Draka Security Directorate. Quantrill has surrounded El Obeid with a Draka legion that he commands. Yet, he says that he accepts the Mahdi's offer of alliance, as enumerated in the documents drawn up by Alexander von Shrakenberg and signed by the Mahdi. He has even accepted the offer to attend a banquet in the city in honor of him and his staff.

Yet, I do not trust him. Quantrill is a swine. He is without honor. Still, tonight might be a perfect opportunity to probe his mind and attempt to catch a hint of his plans, whatever they are. I'm sure that ultimately he's up to no good.

I am sorry my dear sister. I usually don't burden you with my problems like this. Attribute it to my weariness. Still, writing these lines has done me some good. It has helped to clear my mind as to what I must do. Now I shall go post this and (as unreliable as the mail service is) pray that it reaches you eventually.

Please, pray for me, your sinning brother, as I pray for you and our family every day.

Your loving Brother,
C.

VII.

Gordon went out into the night, alone. Despite his recent wounds and weakness, he felt like walking. He felt like more than that, actually, but he couldn't get on a camel and head off into the clear, clean desert to be alone with thoughts that he scarcely could admit to himself. But he simply couldn't stand the thought of being confined any longer. The narrow, winding streets of El Obeid, so much like those of Khartoum, were little better than his closed-in room. He had to get out and be alone and prepare himself for the dinner in honor of Quantrill and his staff. But he couldn't focus his mind.

A hot wind blew like a blast from an open fire. It was unpleasant, of course, but no way near as unpleasant as the flames of Hell, which ultimately he knew was his due.

He was a sodomite. Pure and simple. He was a sinner and when he died he would burn in Hell. Pure and simple.

Almost it was a relief to admit it to himself. Of course he had *known* it. He had known it for years and years, back to his days at boarding school, but somehow he had never *admitted* it to himself. He had certainly never acted on the realization. It had been thirty-seven years since he had touched another with love. He had thought the Mahdi . . .

But, no, of course not. He was fifty, now, hardly in his prime. Old and useless . . .

"Gordon. Fancy seeing you here."

Gordon stopped, startled. He had been wandering with his head down, lost in thought, unaware of his surroundings.

Make that old and stupid, he told himself. Somewhere Agag snickered.

It took Gordon a moment before he recognize the man standing before him in the dark. He was a European in civilian dress. No—he was American. It was Desmond.

"Desmond? What're you doing here? You should be at the Mahdi's palace. The dinner."

Desmond nodded. "I'll make it to the nigger's in time for the festivities. I hope. I have to take care of something first."

Gordon knew. Desmond's right hand was in his bulging pants' pocket, no doubt resting on the grip of a pistol. Gordon smiled.

"I see." Curiously, his depression immediately lightened. Nothing like an assassination attempt, he thought, to focus your mind. "Something you should have handled yourself, a while ago."

"Oh, I quite agree," Desmond said. "Quantrill's orders, of course, but they were my men. They failed though. Never send a nigger or a wog to do a man's work."

"Mind telling me one thing?" Gordon asked.

"What's that?"

"Why?"

Desmond grinned at him. "Well, it's simple, isn't it? You're the go-between. You're the proof, as it were. Without you, there's no evidence that the Mahdi accepted the plan of that traitorous swine von Shrakenberg."

Gordon smiled. "Except for the documents that the Mahdi signed."

"Oh, those." Desmond waved it away. "Those will be destroyed tonight. Along with the Mahdi and the rest of his scum."

"What?"

"Of course. The Mahdi, you see, is the key to this whole thing. Without him, the revolt falls to bits. Without his leadership his savages become, well, worthless savages again." Desmond glanced down to consult a watch he took with his left hand from the pocket on his vest. "The dinner will start any moment now. Of course, under a flag of truce the Draka officers won't be asked to give up their sidearms. Their repeating pistols. Some have smuggled in small packets of explosives as well. They'll kill the Mahdi and wipe out his staff easily. I'm sorry to miss it. It'll be rare sport."

"Sport?" Gordon said through gritted teeth. "Under a flag of truce?"

Desmond shrugged. "Why not? They're only niggers. Oh, sure, there's some white men on the Mahdi's staff, but that's what they get, you see." He smiled at Gordon. "The sounds of gunfire at the palace will be the signal for the general assault on the city. Steam-draggers will batter down the gates. Quantrill's elite legion will swarm in and wipe out the unsuspecting niggers. Easy as pie." Desmond smiled again. "And I'll take care of you."

Gordon's fury increased. He couldn't believe the filthy treachery in Desmond's calm words. Actually—he could. The plan reeked of Quantrill. It was just like him to slaughter unarmed hosts while under a white flag. He would think it clever.

There was the sudden clatter of gunfire from the direction of the Mahdi's palace. Gordon closed his eyes.

"Ah," Desmond said. "There's the signal—"

"One more thing," Gordon asked, his eyes still closed.

"What's that?" Desmond asked, a hint of impatience in his voice.

"Have you killed many men from close up?"

Desmond frowned. "No. Why?"

Gordon's eyes flew open. Boiling with rage he launched himself at the Draka, hand dropping for the jambiyah sheathed at his side. Desmond drew backward as he yanked the pistol from his pocket. But the handgun's hammer snagged on the pocket lining. He pulled harder and it tore free. He lifted the weapon to fire, but Gordon was on him.

They collided, falling backward with Gordon on top, his blade drawn. He stuck it in Desmond's stomach and slashed sideways. His face was inches from Desmond's and the Draka's expression was fear and pain, mingled equally.

"A knife is better for that kind of thing," Gordon told him as he gutted him. Gordon jumped

to his feet, ignoring the blood which soaked the
front of his clothes. His only thought was to get
to the Mahdi. Quantrill, of course, was right. The
Mahdi was the key to the whole thing. Without the
Mahdi, the revolt wouldn't last another month. But
even if he destroyed the copy of the treaty he and
the Mahdi had signed, there was the other copy
Gordon had sent off with Rimbaud. The Draka
would learn of Quantrill's treachery through that
document.

But would they care? Gordon guessed that the
Draka, pragmatic to the end, would care only if
Quantrill failed to end the Mahdi's threat.

Gordon must do all he could to see that the Mahdi
survived this vile treachery. All he could. He ran
toward the palace. Already El Obeid was in chaos.
The gunfire around the palace had died out. That
wasn't a good sign. The legion had begin its assault.
He could hear their vehicles smashing through the
city gates.

God grant him his wish to be in time—

The palace's dining room was full of death. There
were corpses everywhere. Most were native, but there
were some Draka-uniformed bodies as well. He
searched the room but couldn't find the Mahdi, alive
or dead, so there was still hope. Perhaps, Gordon
thought, they had taken him prisoner.

The rest of the palace was chaotic. Soldiers and
servants were fleeing, some looting before the Draka
could arrive. There were no Draka officers to be
seen—and then Gordon heard sounds coming from
the garden behind the palace.

He went through an archway to the torch-lit garden,
and stopped to stare at one of the most horrific scenes
he'd ever witnessed.

He could recognize the Mahdi—or at least his
severed head—even at a distance by his fine white
teeth, visible because the mouth was open in a ric-

tus of false suffering. False because the Mahdi was dead and truly beyond all pain and suffering.

The fine dark eyes were shut, the bladed nose smashed askew, the flesh of his cheeks torn away so that his birthmark was missing. The entire head was caked with dirt and blood.

As Gordon watched, the Draka officers crowded around it as it lay on the ground, and laughed uproariously. One of them stepped back half a dozen paces, drew his sidearm, and fired at it. He missed, and the officers laughed again.

"I'll show you what a marksman I am," someone said. It was Quantrill. There was no mistaking him for another officer. He was a short man, not much taller than Gordon. His arms and legs were lank and thin, making his bloated stomach appear even more colossal than it was. His face was red and flushed, certainly from excitement and drinking both. His eyes were bleary, his nose the size and shape of a rotten potato discarded in the field at harvest. The sight of him made Gordon sick, but his actions were even more disgusting.

He approached the Mahdi's severed head until he stood right over it, undid the fly of his trousers, and urinated upon it. He shook with laughter as his piss struck the Mahdi's head between what was left of his eyes, cascaded down his features and dribbled down his chin to splatter on the dusty ground.

The other Draka laughed like this was the funniest thing they had ever seen, but Gordon went cold, inside and out, though a white hotness flashed before his eyes.

"Is that the use to which you put your peter? That and satisfying your lust upon barnyard animals?"

His voice rang out hard across the laughter, which was silenced instantaneously, and Gordon didn't know who was more surprised to hear it, Quantrill or himself. He scarcely realized that he had spoke and he wondered where the words had come from.

Quantrill whirled, his face scarlet with anger. *"What did you say?"*

In that moment, Gordon suddenly realized he knew to what end he had spoken. He wondered if the words had come from Agag, or from himself, but in the end, he realized also that it didn't matter. He *was* Agag, or at least Agag was a piece of him. He was made up of a multitude of pieces, and he could live with them all. He didn't have to crush them down and hide them away, he didn't have to cut them away from himself. This realization struck him with the force of an epiphany that come over him as hard and fast as a gift from God. Was it? he asked himself wonderingly. Was it?

"You're pissing on your boots," he said to Quantrill politely.

"Huh?" Quantrill looked down, swore to himself, and cut off the flow of urine. He put himself back in his pants, and looked back up at Gordon, who was approaching slowly.

"Gordon? Is that you, Gordon?"

"It is, sir. Charles George Gordon, sir, Field Marshall in the Armies of China and the Ottoman Empire, proud possessor of the Peacock Feather given me personally from the hands of the Empress of China, Governor-General of the Sudan, and lately Colonel in Her Imperial Majesty's Army!"

Agag, loose at long last, simply faded away, disappearing to where Gordon knew not.

"You, sir, on the other hand, are a drunken, filthy, treacherous swine." Gordon added when he'd gotten within arm's reach of Quantrill, "Of course, such behavior is only to be expected from one with the taint of negro blood."

Quantrill eyes bulged until Gordon thought they would literally pop out of their sockets. The veins in his neck swelled and Gordon could see them pulse in time to the blood pounding in his forehead.

"Wha—wha—"

Around them was deathly silence as most of the Draka officers looked on in blank incomprehension, though from the looks on some faces, several had guessed what Gordon was doing. None tried to stop him.

"I wonder. Was your mother raped by a negro, or did she go to his arms eagerly, willingly, because your father—"

Quantrill hit him in the face with his clenched right hand. Gordon's head jerked back at the force of the blow, but he caught Quantrill's left before it could land. No one else moved, though a shudder, partially of excitement, partially of dismay, went through the onlookers.

Gordon twisted Quantrill's wrist, painfully, moved in even closer, and spit right in his face. Quantrill gurgled incoherently and his hand dropped for the hilt of the pistol that was thrust in his belt.

Gordon smiled. Always with the gun, he thought, and his hand dropped to the pommel of his jambiyah and drew it in one swift motion.

Quantrill's pistol had cleared his belt. He was bringing the muzzle up to point at Gordon's stomach, but Gordon was already slashing backhandedly with the jambiyah. It went in shallow at the right side of Quantrill's abdomen and sunk in deeper as he cut across the mass of fat that sheltered Quantrill's guts. Quantrill's finger tightened on the trigger and the pistol discharged into the ground between them. Gordon never even flinched.

"That's for ordering my death," Gordon said into Quantrill's anguished face. With all his strength he rammed the point of the jambiyah as hard as he could into Quantrill's guts. "And that's for the Mahdi, God rest his soul."

Quantrill's breath exploded from his lungs and all the strength flowed from his legs. Gordon held him

up for a moment, then pushed him savagely away. The
knife slipped out of his abdomen, and, as Quantrill fell
backwards his guts came out in great shining coils. He
lay whimpering on the ground, his hands making feeble
motions to stuff his intestines back into his slashed
stomach, flies already buzzing hungrily around him.

"The devil take yours," Gordon told him.

He looked up and around at the Draka officers
who stood in a tight knot, looking from Quantrill,
crying quietly on the ground, to Gordon, and back
again.

"Self-defense," Gordon said, and turned and walked
away.

It was over. He was done with soldiering and fighting and killing. He had a life to live, a dam to build,
a river to tame. It would be hard work, but he'd never
been afraid of hard work. At least from now on his
hands would be dirty with only soil, not with blood.

May, 10 1883
Alexandria

My Dearest Augusta:

I fear that it shall be some time before I'll
be able to visit you and the family again. I have
an enormous amount of work before me, but for
the first time in a long time I feel as if I'll be
able to get it all done. I am done, forever, I
hope, with soldiering. I've had enough of that
to last a lifetime. To last several lifetimes. Perhaps when I am really old and feeble and can
do no more than grip a pen, I shall write my
memoirs. There are stories to be told, no doubt,
if the world is ready to hear them.

I am staying for now with Alexander von
Shrakenberg. There are some questions about
the curious death of a Draka merarch that must

be answered, but von Shrakenberg assures me that matters will work out just fine. The affair ended satisfactorily for the Draka, and that really is all they care about. The Mahdi's Revolt is over and the Sudan is pacified. Not in the way I would have wished, but as you know my dear, that is often the case in life.

I'll find my own lodgings in time, but now I take an odd comfort in living in the household of this strange Draka. He'll probably burn in Hell, though, I'm not the one to judge him. He is a likable man, for a Draka.

He's involved in more activities than any ten men. Cotton plantations, dirigible plants, government projects of all types and stripes, yet he also has time for a full social schedule.

As you know I find that sort of thing tiresome, but just this morning he and his wife Edith were telling me about this new houseguest due to arrive later today. Alexander swears that he's a brilliant conversationalist and great wit and that I'll just adore him. He's a writer, like that Frenchy, Rimbaud. I guess all and all Rimbaud wasn't a bad fellow, but he's hardly someone you'd care to invite to your home. (Hah! Like myself, some would say. Perhaps, like Our Lord Christ, I will learn to practice more tolerance.)

Anyway, he's an Irish chap, name of Oscar Wilde. Ever heard of him?

Your Loving Brother, in Christ:
Charles

Roland Green is a man of letters who dwells in Chicago. He has written fantasy—*Wandor's Journey*—and alternate history, a continuation of the great H. Beam Piper's work in *Great King's War*.

Besides writing, Roland reads a great deal, especially in history maritime and military. He really *knows* the details, and in his hands they're anything but dull and dry; they're the stuff of living, breathing human beings.

In this story, the rising Draka meet the Rising Sun, as two powers of the periphery of the world challenge the older states for room to live.

However bad it was, it could have been worse . . .

WRITTEN BY THE WIND

A STORY OF THE DRAKA

Roland J. Green

I.

Sasebo Naval Airship Base, Empire of Japan
0430, August 18, 1905

A hundred meters aft, one of *Satsuma's* engines
came to life. Horace Jahn felt the vibration through
the big dirigible's aluminum structure before the
sound reached his ears. Once it did, the diesel
sounded like the purring of a cat—a distant cat, the
size of an auto steamer.

Probably Engine #3, the Draka calculated. He could not have told a ground gripper how he made the calculation, but after ten years in airships, it took hardly more thought than breathing. (Say, hiding the need to sneeze at a formal banquet.) But even after he saw lights going on, he wondered why they'd started an engine.

Like the rest of the Imperial Japanese Navy's First Air *Kokutai*, *Satsuma* was snugged down to her moorings, bow locked to the mobile mast and tail just as firmly gripped by the mooring car. Her internal electrics could run off ground power, saving fuel for her five diesels until she lifted off.

Jahn strode forward, remembering to duck as he stepped off the catwalk and scrambled down the ladder to the control deck. *Satsuma* and her five sisters were first cousins to the Dominion's *Harpy* class, but when the Japanese Navy assembled them, they modified them for crews a good ten centimeters shorter than the average male Draka—and Jahn's North German genes ran him up several centimeters beyond that respectable height. The first few weeks aboard Imperial airships had left bruises and scrapes on his forehead, hips, knees, and elbows.

More lights came on. Two crewmen in blue coveralls seemed to sprout from the deck. They bowed to Jahn, then scrambled up the ladder before Jahn could return the bow or take more than two steps forward. He did not believe that the Imperial Navy was really assigning *ninja* adepts to spy on the *gaijin* advisers they were letting watch them fight the Russians, but it was undeniably hard for any of the observers to be awake and alone for long.

At least the Draka had found this easier to adapt to than some of the other nationalities, particularly the British and Germans. Omnipresent little brown men in blue or white were not too different from the household serfs that every Citizen took for granted, from the cradle to the deathbed, however un-serflike their behavior.

The brightest lights and the only noise except the distant diesel seemed to come from the radio room. Jahn looked in through the uncurtained doorway, to see Warrant Officer Chiba at the central table, while a pair of long, blue-clad legs thrust out from what seemed to be the bowels of the radio cabinet.

Jahn didn't need rude magnolia-accented mutterings floating out past the legs to know their owner. He had vivid and mostly pleasant memories of all his encounters with Tetrarch Julia Belle Pope of the Women's Auxiliary Service, and some of the most vivid were also the most pleasant.

Repairs on the radio explained the power-up; the Shalamanzar XVI airship sets ate power like a mine serf attacking his dinner. Pope was a qualified radio operator and instructor, land, sea, and air. Was she aboard for maintenance, or—?

It was less than an hour before the *Kokutai* was supposed to lift out on the biggest airship operation since the Draka burned Odessa. That was slicing time thinly, even with somebody who could work (or play) as fast as Pope.

"Attention!" Jahn called softly.

Scrape, rattle, *thump*, then:

"Shit in your rice bowel, Horrie!" in excellent Japanese. Warrant Officer Chiba tried not to grin.

Tetrarch Pope scrambled out of the radio housing, managed to combine a salute and wiping oil off her forehead, then finger-combed her dark hair as she looked Jahn up and down. He was familiar with her looks of friendly appraisal; this appraisal was hardly friendly.

"Ah had a feeling it might come tah this, when the Archangels borrowed me for *Satsuma*," she said in English, using the term for the Arch-Strategos and Rear Admiral who nominally ran the Draka observation mission. "But Chief Yoshiwara's gone in for surgery. Appendix, ah heard. It came down to me joining the crew or Chiba flying solo. Surely y'all wouldn't want to gladden yo' male hearts that badly, now would y'all?"

Chiba shot Jahn a look that combined mild alarm and complete resignation. Any Warrant radio operator had to understand enough English to know what was going on. The Japanese were up there with the fustiest of British cavalry generals, in preferrring women far behind the shooting line. But preferences were one thing; arguing with Julia Belle Pope was something else.

"You getting killed isn't going to gladden my heart at all," Jahn said. "Or anybody else's."

He thought he saw her shifting her feet, to be ready for a fight if things went that far. Then he raised her near hand to his lips, bowed over it, kissed it, clicked his heels in a perfect parody of *Leutnant zur See* Peter Strasser, and grinned.

"But I suppose you wish to know what happens to me as soon as possible. I take the liberty of assuming that you would miss me—as I would indeed miss you."

He thought his voice had been steady when he said that, as a Citizen's and a soldier's ought to be. Apparently he didn't quite succeed. Pope snatched her hand back, and Jahn could have sworn she was blushing as she dove back into the radio cabinet.

"Yo' ain't good lookin' enough to just stand around lak a prettybuck, Horrie," floated out from the shadows. "So if yo' cain't think of anythin' better to do, check the battery in the Numbah Three worklight and ah'd be evah so grateful."

"Aye aye, ma'am," Jahn said, pointed at Chiba, and switched to Japanese.

"Hard work, Chiba-*san,* and while we're at it, count the rest of the torch batteries."

❖   ❖   ❖

It had been Pope who kissed Jahn first, and that on the first day they met, in the third month of the war. That had been a surprise; most of the rest he'd learned about Julia Belle Pope in the seven months since hadn't been. Frightening, delightful, or outrageous in about equal proportions—and after a while, they could laugh together about even the outrageous parts. . .

He'd been returning to the Draka Mission Compound outside Sasebo after the first airship patrol where the Japanese had allowed him to stand bridge watches alone. Since he'd commanded *Fury* out of Trincomalee two full years before the war broke out, they hadn't needed to take so long to admit that he was a qualified airship officer.

However, Japan's industrial base was limited. Russian front-line strength was two to one against them, and the Americans were using financial influence and the threat of their Pacific and China Fleets to enforce an arms embargo that hurt the Japanese much more than it did the Russians. Modern weapons to the Japanese were like Citizens to the Draka— capital, not interest, to be expended with the same exquisite caution.

Jahn unpacked his flight gear and took a sponge bath in his quarters. He always preferred to be alone for a few minutes, after days in the echoing cramped- ness of an airship's quarters. Then he headed for the palestra—the *dojo*, he corrected himself. Half an hour of exercise or even a few minutes' sparring would unkink the rest of his muscles and make him fit for the company of Citizens, Japanese hosts, or even other nations' observer teams.

The *dojo*, however, was already occupied. Jahn's first proof of that came as he opened the door and saw a tanned bare foot dart toward Lieutenant Commander Goto's head. Goto saved himself from having the foot shatter his nose and cheekbone by a blurringly fast back roll, then pivoted on his thick arms and scythed down his opponent with both legs. An *"Umpff!"* and the sound of a body hitting the bamboo mats marked the end of the bout.

Jahn stepped forward and bowed to Goto and the unknown other. He—no, *she*—was already rolling to her feet, favoring one leg a trifle. She was half a meter narrower and a head taller than Goto, who resembled a pocket-sized sumo wrestler.

Goto and the woman returned the bows. "How was your flight?" Goto said, in Japanese.

The Imperial officer probably already knew more about the patrol than Jahn did. Goto was an accomplished submariner temporarily assigned to the staff job of playing herdboy to the Draka observer mission. He'd abandoned none of his old contacts, even if they hadn't got him the submarine command he transparently wanted.

Jahn looked at the woman, realized that she was not only European but Draka, and decided that the long-rumored Women's Auxiliary Corps detachment must have arrived while he was in the air. He also decided that a little courtesy might put a smile on a very agreeable face. It had vast pools of brown eyes, a wide mouth with dazzling white teeth, a frame of curling dark hair, and only one negative point—a nose so long and sharp that Jahn had a brief mental image both erotic and ludicrous.

He bowed to the woman again. "Lieutenant Commander Horace Jahn, Airship Service of the Navy of the Dominion."

She replied with a salute. "Tetrarch Julia Pope, Women's Auxiliary Corps, at your service." She spoke in fluent Japanese, with a more refined accent than Goto's, or even Jahn's. Then she grinned, and Jahn was not disappointed over what a grin did to her face.

Jahn turned to Goto. "We flew as far as the Bonins—pardon, the Ogasawaras—but sighted little.

Yubari is still aground on Iwo Jima, and nothing remains of last week's cruiser battle but wreckage and a few rafts. We saw no signs of life on any of them."

"Ran has taken them to her," Pope said. Even in Japanese, she sounded as if she was praying. Jahn's eyebrows twitched. He'd heard the Norse gods invoked quite a few times since the Old Faith revival started. Usually the invocation was the gods' private parts, and he'd *never* heard anyone reverently name the goddess of the sea.

"May it be so," Jahn said. Goto also bowed his head and muttered a Shinto prayer too softly for the Draka to catch all of it. "On the way back, we saw an American airship—*Shenandoah* class, I think—who shadowed us for about eight hours until we shook her off at nightfall. They said they were off their course to the Philippines, but they didn't turn when we gave them the correct heading."

Pope's face now twisted into something that only needed a few snakes to be a perfect mask of Medusa. "Damnyankee snoops!" she snarled in English. "What do they think they're doin', messin' around in this war? Think the Japanese are Confederates in disguise?"

The accent was American—Confederate American. Obviously no relative of the Union General, later Senator, John Pope. Her family would have fought the American Civil War in gray and butternut, with Ferguson rifles that Horace's grandfather William might have run through the blockade.

"I doubt that we shall agree on the rights of the United States to be interested in this war," Goto said. "From their point of view, the total victory of either side would endanger their position in the Philippines and western Pacific, not to mention their hopes that the Tai'pings may turn China into a valuable trading partner."

"The only position ah want tah see Yankees in is

on their hands and knees, beggin' the Confederacy
to secede again," Pope said briskly. "But ah suppose
that's too much to ask for, in anythin' but a what-if
novel like that fellah Futrelle writes."

"Most likely," Goto said. "But a word to you,
Tetrarch Pope, speaking as one who is for the moment
acting as your *sensei*. You must remember not to strike
except when you are *completely* centered. You are
very fast and have a longer reach than many Japanese. . . but striking from the true center gives you
the advantage over a non-centered opponent of any
size."

Pope nodded, and looked Jahn up and down. He
felt like a prize bull being judged at an agricultural
fair. "Want tah go a few falls, sir, see if Goto's right?"
she asked.

Jahn shook his head. Pope's face hardened again.
Jahn almost took a step backward.

"Because I'm a woman?"

He shook his head. "Two *good* reasons. I've had
ten hours of sleep in the last five days. Also, my
school didn't teach the pankration style. I wasn't too
bad at Graeco-Roman wrestling—"

"Ha!" Goto said. "Jahn-*san* has five heavyweight
wrestling crowns, two from school and three from the
Navy. Indeed, I would say that he was not too bad."

"Even mo' interestin'" Pope said. "Ah do think a
friendly match might be entertainin'. But some othah
time, ah agree—wouldn't do fo' me to have an unfair
advantage, now would it?"

She stepped up to Jahn, gave him a not-quite-
mocking peck on the cheek, then sauntered over to
where her gear bag stood on a bench. The Japanese
palestra garment, the white cotton *gi*, was loose fitting for freedom of movement, but Julia Pope would
have looked good in a barley sack, either going away
or coming toward you.

Obviously one of the Advanced Women, Jahn

thought, *and a red-hot Rebel as well. Odd combination—but interesting for more than her physical parts. Not that there's anything likely to be wrong with those . . .*

Lieutenant Commander Goto ignored the water still draining from *Number 36*'s bridge platform, that had already soaked his legs to mid-calf. He braced himself between the railing and the periscope housing and studied the horizon with his binoculars. On the other side of the housing, Sub-Lieutenant Yamamoto did the same. Behind them, one seaman made notes as the two officers identified the Russian ships, while another stood lookout.

The Russians had no operational submarines at Port Arthur, or so said the Naval Staff, but the Naval Staff was not infallible. Nor was it impossible that some of their newer undersea vessels, nearly as powerful as *Number 36*, could have made the voyage south from Vladivostok to support the Far East Fleet in its biggest operation of the war.

Meanwhile, less than ten thousand meters away, five hundred or more guns paraded by. The smallest of them would be able to keep the submarine from diving with a single hit. Goto focused his binoculars to get a better look at the ships now passing, *Petr Veliky* and two others of her class of five. Eight 30cm guns, fourteen 150cm, a score of lighter weapons, all cased in 250mm armor and driven by Germania/Danzigwerke turbines at twenty-three knots.

The Germans had an odd taste for supplying a potential enemy, Russia, with so much modern weaponry. But Britain was another potential enemy and Japan a British ally in all but name. "The enemy of my enemy is my friend" was doubtless a popular saying among German shipbuilders.

Three torpedo gunboats now, one-twentieth the battleships' tonnage, seven knots faster, no armor and no guns larger than 10cm, but six torpedo tubes. Then a ship with even more freeboard than the battleships and three even taller funnels, belching a plume of smoke that must have had anyone in her wake coughing like a consumptive. Her decks were crowded with gray-clad troops whose uniforms nearly blended into the superstructure. Goto waited until the transport was out of his field of vision, but before she was gone, another (this one had two funnels and a green hull) steamed into view.

Goto and Yamamoto counted twelve troop-laden transports and nine cargo vessels before the Russian fleet vanished behind its own smoke cloud, still headed south. At least thirty-five warships, probably more, convoying at least twenty-one merchant vessels, was Goto's count. As he asked Yamamoto for his estimate, they both heard the distant rumble of guns.

"We did not see them all," the younger officer said. "They have sent a squadron against Wei-hai-wei."

"Much good may that do them," Goto said. The Japanese had not successfully attacked Port Arthur since it fell to the Russians at the beginning of the war, because of its defending gun batteries, mines, torpedo squadrons, and shore-launched torpedoes. The Japanese anchorage at Wei-hai-wei was just as well defended, with five coastal submarines in place of the shore torpedo tubes. It also now held the coastal defense ships *Fuso* and *Haruna*, which gave Goto a personal reason for wishing that the Russians were only making a diversion. His brother commanded a main-battery turret aboard *Fuso*, and the two old ships were the most visible targets in the anchorage if the Russians tried a serious attack.

Unlikely, though. The agents left behind when the Imperial Navy evacuated Port Arthur had taken full advantage of the Russians being unable to tell a Chinese-speaking Japanese from a native Chinese, and gained full details of the Russian plan to strike far to the south, at Hainan Island. The transports would be carrying nearly five thousand Russian soldiers to spearhead the attack on the island, and the cargo vessels thousands of tons of modern weapons and ammunition, to supply the private armies of the Chinese governors of the coastal provinces. Then either Japan's hard-won foothold on the Chinese coast would be attacked, or the Combined Fleet would have to sortie and meet a superior Russian Far East Fleet at a time and place of the Russians' choosing.

Or possibly both together.

Goto studied the horizon again, then nodded to Yamamoto.

"Trim down until only the radio mast is above water. Then we will transmit our report."

Yamamoto's round young face showed confusion. "Are we not going to pursue on the surface and attack by night?"

"*After* we report, if then," Goto replied. "The courage of the samurai is not in rushing to his death without purpose or gain. It is in serving the Emperor to the best of his abilities, whether by living or by dying."

"As the Emperor commands—"

"—so we are done with sitting about in plain sight," Goto finished. "Clear the bridge and rig for running awash." The soft-voiced command was enough to start the others scrambling through the hatch. Unlike the raucous diving alarm, it could reach no hostile ears.

The meeting of Jahn and Pope at the *dojo* was the first of many, at intervals of a few days over the next five months. Acquaintance ripened into friendship as the war settled into a stalemate both on land and at sea, a situation everyone knew that the Russians could endure longer than the Japanese.

The only unfrustrated Japanese either of the Draka knew was Goto. A month after their meeting, he received his orders—command of *Number 36*, one of the latest Imperial Fleet submarines. His farewell party was memorable, and his relief at getting back into the fighting undisguised.

The Japanese raided across the Yalu River into Russian-occupied Manchuria, and sent occasional airship raids against vulnerable points on the Trans-Siberian Railroad. The Russians sent their long-range cruisers south from Petropavlosk, creeping out behind icebreakers during the long nights, to raid Japanese ocean commerce. The Japanese raided the strongholds of pro-Russian Chinese, while similar squadrons of Russian light craft raided the Japanese coast. Each side tried to interrupt the other's oil shipments from Borneo (*Number 36* torpedoed a Russian auxiliary cruiser off Sarawak, sending it limping off to internment in Haiphong), until the Americans persuaded the British to join them in establishing a Neutrality Patrol around the oil fields. Rumor had it that they'd threatened to occupy the Sultan of Brunei's territory with a regiment of Marines if the British didn't cooperate.

That rumor moved Julia Pope to eloquent fury. "That's the closest the Yankees have come to really messin' with somebody who could mess them back, since ah was a girl. Then they'all have to go kiss and make up. Ah could *spit*."

Which she promptly did, startling two British officers passing by. One of them looked ready to take up the challenge of such unladylike conduct, but Jahn now knew Pope well enough to step back and let her deal with the officer on her own.

"Although if he'd said 'loose Draka morals' one more time, they'd *both* have had a quarrel with me," Jahn said, when Pope had finished an explanation that fell somewhat short of an apology. "Would you have left enough of them for me?"

"If ah was feelin' generous, maybe," she said,

slipping her arm through his. That was Improper Public Contact under the regulations, but even with the Women's Auxiliary detachment, the Draka observation mission was still less than a hundred strong. That was no more than a couple of tetrarchies or the crew of a torpedo gunboat, even if two flag officers commanded it, and all Citizens. Discipline was therefore easy enough so that Jahn and Pope could indulge themselves in the pleasure of shocking the other observers. It probably amused the Japanese, and what the Archangels didn't know wouldn't hurt anybody.

"Right now, though, ah feel closer to *dirty*," Pope said. "Mind if we share the fee for the *ofuro*?"

Jahn started suspecting things when Pope reserved a private bath at a respectable inn. He stopped suspecting and started hoping when she slipped off her uniform and climbed into the tub with him. Nothing he saw disappointed him at all, and his body's reaction to her undraped splendor apparently didn't disappoint *her*.

"You look glad to see me." He would have sworn that she was purring.

"Well, I might call you—ah, *see* worthy. Very."

They went eagerly from looking to touching, and it was quite a while before they had free lips or enough breath to say anything.

That wasn't the last such encounter, either. The Japanese grew cautious about letting anybody's observers aboard their dirigibles, claiming that most of them were on patrol against the Petropavlovsk raiding cruisers, in the dangerous weather over the icy seas off Hokkaido and the Kuriles. Nothing to see, or so Goto's dour replacement told Jahn, "And we can hardly ask foreign observers to expose themselves in areas where we send even our own men reluctantly."

Since the Combined Fleet held most of its exercises as far north as possible, to escape those same foreign observers and "strengthen the spirits of the men," Jahn knew that the officer was lying and suspected that the officer knew that Jahn knew. However, implying either of these things would offend Japanese honor, probably leading to Jahn's being shipped home on a slow Portuguese tramp freighter.

Julia listened attentively, almost affectionately, that night, then gently bit the side of his neck and whispered in his ear, "Somethin' that the serf wenches do, that they say is fun for men too." Her mouth moved downward, until she heard him laugh.

"You'd bettah tell me what yo' find so funny, or ah just might bite."

Jahn tried to control his voice, and finally managed it by stroking her hair. With his eyes on the waxed cedar of the ceiling, he said, "Your nose. It's—that long, that I thought—if you ever did this—you would *gut* me with that—ow!"

The nip was playful, though. After a while, he groaned. "I see I was wrong."

"You cain't see anythin', Horrie. You've got your eyes shut."

"I see Paradise. That's enough."

"Ah thought the Christians say there's no lovin' in Heaven," she murmured, as well as she could with her mouth full.

"They could be wrong."

"Ah most sincerely hope so."

II

Over the Sea of Japan, 0800, August 18, 1905

It was three and a half hours since Jahn saw Pope's legs protruding from under the radio cabinet. It was also three hours and twenty-five minutes into a mystery.

What were the Japanese up to?

He and Pope had still been on the observation platform aft of the radio room when they saw out the windows a convoy rolling by, a long line of the little pneumatic lorries that the Japanese used on major bases. They moved at a walking pace—proof of this: more than a hundred armed sailors marched to either side of the convoy, shouldering bayoneted rifles while their officers marched with drawn swords.

Each lorry towed a bomb cart, with a canvas-shrouded bundle on it. Jahn thought that there were two sizes of bundles, both larger than conventional bombs. As he tried to lean out the window, two of *Satsuma*'s crew came up behind him, politely urged him back, then slid the shutters closed with a fierce rattling and clinking.

A minute later, more metallic noises floated in from outside and from below. Winches and chains were lifting something heavy—*something that they did not want him to see*—aboard *Satsuma* and the rest of the airships. This went on for a good twenty minutes, interrupted once by a gonglike *bwannnggg* and a cacophony of screams and Japanese curses.

Jahn himself had never dropped a bomb in anger, and never seen anything larger than the standard 500-kilo incendiary clusters, direct descendants of the warloads that burned Odessa a generation ago. He knew that several nations had bombs twice that weight. The Draka and the Americans had even used them in combat, on Bushmen in the Sahara and Moro rebels in the Philippines who'd gone to earth too far from roads to allow the peacekeepers to bring up artillery. No doubt the Japanese wanted something even bigger to be a surprise to both friend and foe.

Then trumpets and whistles called *Satsuma*'s crew to quarters for getting underway. Five officers (plus

Jahn and Pope) and twenty-eight petty officers and men saluted the Emperor's portrait (or faced toward the shrine holding the portrait, if they were on duty elsewhere), then all five engines came to life. Now the purring sounded more like a pride of lions who had just feasted on fresh livestock (with perhaps a lion dog or two for dessert). . .

Engine exhaust warmed the air in the superheat cell and *Satsuma* lifted gently into the still morning air, along with five other airships of her lead squadron. Jahn found an unshuttered window and saw that the morning haze was also lifting, except where the ten thousand charcoal fires of any Japanese city created their own murk. Jahn reminded himself that for a country with no local oil supply, burning charcoal was prudent frugality, not primitive filth. . .

His composure didn't survive a good look at the anchorage. Instead of empty water cut only by a few boat trails, he saw at least a squadron of battleships and armored cruisers, flanked by a line of scout cruisers on one side and torpedo cruisers and gunboats on the other. At least they had steam up and the scouts had raised observation balloons, but they amounted to a good third of the already-outgunned Combined Fleet and they were *still in harbor.*

Also, why the observation balloons, when they would be working with the airships?

Speculation ended then, as *Satsuma* glided forward, all five aluminum propellers chopping a wake of wind through the sky as the First Air *Kokutai* headed out to sea. Jahn's speculations only returned two hours later, as the propellers slowed while the engines worked as hard as ever, feeding the superheat so that the dirigibles went on climbing.

At three thousand meters, nearly pressure height, *Satsuma* broke out of one layer of clouds. Through unshuttered windows, Jahn had a good view of most of the *Kokutai*. Two-thirds of the Empire's airpower described slow circles between two layers of cloud, like a school of gigantic silver-gray fish in a god-sized aquarium. The flagship *Akagi* was so close that Jahn felt he could stick a hand out the window and touch the ten-meter square sun-rayed battle ensign flying from her upper fin.

He was raising his binoculars to get a better view of *Akagi's* bomb racks, when he saw a light blinking from the flagship. Something punched him in the back and someone said, "Yes!" behind him, as he finished reading the signal. Then a soft voice said:

" 'The fate of the Empire depends on this day. Let every man do his utmost.' "

Jahn turned to see a grinning Julia Pope. "Ah don't suppose anybody told Admiral Kondo that there's at least one *woman* who's goin' to do her utmost?"

"He's probably too carried away by being the first admiral to lead an airship fleet into action."

"You think we're goin' after the Russian fleet?"

"Our hosts have to be secretive and ruthless. They can't afford to be crazy."

Commander Goto had thought of manning the deck gun as *Number 36* ploughed south, green water swallowing her bow torpedo tubes as she worked up to her full surface speed of fourteen knots. However, the stubby 80mm gun was hardly effective against anything bigger than a junk, and shooting up one of those would merely make noise that might alert the Russians to who was on their trail. The gun's crew would also be more men to get below, if the Russians became suspicious on their own and sent a torpedo squadron racing north to clear their wakes.

Goto would yield to no one aboard in his pride in *Number 36*. But right now he would have considered trading her for one of the French *croiseur-sousmarins de haute mer* or even one of those Swedish submarines that were supposed to have a folding air pipe that let them run their diesels submerged. The Russians could hardly do more to *Number 36* and her comrades than force them to dive, but a submarine's fourteen knots on the surface dwindled to five or six submerged, and a single torpedo gunboat could keep *Number 36* down until nightfall. By then, the Russians would have an unbeatable lead.

Yamamoto scrambled up the hatch and saluted. "Message from Fleet Headquarters, sir."

Goto read the yellow flimsy and nodded. "Let us pray that our best will be good enough."

"I have calculated, sir. If the Russians maintain their present speed and course, it will be."

Yamamoto was too young to have fought the Chinese at sea. He had not faced the surprises that even the unreformed and largely foreign-officered Tai'ping Northern Fleet had been able to spring. In twenty-four hours, if he was still alive, he would be less ready to expect the enemy's cooperation.

The purr of *Satsuma*'s diesels faded to a distant mutter. Jahn felt the deck tilting under his feet, as *Satsuma* turned. Pope tilted against him, sliding her arms around his torso.

"Ah won't pretend that was an accident."

He tightened his grip on her shoulders. "Want to try the Shalimar Gardens, when we make it home? They've got mazes with little nooks where nobody can see you. Some of them even have spring-heated pools."

"Where yo' can wear nothin' and do anythin'?"

"That's the idea."

"Mmmm."

"After the Gardens, I'll have to do it."

"What's 'it'? when it's got clothes on?"

"Visit Alexandria."

"Your mother might not approve."

Jahn stepped back, careful of his footing on the

oily deck. It was level now, but vibrating more strongly as the engines accelerated *Satsuma* on a new course. Looking out the window, Jahn thought that they were still heading south.

A set of repeater gauges confirmed the suspicion, also that they were using a good twenty-five knot tailwind to save fuel. The engines were at one-third speed, just enough to generate dynamic lift and keep up the superheat. A heavy warload and a long flight meant that dropping ballast was a last resort, even if the water condensed from the engine exhausts might replenish it eventually.

"Eventually," Jahn knew, was a dirty word in airship navigation, because it often translated as "too late." His hands again rested lightly on Pope's shoulders, feeling solid muscle and bone (not to mention enticing animal warmth) under the cloth. "I know. I thought I'd have to fight one war at home, before I went off to this one."

They both smiled, remembering the story of his sister walking in on him when he was happily tumbling a kitchen wench, to break the news of the Japanese declaration of war on Russia. His mother had accused him of gross indecency that would corrupt his sisters.

"It can't have been easy on my mother, trying to raise five children in Alexandria, without asking for family charity," Jahn said judiciously. "Seeing me married off will ease her mind a lot."

"Getting out of Alexandria might help some, too. Half that there place is *still* vacant lots and mean-eyed serfs."

Then *Akagi* was signaling again. " 'Russian fleet maintaining present speed. All hands to Battle Stations at 1430.' "

Pope stepped back. "See you at lunch?"

"If we get any, maybe. Save a rice ball for luck, anyway."

"Make that a pickled plum, and ah promise. Ah nevah met a rice ball ah didn't like."

III

The China Sea, 1400, August 18, 1905

The trumpet blowing Battle Stations caught Jahn by surprise. He looked at his Swiss watch. Cursed if it wasn't half an hour early! But on the scale of random variables in war, a half-hour change was barely worth noticing.

Unless the Russians had detected the First Air Kokutai . . .

Jahn needed only a few steps to reach his battle station, at the Auxiliary Control Room just forward of the radio room. He saw Pope sprinting to her post, a pair of chopsticks thrust hastily into the breast pocket of her coveralls. She blew Jahn a kiss, then bobbed gracefully so that not even her hair touched the top of the radio-room door as she vanished inside and pulled the curtain.

Jahn gripped a stanchion as new vibration told him of increased speed. Only slightly, though—this wasn't the crisis that losing surprise would be, then.

Auxiliary Control straddled *Satsuma*'s keel, with machine-gun positions on either side, firing from ball-and-socket mountings through plex-glass blisters that gave them a a 270-degree arc of fire. The blisters also gave anyone in them a first-class view. Jahn insinuated himself between the gunner and loader for the port gun and peered out.

He counted five airships rapidly pulling ahead of the rest of the *Kokutai*, *Akagi* in the lead. He thought he saw the nearest one—*Musashi*, with her white-painted after engine gondola—starting to drop her warload. Then he saw what she was dropping fluttering by, like dirty laundry caught in the artificial whirlwind of the airship squadron's passage. Canvas or treated-silk covers, was Jahn's guess—but *Shokaku* and the rest of the vanguard pulled away into the haze before he could see what the discarded covers had hidden.

Abruptly, the distant rumble of the superheat died. At the same time, the engines speeded up, and Jahn saw the indicators on the control panel to his right go hard over to *Full Descent*. For a moment, the deck seemed to fall out from under him—or was that just his stomach, reacting to the thought of diving an airship at this speed? *Satsuma* was sliding down out of the sky faster than any airborne vehicle Jahn had ever seen, except once when he saw a glider caught in a downdraft at the Alexandria Games plummet into the Nile. Only a water landing had saved the pilot, then he had to be practically snatched from the jaws of the crocodiles.

Around here, it will be sharks.

Skang! The machine gunner had cocked his weapon, with a metallic clashing that would have been ominous under other circumstances. The loader snapped the lid off a second crate of belts and stroked the dull-gleaming rounds as if they might bring him good luck.

Or at least bad luck to the Russians.

Jahn decided that the loader's gesture counted as a prayer, and touched the pocket where the little crucifix rested, that Peter Jahn had worn across the North Sea. The crucifix had helped his great-great-grandfather sail his boat and his family from the Frisian Islands, through Napoleon's patrols and North Sea storms, then kept him alive for six years on the lower deck of a British seventy-four.

What had worked on the sea might now work in the sky.

❖   ❖   ❖

Commander Goto looked at the oily swell through which *Number 36* was trailing a broad white wake, and prayed—to gods bearing different names than the White Christ or the Norse pantheon, but addressed with equal fervor.

The First Air *Kokutai* had gone to radio silence hours ago—the Russians were backward at interception, but not completely incompetent. At sea level, the wind was barely a—a *capful*, Goto thought, savoring the English phrase. Aloft, the heavily-loaded airships would need a good tailwind out of the north to overtake the Russians without burning too much fuel.

Goto raised his binoculars and looked aloft. Visibility was poor enough to hide *Number 36* from anything except a very keen-sighted or very lucky Russian lookout. It was also poor enough to hide the fleet on the sea and the fleet in the sky from one another.

Signaling to the airships meant revealing himself and then having to dive, if he was lucky enough to last that long, then probably missing the battle— another sort of bad luck. Goto lifted the conning tower hatch and called below.

"Battle stations—*gun*. Load with starshell."

Young Yamamoto at least was going to have something to do besides stare at the sky and try to find the wind—the wind that today might write the fate of two empires.

They'd broken out of the clouds at a thousand meters, *Satsuma* and seven other airships that Jahn could count in the improved visibility below the clouds. They were still descending faster than Jahn liked, but none of the crew seemed to be worried. Of course, the Japanese were rather casual about suicide, individual or mass, but he could not see the whole *Kokutai* committing mass *seppuku*—

"I'll be damned."

"I hope not," Pope said from behind him.

"Dump the theology," Jahn said. He was proud that his pointing hand didn't shake. Maybe having the other around Pope's shoulders helped.

Pope's eyes followed Jahn's hand, out past the barrel of the machine gun and the glass, to study their sistership *Shokaku*, barely two hundred meters away.

"Well, ah'll be—never mind. Am ah seein' things, or are those *torpedoes* under *Shokaku?*"

"Either that, or leeches the size of crocodiles."

"Mah money's on torpedoes."

Satsuma lurched. Pope fell against Jahn, so that he could now grip her with both hands.

"What are you doing out here?"

"Chiba threw me out. 'Fraid ah might have learned Fleet code, ah suppose."

If Pope had to take over the radio, she would use Draka Commercial Two for code, a merchant-marine creation that anybody could buy for a not too outrageous number of aurics. This doubtless included the Russians—but Jahn suspected that the Russians wouldn't be listening in on the First *Kokutai*'s radio messages until it was too late to do them any good.

He started calculating. Four torpedoes, assuming the standard 45-cm model, plus what looked like glider wings to let them down into the sea easily. Call it a ton each, times four—plenty of weight to make a big difference in the airships' performance.

Now if only the altimeter isn't jammed and the elevator man doesn't have his thumb up his arse....

Then he saw the starshell bursts ahead, and moments later, blazing through the mist, the bomb explosions.

Commander Goto fired off a curse right after the deck guns fired its third starshell. The vanguard of the *Kokutai* had found the Russians without any help from *Number 36*. Now the five airships were keeping station

over the Russian battle line, raining incendiary bombs
on them.

A modern dirigible with good men at the controls
could keep station over a battleship and practically
shovel the incendiaries out of the bomb bay. The light
bombs wouldn't penetrate, but they didn't need to.
They would start fires—had started them, on at least
three Russian ships that Goto could count. Fighting
fires distracted crews. So did exploding ammunition,
and the Russians' understandable fondness for anti-
dirigible batteries meant extra ready-use lockers on
deck, so that the high-angle guns could go into action
at a moment's notice.

Except that the dirigible bombers had swung
around to either flank of the Russians and hadn't
given them even that much warning.

Ready-use ammunition must already be exploding
aboard one armored cruiser—Goto saw a funnel fly
overboard, a mast sag, and the whole ship swing out
of line. The cruiser narrowly missed running down
a scout, and two battleships had to almost spin around
on their sterns to avoid ramming the cruiser. *Bogatyr*
class, Goto thought, although with a second funnel
now gone and her decks a mass of flame it was hard
to tell.

The Russian fleet formation seemed to be disintegrating before Goto's eyes. Panic-stricken or dying
helmsmen flinging helms over wildly, lookouts unable
to see through the smoke or beating out the flames
on their uniforms—the incendiaries had to be those
phosphorous charges that rumor had mentioned—

The sea grew waterspouts, four of them, twenty
meters high and no more than a hundred meters
behind *Number 36*. This time Goto's curses were a
salvo. As he had feared, the starshells had done no
more than reveal his boat's presence.

Meanwhile, the Russians were not disintegrating
in a panic, as he had thought. The warships were

turning to port, forming into two lines, the battleships in the rear and the lighter craft closer to the submarine. Smoke from funnels, fires, and anti-dirigible guns made the next thing to a fogbank, but Goto thought he saw the bulky merchant vessels holding their course.

Yamamoto wasn't cursing. He was shouting for the ammunition passers to bring up the smoke shells. Goto wondered what for, then noticed a rising chop to either side—just as a second salvo of Russian shells hit the water. Three this time, and if anything a few meters closer. A fragment hit the conning tower hard enough to go *ting*.

Young Yamamoto had a clear head. The rest of the airships would be attacking soon, and the drift of the smoke from *Number 36*'s shells would give them a wind-direction indicator that wasn't lost in the murk over the Russian fleet. They could steer precisely to attack the Russian fleet broadside-on.

The first smoke shell went on its way at the same moment as the third Russian salvo—or was that just one heavy shell? It seemed that hectares of sea reared up, and spray and fragments rained down on *Number 36* even though the shellburst was farther than the first two.

Now Yamamoto was cursing as loudly as his captain. Goto saw why. One fragment had jammed the breech block of the deck gun, another killed the gunlayer, and a third taken the last two fingers off Yamamoto's left hand. He was examining the ruined gun as he wrapped the bloody stumps in a handkerchief.

"Secure the gun and get below!" Goto shouted. He had to repeat the order three times before Yamamoto seemed to hear, and only then did Goto dare to order "Rig for diving."

He hoped he didn't sound too relieved. If the next stage of the battle went as he had begun to suspect, the safest place for *Number 36* would be on the bottom of the China Sea, fifty meters below the sharp prows and hundred-kilo warheads that would soon be filling this area of water.

The port gunner was desperately craning his neck, trying to find a target, with white knuckles on the grips of his machine gun twisting the weapon almost as wildly. The loader, junior but older, finally gripped his arm and said something that stopped the frantic search for targets that still had to be far out of machine-gun range. The gunner sat down in lotus position beside his weapon, while the loader went back to work laying out spare belts. Jahn noticed that the deck had sets of clips on either side of the guns, to keep the ready belts from tangling if the deck tilted.

Typical Japanese attention to detail. I wonder if we could create the concept of an "honorary Draka" to encourage them to join forces with the Dominion. Sooner or later, we will have to start picking and choosing our enemies, instead of just civilizing everybody we meet with a Ferguson.

Then *Satsuma's* deck not only tilted, it seemed that the airship was trying to stand on her tail—*which has to be less than a hundred meters above the water even in level flight—*

Instead of the impact with the water, Jahn felt the whole ship shudder and heave. He didn't need shouts of "Torpedoes away!" to know that the airship's weapons had launched. From the violence of the sudden upward surge, he wondered if *Satsuma* had been carrying only four torpedoes. Then he heard the superheat feed roaring like something vast and *hungry*, increasing the ship's lift by a good part of a ton every few seconds.

I wouldn't fly low over a fleet of Russians in a bad mood either.

Since all he could see out the gun blister was sky,

smoke, and something torpedo-craft sized leaving a
curving wake, Jahn tried to calculate the hammer
blow that was descending on the Russian fleet. Fourteen torpedo-carrying dirigibles. A minimum of four
torpedoes apiece. At least fifty-six torpedoes in the
water, the largest spread ever launched. Unless some
of the airships had maneuvered out to the flanks, to
hammerhead the Russians when they turned to comb
the torpedoes from the first launch? With surface
ships, that tactic went back as far as the Anglo-Russian
War. The Japanese had used it too effectively against
the Chinese not to think of using it with faster launch
vehicles against a more formidable opponent.

Suddenly the torpedo craft wasn't there. Its wake
ended in a rising column of smoke. Jahn saw plat-
ing, funnels, guns flying out of the smoke, and thought
he saw the bow ploughing itself under. He hoped the
Russians didn't maneuver too many of their light craft
into the path of the torpedoes, and with that very
Japanese tactic somehow save their battle line.

Unbelievably, *Satsuma*'s upward lunge stopped at
five hundred meters. *The captain probably vented
superheat. Very shrewd airship handlers, these people.*
Jahn still had to tap the altimeter twice, before he
could believe its reading.

He couldn't see how the Russians were maneuver-
ing, but he could see that they were fighting back.
Akagi was limping off, down by the bow—then some
shrewd Russian put a flare or a starshell into the air-
hydrogen mixture fed by the damage forward. A fire-
ball grew out of *Akagi*'s bow, then swallowed the bow.
Her stern would have risen until it was vertical, but
the glowing remnants of her bow struck the water
first. The flames still swept aft, the cells erupting one
by one, until nothing remained of Kondo's flagship
except a cloud of smoke fed by patches of burning
diesel fuel on the water.

Akagi's killer wasn't the only Russian with sense.

A battleship was firing her main battery into the water, raising tree-tall clusters of shell splashes in the path of the Japanese airships. Some of them were still below two hundred meters, and the glowing foam seemed like the fingers of a sea giant, reaching up to pluck them out of the sky.

Jahn saw *Shokaku* fly directly over one such cluster—and fly away. But one engine trailed smoke, another had stopped, and from two kilometers away Jahn could see rents and wrinkles in her aluminum skin. She wasn't going to make it back to Japan; the Draka could only hope that she could reach a Japanese-controlled portion of the nearest coast.

Then the rest of the torpedoes started hitting. Jahn couldn't watch everything at once, so he focused his attention on a single Russian battleship—*Suvorov*, he thought, the *Petr Veliki* with the second and third funnels trunked together into something that looked like a diseased tree stump or a heating system assembled by drunken serf-mechanics.

One torpedo hit *Suvorov* right forward. She started to slow, which reduced her rate of turn, but with her forward compartments flooding no doubt the bridge officers had decided to reduce the water pressure somehow. That left the ship in the path of two more torpedoes, one striking under the first funnel, the other under the after turret.

Smoke trickled, then gushed, out of the after turret, and the deck and hull around it. Then the smoke turned to flame, steel plates bulged and erupted outward, and the after magazine went up in a single cataclysmic blast of a hundred or more tons of ammunition.

Suvorov's stern was gone—blown into the air or toward the bottom. Her bow continued for a moment, already listing, like some great maimed animal too stupid to understand that it was dead. Then boilers and a magazine for one of the midships turrets both exploded, and *Suvorov* and her eight hundred men were gone.

Jahn looked across Auxiliary Control, to see that the starboard gun blister was gone and so was the gunner. The loader was firing the gun sharply downward—with gravity to help the bullets, he might hit something—but his left leg was a mangled ruin and he would bleed to death if nobody—

The junior elevator man started across the deck to help the loader. Then a giant claw seemed to rip open the deck of Auxiliary Control. Somebody down there still had an anti-dirigible gun in action, and it had just punched a shell into *Satsuma*.

Fortunately the first hit was a dud. It bounced off the overhead and tumbled, sweeping the starboard loader overboard like an old-fashioned solid shot. The hole it left in the deck was large enough to swallow the junior elevator man.

Then a second shell hit, farther aft, and this one exploded. Bulkheads bulged and vomited smoke and fragments. One fragment scored Jahn's thigh. Between that and the dying senior elevator man reeling against him, Jahn fell to the deck.

As he scrabbled for a handhold on the blood-slick aluminum, he heard the port machine gun firing. Next was the sound of metal twisted agonizingly far beyond its limits, and finally a human scream.

Jahn told himself three times that it was *not* a woman's scream.

He did not bother telling himself that *Satsuma* wasn't going down. Somehow the loudspeaker connection to the bridge was still alive, and someone was shrieking "All hands to crash landing stations! Long live the Emperor!" over and over again.

Jahn thought that he was already at his station— if the Auxiliary elevator controls still worked, at least; *Satsuma* was far beyond help by damage control. And while he wished the Emperor Meiji no harm at all, he could not see what prolonging the Emperor Meiji's life could do for his loyal subjects who were rapidly approaching Yasukuni Shrine.

Are worshippers of Christ or the Old Norse gods allowed in there?

Smoke billowed from aft, then Julia Pope staggered out of it. She was covered with blood, and staggered in a way that sent Jahn's bowels twisting like a disturbed nest of mambas.

They do have a point, saying men will panic over a wounded woman.

Except that Julia was where she'd wanted to be, with battle comrades and even a lover close by. If you had to die, that was always one of the better places.

She gripped a stanchion, then shifted her grip as a jagged end scored her palm. "Radio's—dead. Chiba—gone too."

Jahn realized that his own shallow cut had almost stopped bleeding, and decided that Julia needed his battle dressing worse than he did. He started to unwrap it.

"Never mind," she said. "Most of the blood—it's Chiba's. He'd do to ride the river with, as mah father will say when—ah tell him."

Jahn felt even worse gut twistings. Julia's father was *dead*.

Then *Satsuma* gave her most violent lurch yet. The port gunner fired off a last burst and shouted, "We've hit a Russian ship!"

Jahn wondered at the idea of Russian ships flying, then realized that *Satsuma* must have lost considerable altitude from her damage. No fire, so far, but they would be down in the sea in minutes. *Thank God both Julia and I are in shape to swim.*

"Last message, before they hit us," Pope said, sitting down abruptly. "The torpedo squadrons are coming in to finish off the Russians—even towing the coastal boats. The rest of the battle line's going north to surprise Vlad—Vlad—"

She coughed, and rested her head against the metal, as if it cooled a fever. Jahn's fingers flew through the rest of opening the dressing. He looked up, to see blood trickling from the corner of her mouth. In one hand she held out her Thorshammer.

"Take it—take it to a shrine. Or—or Ran's."

Then she twisted the fingers of her free hand, and only let go when he took the amulet. Or when life left her, which was about at the same time.

Jahn didn't have time even to close Pope's staring eyes, before *Satsuma* started breaking in two fifty meters aft. The port gunner and loader were peering out past their empty gun and must have seen something they didn't like, because they both flung themselves through a hole in their blister.

Then Jahn saw it too—an orange glow from aft, where the collision must have ignited escaping hydrogen.

He thought of staying with Julia for only a moment, but that was almost too long. A blast of superheated air flung him out the port blister, and for a moment he thought he was going to come down on the Russian's deck.

But he missed, dove deep, and came up just in time to see *Satsuma's*—and Julia's—hydrogen-fed pyre cremate everything above decks aboard the Russian ship—a freighter, he thought.

But the Russian must have been carrying fuel or ammunition, and the hydrogen flames had reached it. Explosions sprayed the sea with flames and wreckage, as well as all the Russian crew who hadn't already been reduced to ashes on their own deck.

Bodies and parts of bodies rained down around Horace Jahn. One landed almost on top of him, and he was obscurely relieved to see that it was a man.

The explosions continued, as he swam away from the burning Russian ship. . . .

IV

China Sea, 1950, August 18, 1905

Commander Goto had double lookouts posted and a machine gun mounted on the bridge, as *Number 36* cruised through the graveyard of the Russian Pacific Fleet. The Combined Fleet's torpedo squadrons were still patrolling the area, to sink or capture any surviving enemy ships that hadn't beached themselves on the Chinese coast, and they would have quick hands on the gun lanyards.

So, for that matter, would Sub-Lieutenant Yamamoto, even he would be firing the machine gun with his right hand only. Morphine controlled his pain, and he was determined to end the most glorious day in the history of the Imperial Japanese Navy on his feet, at his post, ready to deal with any Russians not yet out of the fight.

None of the living Russians they'd found so far had any fight left in them. In fact, several had begged to be rescued. *Number 36* had no space for prisoners, so the radio operator had just given the torpedo-gunboat *Furutsuki* the position of the latest boatload, when a lookout called out a lone swimmer dead ahead.

One man we can take, and perhaps his gratitude will make him talkative.

In the fading light, the man was certainly a European, and fair-haired like so many of the Russians. But he was wearing Imperial Navy airship coveralls, and Goto remembered that seven of the nineteen airships who had delivered the first and deadliest stroke were lost or missing.

As *Number 36* slowed, the man released his grip on half of a wooden deck grating and swam over to the submarine. Gripping the port bow plane, he hauled himself aboard even before the deck party could reach him. It was only when he stood up that Goto recognized Lieutenant Commander Jahn, last heard of aboard the missing *Satsuma*.

"We may have other survivors in the area," he said. He seemed afraid to let out more than a few words at a time, and Goto did not bother asking about the fate of Lieutenant Pope. The big Draka seemed smaller than before, as though his body had shrunk to fold itself protectively around his wounded spirit. Goto thanked the gods for his brother's survival and asked them to give peace to Julia Pope along with all the other warriors who had died for the Emperor this day.

He was about to urge Jahn below, when the man held out something in his hand. It was a sea-tarnished, smoke-blackened silver amulet in the shape of a hammer. Goto recalled seeing Julia Pope wearing it at his farewell party—a religious emblem, like the Christian cross.

Jahn looked at the amulet for a long moment. Then he thrust it into a hip pocket and saluted Goto.

"Lieutenant Commander Horace Jahn, Navy of the Dominion of the Draka, reporting aboard. Do you know if there is a shrine to Thor or Ran in the Empire?"

Dave Drake is an ex-lawyer, ex-soldier, and present writer from Iowa who currently resides in the woods of North Carolina. He has many praiseworthy attributes—for instance, he preferred driving a bus to practicing law. He's also a classical scholar who's as much at home with the meditations of Marcus Aurelius as with motorcycles and pistols.

Most of the SF field is familiar with his *Hammer's Slammers* series, perhaps the defining example of future war fiction. He's also written fine stories set in places as far apart as the Roman Mediterranean and the Congo Free State, and once had the honor of having a horror story censored in England . . . because it was too horrible.

Drake can show the dark side of the world without for a moment slipping into the pornography of violence. He knows it's real, not a slasher flick. He's been there, and he can show what it does to the human soul better than any of us.

In the Draka universe, there's an analogue to World War Two, which the inhabitants of that timeline call the Eurasian War. It's *worse* than World War Two, which is saying something. Drake shows why.

THE TRADESMEN

David Drake

AUTHOR'S NOTE: I'M INDEBTED TO WILKESON O'CONNELL, WHOSE WORK SHOWED ME THE WAY TO SOLVE A PROBLEM THAT HAD BEEN EXERCISING ME FOR SOME TIME.   —D.A.D.

Colonel Evertsen heard voices in the outer room of his office in the Tactical Operations Center. An outbound convoy—a convoy headed from the interior to the front—had reached Fort Burket a half hour before; District Administrator Kuyper, Evertsen's civilian counterpart, would be coming to discuss the latest dispatch from Capetown.

Evertsen turned, closing the maintenance log he'd been studying in a vain attempt to change the numbers into something Capetown would find more acceptable. The roads in this Slavic hinterland had been a joke before they were made to bear the weight of mechanized armies. Now they'd been reduced to dust, mud, or ice. Take your choice according to the season, and expect your engines and drive trains to wear out in a fraction of the time that seemed reasonable in an air-conditioned office in Capetown.

Instead of the rumpled Kuyper, a tall, slim officer turned sideways to enter the narrow doorway and threw a salute that crackled. He was wearing battledress in contrast to Evertsen's second-class uniform, but the clean, pressed garments proved he was a newcomer to the war zone.

"Janni!" said Evertsen in pleasure. He rose to his feet, stumbling as he always did when he tried to move quickly and his right knee betrayed him.

"Lieutenant Jan Dierks reporting to the base commander, *sir*," the newcomer said. He broke into a grin and reached across the desk to clasp Evertsen by the arm. "You live in a maze here, Uncle Jan. Is the danger so great this far from the front lines?"

Evertsen bit back the retort—because Dierks was his nephew, and because anyway Evertsen should be used to the attitude by now. He got it every time he went home on leave, after all. *I see, colonel, you're not in the fighting army any more . . .*

"Not so dangerous, not now," Evertsen said, gesturing Dierks to a chair. The room's only window was a firing slit covering the east gate. There were electric lights, but Evertsen normally didn't bother with them until he'd shuttered the window for the night. "The fort was laid out two years ago, after all. But although the danger has receded, one gets used to narrow doorways and grenade baffles more easily than one might to a sapper in one's bedroom."

"Oh, I didn't mean to imply . . " Dierks said in sudden confusion. He was a good boy; the sort of son Evertsen would have wanted if things had worked out differently.

"No offense taken, Janni," he said easily. "Though in fact the constant advance causes its own problems. The point elements always bypass hostiles, and some of those are going to decide that a logistics base guarded by cripples and transients is a better choice for resupply than trying to get back to their own lines."

Evertsen tried to keep the bitterness out of his voice when he said, "cripple," but he knew he hadn't been completely successful.

Dierks looked through the firing slit, perhaps for an excuse to take his eyes off his uncle, and said, "There's a convoy from the front arriving. Do they usually come in at the same time as an outbound one?"

"Not usually," Evertsen said in a dry voice, "though they're supposed to. We won't be able to send your trucks forward without the additional escort that accompanies the inbound convoy."

He rotated his chair to view the east gate. There were about forty vehicles, meaning a score or more were deadlined at one of the forward bases. That was par for the course, but Christ! why couldn't Capetown see the Russian Front needed mechanics worse than it did more riflemen? Around and beyond the convoy, the plains rolled on forever.

The leading truck was a standard 6x6, empty except for the load of sandbags that would detonate any pressure-fuzed mine. The duty of driving that vehicle changed every fifteen minutes.

Two armored cars followed. There should be four more at the middle and end of the line, but Evertsen saw only two. The four guntrucks, each with quad-mounted heavy machine guns behind walls of mortar boxes filled with gravel, were spaced evenly among the non-combat vehicles.

"I suppose returning convoys are to reposition the trucks?" Dierks said.

"That," Evertsen said. He turned from the window. "And for casualties and leave-men. Mostly casualties."

He cleared his throat. "A fit young man wouldn't be posted to Fort Burket, Janni. Where do your orders take you?"

"The Fourth Independent Brigade, sir," Janni said with pardonable pride. The Four Eye was a crack unit whose neck-or-nothing panache made it a fast route to promotion ... for the survivors. "I could choose my itinerary, and when I saw an officer was needed to escort specie to the District Administrator at Fort Burket, well, I volunteered."

There was an angry mutter in the outer office. Administrator Kuyper squeezed through the doorway with a document in his hand and shouted, "Evertsen, do you know what those idiots in Capetown have done? They've—"

Janni jumped to his feet. Kuyper noticed his presence and said more mildly, "Oh, good afternoon, lieutenant. I didn't realize. . ."

"You've met the Lieutenant Dierks who brought the discretionary fund supplement, Kuyper," Evertsen said from his chair. "Allow me to present my nephew Janni, who's been posted to the Four Eye."

"It's about the damned discretionary fund that I've come, Evertsen," Kuyper said. "They've reduced the bounty authorization from a hundred aurics to sixty, and they've made an immediate cut in the supplement to the discretionary fund."

Evertsen's fist clenched. "Do they give a reason?" he asked, more so he had time to think about the implications than because any reason could justify Capetown's action in his mind. He wished Janni wasn't present for this, but he couldn't very well order the boy out.

Kuyper waved the document, obviously the one Janni had brought with the paychest. " 'At this crisis in national affairs,' " he quoted, " 'the fighting fronts must take precedence for resources over the lines of communication.' By Christ, Evertsen! How much use do they think those greater resources will be if the convoys carrying them are looted by guerrillas?"

Dierks looked from one man to the other, hearing without enough background to understand the words. The hefty administrator was between him and the doorway. Because he couldn't easily leave, Dierks said, "The specie I escorted was to pay the Slav irregulars, then, the Ralliers? Rather than your own troops?"

"Yes," Kuyper said, "and there'll be hell to pay when they—"

Kuyper's eyes were drawn to the viewslit because it was the brightest thing in the room. "Oh, *Christ!*" he said, staring toward the gate. "It never rains but it pours. There's Bettina Crais, in with the convoy and coming toward the TOC. Three guesses what she's going to want!"

"And how she's going to react," Evertsen agreed grimly. He'd rather have had a few weeks to figure a way out of the impasse; but if he'd been a lucky man, he wouldn't be commanding a line-of-communication base. "Well, we may as well get it over with."

"Lieutenant, give me a hand with the paychest if you will," Kuyper said. "Even in its present anemic state, that much gold is a load for me. Besides, it won't hurt to have a fit young officer like you in the room when Crais gets the news."

The two men started out. Evertsen said, "Kuyper, perhaps Lieutenant Dierks shouldn't be . . . ?"

Janni stiffened in the doorway. "Sir," he said, "I'm cleared at Most Secret level. I'll obey any order from a superior officer, of course; but I remind you that to treat me as a child because of our relationship would dishonor the uniform I wear."

He thinks I'm trying to protect him from violence

by an angry Rallier, Evertsen thought. *And he's young enough to worry about honor!*

"Yes, of course," Evertsen said with a curt nod. "You'll find the experience instructive, I'm sure."

The colonel stared at his hands while he waited. Once he'd dreamed of commanding a unit like the Four Eye himself. He'd had a lot of dreams. Once.

Janni and Kuyper returned from the latter's office with a metal chest which they set on the corner of Evertsen's desk. The administrator waited beside it; Janni stood at parade rest on the other side of the desk, facing the door.

The maintenance log was still out. Evertsen sighed and slipped it into a bookcase behind him as voices murmured in the outer office.

Bettina Crais entered.

She was a petite woman; that was obvious even though a felt camouflage cape, worn dark-side out in this season, covered her from neck to ankles. She'd slung her long-barreled Moisin-Nagant rifle muzzle-down over her right shoulder; a swatch of rabbitskin, bound fur-side in, protected the bolt and receiver against the elements. Mounted on a stud in her left ear was half a gold coin the size of a thumbnail, so worn that the fractured portrait of George III was barely a shadow on the surface.

"Colonel," Crais said, nodding. "Mister Administrator. I've come for my pay."

Dierks blinked in amazement. Despite Crais' fine features and short blond hair, he'd assumed she was Slavic until she spoke—with a Vaal-District accent you could cut with a knife.

"Mistress Crais," Evertsen said, "allow me to present my nephew, Lieutenant Jan Dierks."

She turned her head. Janni drew himself to attention reflexively. Crais grinned and said, "A pretty boy you've got here, Colonel. Want to send him out with me to blood him?"

"Lieutenant Dierks is on his way to take up a combat appointment," Evertsen said, trying hard to keep the disgust out of his voice. He didn't want to anger Crais, particularly not now.

"And d'ye think what I do isn't combat, Colonel?" she sneered. "Without me and the Ralliers, the truck drivers and invalids you've got staffing this place would find out what combat really is."

"Well, Crais," said Kuyper with false warmth, "you'll probably want to relax for a few days before you head back. I'll arrange a room for you in the transient officers' billets so you won't have to doss down in the civilian lines. You can run a tab at the O Club as well until we get the finances straightened out."

Crais turned her ice-blue eyes on the civilian. "I don't owe anybody, Mister Administrator," she said in a voice that came straight down from the Arctic Circle. "And I'll find my own bed. It's for the one night only, because I'm heading back at dawn with the inbound convoy. I've got my husband Lute up with the three kids, and I want to get back to them."

"You've brought your family to the Zone?" Evertsen said in amazement. "Good God, I didn't know that!"

"I shouldn't wonder if a lot goes on around here that you don't know about, Colonel," Crais said with not quite a sneer. "We've got a dugout as snug as you please with paneling inside. Lute doesn't hunt with me—it's no more his thing than it would be your nephew's here, I reckon—but he takes care of the kids and the garden. We'll have all our own food come this time next year."

"Where is it you live, Mistress Crais?" Janni asked with careful politeness. He was too much a gentleman to allow Crais' belittling to affect him openly, though Evertsen had seen a vein throb in the boy's throat a time or two during the conversation.

"Nowhere, now," Crais said, turning her cold eyes onto him, "but it'll be an estate in a few years when

things settle down. Me and mine'll be here on the
land, and no rich party-boy from Capetown will take
it away from us. There'll be no more scraping a crop
from sunbaked clay the way my family's always had
to do."

She caught the line of Janni's eyes and tapped the
broken sovereign. "This, you mean?" she said. "This
came from Lute's family. My folks arrived at the Cape
without a pot to piss in, but that'll change, boy. My
son and the girls, they'll be folk as good as any
walking the streets of Capetown!"

Crais looked out the viewslit. Vehicles were still
grunting and snarling through the entrance baffles.
It might be an hour before the last of the convoy was
safely within the perimeter of Fort Burket.

"The outbound convoys drop me on the road and
I hump my goods home myself," she said. She was
obviously pleased to tell a young aristocrat how hard
her life was and how well she succeeded. "From a
different spot each time. Most of the hostiles couldn't
track a tank over a grass lawn, but I don't make it
easy for them. When I come in, I wait at Depot
Seven-niner for an inbound convoy."

She grinned. "You don't stand out in the middle
of the road and flag a convoy," she said. "Not even
me."

"How do you get into the fuel depot?" Evertsen
asked, both from interest and because he saw that
the chance to talk—to brag—put Crais in a better
mood. "I'd have thought the garrison would be just
as quick to shoot as the convoy escorts are."

Crais shrugged. Even the simplest of her movements were as graceful as a gymnast's. "We have click
signals on the radio so they know I'm coming," she
said. "And they know they need me. Depot Seven-
niner would do better to take down its barbed wire
than to lose me patrolling the district."

Her left hand reached under her cape and came

out with objects on a string. "That's talk enough," Crais said. "I've got six hundred aurics coming. Pay me and I'll arrange for my needs."

She tossed the string onto the center of the desk. There were six items tied on a strand of sinew. Shrivelled up the way they were, they could be mistaken for mushrooms or nutmeats, but of course they were—

"Those are human ears!" Janni said. "Good God! Some of them are from children!"

"Your uncle don't trust nobody, boy," Crais said with a sly grin toward Evertsen. "Not the Ralliers and not even a fellow citizen from the hardscrabble part of his own country. He wants proof, so we bring him the left ear from every kill."

She looked at Evertsen. "So here they are, Colonel. Want to soak them open so you can be sure I'm not trying to cheat you with a right ear or two?"

"That won't be necessary," Evertsen said without inflection. He and Kuyper had seen more ears than Crais had, many more of them. They were experts by now, well able to make sure the State wasn't cheated by the irregulars in its service.

"The lieutenant's right," Kuyper said. "Four of these are children. Stay-behinds, and all the men able to carry a gun off with the guerrillas."

"Aye, that's right," Crais said; her voice calm but the look in her eyes as she gazed at the administrator . . . less calm. "A family, still working their plantings from a cave-in in the wall of a ravine. Pretty well hid, too. I wouldn't have found them, I guess, without the smell of wood smoke to draw me. That's why I pack in block alcohol for our fire, you see."

Janni didn't speak again, but neither could he draw his eyes away from the wizened trophies. Crais grinned more broadly and went on, "I hid at the treeline for three hours till I got the woman and the older girl, she was maybe twelve, together. Nailed them both with one round. The grampa came out of the house with a rifle and I shot him too. Thought I could use his ammo belt, but he had an old single-shot Berdan, so I was out another round. Cartridges cost money in the Zone, Lieutenant."

Janni stood iron-faced. It was hard to tell whether he even heard what the woman was saying.

Vaguely disappointed at the lack of response, Crais continued, "I tossed a smoke bomb into the dugout and waited to see if anybody more come out. I use sulphur and tar and enough gunpowder to keep it going if they try to douse it, but nobody did this time. They all choked. I went in when it aired out and found a girl of eight and a boy of six. And a baby, but I didn't bother to sex that one."

Her left index finger, as delicate as carved ivory, indicated the tiny last lump on the string.

Crais looked directly at Janni again. "You may wonder why I used a smoke bomb instead of a grenade, Lieutenant," she said. "I'm a working girl and can't afford to lose a trophy. Your uncle wouldn't have paid me for the baby if all I'd been able to bring him back was the foot and a few toes. Would you, Colonel?"

"Good Christ, woman!" Evertsen said. "We have to do this; we don't have to like it."

"*Some* of us have to do this, Colonel," Crais said. "Some of us don't have estates we could retire to if we felt like it."

"Ashkenazy's band brought twenty units to Fort Schaydin last week," Kuyper said. "All of them were real guerrillas, too."

Crais turned to the administrator like a weasel preparing to spring. "Real, were they? Aye, I suppose they were—if you want to call people who get drunk around an open fire in the Zone real guerrillas. They were under a political officer from Berlin who was going to show the locals how to do it."

The woman stood like an ice pick stuck into soft flesh, looking disdainfully at the three men. "You know the real danger's locals from the Zone who filter back and hide with stay-behinds till they're ready to cut throats, Kuyper," she said. "Ain't that so, Colonel?"

Evertsen nodded curtly. "Yes," he said, "I suppose it is."

Kuyper peered toward the viewslit. "There's a lone truck following the convoy," he said. "I think it's Bruchinsky's lot."

Colonel Evertsen stood and looked, in part because it gave him a chance to turn away from Bettina Crais. A 6x6 truck had caught up with the convoy just as the last armored car grunted through the gates. It was originally a German Horch, Evertsen thought, but with a wood-burning gasogene adapter and repairs which used parts from many other vehicles. At least twenty Ralliers filled it, already whooping with anticipation of their next few days.

One man jumped out of the cab and started purposefully toward the TOC, however. Unfortunately.

"Yes, that's Bruchinsky," Evertsen said heavily. "I'd have appreciated some time to untie the knot Capetown's bound us with; but if there's any luck, it doesn't come to poor bastards with gimp legs that keep them out of field commands."

"I'm not holding you up, Colonel," Crais said, misunderstanding the comment. "I'll take my pay now and leave, so you needn't to share your pretty office with me and Bruchinsky both."

Evertsen turned. "Explain the new situation to Mistress Crais, Kuyper," he said.

Kuyper nodded calmly; the plump civilian had never flinched from the unpleasant duties of his position. "We've received a dispatch from Capetown changing the amount of the bounty," he said. "From now on we'll be paying you sixty aurics per assessed unit instead of the hundred you've received in the past. That means three hundred and sixty aurics will be paid for the present string."

"The hell you say, lardbelly!" Crais shouted. Her left hand moved beneath her cape and clenched on something hidden. "The *hell* you say."

She looked venomously at the men, her lips working without sound. The flesh was drawn so tight across Crais' cheekbones that her face might almost have been a skull. "Do you know what it costs me to live in the Zone? Nobody issues *me* food and fuel. Do they think I could patrol every day and tend crops besides?"

"Capetown believes that since the threat has diminished," Kuyper said, "the bounty can also be cut. In my capacity as District Administrator I'll make representations to Capetown about the changed policy, but—"

"How diminished will the threat look if me and the Ralliers stop hunting the Zone, *mister*?" Crais said. "In a month, in a week even? And what happens if some of us start hunting for the other side, hey? How many ears are there on a convoy inbound with a load of wounded, hey?"

"You can swallow that sort of nonsense, for a start!" Evertsen said. "Berlin might be willing to take on the Ralliers—for the duration only, of course—if they decided to turn their coats again; but the only use they'd have for you, Crais, is the same one they have for every Draka they capture. And if they were going to make distinctions among Draka—that wouldn't be to the advantage of any of the three of us, would it?"

"Damn you, it ain't right!" Crais said, but there was more despair than anger in her voice this time.

In a gruffly conciliatory tone Evertsen said, "It isn't my job to explain Capetown's policies, Mistress Crais. That's just as well, because sometimes I find those policies completely inexplicable."

"See here, Crais," Kuyper said mildly, "I think

there's a way we can work with you. Capetown's right
about the number of units dropping these past
months. The guerrillas have been steering clear of the
district, and you've rooted out most of the stay-
behinds. I think there'll be enough in the account to
pay you at the old rate for adults; but children will
have to go at sixty aurics per unit, I'm afraid."

Crais looked at the two older men. Her expression couldn't be said to have softened, but Evertsen
no longer felt there was a real chance that she was
going to lunge for his throat with a skinning knife.

"I understand your concern about the cost of
supplies, Crais," he said. "I'll give you a chit for my
steward, directing him to sell you food and fuel from
my personal stock at the delivered cost to me. I think
you'll find that more reasonable than dealing with
drivers for supplies that've fallen off the back of
quartermaster trucks, so to speak."

"Still ain't right," Crais muttered. "But I guess I
oughta be used to the short end of the stick. All right,
I'll take your bargain."

Evertsen stripped an order blank off the pad and
began writing directions to his steward on the back
of it before Crais had an opportunity to change her
mind. She added in a mixture of explanation and
defiance, "It won't matter so much next year because
we'll have the crops in. But we need to make it
through the season, you see."

A heavy Slavic voice sounded at the entrance to
the TOC. Kuyper had already raised the lid of the
strongbox. He paused and said, "Say, Crais? Would
you mind waiting a moment to be paid? I want
Bruchinsky to see that everybody's being treated the
same, if you see what I mean."

"Afraid Bruchinsky might fly hot when you tell him
to bend over, hey?" Crais said with a cold smile. She
straightened her trophy string on the metal desktop.
"Yeah, all right, I'll help you with him."

She frowned in concern and added, "Bruchinsky keeps pretty good discipline in the field, you know. You only see his lot when they come in to tie one on, but it'd take a battalion to replace them."

"But you bring in two units for every three we get from Bruchinsky's whole band, Mistress Crais," Evertsen said. He was flattering her, but the words were still the cold truth.

Crais grinned. "That's so," she said. "Hunting's a job best done alone, *I* think."

There was a boom of laughter and a huge Slav squeezed through the entrance. His hair and beard were matted into a sheepskin vest worn fleece-side out, and a large rosary hung from his neck. "It is I, the great Bruchinsky, Colonel!" he said. "Eight hundred gold you owe us! We celebrate tonight!"

Evertsen saw his nephew's nostrils flare, then tighten. The Rallier's effluvium was a shock even to those prepared for it by experience. Well, Janni would smell worse things when he first stood on a battlefield fought over for several days in high summer; as he surely would, if he survived.

Crais and the Rallier exchanged brief comments in Zone Pidgin, a mixture of English, German, and several Slavic dialects. The two irregulars respected one another, though Evertsen knew there were undercurrents of mutual disdain as well: for a Slav on the one hand, for a woman on the other.

"We'll be with you in a moment, Captain Bruchinsky," Kuyper said. "We were just paying off Mistress Crais."

He took out a roll of ten-auric coins and broke the paper on the edge of the strongbox. He stacked ten pieces of new-minted gold behind each of the larger ears. "That's a hundred apiece for the two adults, and . . ."

Kuyper set six coins beside the first, the second, and the third of the small ears, then paused to break another roll. "And the last," he said. "Sixty aurics apiece for each of the children, two hundred and forty in all."

"What?" Bruchinsky said in amazement. "What's this fucking shit? You pay for ear, not fucking man ear and kid ear!"

"Not any longer, Captain Bruchinsky," Evertsen said coldly. "Capetown has decreed a change in the bounty, and of course we're bound by their decision."

"No fucking way I let you Draka bastards cheat me!" the Rallier shouted. "No *fucking* way!"

He flung back the sheepskin, exposing the sub-machine gun he slung beneath it. Like Crais' rifle it was of Soviet manufacture, a Shpagin with a 71-round drum. Soviet weapons had a rugged willingness to function that made them favorites among troops who operated without the luxury of a unit armorer.

Neither Evertsen nor Kuyper spoke. Janni stood like a statue, his face unreadable. The only sign that the boy was aware of his surroundings was the way his eyes traversed the room: back and forth, taking it all in.

Bettina Crais bent forward and scooped her coins, stack by stack, into a calfskin purse. The gold chimed musically. She folded Evertsen's note to his steward and stuck that in her purse as well.

"Crais!" said Bruchinsky. "You let them shit on you this way? You take their fucking sixty?"

Crais looked at the Rallier. Evertsen had seen gun muzzles with more expression. "It doesn't look to me like there's much choice, Bruchinsky," she said. "You want to buy my string off me at the old price?"

"Fuck!" the big Slav said. "Fuck all fucking Draka!"

He laughed as explosively as sudden thunder and slapped his string down on the desk beside that of Crais. There were eight units, four of them so fresh that a drop of blood oozed from the adult's torn lobe.

"Sure, pay me the fucking money," he said cheer-fully. "The boys all be so drunk in the morning they

don't know how much money we get. Me too, by
Jesus!"

Crais settled the purse back under her cape. She
gave a nod; more a lift of her chin. "I'll be on about
my business, then," she said. "See you in a week or
two, I reckon, Colonel."

She stared at Janni again with her expressionless
eyes. "Watch how you go, boy," she said. "It'd be a
pity if ears as cute as yours wound up hanging from
a string."

Bruchinsky laughed uproariously as Crais left the
room.

Kuyper began stacking coins with unobtrusive
precision. The administrator made a show of every
payout. Partly that was because the Slavs generally
liked a bit of ceremony, but Kuyper himself was the
sort of man who wanted order and dependability in
all things. It was difficult for Kuyper to be stuck in
this wilderness with Capetown's whimsies grinding him
from one side against the flint realities of the Zone
on the other, but he served the State as well as
humanly possible.

So did Colonel Evertsen; but it was hard to remember that as he read the disgust under his nephew's
blankness.

"Shit on Capetown," the Rallier said cheerfully. "We
still richer than I think when we start in. We break
down and get lucky."

"A breakdown in the Zone lucky?" Evertsen said,
frowning slightly. "Lucky you survived, you mean."

"Aw, our fucking shitpot motor, you know," Bruchinsky
said. "Still, she not fancy but she get the job done okay.
Just like me and the boys, that's right?"

He laughed and fumbled a bottle out of a side
pouch. It was empty, as Bruchinsky decided after
frowning at it for some moments. He cursed and
deliberately shattered it on the floor.

Evertsen said nothing. His batman would sweep

up the glass. It was the colonel's duty to the State
to deal with the irregulars. . . .

"Naw, the luck's good because we walk around
while Oleg fixes the motor," Bruchinsky resumed,
sunny following the momentary squall of the empty
bottle. "Pedr thinks he sees a track. I don't see shit,
but Pedr, he good tracker. Near as good as your blond
bitch-dog, Colonel, that's right?"

Evertsen offered a thinly noncommittal smile. He
didn't like to hear a Slav animal refer that way to a
Draka, but more than policy might have kept him
from reprimanding Bruchinsky in this particular case.

"We go a little ways in and I think 'a rag,' but we
look at it and it's a doll," the Rallier continued. "So
Pedr's right, and six of us we follow up fast while the
rest stays with the truck."

Kuyper broke another roll of aurics with a golden
tinkle. There were five adults and three children in
the string. The latter were very fresh.

"We find the place three miles, maybe, off the
road," Bruchinsky said. "It's hid good, but a kid's crying
before we see anything and we crawl up close. There's
a man hoeing squash and corn planted together, but
he's patting a kid who's bit on the neck by a big fucker
horsefly. One burst—" he slapped the submachine gun
"—and I get them both. Not bad, hey, even though
the boy wiggles till we twist his neck."

Kuyper set six coins behind the first of the small
ears, then looked at the Rallier with an expression
Evertsen couldn't read. The administrator resumed
counting, his fingers moving a little slower than
before.

"There's two girls in the dugout," Bruchinsky said.
"They got good gun like this—"

He pumped his submachine gun in the air for an
example.

"—but they little girl, they cry and cry but they
can't cock it, you see?"

Bruchinsky racked back his charging handle. *His* weapon was already cocked, so it spun a loaded round out onto the floor.

Evertsen managed not to wince. He supposed being shot by accident in his office by a drunken Slav would be a fitting end to his career.

"Pedr finish them with his knife after he have a little fun, you know?" the Rallier said. "So we run back with four more kills, the truck fixed, and we drive like hell to catch up with the convoy almost. Lucky, not so?"

"That completes the count, Captain Bruchinsky," Kuyper said, closing the lid of the strongbox. "Six hundred and eighty aurics."

"Shitload of money," the Rallier said admiringly. "It all be shit gone soon, but we party tonight!"

"If that's all . . . ," Evertsen said. It had gone better than he'd dreamed a few minutes before. Not that his superiors would care about the skill with which he and Kuyper had covered Capetown's idiocy. . . .

"One thing," Bruchinsky said, fumbling in another of his pouches. "This I get from the farmer today. Does it spend? It's broke, but it's real gold by Jesus!"

He held it out for the others to see. It was a sovereign, snapped in half and mounted for an ear stud. The legend and lower portion of the bust of George III were worn to shadows.

Janni began to laugh. The sound started normally but rose into hysterical peals.

Bruchinsky, the only man in the room who didn't get the joke, looked in growing puzzlement at his Draka companions.

Jane Lindskold is a former professor of English; despite that, she is also a crackerjack storyteller and wordsmith. She lives in Albuquerque, New Mexico, with her archaeologist husband Jim Moore (who I pump unmercifully for research material) and the inevitable writerly pride of cats. Her work includes science fiction, high fantasy, and the recent and unforgettable tale of supernatural creatures among us, *Changer*. I particularly liked the Yeti who compulsively haunted Internet chat rooms and King Arthur's consulting business in the sunbelt.

When I wrote *Marching Through Georgia*, the first of the Draka books, I aimed for a tone of tragic intensity. Jane rather effectively sticks a pin in my hero's self-image, using a cheerful ruthlessness in the service of her art. It's also an homage . . .

THE BIG LIE

Jane Lindskold

To George MacDonald Fraser and David Case

Well, I suppose you've heard it all and believe it, too, the more fool you, but I was there and I can tell you. It wasn't anything like that, nor were the Draka anything like you believe. The whole pot of rot is a big lie like God or love or the perfect deviled egg.

Trouble is, people believe what they want to believe and those books—those damn novels—they've been taken for fact when there are plenty who could tell you otherwise, but if they did they'd have to admit the truth about themselves and who wants to do that when the Lie is so much bigger and grander and finer?

I'm an old man now, old as Sin or Eric von Shrakenberg, which is about the same thing as I see it. When you read this, I'll be dead, so the Big Lie won't matter to me any more. In fact, I get rather a chuckle out of the idea of your reading this, of shattering the Lie for you when it has served me well enough all my life.

You might ask why would I do that when "Glory to the Race" has replaced "Please and Thank You," "Hello and Good-bye," and "By Your Leave" for the Draka people. Well, as I see it those long-limbed, high-cheekboned, super-strong, genetically engineered mutants are no more my race than are the chimpanzees that the Draka geneticists used for their early experiments.

White Christ! The divergence between us is probably greater. Think about that for a moment, then maybe you'll understand why I'm telling you this story, why I'm breaking down the Big Lie.

Then again, you might not understand. After all, you're one of those mutants, aren't you?

I was born in 1918, the same year as Eric von Shrakenberg, the same year that the Draka Women's Auxiliary Corps was abolished and women were integrated into the military. Unlike Eric, who was born a plantation owner's eldest brat on the Oakenwald Plantation. I was born in Cairo, Egypt. My parents named me Covington.

That's right. Start and look amazed. Your humble author is none other than the much decorated, ever-so-famous Covington Coemer, Arch-Strategos, Retired. I did say that the Big Lie had served me well, now, didn't I?

Growing up as I did under the shadow of the Great Pyramid, I never did quite buy into the myth that the higher-ups were pushing even then—the myth that Draka Citizens were the pinnacle of human evolution and that the rest of the world's populations were mere serfs. There was just too much evidence to the contrary.

Oh, I didn't waste my time griping and moaning about the way of the world as Eric would have you believe he did. I enjoyed the power and privilege that being at the top of the food chain brought me. I just didn't believe that somehow we Draka were better than the rest of humanity. Meaner, tougher, better trained—I had no problem with believing *that*. Thor's Hammer! Hadn't I been hustled off to boarding boot camp at an age when most children were still toddling about under their parents' loving care? If such brutality didn't produce a better trained product, then what was the use?

After boarding school ended, I went into the military just like every good, obedient Draka does. There I ran and jumped and crawled and sweated and learned what I was best at—sharpshooting. Although I didn't escape the normal grind, from my first year in I was given extra training on all sorts of distance rifles: ours, the Fritz's, the Ivan's, the Abdul's, anyone and everyone's. The idea was that wherever my company found itself, I would be prepared to kill the inconvenient enemy from a distance, opening a door for those whose duty it was to rush in and die valiantly. It's almost as safe a job as being Arch-Strategos.

The other thing I learned to do in the Army was to bunk and run—not letting my commanders know what I was about, of course. In the process of perfecting this art, I learned how to claim credit for other soldiers' achievements. This was easier to do than you might imagine, since most of the real heroes were reduced to artful red smears on the landscape.

Yes, those were golden years. As I was promoted and decorated for what I knew was arrant cowardice, well now, the cynicism that my Egyptian birthplace had nurtured got a healthy dose of fertilizer. Then my presumed heroism gave me a kick in the butt when in the spring of 1942, I found myself assigned to the First Airborne, Century A. That was where I met Eric von Shrakenberg, one of the primary architects of the Big Lie.

Now wait! Before you crumple up this memoir and toss it in the trash, you hear me out. I'm no crank. I was there and I know what I saw and heard. Hel! I know what I did and said. And I know what Mr. Perfect Draka, Eric von Shrakenberg did and said, too. I'll swear on anything you like that his version of what happened that Spring is about as true as Father Christmas.

I can imagine you frowning (an elegant expression, stern yet fierce on that high-cheekboned viz) despite my reassurances. Therefore, before I proceed any further, let me point out something that is damned suspicious when you bother to think about it. (Not that you young mutants are trained to think—just to plot and analyze, but that's neither here nor there).

The novels that have done the most for creatively presenting the image and philosophy of the Draka to the world at large have also served as propaganda for one of the most prominent Draka families—the von Shrakenbergs. Chew on that while I tell you the truth behind the campaign that pulled dear Eric out of reach of the Politicals and injected him firmly into the Draka ass.

As I was saying, I was assigned to the First Airborne, Century A, as a sharpshooter under the command of one Centurion Eric von Shrakenberg. Now all of you think that you know what kind of man dear Eric was during that period in his life. You've read the biographies of our famous Archon. You've read his own *The Price of Victory*, that sensitive novel that became such a best-seller among the young World War II veterans.

Dreck! I tell you. Dreck and drivel. Far from being a sensitive young warrior, handsome and genteel, nursing doubts about the righteousness of conquest, but ready nonetheless to die for his people, the Eric von Shrakenberg I met when I reported for duty was a stoop-shouldered, dead-eyed young brute who looked like something right off a Fritz recruiting poster. He even wore his pathetic bristle of a mustache in the same style as the Fritz dictator, Adolph Hitler. This pathetic item of facial decoration was, as I recall, not "yellow" as is usually reported (I suppose he thought "blond" would sound too effeminate, a thing only a man uncertain of his masculinity would fear) but mouse brown. I suppose he bleached it in later years to help man match myth.

When I reported for duty, Centurion von Shrakenberg positively sneered upon hearing my accent. You see, like many of those born and raised in Egypt, my accent is British in flavor rather than the lazy, plantation drawl affected by South African aristocrats like our dear Eric. Moreover, where Eric was fair with a tendency toward sunburn, my complexion was slightly swarthy with the usual accompaniment of dark eyes and hair. My bluff, good-natured features were graced by a set of truly fine whiskers. Our meeting was like night outshining day and putting day into a right funk, if I do say so myself.

Well, I could tell from that first meeting that Eric was a bigot and I knew there would be trouble between us. Still, faithful to my training, I snapped off a pretty sharp salute. The pompous son of a bitch even managed to belittle me for that courtesy.

"At ease, Coemer," he drawled. "Yo' don' need be so formal with me here. In Century A, we're all Draka."

I blinked, uncertain how to reply to such nonsense.

Of course we were all Draka. What else could we be? Century A was a Citizen's unit, not some hoard of jungle bunny Janissaries. I held my tongue, resolving to keep my eyes wide open and my mouth tight shut while I learned as much as I could about our commander.

Quickly enough, I discovered Eric's great "secret." Secret! Faw! He all but bragged about how he'd had the chit he'd fathered on a favored serf wench smuggled out of the Domination.

Later Eric's own writings would lovingly lick the liberal ass, garnering sympathy by implying that he committed this crime against Draka law out of the greatness of his heart—that he couldn't bear to see his own daughter (no matter that her mother was a wench bought for a few aurics so Eric'd stop tupping the kitchen staff and delaying dinner) raised as a slave. In this fashion, Eric presented himself to the non-Draka world as being possessed of great sensitivity, deeper than what most Draka are capable of feeling. The rest of us, of course, have had ample opportunity to recognize the discrepancy between what he wrote and how he has acted.

Let me set you straight. Eric smuggled his serf-spawn, Anna, out of the Domination not from any love for her or her mother, but out of hatred and distrust of his father. It's well-known that there was tension between old Karl and his son—tension that came to the fore when Eric became heir upon the death of John, the old man's favorite, who was killed while mishandling a serf uprising at some mine.

In the early years of his career, Eric never had the sense to know when to put on a pleasant facade or stop his gob. By the time he became famous, too many people knew about the tension between him and his father for him to deny it. Therefore, in an effort to save face, Eric portrayed his relationship with his father as one of like spirits possessed of different philosophies.

One has to admire old Eric for this. He's almost as much of a sneak as I am. By claiming a similar spirit to Arch-Strategos Karl, Eric managed to co-opt the greater man's reputation into his own. In his self-created mythology, Eric von Shrakenberg becomes the best and finest product of a great line, the one in whom everyone else's deeds find their culmination.

Dreck! The truth was, Eric hated his father for preferring his brother, John. Karl, for his part, hated Eric for living when his favorite son was dead. When it became evident that little Anna was going to resemble her mother—about whom Eric had been obsessively possessive, just ask anyone who ever tried to borrow her for a bit of fun—Eric realized that Karl could use Anna against him. The mind boggles at the possibilities.

So Eric had seven year-old Anna smuggled off the family plantation and into the United States. There she followed in the tradition of her loving and loyal family by writing nasty (but true) things about her papa's people in books such as *Daughter to Darkness: A Life*.

I know I've wandered off the subject of Century A's great deeds on the North Caucus Front, but it's important that you understand the vile sewer lurking beneath Eric's aristocratic veneer. In fact, there's one rumor—rumor only, mind you—that circulated in our company during the dark watches while Eric and his snoops slept. Keep in mind, though, that it's just a rumor.

There were those who said more sinister things about Eric and his daughter, and these others knew him well. These said that Eric was tempted to incest with the little Anna and got her out of reach before he could give into the impulse and be reprimanded for it. Child abuse—even of serfs—is one of the few things we Draka find abhorrent. It's such a waste of good property.

But I'm not saying that Eric von Shrakenberg really wanted to screw his own daughter. I wasn't present— like those of our company who had known him from a child—to make a fair judgment. All I can say for certain is that Eric von Shrakenberg hated his father with a passion so fierce that his entire military career was in one way or another an attempt to one up the old solider.

This Eric was the man I found myself serving under on April 14, 1942, when at 0400 hours we readied ourselves for our parachute drop into the partisan infested, German-held lands in the Caucasian Front. While I busied myself making certain that my gear was properly packed, I noticed the centurion idly smoking and staring at the wall while Sophie Nixon, our comtech, leered at him with what I guess she thought was hidden lust.

Eric wants everyone to believe that he was thinking deep thoughts during those ten minutes before we leapt out of the plane, but my sincere belief is that his bowels were in as much of an uproar as were mine.

Don't believe the nonsense they tell you— jumping out of a plane is not as good as sex. (Well, maybe it is for Eric. I've heard what the wenches at the officers' Rest Center snigger about his equipment.)

Jumping out of a plane is a terrifying thing. As you walk to the hatch, your mind is flooded with memories of classmates who died during training. You see their broken, mangled bodies etched in sharp relief against the dirt. When you try to distract yourself, the statistics on how many trained skydivers die or are seriously injured during a jump rear their ugly heads for inspection. You find yourself considering which would be worse. Having a broken leg on enemy turf is no picnic, but Draka armies don't like to haul the wounded along.

Then you make the jump, your bowels turning to water, your dry lips counting the seconds until you can pull the cord, an overstimulated imagination dreading that the parachute you so carefully packed will fail you in the end. Even when it doesn't and you're jerked up, harness straps digging into your shoulders, there's the landing to worry about. All it takes is a patch of uneven ground and you're presented with that shattered ankle or blown knee. You dangle weightless from the 'chute, straining your gaze downwards, trying to see what portion of real estate you've drawn. All around, more solid spots against the friendly darkness, are the silent figures of all those who are falling with you.

I'm a fair man. I don't blame Eric von Shrakenberg for the loss of our legion armor, but it was a blow nonetheless. By some miracle, Century A came down with personnel and communications gear intact, but the armor we'd counted on to make our job possible landed in a gully. There was no possibility of fetching it out in time, not with our fellow Draka sprinkling onto the landscape all around, geared up to carry out their parts in the battle plan. So we left the armor where it fell. I suppose someone fished it out later. I never bothered to find out.

No, I don't blame Eric about the armor, I don't even blame him for our being separated from the main Draka force. He isn't responsible for the vagaries of wind and terrain. On the other hand, perhaps I *should* blame him.

According to Eric's own account of the battle, Century A came down pretty much on target—that is, we were *meant* to be the northernmost element of the Draka attack force. Someone has to be stuck out alone—I know that as well as any man and better than some—but I find it rather interesting that Arch-Strategos Karl von Shrakenberg's much hated son and heir was dropped in the ass end of nowhere, voted most likely to die. Consider that the old commander was at that very moment courting an eligible Citizen of unimpeachable credentials and you wonder if he wasn't counting on the Fritz to sweep his family slate clean and give him a chance to start over.

Ah, but that's neither here nor there. Eric didn't die—and I'm here to tell you why it's no credit to him that he didn't.

Once we were down and gear handed round, Eric ordered us to move on Village One. In his own accounts, he gives an almost accurate account of that early battle. Oh, he beefs up the number of Fritz holding down the shop and minimizes our casualties, but he's hardly out of line there. Most military historians lie. Victors lie more than losers—it's one of the spoils of war.

Now Eric doesn't tell you what I was doing during this particular battle. There are two reasons for this. One is that the members of his Century are with the exception of Sophie Nixon—for reasons I'll explain later—fictional versions of real people, usually composites of three or four real Draka. So there is no me in all his tales—part of the reason his depictions of the Draka are so shallow, I like to think.

In interviews Eric has explained that this was artistic license, that he couldn't hope to deal with the heroism of a hundred and ten individuals in one short novel, so rather than slighting one or the other he combined people. I still get a sour taste in my mouth when I recall the saccharine way he referred to "those brave members of my Century, living and dead, whose courage inspired me to the best of which I was able."

I wash the sour taste away by recalling how little

Eric knew about what one of his "brave warriors" was up to.

Now, in the battle to take Village One most of our Century was ordered to rush into that Fritz-held horror leapfrog style: shoot, drop, move, shoot again.

Eric sent the Century's four best sharpshooters to scout out good positions. From these we were to pick off Fritz commanders or any other tasty targets. Due to the lack of armor, we sharpshooters were particularly essential. I recall with a grin how Eric admonished us to do our part with dignity and verve.

This was the kind of assignment I liked the most. It kept me out of the direct action, but gave me opportunity for safe kills so that I could brag with the best when we were all safely in camp and the fighting was over. I won't tell you how many times I simply snugged myself down in a cozy fork in some tree and waited for the worst to be over. Later, when the fight was being dissected and someone mentioned a miracle shot out of nowhere that saved his or her ass I wouldn't say anything, just look at my boots and polish my knife. Pretty soon some wise fellow would "realize" where credit was due and I'd mutter something stern and manly about just doing my duty.

Ah, it was marvelous, it was, and it didn't hurt that my shooting on the range or on the rare occasions that someone was watching was pure art—if I do say so myself. You see, even Draka aren't immune to the desire for a Guardian Angel. I've been told more times than I could count how someone went into danger all the more willingly knowing that I'd be lurking in the darkness to get them out.

"Homicidal children who believe in fairy stories, even with their legs ripped off and their faces ground to sausage meat." That's what someone once called the Draka and he was right, too. And like any children, they're happiest with the reassurance that someone is looking out for them. The way I see it, whether or not I actually helped anyone, I provided that reassurance, so I did my duty even when safely ensconced in some blind.

On this particular grey dawn in 1942, I loped off into the forest surrounding Village One ready to take my ease in some tall tree. I planned to shoot a Fritz or two if opportunity permitted, but I wasn't going to put myself into any particular danger while I was about it.

Right away, I could see that the countryside wasn't going to cooperate with my idea of a pleasant morning's work. The trees were barely budding, black limbs making dark lacework against a sky that held either traces of moonlight or the beginnings of dawn. The air was chill and the ground kissed with frost—not ideal conditions from a desert-born's way of seeing things.

I was silently cursing my bad luck and casting around for an alternative fox hole when I heard something stirring in the brush behind me. A branch snapped under a boot. As my heart tried to exit via my mouth, I flashed my knife out faster than you can say "Covington Coemer," but the fellow emerging from the shrubbery to my rear held a heavy P-38 with a calm, deadly assurance that left me no doubt that he knew how to use it. Even in the semi-light, I couldn't fail to see that he held it aimed at my torso so that even a near miss would spill a whole lot of my precious blood.

My new acquaintance was a skinny fellow, but the clothing that hung loose on his frame testified that once upon a time he hadn't been nearly so gaunt. I guess his eyes and hair must have had color, but I couldn't tell what shade they were in this dim light and I didn't really care. As far as I knew, this grey specter was Death with his lips puckered up round and ready to deliver one honey of a kiss through that unwavering gun barrel.

"Lean your rifle against that tree," the shadowy
figure ordered, his English heavily accented with some
other language I didn't recognize, "and take three
steps back from it. Remain in the open. Move any
way but that which I command and I shoot!"

I obeyed, leaning my rifle against the trunk of
something that might have been an oak. Even if I
wanted to try to escape, there was no cover and at
close quarters I was nearly as deadly without the
blamed thing. Yet, even as I was divesting myself of
my weapon, I was wondering why he didn't just have
me throw it down. I guessed that he was a partisan
and that weapons were dear just then. I was partially
right.

"Now, fold your hands on the top of your head and
stand on one leg."

I did as directed, feeling like a fool and wishing
something would distract him for just a moment . . .

My new friend continued, "You are going to do two
things for me or I will kill you."

I nodded and he studied me. I expect that I was
a bit of a disappointment for all my height, broad
shoulders, and fine whiskers. Surely he expected a
Draka to wither him with curses or spit fire. I suppose some of my fellows would have done just that,
but I've never seen it as part of my duty to die when
living seems a viable option.

"Speak on, old chap," I encouraged.

"First, you will carry a message into the village."

I liked this. I couldn't do that if I were dead. Then
I thought of some of the things I'd seen my comrades do in Italy—things that left a man technically
alive and capable of carrying messages, but not long
for this world. My blood chilled. Surely this fellow's
accent wasn't Italian, was it?

"Give the message to the old patriarch," my captor continued and I nodded though I had no idea who
in Thor's mitten he meant. "You will tell no one of

this message. If you do, the message itself will condemn you. Understand?"

"Completely."

"Good."

He glowered at me a bit more while I concentrated on the trickle of sweat from my armpits down my sides. It tickled and I had to fight back a perverse urge to grin and wriggle. I rocked a little on my one leg and wished he hadn't chose to have me imitate a stork. It's hard to feel dignified, you know?

"I selected to follow you," he said, sounding less than certain for the first time, "since you go by yourself with the rifle with the great scope. You are a sniper?"

"Right!" I agreed. "The best."

He snorted, obviously doubting me, which stung a bit. It's hard to be taken for a liar when all you're doing is telling the truth—especially when you *are* a liar. My captor continued:

"Since you say you are a sniper, the other job I have for you is this."

Stepping forward, he picked up my rifle carefully, keeping the deadly mouth of his P-38 on me so that I had no opportunity to jump him. As he did so, a white flare burst in the general vicinity of Village One, making the forest shadows go crazy. For a weird moment, I actually thought my captor was responsible, then I remembered Eric's briefing. From the near distance, gunshots, screams, and shouts of "BuLala!" announced that my Draka fellows were in the process of ruining someone's morning.

"Move quickly, Drakanski!" my captor snapped. "Be good and I shall give you a chance to do your job."

He hustled me over to a spot that provided me with an ideal overlook of Village One. It was just the sort of spot I would have chosen for myself given time—a grand vantage, but completely secure from observation. In the flare's early light I could see long-robed civilians hustling for cover. The Fritz in their grey uniforms stared in confusion. The smarter ones joined the ragheads in the general move toward cover.

"See the mosque?" hissed the voice behind me. "Aim at the one who is coming out. Now! Fire!"

I did, noting through the scope that the man he had ordered me to shoot was a handsome young buck in local attire. No matter who he was—he could have been my own brother—with the hard muzzle of the P-38 ready to separate my spine I wasn't arguing target choice. As the handsome Abdul's head exploded, I heard a satisfied chuckle from behind me.

"Now, the next who come after him. Shoot them too," came the order.

I was aware of the stench of foul breath and realized that my captor was so close that he must be practically touching me, but I didn't dare get in a wrestling match now. As I popped off three more— a woman and two men—the chuckling deepened.

"Collaborators," he whispered as if I needed any more explanation than the gun in my back for doing what I was doing.

"Now the Germanski," he said. "They will come from two buildings to the right of the mosque."

Damn him if he wasn't right. I guess the Fritz had taken over the buildings as a barracks or club or something. For a minute there it was like shooting serfs on the dunes back home. Then the Fritz got smart and dove back inside, but I fancied that the last fellow through the door wouldn't be sitting any time soon.

I was so absorbed in my fun that I didn't notice when the pressure at my back altered and the hali-tosis miasma lessened. Glancing over my shoulder, I saw that my captor was at the edge of the tree line, already in half-cover, though the P-38 was still aimed at my gut.

"Farewell, Drakanski," he said. "The letter is in your pocket. Think this: If you do not deliver it or otherwise cross me, I know of many places like this one that overlook the village. I, too, may have a rifle."

He vanished into the pre-dawn gloom and I assuaged my wounded vanity by banging away at the Fritz down below. I avoided shooting natives if I could, not wanting to prevent the planned postal delivery. My back shivered the whole time I was about my fun though, fearing a bullet was due to pierce it any moment. Knowing what horrors lurked in the darkness, that damned letter seemed a pretty fragile shield.

When I rejoined the rest of Century A we were the proud owners of a stone and dirt village without any of the comforts of home. We were still the northernmost Draka unit, but now we were a battered and bloodied northernmost Draka unit.

I've mentioned the right to lie as one of the spoils of the victor. A more specific spoil of that particular battle was the residents of Village One themselves. They were Circassians, dirty Abduls, half-starved and so accustomed to being beaten on that we were viewed as no worse and no better than the Fritz or the Ivans. All in all, we had captured about two thousand potential serfs.

Among them was a scrawny old raghead who seemed to make most of the palaver for his people. I guessed this was the patriarch and as soon as possible I slipped him the mysterious letter. It couldn't do me any good anyhow. I'd taken a glance at it and it was written all in those funny Arabic curves and sticks. The patriarch, however, trotted off with it right away. Later, I saw him studying me and looking really thoughtful. His gaze made my blood run cold.

In his accounts of these events, Eric makes himself out to be some sort of genius for thinking to use the Circassians to replace the Draka labor we didn't have. He also seems to think he was clever in bribing them to work for us instead of cracking the whip over them. He wasn't. Whip cracking would have taken Citizen soldiers that we couldn't spare. Moreover, once we were done cracking those whips, we would have had to deal with our less-than-tame serfs.

The Security Directorate was still lurking in the background, letting the Army take care of the messy business of pacification, so they weren't an option. We could have shot the Circassians, but that would have been a waste of some 2,000 bullets. We could have stuck them in a basement or two and tossed in a grenade, but that wouldn't have served our purposes. We needed those basements. Besides, killing the ragheads, whatever the method, would have left us with a heap of corpses breeding disease and stench.

So we let them live. Turning them loose in the countryside with food and blankets meant that they were out of our hair and in to the Fritz's. It also made certain that any guerrilla fighting on the part of their hotheads would be directed toward the Fritz not toward us. We'd given them food and a promise of enough more to survive the coming year. They weren't going to trouble us until they had an opportunity to find out if that promise was good. By the time they found out that the food came with a serf tattoo attached, Century A would be long gone.

That's why I don't think Eric was particularly clever. He simply did the only reasonable thing. Those Circassians worked like the serfs they already were— for all they weren't yet wearing orange neck numbers— and then got out of our way under their own steam.

Brilliant? No, no more than keeping your head out of water is brilliant when you're spilled into the ocean out of a sinking ship. Eric's brilliance came later, when he wrote up his account for the masses and portrayed himself as a liberal showering mercy upon the defeated.

As I write those lines, I can just imagine your all-too-similar mutant faces crinkling up in confusion every time I discuss Eric's deliberate representation of himself as a tenderhearted liberal. After all, why would a Draka commander, one with both political and military ambitions, do such a foolish thing?

Ah, well here you underestimate the sinister cunning of the Draka mind. Eric von Shrakenberg rose to power during the years when the Alliance didn't even exist, when we still had to deal with individual countries each with its own political and social philosophies. During the Eurasian War, we were allied with the United States. It was an alliance of convenience, not of sympathetic natures, a thing American war reporter Bill Dreiser makes perfectly clear in his book *Empires of the Night: A '40s Journal*.

Even back then Eric was, if nothing else, a cunning old snake. He realized that for him to rise to power in the Domination he had to be accepted not only by the Draka but also by the United States and her weak-willed, freedom-worshiping allies. Assassination is a tool that the U.S. of A. has stooped to time and again when the leader of another country behaves in an inconvenient fashion. Doubt me? Look at South American history both of that time and in the years that followed.

Eric deliberately promoted himself as a Draka who had been a sensitive, thoughtful, even liberal youth. The Draka who got to know him well realized that he had outgrown those failings. Some of us—myself included—doubted that he had ever possessed them. We saw up close and personal what a nasty, scheming, credit-stealing bastard he was. To most Draka those traits made him a man worth following whether in battle or in the political arena.

The tales of Eric's liberal youth, however, made him acceptable to the Americans and their allies. They sopped up Dreiser's account. They read Eric's own

novels. They believed the half-truths and outright lies
that Eric spouted for their benefit. And so they let
him live. A CIA assassin never slipped heart-attack
poison in his wine or bribed a serf wench to sacrifice her own life in taking the Master's.

Don't you ever forget as you read this, smug in
your late historical superiority with all the Earth
ground beneath the heel of the Domination and liking
it, too, that assassination was a very real risk during
the years following the war against the Fritz as we
set out to pacify the lands that had been Hitler's and
were now our own. So don't forget that Eric had
every reason to want the Allies to view him as a lesser
evil than most other Draka politicians. But I stray
from the point.

Once we had the Fritz out of Village One, and the
labor problem solved, we set about making the place
more Draka-friendly. Fortunately, our radio had come
down intact, so Eric contacted the quartermaster and
requested some supplies. As our defensive plan and
fortifications are a matter of history, I'm not going
to bore you—and myself—with a repetition.

Let me just add that digging and blasting and
clearing away rubble for six hours straight gives you
more than blisters. Trust Eric to whine about his own
blistered hands and to brag that doing a bit of light
digging was his way of leading by example.

For my part, I was down on the basement level,
helping create what would become our tunnels. We
did this by blasting out connecting walls and then
setting a gang of the wild Circassians to clearing out
the rubble.

After that narrow brush with death out in the
forest, I was quite edgy. When I get edgy, I get horny.

Psychologists will tell you mine is a natural enough
reaction, one shared by a large portion of the human
race. They say that proximity of death creates a desire

to create life and other psychobabble along the same
line.

Well, I really can't say whether it's a desire to
propagate the Race that makes me want a wench as
soon as the worst of the danger is over or whether
I simply prefer rogering to getting drunk as a way
of forgetting the horror of it all. What I do know is
on that particular post-dawn I realized that one of
the Circassian wenches in my crew was somewhat
better fed and less filthy than the rest.

Eric hadn't given us any time for recreation once
we took Village One. Now that the place was just
about secured, I figured it was time for me to have
some fun. I tapped my chosen wench on the shoulder and jerked my thumb in the direction of a room
off to one side.

This particular room had probably begun life as
a root cellar. Now it remained only because the
engineers had ruled that its walls provided significant
support. It was empty now; whatever it had held had
long ago been taken by the Fritz or maybe even by
the Ivans before them. The floor was dirt, packed
hard from years of trampling and cold as ice, but I
had heat enough for us both.

With signs, I directed my girl to get on all fours,
pausing long enough to make her somewhat comfortable by folding a rag of blanket under her knees. She
didn't protest. I had no doubt she'd been through this
before. I've heard that these shepherd peasants don't
know how to do it any other way. In any case, the
Abduls aren't exactly romantic toward their ladies.

Maybe it was that last thought, maybe it was the
resigned look in the girl's big brown eyes, but before
I flipped up her skirts and hauled down her ragged
underthings, I put my arms around her and kissed
her warmly. She started slightly. Then the saucy thing
kissed me right back!

When our lips parted, she rolled onto her back,

making quite clear that she preferred the act this way. I wasn't about to argue. I'd thought I might need to club her to keep her from screaming and here she was inviting me to have at her! I supposed she thought that rogering was more to her liking than hauling rubble in a dark tunnel.

I was too damn fired up to manage much in the way of warm-up activities, but I did give her bubbies a squeeze before mounting up and getting on with the business. Just to make certain she stayed quiet, I put my mouth over hers. She nibbled my lips, moaning gently, a sound I felt more than heard.

It was over faster than I'd have liked, nor could I risk a second go, not with my crew laboring maybe three meters away. I straightened my uniform and, locating a chocolate bar in my pocket, I gave it to the Circassian wench.

"Think me," she whispered in very broken English, "when you get loot?"

I gave her soft parts a squeeze to show her that I would indeed, though I did wonder if she realized that she herself might be part of that loot rather than on the receiving end of any gifts. Given what I learned about her later, I wouldn't doubt it. Then I slapped her across the rump, handed her a shovel, and sent her back to the labor party. I joined them a moment later, well pleased with the interlude.

When the fortifications were complete, Eric sent our erstwhile laborers out into the wilds to fend for themselves. They went burdened with food and blankets, the latter from a store the Fritz were too stupid to destroy when we attacked. I found my wench and slipped her a few extra pieces of chocolate, not out of any softness, but because I'd been playing with the idea of hunting her up again next time Eric sent me out on sniper duty. Finding her would be a long shot, but then I wasn't paying for the candy.

After the Circassians were gone, we settled in, waiting for all hell to break loose as we knew it must in time.

I suppose this is the best place to set the record straight about Eric's relationship with our comtech, Sophie Nixon. In his own accounts he represents his relationship with her as one of those wonders that blossom under fire. She is the voice of practicality when he lapses into too deep thoughts. Her no-nonsense approach to life and death is a natural antidote to his Byronic brooding.

Well, I've said already that Eric von Shrakenberg was not the person he presented himself as being. Neither then was Sophie Nixon, but I don't suppose that even in fiction can a man tell the truth regarding the woman he eventually married.

About the only true thing in Eric's portrayal of Sophie is her age. She was nineteen and a half in April of 1942. I checked the record later, curious as to whether he had left any scrap of the truth intact. He portrays her as a cute, round-faced wench with features lacking the aquilinity so prized by the Draka. Of course she was in perfect condition, but who among us wasn't after paratrooper training?

I recall Sophie as round-featured, but not at all cute and I wasn't the only man in the company to make that assessment. She smoked constantly so her horsey teeth were yellow stained. Her hair and breath reeked of sour tobacco smoke. Her skin was dull and flat—again from those damn fags.

Like most of the men in Century A, I knew that Sophie was as lusty as a cat in heat. She preferred men to women, but would take women and if she couldn't get women just about anything would do. I'm not kidding—the stories about her role in the girl-and-pony show at the Legion Hall were common currency back then. I understand that the Politicals considered going after her for it, but she hadn't broken any laws but those of good taste.

You must recall that in those days the Race Purity laws were in full effect. I might go and have a romp with a captive wench, but any Citizen woman caught taking her pleasure of a male captive in a similar fashion would be liable for criminal proceedings. So when Sophie had an itch to scratch, she needed a Citizen male for her toy.

Well, I'd had my go at Sophie and found her too pushy for my tastes. I like a woman who will play, not one who wants to ride me like a fire fighter who's just heard the bell ring. It's undignified and takes some of the fun out of it. Most of the men felt the same and the women in our Century were off Sophie for some obscure reason based in feminine politics. That meant that if Sophie Nixon wanted her ashes hauled there was just one man left in the Century who could do it for her—Eric von Shrakenberg.

Now Sophie was never a woman to turn down a challenge. Her posting as a comtech in those days of primitive radio was proof enough of that. Bedding Eric would make keeping vacuum tubes unshattered during a parachute jump seem a lark. We all knew Eric preferred sex with serf wenches—I suppose it went back to his childhood. Once a week he'd trot down to the officers' Relief Station, take a half-hour with a girl—any girl—and then his itch was scratched. In all the gossip around the mess hall, I never met anyone who could swear Eric had done it with a Citizen.

So to be fair to Sophie, maybe it wasn't just because no one else would have her that she made her play for Eric; maybe she wanted to be the one to get his cherry, to force him to do the capital act human to human, rather than master to serf.

Whatever her reasons, she sniffed after him like a dog in heat. It became something of a company joke—

one we kept from Eric and Sophie, of course. There was even a betting pool going about when she'd get him, where, and how publicly. I would have won, too, but the circumstances under which I was witness were such that I preferred to keep my lips buttoned.

But I'm getting ahead of my story.

Hell broke loose at around 1600 hours that same interminable April fourteenth. The Fritz, in the person of a fighting SS unit, brought the battle into our fortified little village, winding up the road with tanks and various other vehicles. They were armed to the teeth, ready to smash through what they imagined was a medieval village held by a rather lightly armed and armored paratrooper unit.

They were wrong and we punished them severely for their conceit. For once I was in the thick of it, not liking *that* at all but not wanting to risk my hard-won reputation as a hero. If I died here, that reputation wouldn't matter much, true, but I planned on living on and living well.

After the fight was over, we knew the trap was sprung. There was no way we'd pull the Fritz into it twice—especially not this particular unit. The SS were pure slime, but cunning, too. And, sadly for my hopes of a solid eight hour's sleep, they weren't afraid to work nights.

About 0230 on April fifteenth—less than twenty-four hours since we'd made that damn parachute drop, if you've forgotten—one of the Circassian scouts came in with the news that the Germans were moving into position to crush us, probably with first light. We didn't have the luxury to wait for them to come to us. If we did, not only would they most certainly win, but they would also roll up and pinch our fellow Draka between their advance and the Fritz already in position.

I'm no empty-minded hero with stars in my eyes

and the flutter of dragon's wings in my ears. I suppose that's apparent enough. Still, even I felt a burning anger that the losses we'd already suffered might go for nothing. I was also determined that I wouldn't join the casualties if I could help it. A brilliant idea born of desperation sprang to mind.

When Eric scanned our group looking for volunteers to round out Tetrarchy Two, the unit he had nominated for certain death, I stepped forward.

"Take me, Eric," I said boldly, thinking of treetops and the two dozen ways a man could honestly claim to get lost in the dark during a battle. I'd be a hell of a lot safer out there than waiting in this death trap of a village.

He nodded. Tetrarchy Two's shooter had been killed in our second action. While Eric named the others who were being sentenced to death and lust-sick Sophie Nixon proclaimed her right to sacrifice more radio equipment to her desire to get laid, I stuffed my pockets with things that would make survival in the damp forests more tenable. So eager was I that I was ready to go before Tetrarchy Two assembled, so I made myself useful at Eric's right hand.

He smiled at me. The vicious light in his eyes said: *"Now I'll have my chance to get rid of you, Egyptian."*

Mere minutes after the Circassian scout's report, the augmented Second Tetrarchy filtered out into the night. Our faces were smeared with black, our bodies weighted down with two kilos of gear apiece. Rain poured from an unseen sky where clouds obscured what little light stars or moon might have offered. I can sincerely say that I have been in brighter mines.

Despite the icy trickle of rain that ran from my hair down the back of my neck, I grinned into the darkness as I ran along the muddy road. Red-haired Loki must have smiled upon my plans. There could hardly be a more perfect night for slipping away from trouble.

After about ten klicks of jogging along through perfect darkness, a soft whistle sounded a halt. We clustered round while the native scout reported that we had reached the trail that would take us to the Fritz. Eric snapped out orders. Most of the Second Tetrarchy—myself included—were to go west and cover the other trails, picking off the Fritz as they headed along them toward Village One. Another group under Eric's own command was to escort some satchelmen from the combat engineers to blow up the Fritz tanks.

Well, we'd all have done a hell of a lot better if Eric'd just stayed back at the village and let us do our jobs without his damned leading by example. If what Eric pulled that night was an example of the best Draka High Command can offer, well, no wonder breeding *ghouloons* and mutant Citizens became such a priority in later years.

And how did I happen to be there to witness Eric's muff when I'd been sent off with the bulk of the Second Tetrarchy? Once again, I'd been clever and screwed myself good in the process, but then if I hadn't, I suppose I wouldn't have been in position to win the battle for the Draka.

As soon as we split to cover the various paths, I left my partners. No one questioned this, not with my cool assurance that I'd be there when they needed me. It's that Guardian Angel thing again. Also, as Eric is fond of noting when his own disobedience is mentioned, Draka encourage a certain amount of independence and innovation among even the lowest ranked troopers, and I was a decorated hero.

I melted back into the darkness and here my own ignorance of forests defeated me. Egyptian-born as I was, I was more comfortable with deserts or river swamps and marshes. I'd trained in places similar to these dark, wet forests, but training isn't the same as having a terrain imprinted in your blood.

To make the least fuss about an interminable time spent creeping around in the damp, looking for a place away from both the Fritz and my homicidal buddies: I got lost.

A dim flicker of light, barely glimpsed through the hateful black tree trunks gave me my first landmark. I closed, moving across the sodden forest floor with supreme stealth. Soon I could distinguish the faint sound of boots and the swish of rain capes. I matched the cadence of my movements to theirs and closed further. My plan was to trail long enough to get my bearings and then beat cheeks in the opposite direction.

I only realized how far off course I'd gotten when I heard Eric von Shrakenberg's voice, hoarse and low, reminding his small troop of their orders. Ahead, just visible through the trees, were the Fritz with tanks, trucks, and troops. I didn't need to be told that they were also far better rested than we were. I hated them for being dry and asleep when I was out here sodden, my head pounding with fatigue as the effects of the chocolate and coffee I'd bolted down burned off.

What I did next wasn't cowardice but prudence— at least I'd like to think so. If I joined Eric and his brave band, I'd have been damned for disobeying orders. If I tried to slip away, I might be caught in the crossfire. There was a sturdy tree just ahead, an old monster with vines and moss hanging from the limbs and a thicket at the base. In two seconds I'd imitated a squirrel and slipped into the boughs, finding myself a position in which I could lie hidden.

Darkness was my friend at that moment, darkness and pouring rain. I felt almost cheerful, like when as a boy I'd slipped into the old brothels in Cairo and watched my elders fornicating in what they thought was decadent privacy. They'd never dreamed that a little boy lay silent and aroused on one of the ceiling joists, observing them through the cracks in the lath and plaster. Now once again I figured I'd play voyeur from perfect safety and maybe learn something I could turn to my advantage.

Turns out, I proved more a prophet than I'd ever dreamed.

Eric and his little band closed on the Germans. From my vantage, I saw the sentry before Eric did, but I couldn't very well give warning.

"*Halten sie!*" came the nervous challenge.

Then Eric blew it.

"Ach, it's just me, Hermann," he said in German. "Where's the *Herr Hauptman*?"

To this day I hold that if Eric hadn't been so busy trying to be clever—I mean, why bother calling the sentry "Hermann" as if he knew him?—he might not have forgotten something as elementary as the fact that the SS doesn't use the German Army rank system. No matter, the cat was out of the bag.

The Germans opened fire and I ducked close to my guardian tree trunk. Nothing came near me, however, and in the wild light of flare fire I was more safely hidden then ever. No one, Draka or Fritz, would have believed that my black-painted face was anything but an illusion wrought of shadows and fear, even if they did catch a glimpse of me.

Slowly, I worked my rifle into position. I no longer needed to worry that the flash from my shooting would be seen, and I had a fancy to lessen the odds that some Fritz might get lucky and take me out.

As I sought targets and fired, I caught glimpses of Eric behaving like a raw recruit. Spotting what any idiot could have realized was the command truck, did he draw back and fire into the body from safety?

No! The idiot pounded forward and tossed something—I guessed a grenade and a muffled "whump" a couple seconds later confirmed my guess—into the back. Then, without checking or even firing a few shots through the canvas to make certain that the grenade had done its job, Eric went loping toward the back of the truck.

I'm not certain to this day what he was after. Maybe the radio. Maybe the commander. Maybe a safe place to hide. What he got was a boot soundly in his jaw as a big German came barrelling out. Then the two of them were in the mud, wrestling like mad dogs. If it hadn't been for Sophie Nixon's desperate need for Eric, we would have been spared his continued troublemaking. As it was, she rescued him from his own stupidity.

Kicking the Fritz in the balls to distract him, Sophie proceeded to beat him to death with the butt of her machine pistol. It was pretty ugly. I distracted myself from the sight of Draka femininity in action by picking off a couple of opportunistic Fritz—one of whom had fled into the woods, chanced on our native guide, and would have killed him but for me.

The once quiet, rainy night now echoed with manmade thunder. The air reeked of explosives, burning fuel, and roasting corpses. As if in an effort to reclaim the night for Nature, the storm grew in force. To me up in my tree, it was evident that despite his crew's valiant effort to make up for Eric's mistakes we Draka were losing the battle.

After Sophie forced a stim between his lips, Eric caught on. He hollered the call to retreat to those few sodden and battered Draka who still lived. They dropped back and damn me if Sophie and Eric didn't take refuge under my own favorite tree!

Somehow Sophie had managed to keep hold of her radio, even while saving Eric's bacon. I saw her thrust the handset into his palm, urge him to do something. The stim had taken effect by then. Trembling in my perch, I damned Eric's eyes as he called for firefall—

a bombardment of the very area in which we had taken shelter!

Didn't the idiot realize that our people would be using captured ordnance—ordnance that they couldn't trust or aim? Didn't he realize that *we* could get killed? Let him die a hero if he wanted! I knew that the only way to be a hero was to live and enjoy the benefits!

I wanted to leap down, to drag the handset from his mouth, to shout a counter command, but the memory of Sophie beating the Fritz to death with the stock of her machine pistol stopped me cold. Then . . .

Well, according to Eric's account, what happened next was that he ordered his troops to retreat "firing for effect". Wotan! As if with the skies raining fire and explosion our little guns could have any effect! Anyhow, that's the official story and many a Draka has thrilled at the drama of those blood-smeared survivors hauling ass up the trail, led by a commander who collapses in pure exhaustion at the brink of safety.

Rather reminds you of the tale of Moses and the Promised Land, doesn't it?

There isn't a word of truth in it. What really happened is that the remnant of Eric's band hugged the dirt, praying to whatever gods they believed in that they hadn't just gone through hell to die by friendly fire. And hidden in the thicket at the base of my mighty oak, Sophie Nixon tore open Eric von Shrakenberg's trousers, straddling him then and there in the mud and rain.

He didn't protest. Maybe like me he was remembering the battered Fritz. Maybe he was enjoying it. Maybe he was just too tired to do anything but comply. I told you that I could have won that betting pool, but circumstances rather robbed me of the opportunity.

Sophie finished with Eric about the time it was

certain that our distant gunners had the range. Tucking
himself back into place, a foolish grin on his face, Eric
commanded the remnants of his troops to retreat. He
might have even told them to fire for effect, but if he
did it was with a slap at Sophie's rump and a shy grin.

I stayed in my tree. By now the team I was supposed to be with had probably given me up for dead.
Once Eric and crew were out of the way, I'd find
my own way back. It occurred to me then that I'd
better find some freshly dead corpse to donate an
artistic bit of blood. It always pays to advertise.

My plan would have worked, too, but for that damn
forest. Somehow, I stumbled into a gully awash with
rainwater and had to sidetrack. I'd just checked my
compass and was reorienting when there was a rustle
to one side, slightly behind me. A terribly familiar
voice said:

"Lost, Drakanski?"

I wheeled. There stood my partisan of the dawn
before. At his side stood a someone I also knew—
my woman of the tunnels. Both held guns. My senses
reeled. Had I been any but a Draka, I believe I might
have fainted. This was too much. I was sodden,
starved, cold, and wet. My head rang from the bombardment. And once again, I was a captive . . .

They hustled me away with an efficiency that
bespoke familiarity with these horrid woods. Then,
when we were safe within a shelter of some sort, the
girl made tea. She offered me a cup, along with a
hunk of that very chocolate I'd stuffed into her hands
moments before Eric banished the Circassians into
the wilderness.

I sipped the tea. It was strong and bitter. I suppose I must have grimaced, despite the warmth that
coursed through me. The girl grinned evilly and said:

"Too bitter, Master Covington? Let me sweeten it."
Leaning forward she spat into the cup.

As I stared at the gob of slime floating in the brown liquid, she snarled, "Drink it! It's no worse than what you did to me! We've shared body fluids, eh?"

"Enough, Anya," the man snapped. "We are the Drakanski's friends. For now . . . "

He must have been a powerful man among them. The vixen not only lowered her gaze, she actually poured me a fresh cup and added a bit of honey. Her gaze was acid though, and I had no doubt where I stood with her. As I sipped my tea, I gave her a cordial nod and said to the man:

"We meet again, I see. Do you need any other messages delivered?"

He seemed to admire my coolness, for he gave me a broken-toothed grin. "In fact, we do. How would you like to be the great hero of this battle?"

I allowed as this idea suited me fine and he explained. The remnants of Century A holding out in Village One didn't have a chance. They could hold the ground for a while, but the main Draka forces were hard pressed and could not send relief through known routes.

Abdul's people, however, knew some tricks even the Fritz did not. They would guide me to the Draka headquarters. Once there I would act as go-between for them and the Draka command. With luck, our forces could reach Village One in time to preserve our line.

The plan rather pleased me. It would keep me alive and out from under whatever hell the Fritz would surely be bringing down on Eric's head. If we did pull it off, I'd be due for a commendation. Only one thing troubled me.

"Why would you do this for us?" I asked.

"Not for you!" The girl spat—on the floor this time. "For us! Germanski and Russki alike only wish us dead. Draka at least would keep us alive and you have given us the means to live . . . "

Something in those fiery eyes told me she wasn't telling me the whole truth, but this at least was a lie I could live with. What had been in that message I carried to the patriarch? I'll tell you here and now, I don't know, but I found it an interesting coincidence that Security never did recapture all the former residents of Village One.

"Very good, then," I said. "When do we start?"

There was nothing I wanted more than to sleep, but I couldn't show a bit of fear or tiredness now. To my great and secret joy, the man shook his head.

"Not for some hours now. The woods are filled with Germanski and even with some Drakanski and the Russki they have tamed. They seek their dead and wounded—what will they think when they don't find you?"

I shrugged. "It's a big forest, my good man."

"Rest now," the man ordered. "Anya and I will take turns watching over you. Do not think to escape."

"When you've given me the best chance to aid my people?" I said with what I hoped was becoming indignation. "I should think not!"

To tell the truth, I was happy to be there in that cave. The tea had only just kept exhaustion at bay. I had barely stripped off most of my outer gear, tucked my knife in my fist, and laid my head down on a pillow made from my folded rain cape before I was sound asleep.

I awoke a few hours before dusk, ravenous and horny. My captors fed me well, mostly from the stores we'd given them. My other hunger shriveled and vanished when I saw how the girl Anya was glowering at me. I wondered why she had been so cooperative when we'd coupled down there in the tunnels. All I could figure was that it must have been my dashing whiskers.

Musing on imponderables such as the workings of

a woman's mind, I cleaned up, checked my gear, and got ready for the trail.

We left as an early dusk accompanied by more rain was gathering. The chief partisan had told me to call him Abdul; his expression had been so sour that I knew he was well aware that this was our derogatory slang for all ragheads. In addition to Abdul and Anya, there were a half-dozen other partisans, all scrawny, but all as silent in the woods as ghosts.

They set a fast pace for all they were half-starved. Their mood was good. Apparently, last night's battle had been a windfall for them. They'd scavenged weapons and food from the remnants of the Fritz encampment. I tried not to listen too closely though they politely chattered in German and English for my benefit. Devotees of Islam often follow Jewish dietary laws, but from what I could gather, long-pork was on these ragheads' menu. I wondered if they intended for me to end up in the larder at the end of this venture and tried not to tremble.

With the skies overcast, I felt as if we were hiking through a timeless void, but a glance at my watch told me that we had been hiking for six hours when at last Abdul called a brief halt. We ate (I tried not to think what was in the sandwiches) and trudged on. When daylight came round again, we crept into some hole and slept. The next dusk, we moved on again. It was full dark when we reached the main Draka lines.

I took over then and my name and reputation got us through to the strategoi in charge of the area. Muddied, bloodied, worn from hours of hiking, I must have cut a dashing figure, but that wasn't enough. I had to talk as I've never talked before. Most of what I told them was the truth—though I left out my role as captive.

Freya's Tits, but I was eloquent! The chaps in charge not only listened to me, they listened to Abdul and believed in his good faith. Doubtless the fragmented messages from Village One added credence to my report. I was given a chance to wash, eat, and even rest a little, then it was Covington Coemer to the rescue with my faithful native guides giving directions.

This is the kind of heroism I like. While Eric and the remnants of Century A—down at this point, I later learned to around half-strength—were being bombarded by furious Fritz, I rode easy and alert in a *Pelast*-class, light, eight-wheeled personnel carrier. Our local guides had done well by us and I couldn't really complain when one by one, they filtered off into the forest, ostensibly to scout, in reality to escape their dangerous allies.

Anya was the first to go and I was glad. Any thoughts I'd had of acquiring her for a play toy had vanished over our two days of intimacy. She'd never sweetened to me again, but something one of the others said led me to believe that our one friendly tumble had been her way of rewarding me for getting that mysterious message to the patriarch. Shortlived thanks, that, as I see it.

Abdul was the last to leave us. I can still recall his sardonic face, dirt-smeared and weary as he saluted me from the edge of the wood. Then he was gone. I'm delighted to say I never saw him again.

No one made an effort to stop him or any of the others. Like the rest of our new property, they could be herded up when the battles were fought. I had my doubts though that Security would catch Abdul. I suspected he'd be out there causing trouble for any and all until he laid down his life and became part of the soil he'd worked so valiantly—and futilely—to defend.

Our rescue team arrived in the eleventh hour, only to be nearly shot by a wild-eyed, desperate Eric von Shrakenberg. My heroic initiative was made much of at the time. Trust Eric to neglect telling in his own

account just how the Draka reinforcements happened
to show up in the nick. No, he was too interested
in his own personal drama to give credit where credit
was due.

Well, I know the truth and now you do, too.
There's one last point on which the record needs to
be set straight.

After the mopping up was over, Eric insisted that
what remained of Century A—down to fifty from one
hundred and ten after the worst of the wounded were
taken out—be permitted to hold Village One. It's part
and parcel of that man's incredible ego that he would
insist an under half-strength Century be given such
a tremendous responsibility.

Still, I think he knew what was coming for him.
He'd freed potential serfs, armed Russian madmen
(I skipped the details of that as you can find them
in numerous accounts), and acted even beyond the
usual parameters of military initiative. Besides, he
knew that the Security Directorate wanted his ass.

By then, I'd rejoined Century A. What else could
a hero who'd risked all to save his buddies' lives
believably do? We'd taken over the ruins of the
mosque as our headquarters. Those who weren't on
guard had gathered within the shelter of the mosque's
battered walls when two green-painted vehicles with
the Security Directorate's badge on their sides rolled
through the entrance.

Eric blanched. His crimes had caught up with him
before he had a chance to disperse news to the
Domination at large of his valiant efforts to hold
Village One. It looked like the end for him.

I lit a cigarette, idly wondering if Eric had chosen a mosque as headquarters on purpose. As his own
writings have shown, he does have a bit of a mes-
siah complex. Being arrested in a holy building may
have made up for the lack of local olive groves.

However, calm as I seemed, I made certain my rifle was near at hand. Security can be a bit indiscriminate and I wanted to have the means of reminding them who was the real hero.

The chiliarch who dismounted from the vehicle was neat and polished. Given how much mud, sweat, and blood I'd seen these last few days, I hated him on the spot. It's a wonder he didn't wilt under the force of Century A's collective resentment, but he just strode forward with his two pet Intervention Squad troopers—three of them into the arms of nearly two score. They must have been more insane than even dear Eric.

None of us loved Security. Some from fear, some from resentment, and now here were just a few of their polished policemen come to seize several of our number. Eric makes out that they wanted him—and certainly they did—but they would not have settled for him alone. You don't bring in two vehicles to take away one man.

Eric's account (one he was forced to release after Bill Dreiser, the American reporter, said more than he should have) made out that Security planned to take Eric, Dreiser himself, and one of the Russian partisans. Maybe that's true, but the rest of us knew that they'd take a sampling from Century A for good measure.

So when Eric leveled the P-38 he carried in his waistband at the chiliarch, the rest of us were more than willing to follow suit—not for love of Eric, never that, but to save our own bonny, bright hides. Once you've been tarred with Section IV of the Internal Security Act of 1907 there's no one—hero or villain— who is safe.

Well, I fired with the rest and I'm proud to say that my shot took out the chiliarch when Eric's went wild. No, the dramatic speech, the proof of Eric's "guts" in defiance of what was in his dossier never happened. That's trim on the Big Lie. Eric simply fired at the chiliarch in panic and missed. I'm the man who took the chiliarch down—though from the number of bullets in the body even a forensics expert would be hard-pressed to say just who killed him.

The Intervention Squad Troopers came in for their own fatal dose of lead poisoning, but Sophie cut the throats of the serf drivers. I guess finally getting Eric had softened her heart.

So there's the truth, believe it if you can. I doubt you have the courage though. Those were the days when Draka were humans and you, well, you're just poor mutant scum, programmed to duty and death.

Carry on, grandchildren. Know that from some odd Valhalla, Grandpa Coemer is looking down at you and laughing.

Lee Allred installs fiber optic networks for the U.S. Air Force, which may involve high technology or pick-and-shovel work. He's also chaired university symposia on SF, and been named a finalist for the Sideways Award for Alternate History; he made his science fiction debut with "For the Strength of the Hills," a novella which won first place in the Writers of the Future contest for 1997.

Here the Eurasian War draws to a close, and the Draka bring methods honed in the colonies home to the heartland of Europe.

THE GREATEST DANGER

Lee Allred

Late September 1944
St. Peter Port, Guernsey Island
Channel Islands

Admiral Hans Laban Verwoerd lay sprawled in the center of Cornet Castle's ancient courtyard. A heavy boot ground itself into his spine, pinning him to the rough stone flagging.

Banners, printed with motivational slogans, hung limp in the dawn air. Verwoerd turned his head, scraping his cheek against the rough flagstones. *I want gremlins around me*, the nearest one read, *for I am courageous*.

Verwoerd spat out a tooth chip.

The boot in his back shifted slightly. "Service to the State," the voice above Verwoerd barked.

"Glory to the Race," came the reply.

Verwoerd knew that voice well.

Brekenridge.

Five months earlier . . .
Late April 1944
Government House, Archona
Domination of the Draka

Verwoerd stood at attention for a long time before the Archon finally closed the manila folder marked MOST SECRET.

"An interesting proposal, Admiral. Totally unfeasible, of course, but interesting."

She slid it back across the desktop.

Verwoerd studiously let it lay. He was in his late fifties, of an age old enough for the years to turn his hair steel grey, line his craggy face; young enough he could still keep trim and fit if he kept to the strenuous Draka military regimen. Even so, the length of time he'd stood in front of the Draka ruler would have challenged even a younger man.

He continued to fix his gaze at a point centered on the window behind the Archon's desk. The window looked down the length of the Avenue of Armies. The view was distorted by the thick armorglass. Over six million serfs were in the Janissaries now. Far too many serfs had access to weapons for comfort these days. The war, of course.

Noor leed bid, as Verwoerd's old Afrikaaner grandfather used to say.

The Archon reopened the folder, then let it fall closed again. "I take it the Army's already turned you down. And Security."

The Army had told Verwoerd no; Security had told him Freya, no.

"So why bring it to me?" she asked him, half-rhetorically. "You used up a lot of favors getting here. The Navy doesn't have many favors to spare." Nor, she left unspoken, did the Rationalist Party.

Verwoerd knew fears of offending the Navy hardly kept the Archon awake nights. After all, Security Directorate's operating budget for their coastal patrol and brownwater flotillas was bigger than that for the entire bluewater Navy. But the Navy and the Rationalist Party did have close ties; most Rationalist politicians were former naval officers. Most naval cadets came from Rationalist families.

After four years of ever-increasing casualties, war-weariness was setting in. The Rationalist minority was gaining support—worrisome for the Draka League and the Archonship; they'd held an electoral lock for the last sixty, seventy years.

The Archon steepled her fingers.

Abruptly, she flipped a button on her intercom. "Please tell Dominarch Heusinger I'd like to see him at his convenience. East map room." She released the button.

She glared sharply at Verwoerd. "If you have something to say, Admiral, say it. I don't like having people cock their eyebrows at me." She paused. "Ah. My not inviting Security along?"

A chuckle. "Admiral, anytime I send for the Dominarch, somebody from Skull House invariably comes trotting along behind."

The projectamap showed the ongoing campaign in western Europe. Draka forces had smashed their way across the Rhine, ready to hook southward through the Low Countries towards France. Bilious green ovals marked the contaminated areas where atomics had been used in the Rhine and in Brussels. The amphibious thrust into southern Spain had fizzled out, but the beachheads were secure, if unfortunately stationary.

It was those Spanish beachheads that Dominarch Felix Heusinger pointed to. Heusinger had recently replaced John Erikssen as the Dominarch—Draka Army Chief of Staff. Ack-ack shrapnel over the Vistula had put Erikssen in the intensive care ward. The drive across the Rhine had been Erikssen's planning; the landings in Spain Heusinger's.

"We're simply spread too thin," he told the Archon. "We can't even scrape up enough troops for a breakout in the Iberian Peninsula. We certainly don't have spare resources for absurdities."

"Absurdities such as Verwoerd's proposal?" The Archon smiled. "Or such as the Navy?" She leaned back in her chair and fumbled in her jacket for a smoke. "You've of course already explained all this to Admiral Verwoerd?"

The Dominarch snorted. "Of course not. That's why we have lowly decurion clerks at Castle Carleton sitting at desks with rubber stamps." He slapped the back of his fingers on his folder. "To reject twaddle like this and not waste my time."

The Archon lit a thin brown cigar and drew on it until it caught. "So actually this is the first time you've seen this."

The army man flushed.

She blew a smoke ring. "Admiral?"

Verwoerd got up out of his chair and walked to the projectamap. He tapped his wooden pointer right on the Spanish beachheads.

"The Dominarch is quite right. We *are* stretched too thin." Verwoerd spoke in a clipped Oxford accent. The accent was quite genuine, the legacy of schooling and a youth spent abroad back when the Domination was still but a Dominion of the British Empire.

"That's precisely the reason for my proposal."

Heusinger muttered about circular logic.

Verwoerd ignored him and continued. "The Domination is trying to conquer the whole of Eurasia with an army of four million, roughly ten percent of our free population."

He nodded in the direction of the Security Directorate liaison, Brekenridge. Erikssen had rated a stategos for a liaison; Heusinger a mere cohortarch. "And that's not counting who knows how many Draka Security personnel—the Order Police, Krypteria, Compound and Camp Guards needed to pacify the areas we already have overrun."

"Or the Navy," added the Archon.

"Or Navy," Verwoerd nodded. "Or Air Corps personnel." He lowered the pointer. "There simply aren't enough Draka to go around."

" . . . Janissaries . . ." Heusinger muttered.

Verwoerd shook his head. "Ask Brekenridge if he wants a larger serf army."

It was Brekenridge's turn to snort.

"I'll take that as a no. Also, we're running short of free Draka to run the homefront. Key industries are limping along—"

"Like shipbuilding?" Heusinger asked, mocking the Navy's perennial complaint.

"—And it's only going to get worse."

No one in the room wanted to argue that. War production shortfalls were at near-critical level. And meanwhile the Americans were pouring out tanks and guns and planes in ever increasing numbers that the Draka could only dream of matching. They weren't at war with the Americans yet, but it was only a matter of time.

"We're teetering on a knife edge. The slightest reversal in Europe, the tiniest setback and—" Verwoerd cracked the pointer on the table. "It could all come crashing down."

The Archon frowned. "Don't tell me the problems, Admiral; tell me solutions."

"The solution? Increase the free Draka population."

He thumbed a rotary switch on the projectamap. The slide mechanism clacked and slid in a new map: Great Britain.

Brekenridge threw up his hands. "Sweet Land of Canaan, no! Not mo' Rationalist sennament for the Mother Country."

Brekenridge's drawl was sloppier than even the Draka norm. Like most Security headhunters, he was a descendant of bitterenders, poor white trash Confederates who'd fled to Draka rather than submit to Yankee rule. They'd arrived too late to join the hereditary plantation families' land grab, lacked the skills needed for the emerging technocratic class, but were just what was needed to fill the swelling ranks of the Security Directorate. The overseer's whiphandle had nestled comfortably in their palm.

"Don' know why y'all call yo'selves 'Rationalist,' anyway. Anybody with half a lick of sense knows the limeys ain't never goin' a join us."

"I'm not here to comment on political platforms. This is a military proposal," Verwoerd said stiffly.

"Shore. Like everybody don' know the Navy ain't nothin' but an adjunct of the Rationalists—"

"Would that be the same 'everybody' who also knows Security is nothing but an adjunct of the Draka League party?" A slight Draka slur crept into Verwoerd's speech, overlaid with a touch of guttural Afrikaans. "Or is it the other way around? I forget."

The Archon tapped her fingernails on the conference table. "Gentlemen. Could we get back to the discussion at hand?"

Brekenridge lazed back in his chair and hooked his arm over the high back. "Oh, shore, shore. I got plenty of time to waste."

"Actually," Verwoerd said, "Cohortarch Brekenridge's objection *is* very germane to the discussion."

"I'll say it is," Brekenridge snorted. "We're some Frankenstein monster the limeys created for themselves. They hate us nearly as much as the Nazis."

"So." Verwoerd faced the security man. "Britain would be as likely to cooperate with us as they would the Nazis?"

Brekenridge, sensing a trap, kept silent.

Verwoerd turned the thumbwheel again. This time it showed a portion of the Bay of Biscay and France's Cherbourg peninsula. He pointed to a cluster of dots off the Cherbourg tip.

"These are the Channel Islands. The northernmost island is roughly sixty miles south of Britain, about eight miles west of France."

He switched to a close-up of the islands.

"Four main islands: Guernsey, Jersey, Alderney, Sark." He tapped his pointer as he named them. "A duke named William grabbed them in 933—sort of a dry rehearsal for a conqueror named William in 1066. Part of the British Empire ever since—even before Britain proper, as the Islanders are fond of saying."

The next slide showed Wehrmacht troops marching down a city street, past a Lloyds Bank office. "Since the Fall of France, four years ago, the Channel Islands have been occupied by German troops— excuse me—Pan-European troops."

Brekenridge feigned a yawn. "Y'all missed yo' callin'—you shoulda been a h'stry *professor*."

"The sizable German garrison," Verwoerd continued, "is, in a word, starving. In fact, everyone on the islands is starving. Between the RAF, German U-Boats, and our own Air Corps, no supply ships have been able to reach them for months. A Red Cross ship, Swedish, in fact, did try last month. Ended up sunk by one of our planes."

Draka pilots joked that a Red Cross was really a red crosshair.

The Archon tapped ashes from her cigar. "If the garrison's so weak, why haven't the British tried taking it back?"

"Civilian casualties. One thing to bomb French ports and kill a few thousand Frogs. Quite another to kill your own people. Also, Hitler was fixated on defending the islands. Starving or not, Fritz has spent years fortifying them. Rather surprised the islands haven't sunk from all the concrete."

Verwoerd flipped to a map detailing the island defenses. He pointed out the extensive fortifications, shore batteries, minefields, and trenches.

Heusinger whistled. Maybe he had learned something from Spain after all. "Where did you get this information?"

"From the same person who can hand over the islands to us without a shot." The projector clacked again. "Admiral Canaris."

Brekenridge was on his feet, sputtering. Verwoerd smiled. "Yes, rather a shock, isn't it? It was to Naval Intelligence, too. That charred corpse in the recent newsreel must have been somebody else. Turns out Canaris has been a guest in one of Skull House's countryside inns."

The corner of the Archon's mouth turned up. "Most likely a simple clerical error on Security's part, wouldn't you say, Cohortarch?" Brekenridge glared at Verwoerd.

"It might be convenient to have Canaris placed in Naval Intelligence's care," Verwoerd said. "I'd hate to have him wind up dead again before he completes his bargain with the Navy."

The other corner of the Archon's mouth turned up. "I'm sure he'll be happy in his new lodgings. Continue."

A slide of a German officer asking a British bobby street directions. "The Germans have conducted a 'model occupation,' a real kid-glove approach. Particulars are in your briefing documents, but simplistically stated, of all the Nazi conquests, the Channel Islands unique in never having had a Resistance movement. In fact, when the British attempted covert operations on the islands, the locals actively assisted the Germans in countering them. And this despite Cohortarch Brekenridge's assertion that Britons would never cooperate with Nazis."

Verwoerd brought up the lights.

"If they'll cooperate with Fritz, they might cooperate with us. We might just be able to find a way to bring the British in on our side."

He shrugged. "A long shot, I know, but it would cost us very little even if we fail. If we succeed . . ."

He let the myriad possibilities hang in the air.

"That small cost you mentioned?" the Archon asked.

"Initial resources would require a bribe for a French politician and a cargo ship full of food. If you will turn to the second tabbed section in your briefing . . ."

The Archon had insisted on taking Verwoerd back to his office at the Admiralty Building in her private autosteamer.

Light rain clattered on the roof and streaked the windows, adding to a sense of gloom the Archon carried along with her.

She took a long pull on her cigar and slowly exhaled. "Army and Security might squawk a while longer," she said, "but I'm approving your project.

"Not," she held up a hand, "because I think it has any hope in succeeding." She shook her head. "Huesinger's idiocy in Spain has gone on far too long. We'll have to take Gibraltar; when we do, we'll need some leverage on the limeys. Something a little less coarse, I think, than the threat of atomics."

"I . . . see."

"I'm sure you do. I really should have you running Skull House instead of this harebrained project. Or perhaps not. You're too clever by half; you know that don't you?"

She sighed. "Keeping those islands of yours, that's a given, no matter what. Too much mischief can be made that close to the French coast." She drew a last puff on the cigar. "The inhabitants will serve nicely as hostages, though. Might as well keep them happy with your silly project until we're ready to use them for Gibraltar."

"I don't want Security forces anywhere in my jurisdiction. They can have Alderney island and play prison guard with any Germans we capture, but all locals are to be sent to me first."

"Security will have spies among your people, you know that."

"Fine. They can spy all they want. Just as long as they stay away, otherwise."

The Archon stubbed out the cigar and turned to face him. "Tell me, Admiral. Why do you Rationalists care so much what the rest of the world thinks of us? Why are you so desperate the Draka be liked?"

"The Superman shouldn't care what the *ondergeskik* thinks of him, you mean? 'I teach you the Superman.'" He shook his head and fell silent for several moments.

"Maybe," he said at last, "in terms of education, physical training, wealth, eugenics, perhaps soon even genetics—maybe by some standards we Draka have become Nietzsche's superman. We certainly like to flatter ourselves into thinking we have."

He shook his head. "But one would think that a superman shouldn't have to fear. And we do. We fear everybody else on the planet."

"With good reason," the Archon said. "Everybody else on the plant fears *us*. Hates us, too. It's destroy them first before they can destroy us. The fox knows many things, but the hedgehog only one—one big thing. Our fear—and the ferocity it feeds—is that one great thing we've learnt well. If we try to become a fox at this stage . . ."

The autosteamer hissed to a stop as it passed through the Admiralty compound gates. The Archon grumped. "If you want to be liked, Admiral, I suggest you get a dog."

Verwoerd gave a thin smile as he reached for the door handle. "I prefer cats myself. A dog will lick anyone's boot. When a cat shows affection, it *means* something somehow."

The Archon sniffed. "Cats are far too independent for me. Think themselves their own masters. They claim cats are domesticated, but most days I have my doubts."

Verwoerd opened the door and began to get out. The Archon laid a restraining hand on his arm.

"Admiral, remember: it's taken millions of years to domesticate cats," she said. "You've considerably less time."

Soon after that Draka armed forces fought their way into Flanders. Soon they would be rolling across France.

Time.

Verwoerd pulled out a thick stack of binders from his safe. The folders were delivered to Signal Ops. Encoded messages began to flash across the Domination. "Initiate Operation Hedgehog."

Verwoerd then went to dinner. He ate as usual at a restaurant frequented by Naval officers and Rationalist party officials. Verwoerd finished his meal and left. Tucked inside the used linen napkin he'd tossed on the table lay a handwritten note in no code the Navy used:

"Initiate Operation Fox."

❖   ❖   ❖

Early August 1944
St. Peter Port, Guernsey Island
Channel Islands

The British airship *R 100* settled over the airfield.
A hundred Draka sailors manned the drag ropes,
pulling the lumbering beast to the docking tower.

The old ship was barely airworthy. Her canvas
cover sagged and drooped. Her covering rippled from
stem to stern with the slightest forward motion Her
aluminum-colored reflective paint had all but flaked
away.

She was old and she'd been mothballed for twenty
years, but she was all Britain had for the job. She
could fly over the still lurking U-boats, and she could
carry fifty-one tons of cargo: badly needed foodstuffs,
medicine, clothing, blankets, shoes, and children's
teddies.

Fifty-one tons of cargo, including the official British
observer the Draka themselves had requested.

The *R 100* finally settled into place. The gondola
hatch opened up, and the airship's captain and its
single passenger stepped out onto the tarmac.

Verwoerd, resplendent in his dress uniform, waited
to greet them. Behind him, lined up along the airfield, were captured German flak wagons, their deadly
barrels aimed at the giant hydrogen-filled airship—
a gentle Draka reminder that they, not the British,
were in charge of these islands now.

The airship captain, Nevil Norway, saluted Verwoerd.
Norway, like his ship, had been taken out of mothballs.
Most of the British airmen who had worked on the
British dirigibles in the 1930s were long since killed
in the war.

Beside him stood a young woman in her early
twenties. She wore a Royal Air Force uniform. The
ribbons on her jacket marked her a combat pilot—
Britain was running desperately short of soldiers, too.

"Good afternoon, Admiral." Norway said, frowning at each word. "May I present Flight Lieutenant Sally Perkins. She's to be our official observer, as per your request."

"Flight Lieutenant," Verwoerd saluted.

"Admiral."

"I understand you were born and raised here in St. Peter Port."

"Of course you do. Isn't that why you requested me?" Contempt dripped from her voice.

Verwoerd sighed and turned to an aide. "Would you please escort Flight Lieutenant Perkins to my staff car?"

"Shoving me out of earshot already, Admiral? Is this how I'm going to spend my time as an observer?"

"Goodbye, Lieutenant," he said.

He turned back to Norway. "Captain, if you would be so good as to remove your crew from the ship while we unload the cargo?"

Norway bit his lower lip, then turned and called out to his executive officer. Soon the British crew-members marched off the ship to a designated spot several hundred feet away. Draka sailors began swarming aboard.

"You seem unhappy, Captain," Verwoerd said.

"She was a good ship," he said stiffly.

Verwoerd started, wondering as anyone familiar with Draka airships would how anybody could possibly think that British monstrosity a "good ship."

Then it dawned on him. "Oh," he said with a chuckle. "You think we're going to keep that bucket of bolts. Captain Norway, the Draka are not in the habit of keeping what isn't theirs."

Norway turned on him. "Really? I remember hearing about a little tea party called the Versailles conference. I remember a spot of land on the map called Turkey."

"So do I," Verwoerd replied. "I remember both of

them quite well. I was there." Above his chest hung
among all the Draka ribbons was a series of British
Navy ribbons dating from the Great War, including
one for Gallipoli. "Mesopotamia was bought with
Dominion blood. It was only right we keep it."

"Just as it's only right you keep *this*?" Norway swept
his hands to include the whole of the island he stood
on. "You spilled no blood here. It isn't yours to keep;
it's ours. It's British."

"The plebiscite—"

"Null and void!" Norway shouted. "A fraud and you
know it! How do you think starving people are going
to vote with a freighter full of food in the harbor,
the Frenchie who proposed the vote standing on the
dock?"

"Nevertheless," Verwoerd shrugged, "the plebiscite
took place. If the Channel Islands' inhabitants vote
to sever ties with Britain, our ally, and vote to be
annexed into the Pan-European Union, our enemy—
what are we supposed to do?"

Norway fumed. "Trumped up legal technicalities—"

"Trumped up they may be, technicalities they may
be, but legal they are: your government has agreed
to honor them until final ownership of these islands
has been adjudicated by an international tribune."

Norway muttered something about atomics and
blackmail.

Verwoerd shrugged. "You and I—we're only simple
soldiers. We just follow the orders we've been given."

They watched in silence as Verwoerd's men
unloaded the cargo into waiting lorries.

"Captain," Verwoerd said quietly, almost in a
whisper. "I give you my word that the Islanders will
be humanely treated."

"As if the word of a Draka slaver meant anything!"

Verwoerd pointed to the Victoria Cross pinned
above his battle ribbons.

"I served in the Royal Navy during the Kaiser's War back when we Draka were British subjects. The Islanders are our kin. How could we not treat them humanely?"

Norway refused to answer, but his face softened somewhat.

Soon the airship was emptied of all cargo. Her crew marched back inside.

"Will you require a Draka fighter escort until you reach British airspace?" Verwoerd asked.

Norway frostily declined.

"Very well, Captain. A safe journey home."

Norway saluted and turned about on his heel.

"Oh, and Captain?" Verwoerd called after him.

Norway looked over his shoulder.

"You may not want it," Verwoerd said, "you may not believe, but you still have my word."

"I apologize for the delay," Verwoerd told the British woman as he climbed into the staff car.

"Hardly a way to start out as an observer," Sally Perkins said, her voice ice. "Being shoved aside—"

"Being shoved aside where you can't overhear one old man be forced to humiliate a proud younger man?"

The woman stared ahead stonily.

"Flight Lieutenant Perkins. You and I are going to have to learn to work together. Our good relationship, our trust in each other, are about all that stands between the Channel Islanders and the auction block."

"Is that a threat?"

"It's a plea. I'm begging you: help me save these people."

She stared at him closely, thoughts flickering across her eyes.

Slowly, she nodded.

A small crowd gathered behind Verwoerd as he set up his easel on a bluff overlooking Moulin Heut Bay.

The first weeks of Draka occupation had gone exceedingly well. Verwoerd's hand-picked naval gendarmes had been nothing but unfailingly kind. After the second day they even went about unarmed save for the same nightsticks carried by British bobbies.

The Draka had distributed great quantities of food, new clothing, shoes, medicine, and little essentials the islanders hadn't seen since before the German occupation. Things like sewing needles and toilet paper.

The Draka had initiated a spate of sporting events, musical concerts, and theatrical shows. What proved most popular was their bringing to the islands several new Hollywood motion picture films. For the last four years the only motion pictures to be seen were those that had been playing at the Gaumont Palace the day the Nazis had landed—*Top Hat* and *The Barretts of Wimpole Street*—of which the islanders were thoroughly sick. *The Dancing Cavalier*, with Errol Flynn and Carole Lombard, had been a big hit, even if it was two years old.

But the biggest local attraction soon proved to be Verwoerd himself.

He'd put away his military uniforms and had taken to wearing smartly-cut Savile Row civilian suits, with his Victoria Cross pinned to his jacket lapel. He seemed to be everywhere on the island at once, to know all of the local children by name, and to be more British than the Islanders themselves.

He'd taken up headquarters in the old Castle Cornet and had immediately set out to repair the minor damage the old historic landmark had suffered during the brief German invasion. The regular Draka Navy forces on the island were barracked there or in other closed compounds, out of the eye of the local islanders.

Where Verwoerd went, Flight Lieutenant Perkins went with him: concerts, the cinema, and Verwoerd's strolls around St. Peter Port's Candie Park. Local wags began wondering just what the young RAF officer was supposed to be observing. But most of the islanders warmed to her; one of their own was a genuine war hero, and after four years of Nazi occupation, the islanders sensed that Draka good will depended in part on Sally's daily Draka-monitored reports to London.

Today Verwoerd had decided to watercolor and had imposed upon Sally as his model. He posed her so she was seated on a large rock, then returned to his easel.

Verwoerd painted for a while.

"You've lost your audience," Sally said.

"Hmmm?" The audience had been behind him. He looked over his shoulder. They were alone on the bluff.

"I rather suspect the novelty wore off," he said. "The first few washes of a water color do look somewhat random." He swirled a brush in a jar of water and dabbed it in an awful earth tone color.

"Renoir painted this bay, you know," he said. "If I had any talent, I'd try to capture some of what he saw here." He shrugged. "Oh, well. I have a much better model than he did."

Sally ignored that last comment. "Lots of famous people have lived here: Victor Hugo . . ."

" . . . Victor Hugo. Oh, and Victor Hugo." Verwoerd smiled. "Yes, I know. 'The Channel Islands are little pieces of France dropped in the sea and scooped up by England.' " He took a step back to stare at his progress, then started painting again. "There's a statue of him in the park, and little plaques all over St. Peter Port, I imagine: 'Victor Hugo Slept Here.' "

Sally looked at him. "You're an odd one. Out and about the city you act like a kindly old grandfather. Yet back at the castle you hang those dreadful banners all over the courtyard."

" 'What is the best remedy? Victory!' Or 'I want gremlins around me, for I am courageous'?"

"Yes. What ever does that one mean?"

"What do Nietzsche's syphilitic ramblings ever mean? 'Courage creates gremlins for itself' is the rest of that particular quotation." He washed out his brush and dabbed a new color. "Just be glad I'm not hanging those banners all over town the way Security wants me to. They're supposed to remind my troops they're Draka supermen." He made a face.

"Are they? They don't act like it."

He set down his brush. "It may surprise you that there are actually a number of Draka like them. Not all of us are your Hollywood stereotype villains."

"Your men all seem to have Dutch names."

"Very observant." He selected another brush. He sucked on the bristles to form a hard tip. "When the British first started arriving in droves in the then Crown Colony of Drakia, they pushed the original Dutch Boer farmers right out of the way. The British expanded northeastward across the Orange and beyond into the power vacuum left by the *difaqane*."

He dipped his brush in a bright vermilion. "Millions slaughtering each other with stone age weapons, if you can imagine. Three million dead, thirty million dead—nobody knows for sure." He swept the brush over the canvas. "Maybe if the *difaqane* had never happened . . ." He selected another brush.

"A Draka would say they brought their fate on them themselves."

"*Some* Draka would," he said quietly. "As I'm trying to point out, we're not all alike."

"No. Some are faster painters. I think my leg's asleep."

"Oh. Sorry." He got back to painting. "The Dutch, those few left who refused to be swallowed up by the British at any rate, struck out northwest into the Kalahari. Our *Voortrek*. Windhoek. Walvis Bay. A rough life, and one with few natives to lord it over."

He shrugged. "We developed a bit differently. Rationalists and Navy men now, mostly."

Sally almost smiled. "Is that why you don't like Nietzsche banners like all good little Draka are supposed to?"

He daubed his brush in a mixture of colors. "There was a time in my life when I thought of little else but Nietzsche. I was a young man at the time; I'd spent my life in British boarding schools, thought of myself as British, but I was still Draka. I guess I was trying to discover who I was."

Sally rolled her head around, stretching her neck muscles. She resumed her pose. "He's almost your state religion, isn't he?"

Verwoerd snorted. "The Draka worship nothing but themselves. 'Serfs look up because they wish to be exalted; the superman looks down because he already is exalted.' When you're the *oppermans*, it's rather hard to admit some entity might be superior to yourself. That's why the attempt to revive the Norse mythology, Naldorssen and all that, failed so miserably. Probably also why religion has always fascinated me so."

"I'm having a rather difficult time picturing you as a priest."

Verwoerd laughed. "Actually, before the war—the Kaiser's war—well, I intended to become a theologian."

"Then the war changed all that?"

He poured the dirty rinse water out of the jar and filled it with fresh, clear water. "Not in the way you imagine. Living, if you can call it that, in the trenches in the Dardanelles changed my intentions, true: it intensified them. Somehow the idea of somebody somewhere having the answers seemed more precious to me than any pearl of great price."

Sally nodded. She had seen combat, too. " 'Thou pure, thou luminous heaven! Thou abyss of light!—because they rob thee of my Yea and Amen,' " she said. "Only in your case, you were looking for your Yea and Amen."

Verwoerd smiled weakly. "Since when did you start reading Nietzsche?" he asked.

"Since you started hanging it up in courtyards."

He gave a truer smile. "After the war, I spent a year studying in the Vatican. Another year in Canterbury. Six months touring the American Bible Belt. Finally three days in Salt Lake City."

"Only three days? You seemed to have given the Mormons pretty short shrift in your studies."

"Sometimes three days are enough." He jabbed his brush once or twice, then set it aside. "There. Done."

Before he could stop her, Sally raced over to the easel. "Let me see."

Verwoerd's painting was a beautiful, intricate seascape of the bay below. Every detail, including the rock Sally had sat on, was in the picture. Sally, however, was not.

"You had me sit like a human pretzel on that hard cold rock for hours and you didn't even paint me?"

"My dear," he laughed, "I couldn't paint a portrait to save my life. Let's eat."

They sat down on a nearby grassy knoll. Sally opened the wicker basket. "Ploughman's lunch, I'm afraid. I'm a better fighter pilot than I am a cook."

Verwoerd sliced off a huge hunk of cheese. "I've spent all morning talking about myself. What's your story?" He broke open his loaf of French bread.

She shrugged. "Not much to tell. I was sixteen when the war started. Seventeen when they started evacuating women and children off the Channel Islands before the Germans came. Twenty when the RAF was desperate enough to start recruiting women fighter pilots. Twenty-and-a-half when I pranged my plane and banged myself up. Now I'm on the RAF dog-and-pony circuit giving hero speeches."

"That's all?"

"That's all." She rooted around in the basket until she found the sour pickled onions. "What made you leave Salt Lake City after three days?" Her eyes narrowed. "You didn't convert, did you?"

He laughed. "Those Mormons have the craziest ideas. They usually manage to get everything backwards. Take for example: the New Testament has the Pharisees use the excuse 'it's better that one man die than a whole nation perish' to kill the Nazarene. The Mormons stick that same excuse in the front of their scripture, only they have one of their prophets use it as an excuse to cut off the head of an evildoer."

Verwoerd licked his fingers. "That wasn't their craziest saying, though. Try this one: 'As man is, God once was; as God is, man may become.'"

"Crazy is right."

"All I was struggling with was the concept of setting myself up as one of Nietzsche's supermen. Here were what I was supposed to think of as serfs, dreaming of themselves as Gods in embryo." He shook his head.

He brushed the crumbs off his clothes. "The belief may be absurd, the belief in it is not. I had the son of a friend tell me that a while ago."

"But what made you leave?" she asked again.

He paused before he answered. "In a way, I suppose I found what I was looking for."

She looked at him sharply. "No you didn't. You found something else. What?"

A longer pause. He fingered the Victoria Cross on his jacket.

"Something to be frightened of. Something that scared me so bad I ran away."

She waited for him to tell her, but he wouldn't.

"You'll know," was all he said. "One day you'll know."

❖   ❖   ❖

Late that evening—long past midnight, in fact—Verwoerd sat in his office in Castle Cornet with his intelligence officer. An American Williams-Burroughs tape recorder lay on the table. The aide rotated the chrome dial to *Play*.

" . . . your judgement's a bit suspect, dear," an old woman's voice said. "You're sweet on him."

"Nonsense." That was Sally's voice. "I am not. I—"

"It's all right, dear. You're young and these things happen. Heaven knows enough of our girls fell for the Germans when they were here."

"Now wait just a minute—"

"How long do you think they can keep up this act of theirs?" A man's voice now. Several voices murmured assent.

The aide switched the tape off for a moment. "We think there were at least a dozen present. Hard to be sure, even with telescopic lens. Too many ways in and out of that old abandoned factory. We have pictures of some of them."

Verwoerd impatiently waved his hand for the aide to start the tape again.

Sally's voice: " . . . I keep telling you—I don't think it is an act. I think for the first time in their lives they don't have to be Draka supermen, they can be plain human beings. I think they're *enjoying* it."

"Sure, maybe—the ones we see." A younger man's voice. "And what about the ones we can't see? What about the ones on the mainland? What about the ones back in Draka-land? The Intervention Squads, and the Order Police, and the Krypteria?"

An older man grunted in agreement. "At least the Germans saw us as fellow human beings. These Draka—" he spat out the word like it was deadly poison "—when they look at us they don't see anything but an animal to be tattooed and chained and worked in the fields until we drop in our tracks and die. I say we fight."

Choruses of agreement.

"Amateurs!" Sally said in disgust.

"Maybe so," the old man said, "but we're all you've got."

The aide clicked off the tape. "I also have a further report from the *Uitdager*."

Verwoerd snorted. The *Uitdager* lived up to her name, although she challenged her creators more than her opponents. The Domination was woefully behind in submarine and torpedo technology. Lurking and spying were about all Draka submarines could hope to do and survive.

"The *Uitdager* took up station in Rocquaine Bay as you suggested. Shortly after this meeting, they spotted a flashlight on shore blinking what could only be a coded message. Presumably to another submarine in the vicinity. Allied, undoubtedly. British, presumably."

"Presumably." Rocquaine Bay lay on the west tip of the island. A light flashed from there wouldn't be seen from the French coastline, or by the Draka Security troops on Alderney to the north. Verwoerd half-dreaded the next item of information.

"My men followed Flight Lieutenant Perkins out of the recorded meeting. They place her on the shore of Rocquaine Bay at the approximate time the coded message was sent."

Verwoerd nodded. None of the night's events were much of a surprise. Still, it was unpleasant to confirm as fact what could pleasantly be considered only a possibility.

"Initiate phase two," he said.

The intelligence officer picked up his own flashlight laying on the floor beside his chair.

He set out for Rocquaine Bay.

Four bodies were laid in a line side-by-side on a table inside the airport's hangar. A wool blanket had been draped over each of them to cover their faces.

Verwoerd looked down on them and sighed. "A British Catalina float plane was mistakenly shot down over the island early this morning. The bodies were recovered in the wreckage," he told Sally.

" 'Mistakenly!' " Sally spat.

Verwoerd looked at her. "Do you want me to say I'm sorry? We're at war, still. Mistakes happen. How many times did you shoot at one of your own planes?"

Sally turned her face away.

"I'd like you to arrange a public funeral," he told her. "A very public funeral. Saying I'm sorry won't help matters any; showing I'm sorry, perhaps, just might."

Red, white, and blue bunting was hung in Candie Park. The white gingerbread-style bandstand where the coffins lay in state was festooned with Union Jacks. Portraits of the British king were hung in all the shop windows facing the park.

Nearly the entire island population attended the services. Over two thousand wreaths were laid.

Verwoerd had insisted every available man in his command attend as well. A few Draka gendarmes stood their post around the park, but the vast majority of Verwoerd's men were lined up beside him in their dress uniforms. Even Verwoerd himself wore his uniform, the first time in weeks.

The looks the islanders gave them turned from unease, to baleful stares, to bitter resentment. The Draka, too, were uneasy. The holsters hanging from their dress belts were empty on Verwoerd's orders.

Then, spontaneously, before the services were even finished, someone in the crowd started singing "God Save the King." The audience picked it up. Then, once that anthem was finished, they began singing *Rule Britannia*. With each verse, their voices grew louder.

Rule, Britannia! Britannia rules the waves!
Britons never never never shall be slaves!

Over and over they repeated it until the very
ground shook and the roar became a single voice, a
chime, a chant:

Britons never never never shall be slaves!

Verwoerd's men fingered their empty holsters,
helplessly waiting for the tumult and the shouting to
die.

Verwoerd grabbed Sally by the shoulders and shook
her until she stopped singing, until she finally stared
up at him with tearstained eyes.

"You wanted to know what I was frightened of?"
he shouted above the roar of the crowd. He pointed
at the swaying crowd.

Britons never never never shall be slaves!

"Run," he told her. "Hide. Because when the Draka
are afraid . . ." He shook his head.

She placed the tips of her fingers to his cheek, and
stroked gently, cat-like. The first and last time they
would ever touch.

She vanished into the crowd.

Rule, Britannia! Britannia rules the waves!
Britons never never never shall be slaves!

The chant continued long after Sally had gone. And
somewhere, Verwoerd knew—somewhere in the ranks
of men next to him—Skull House's spy was afraid.
Very, very afraid.

❖   ❖   ❖

Late September 1944
St. Peter Port, Guernsey Island
Channel Islands

It was soon after that Verwoerd found himself face down on the flagstone of Castle Cornet's courtyard.

He was surrounded by gremlins, all right. Gremlins wearing the dark green uniforms of Security and the cobra badges of the Intervention Squads.

Somehow, being surrounded by gremlins didn't seem to give him courage.

But then, he wasn't safe in the Swiss Alps sitting at a desk writing aphorisms.

"Hello, Hans, ol' buddy."

Brekenridge leaned lazily on the front fender of Verwoerd's own staff autosteamer. He was paring his nails with an SS ceremonial dagger, undoubtedly a souvenir from one of his Alderney playthings.

He clucked as he looked over the squad he'd sent to fetch Verwoerd. "That's shore a purty shiner you got yourself there, Yancy," he said.

She started to explain.

Brekenridge cut her off with a snort. "Didn't I warn you sweetlin's ol' Hans was pretty spry for a man pushing sixty?" He stuck his ring finger in his mouth and daintily bit off a cuticle. "An' what else do I see? Couple lips busted open? Bloodied noses? My, my."

He spat out the cuticle. "Let that be a lesson t'y'all—stick to yo' regimen, and when you git to be as old a crock as Hans, you'll be in just as good a' shape."

The SS dagger went back in its sheath. He walked over and crouched down on his haunches to peer at Verwoerd. " 'Course, this mo'ning Hans looks a bit worse for wear. Right disappointed in you, Hans. Usually you's so impeccable. Shore waited long enough for you to roust yourself up outa yo' bed an' git shaved, showered, an' sissyfied 'fore we came knocking. Then you go an' almost fall in the mud."

Brekenridge got back to his feet. "Pick him up 'fore he gits all dirty."

Verwoerd was hauled roughly to a standing position. He shook himself free. He smoothed his hair back into place, then brushed at the front of his tailored Savile Row English-cut suit.

The courtyard was empty save for Security troops. "What have you done with my men?"

"Shush now, don't you fret none. Your cute lil' old sailors are lazin' about their barracks in their purty lil' sailor suits, havin' a fine ol' time. Not like they's much use anyhow. My boys worked up a harder sweat fighting the Eyeties."

"Where's my staff?"

"Playin' cards with yo' sailors, I 'spect."

"Am I under arrest as well?"

"Now who said anything 'bout arrest? My boys just helping an old man down some stairs so'n we two can have a visit." Verwoerd chucked his dropped hat. "We gonna take a ourselves a little drive, Hans."

Verwoerd looked around at all the Tolgren machine pistols pointed his direction. "I suppose this is the part where I'm supposed to make a desperate leap like some Hollywood hero?"

"I'd shore like it if'n you was to try, old man. Less fuss for me in the long run."

Verwoerd calmly put his hat on. "Sorry if I disappoint you; I'm a little too old for Hollywood derring-do. Besides, I prefer the more cerebral approach." He nodded at one of the slogan banners. "After all, 'victory is the best remedy.' " He got into the staff car.

Brekenridge unsnapped his pistol holster and walked around to the other side. "I 'spect I'm going to enjoy this. Yes, indeedy."

❖   ❖   ❖

The leather dispatch pouch lay on the seat beside him. The typed orders with the Archon's signature lay neatly tucked back inside the pouch.

"So. It isn't entirely a coup. The Navy remains in charge here—but only as long as I do things your way."

Brekenridge ran his finger across the edge of his dagger and smiled. "That's 'bout the gist of it."

Verwoerd leaned back in his seat. "It still looks like a coup to me."

"Not at all. You're still *baas* around here—as long as you play the game. And the word's not 'koo,' it's 'koop,' " he said, giving the Draka pronunciation. "You know what yo' problem is, Hans? You dress like a limey," he flicked his dagger point at Verwoerd's suit, "you tahk like a limey—rawhthawh—" he mimicked Verwoerd's accent, "and some say you even think like a limey. Dangerous habits, Hans. Start dabblin' in dragons, better take care lés'n you want to turn into one.

"An' they be dragons here, yes indeedy." They passed a store with a faded picture of the British monarch taped in the display window. "St. Georges a'plenty, too. Question is, which'n are you?"

The autosteamer slowly wound its way through the narrow streets of St. Peter Port.

Little bits of England flashed past the windows— a Toby The Chemist shop, a Lloyd's Bank, even billboards for Guinness beer and Players tobacco. A glimpse of England that now would soon vanish.

Out in the harbor, Verwoerd could see the hazy smudge of the French coastline scant miles away. He could see the fires from the looting still going on there. That was St. Peter Port's future now, too.

The autosteamer hissed on. The city streets were deserted.

Verwoerd was just about to ask Brekenridge what he'd done with the locals, when suddenly he knew.

He saw rows of open lorries parked along Candie Park, packed full of people. Security troops were yelling for the dazed, frightened Channel Islanders to get out of the truck, herding them by gunpoint into the park where bunting and Union Jacks still hung. The pigeon-stained statue of Victor Hugo looked down at the tangled curls of concertina wire beneath its feet.

Holding pens.

Blood roared in his ears and he turned.

"I wouldn't try it, Hans."

The point of Brekenridge's dagger pressed against Verwoerd's Adam's apple. Verwoerd realized he'd been tensing himself to leap at the security man.

The dagger point pressed harder. "G'wan—live dangerously, like yo' precious Neechee says."

With an effort, Verwoerd relaxed and sank back into his seat. Brekenridge lowered the dagger. "Tsk. I thought we were goin' to use the more c'rebral approach."

"The Archon said nothing about rounding up locals into serf pens."

"But Skull House shore did." He pulled a slim leather wallet from his jacket pocket and wiggled it.

"We wuz only grudgin'ly allowing yo' lil' pet experiment—providin' you started t'show the results you promised. An' providin' it don't endanger the state."

Brekenridge leaned back. "The other day your pet limeys nudged up agin that line in the sand, if'n they didn't jump right over it with both feets. Time now to pay the piper."

"The yoke?"

Verwoerd's voice was barely audible. Courage did create its own gremlins: the courage to hope.

Brekenridge shook his head sadly. "Not the yoke. 'Least, not yet."

The car slowed in the middle of the block, then

pulled over to the curb and parked outside the Gaumont Palace cinema.

"Jus' the next best thing."

A circle of Security troops waited outside the Gaumont.

They pulled Verwoerd out of the car. Brekenridge slid out behind him, hand resting lightly on his holstered pistol. His eyes, however, were on the Gaumont.

The Gaumont was a tiny thing, not even as big as the lobby of the average London cinema, not even big enough to have a lighted marquee above its entrance.

"Imagine this dinky ol' island having a palace like this. This is bigger than any showhouse in Alexandria."

Letting serfs watch movies or even run the projector was dangerous. The might get ideas of the outside world. Most Draka theatres were really small private screening rooms in plantation homes—one of the many reasons Virconium studios lagged far behind Hollywood.

Verwoerd looked at him and clucked his tongue. "See what you're missing? You need to travel more, Brekenridge. Broaden your horizons."

"The only horizons I'm interested in broadenin' are the Domination's. An' when I visit a foreign country, it ain't foreign no more; it's conquered." He waved a hand at the cinema. "Serf nations squanderin' their resources on frippery like this, that just makes the job easier."

"I wouldn't discount it too fast. That's the stuff dreams are made of. And serf dreams are dangerous things."

Brekenridge snorted. "You'd know, wouldn't you? Dreams of rulin' the waves an' escapin' the neck collar—and boastin' about it in song! That's the reason

all your limey friends got one foot on the auction
block today: dreams like that. Well, we're just going
have to give them some nightmares instead."

He turned. "G'wan, paste it up there, Benning,"
he snapped.

A security trooper smashed the glass door of the
poster box with the butt of her Tolgren's collapsible
stock. She ripped out the poster for *The Dancing
Cavalier* and slapped up in its place a plain white
sheet of paper with *Initial Orientation Film* printed
in plain block letters.

"Little training movie Security whipped up in
Denmark," Brekenridge explained. "Seems to have
worked wonders up there preventin' any uprisin'." He
squinted at the stenciled movie title. "Hmm. Do
believe the title lost sumthin' in the translation. In
Danish it's *Slaves' First Day*." He chuckled.

"I'm to round up every limey on this island and
show them this lil' cinematic masterpiece. Some of
'em are hiding yet, like that girlfrien' of yours, but
we'll find 'em, never fear."

He plucked a bit of lint off his shirt. " 'Long as
your limeys behave themselves, this is as close as they
git to going under the yoke, an' you kin continue with
what's left of Project Hedgehog. They misbehave,
though," his white teeth flashed a shark's smile, "they's
mine."

"But that will kill whatever chance . . ." Verwoerd
shook his head. "You can't be serious!"

"Serious as a shockstick, 'old bean'—an' it just keeps
gittin' better. It's you who's gonna stand here taking
their tickets personally, letting 'em know their pre-
ciously nice, humane, decent Hans Verwoerd is a part
of all this. They'll remember you as the one forcin' this
film upon their poor unsullied sensibilities."

A security detail began unloading sandbags out the
back of a lorry. They starting stacking them into the
beginnings of a machine gun nest.

"Jus' in case the natives git restless."

"*Vieslik—!*" Verwoerd spat in his birth tongue. "I want no part of this."

"Oh, but you's already a part of this, whether you like it or not, Hans: you's Draka and this *is* what bein' Draka means. We's Draka. They's serfs. Ain't nothin' in between. Yo' ain't gonna change that, don' care what the Archon said you could try here."

A heavy machine gun, its tripod, and several boxes of ammo were placed behind the sandbags. Another lorry with a squad of Security troops arrived.

Brekenridge's face almost softened into something human. "I'm just speedin' up the process, Hans. Kindlier in the long run, not givin' these po' souls any hope."

Brekenridge's men began stringing barbed wire.

"Pity's the greatest danger, Hans. That's what Neechee says, an' it's true. Dangerous for them. Dangerous for us."

"Reckon they don't like our trainin' film none." Brekenridge said. He was sitting with Verwoerd in the back of the theater, watching the audience more than he was watching the movie.

The sour stench of vomit and urine fouled the air in the cramped theatre until Verwoerd choked on it.

Security troops stood in the aisles and at the exits. Levelled weapons kept the locals in their seats.

"But," Brekenridge went on, "I reckon they'd like it a whole lot less findin' themselves in it rather than just watchin' it," he said for effect, his voice carrying across the theatre.

Stark images of black and white danced across the screen. The screams from the original Danish soundtrack and the sobbing and retching from the audience at times drowned out the dubbed English narration.

The narrator was obviously a fresh-caught Danish

serf. She stumbled through the script in clear, but highly accented English. She was also clearly frightened out of her wits. A terse Draka voice prodded her on when she faltered.

At one point, the scene shifted to a expensively furnished stable. A group of people were dragged in by their collar chains. They were bruised and bloody, their clothing nothing but shreds.

The narrator's voice started sobbing, then pled rapidly in Danish. The Draka voice barked once, twice. The Danish voice only grew more desperate. The audience heard the meaty sound of a slap. The narrator sobbed hysterically.

A gunshot, then the thud of a heavy object hitting the ground. The clank of chains, and a new voice—male this time—identified the people on the screen: "L-ladies and gentlemen, the Danish Royal F-family."

The camera zoomed in on the once proud faces, then panned to what awaited them in the stalls.

"Enough," Verwoerd growled. He stormed out the back of the theatre into the lobby. Brekenridge sauntered behind him, smiling.

"Bit squeamish are we?" he asked. "From the film? Or just from the aroma of *eau de serf*?"

Brekenridge ran his fingers over the lobby's faded wallpaper. The wallpaper had started to peel from neglect in the four years of Nazi occupation. He poked his finger into a fresh bullet hole, one of several peppering the walls from the four hours of Draka Security occupation. Security called firing automatic weapons over prisoner's heads to get them to take their seats "gentle persuasion."

"You might be able to walk away, Hans, but them poor souls in there can't." He dug deeper. The plaster crumbled until his whole fist punched through.

"These past few weeks, you've been the carrot. T'day, I'm the stick." He pulled out his fist. "Never did put much stock in carrots. Seein's is, there ain't an animal in the world who remembers they're a vegetarian when they're pushed into a corner."

They waited in the lobby until the movie ended. The guard started herding the audience out of the theatre, back through the lobby.

The faces of some of the islanders were sullen, others terrified. A few were white with rage. Those were the faces Verwoerd could feel Brekenridge memorizing.

A number of them had voided themselves, or had vomited on themselves, or both. That only made Brekenridge laugh.

"Don't bother breakin' out the mops, sweetlin's," he called after them. "Havin' each of yo' groups muck in through the swill of previous ones adds a certain . . . *ambiance* to the film."

As the last of them filed out, Brekenridge called one of his men over and told them to distribute handfuls of each group that had seen the film into the holding pens of those groups they wouldn't get to until tomorrow or the next day.

"That should have the desired effect," he told Verwoerd.

Yes, thought Verwoerd. It will indeed.

Brekenridge had made a mistake. Actually, he had made several, but this particular mistake could prove fatal. Verwoerd would see to that.

Verwoerd was locked in his own office. The office had been stripped bare. Everything was gone—desk, chairs, books, files—everything down to the paper-clips. Everything in the room had been taken, every possible hiding place searched.

Except one.

Verwoerd cradled the tiny pistol he'd retrieved from its hiding place. It was hardly larger than a cigarette lighter. It held but a single bullet.

Sometimes, a single bullet was all you needed.

He slipped the pistol up his sleeve.

Verwoerd was curled up on the hard wooden floor asleep when he was awakened by the chatter of machine guns.

Screams and the sounds of boots running across the flagstones below echoed in the once quiet night.

Footsteps pounded up the staircase.

Sally Perkins, her face blackened with burnt cork, dressed in a black sweater, slacks, and stocking cap, and carrying a Sten gun, burst into his room.

"I was afraid you weren't coming," Verwoerd said calmly.

She stared at him. "You knew—?"

"That you were an SOE agent? Of course." His smile was thin. "Who do you think your 'Agent Fox' was?" He gave the code phrase that confirmed it.

Two more commandos entered into the room. One of them was Captain Norway.

"Area's secured. They're starting to load up the islanders now."

Verwoerd cocked his eyebrow at Norway. "I was wondering how you were going to evacuate them."

Norway snorted. "On the old *R 100*? You've gone potty, old man. Hardly room for sixteen thousand. Besides, the old girl crashed on the way back from here. She wasn't a very good ship after all." He looked down at his commando uniform. "That's why I had to look for another line of work."

Sally tilted her head at the window. "The Americans loaned us some troop carrier subs from the Pacific. They're in the bay now." She pulled off her stocking cap and shook her hair. "You know, I really must get around to thanking Brekenridge. We couldn't have pulled it off without his unwitting help— stripping your men off the defenses, rounding up all the locals in one place."

Verwoerd shrugged. "Security's first instinct is to

shoot anything that moves. Anything that survives afterwards gets herded behind barbed wire."

"We've got him downstairs. All trussed up like a Christmas goose."

Verwoerd got to his feet. His muscles were stiff from the hard floor. "Would you mind taking me to him? I've my own thanks I'd like to deliver."

Verwoerd almost didn't recognize him. Brekenridge's face was crisscrossed with white surgical tape. The tape was holding in place a specially-designed gag. The device prevented any nasty episodes with cyanide pills, hollowed teeth, and other assorted Skull House toys.

"*Hmgghf! Ggmmphrnnf!*" Brekenridge mumbled through the gag, thrashing on the floor in his straight jacket.

Verwoerd squatted down beside him. "This seems to violate the Geneva convention, somehow. Get up off the floor. I'd like to have a little chat."

Brekenridge was lifted up and set in the chair.

"Much better," Verwoerd said. He stood inches in front of the chair. "I don't think he's enjoyin' our little trainin' restraints," he said in the same Draka drawl Brekenridge had used that day at the Gaumont. Verwoerd tapped his finger on the gag. "This is special equipment we got from all the way up in Denmark. We call it 'Slave's First Gag.'" Before the British could stop him, he backhanded Brekenrdige in the face. The security man toppled to the floor.

"Get him up!" Verwoerd's voice was hard, not to be disobeyed.

They sat Brekenridge up. The man was crying, almost hysterical.

"So much for Nietzsche's Superman," Verwoerd spat.

With the speed only another Draka could match, in one smooth movement Verwoerd reached in his

sleeve and pulled out the tiny pistol, then pointed
square between Brekenridge's eyes.

The British commandos grabbed for their guns.
They might as well as have been moving in slow
motion. Verwoerd swung his tiny gun back and forth
in an arc.

"Drop your guns!" he barked.

The commandos hesitated.

"I said drop them!" Verwoerd shouted. "On the
floor. Good. Now kick them towards me."

Sten guns clattered across the floor.

Sally glared at him with contempt. "You're one of
them after all, aren't you? You're just like them."

It tore his heart, but Verwoerd nodded.

"You fight monsters, you become one," she said,
tears welling.

"Now you know what I learned spending those
three days in Salt Lake City." He slowly edged over
to the door and closed it, locking it shut.

"There's no way you can escape, Hans. The courtyard is swarming with commandos."

"Nietzsche was right all along," Verwoerd said as
if he hadn't heard her. "Right about so many things.
'Once I thought of little else but Nietzsche'—would
that I had ever been able to stop!

"Those three days I stared into the abyss—'thou
heaven above me, thou pure, thou luminous
heaven! Thou abyss of light!—and it stared back
at me.'"

His words sounded crazy, but his voice was level,
his face a cold stone blank.

" 'And what have I hated more than passing clouds,
and whatever tainteth thee? And mine own hatred
have I even hated, because it tainted thee!' "

He edged back over to Brekenridge and pressed
the tiny muzzle of the gun to his forehead.

"Understand a thing to its depths, dear Brekenridge,
and seldom will you remain faithful forever, for

bringing the depths into the clear light of day reveals what is in the depths is not pleasant at all."

The two commandos looked at each other and dove for their guns.

Not fast enough.

Verwoerd kicked the guns away from their outstretched hands. "Stand up," he told them. "You, too, Sally. I mean it."

"You're crazy, Hans." she said, tears on her face. "You're raving."

"Of course I am crazy—I'm a Draka! A coldblooded kind of crazy. The kind that lasts a lifetime."

But tears were trying to well in his eyes. He blinked them away.

" 'You must become what you are.' The Will to become the Superman, to rise above 'slave morality'—that makes us the Superman. It was our Will that made us better than the rest of the world.

"Then I visited that accursed city, saw that same Will channeled into their serf morality, their serf dreams. To 'never never never' fall under the yoke, to be gods looking down in pity on mere superman. To will the absurd fantasies of religion into reality—entire nations that don't have to conquer or murder or . . ."

He composed himself. "I knew then my people were too evil to let them continue to exist. I dedicated my life to destroying the Domination."

"You've made a good start," Sally said. "Rescuing an entire population out from under the noses of the Draka will give conquered people all over the Domination hope—"

"And don't you see how much like them that makes me?" He threw his head back and laughed, a horrible snake hiss.

"Never again will the Draka attempt to soften a conquest. The Rationalist Party is through after this. They'll be lucky if they're all lined up and

shot rather than forced under the yoke. I've know-
ingly and premeditatedly killed my friends, my
family—killed the last vestige of decency in the
Domination."

Sally stared at him in horror, seeing what he was
for the very first time.

"I had to, don't you see?"

He pressed the gun to Brekenridge again.

"Better that one man perish. Better that an entire
nation perish. Better that one man . . ."

He spat on Brekenridge and shoved him backwards. Man and chair went tumbling onto the floor.

Verwoerd wiped his eyes with the back of his free
hand. His Will was no longer strong enough to stop
them from tearing.

"The greatest danger was that you would pity us.
Now—now you will hate us. Now you will learn our
hedgehog's trick. Now you will fear us."

Verwoerd stared longingly at Sally, then fell to his
knees in a supplicating posture known across half the
world, known where ever the Draka ruled.

"Now you can destroy us."

He turned his tiny pistol with its single bullet
around and pointed at his own heart.

William Barton writes things about human beings so un-
bearably true that they're difficult to publish; if you want to
know what I mean, read *When We Were Real* . . . or this story
about a German scientist making the best of it in a world
he never made . . .

HOME IS WHERE THE HEART IS

William Barton

The dream becomes the dreamer, as with mandarin and butterfly. Silly. Strange. Like the dreams you have when you're in the hospital and they've pumped your ass full of drunks . . . drunks. Ah, can't think. What the Hell . . . oh, *drugs*. That's what I meant. When they fill your ass with drugs.

Two men talking, speaking some funny kind of English, nothing like the clipped Brits and twangy Yanks I'd known between the wars, the years between the wars, in Paris, when . . . Oh, Hell.

Men with funny, muddy voices, language less like German than any English I'd ever heard before, men talking as if I were. No. Flinch away from that. Now.

"Whyn't we jes kill this pony, suh? We'un got owah *own* engineeahs."

The other, von Something? Von Frankenstein? Fading in and out now, sharper voice, a little less mud in it, "Not like these we don't. And most got away 'fore we could get 'em."

One of them touched me, lightly, on the shoulder, smearing old, cold sweat, grease of fear sending a thrill from there to . . . *Grüss Gott*, making me shiver, stopping the breath in my throat. Von Somethingburg said, "There, there, Hans. All over now. You've told us what was needful . . ."

Hans? Not my name. Is it? Hans . . . Hansel and Brutal . . . I started to giggle, feeling those warm fingers press into my shoulder, oh-so-reassuring, then I started to cry and . . .

Morning. Rosy-fingered dawn lights the window. Some afterecho of a second dream, dream forgotten, surrounded by dreams of torture and redemption. Me, in a coffle, coffle led by dark, black men, men with guns, staggering on bare, bleeding feet down a bombed-out bleeding street. *Boom!* Flash of light, looking up just in time to see a rolling ball of fire, smoke, orange and black all mixed together, rising from the roof of the Reichstag, black swastika spinning like a galaxy as it tumbled to the street below.

Pictured those famous faces, *der Führer*, *der Dicke*, stumbling in a coffle like mine, then moved on quickly, responding to a gentle tug on the neck chain, not wanting the black man's whip.

Bed. My bed. My home. The home they've given me. Safe. My God. Safe. Rich, crumpled cotton sheets under my back, sheets better than anything I'd ever had in Germany, clammy with night sweat now. Night sweat and dreams. Plaster ceiling, lit by red dawn, stripes of light and dark picking out irregularities, color and shadow.

I got up, sat for a minute on the edge of the bed,

wishing. No. Not wishing for anything. Just looking
down at my smallish gut, middle age settling in, round
dome of hairy belly, black hair over fishbelly white.
Well. Slippers and thin cotton robe, white with a pale
print, ibises and river reeds, boy-slim Pharaoh knee-
deep in Nile, bow well-drawn. Got up and walked to
the kitchen, water from the tap, tepid but fresh, safe,
just like this was Europe or America.

Safe.

Reached up to the little shelf over the sink and
turned on the radio, little green Zenith, not new, not
old, AM still staticky with night as I twisted the big
plastic dial. Outside, the sky was turning blue over
scrubby subtropical bushes, my neighbor's lawns,
distant city buildings low on the horizon.

Announcer's voice with the Brit-like accent you still
hear from people down around the Cape. Something
about ongoing border negotiations with the Allies.
India. Christ. What do they *think* is going to happen?

Well. Prepared the pot. Beans ground, water from
the tap because that's what I had, put it on the gas
ring, thud of ignition and hiss of gassy flame.

There was another sound in my head. Same thud
of ignition, swirl of orangy fire and greasy smoke on
the ground, then the pumps would run up, and there
would be that wondrous waterfall roar. *Aggregat Vier*.
Beautiful spear of yellow-white fire in the sky, rising, tipping over toward the west.

Fat man in the news. He never did get to piss in
the Rhine.

A moment suppressing hysterical laughter, keeping silent.

Outside, the air was still cool, but with a sharpness
promising the hot day to come, when the sun would
burnish the sky, burning the wilderness lands around
the base their tawny lion-colored shade of gold.

Bottle of milk in the cooler, newspaper at the end

of the driveway, near the rear bumper of the old
prewar Ford steamer they'd given me.

"Good morning, Mr. de Groot!"

The soft, musical voice of my next door neighbor,
probably put me here so he could keep an eye on
me for the bosses, dark man with sharp, alert features, deep black eyes, shiny, oily-looking black hair
falling over a broad deeply-tanned brow.

"Ah, good morning Dr. Groening . . ."

Why the Hell would an Anglo-Indian chemist,
product of the *finest* British schools want to be here,
and work for these . . . these . . . Shut up. Those white
buildings poking over the horizon. Archona. Remember just where the Hell you are, Helmut . . . no. It's
Hans. Hans de Groot. Don't forget.

He walked up, grinning, and said, "Well . . ."
Having as much trouble with W's as me, though
English was certainly his native tongue, that special
accent making it come out a bit like *vwell*, "today's
the big day, eh? I'm sure you're looking forward to
getting busy?"

A slow nod. "I . . . I am. Yes, I am, Dr. Groening."

He said, "Please, you must call me Apu . . ."

"Apu . . ." I remembered seeing his work under a
very different name, before the war, gracing the pages
of every chemical journal you could name. The Draka
were our allies. Why shouldn't he have gone to work
for them?

A soft hand on my forearm. "And you must remember, they say 'Grooning' here, not 'Grehnink.' "

"Sorry."

"Well, we all know who we are, Hans."

Closer to the equator, the midday sun is always
high in the sky. Always summer here. Mad dogs and
Englishmen. Well. I'm sure as Hell not an Englishman. I guess mad dog will have to do.

The sky seemed too dark a blue for all this heat. Too dark and too low. I remember back in the early Thirties, honeymooning with my young wife in the American southwest, seeing the haze of the Grand Canyon, making it looking like some cartoon canvas, more a work of art than a work of nature, under an impossibly high sky, pale blue so terribly far away, hinting at the depths of the *planeteraumen* beyond . . .

Planetary space. And that young wife . . . No will to wonder where she . . . Here, the sky seemed flat, as if there were no beyond. Flat blue sky over a sea of pale brown grass, amber waves rolling in the hot, dry wind. Far way, closer than the horizon, were the tiny figures of elephants walking.

Nearby, muscular black men, men burnt the color of coal by the sun, shining like anthracite, sweating in the heat, sang as they worked, snatches of Swahili and English, tribal chanteys and popular prewar radio tunes mingled as they took the crates from the backs of flatbed drags, breaking the straps and pulling them down, piling them in orderly arrays.

"No, dis vun over hier, Sambo . . ." says Hartmann, who can't remember his new name, and can't get the story straight. *Verdammt* idiot. No tigers in Africa, Hartmann. The story of little black Sambo comes from Dravidian India.

I remember how Apu laughed when I said that. Little black Hindoos . . . Funny. I expected our workers would be Frenchmen or something, excess labor being run into the ground, but . . . Right. Mad dogs and Englishmen.

The medium-brown overseer, toasty skin dressed up in white linen, had shrugged, running the whip between his fingers, assessing his line of workmen. These boys, sah, will get the job done. They's *good* men, these boys.

They worked like machines, glittering in the sun,

sweat beading on black skin as lovely as a healthy
horse's hide, singing, taking turns with the water
barrel, bringing the crates on down.

"This one first," I said.

A black man came with a crowbar and opened the
lid, nails squeaking as they pulled from wood. Shine
of sunlight on silvery chrome, gray steel, golden brown
copper. Not a bit of corrosion. Not a bit.

I reached out and touched the A-4 motor, running
my fingers over the peroxide turbine's casing, feeling the edges of the stamped-in serial number . . .

Magic.

Magic that will take us to the stars.

I remembered a big, dark cavern. Bridge cranes
rumbling overhead, conscript labor down in the squa-
lor and darkness. *Nordhausen*. I remember how they
starved and died. But they worked, and built these
wonders for us, working by the numbers, dying in
turn, so the missiles could spear up from Holland and
Normandy, crawling away into the sky, on their way
to holdout England.

Vergeltungswaffen too late. Jets too late. Maybe if
we'd had the industrial organization of the Americans,
the utter, all-consuming confidence of the Draka . . .

Common sense Draka knew how not to waste serf
labor, unlike our fat engineers and *kränkliche* politicians.

These blacks now, working, singing in the sun.

I remembered being at some country estate, in the
hill country north of the Zambezi, the day they took
off my collar, the day . . . Handsome man with tawny
brown hair, sun-streaked hair, casting the collar aside.

"You're a lucky man, Hans. Most landed immigrants
had to have come over before the war started, or
come over to our side before we got into Europe
proper. Some of your old friends did, and they've
asked for you as a coworker."

Humble. Oh, so humble, "Thank you, sir . . ."

"Don't thank me, Hans. If we'd had the reach to take America, there'd be no need for your kind. No need at all."

In the background, carefully sprawled on a brocaded divan, there was a naked woman, long, shiny black hair and pale white skin, maybe French or Italian, pretty like a movie star, half-reclining with her legs just slightly apart, staying the way he'd left her when they brought me in the room.

He saw where I was looking and smirked. "Get out Hans. There's a car waiting that will take you to Archona."

Hand on my shoulder in the here and now, under a sun so bright its rays seemed to punch through white clothing, through my tropical helmet, ultraviolet light cooking the substance of my brain. Musical voice, "Beautiful work you did. Incredible precision."

I nodded. Nothing to say. Still looking at the workers, so tireless.

Apu said, "Like's Rossum's machines, eh, Hans?"

I wonder where Karel Capek is now. Escaped to America? Slaving on a plantation somewhere? Or just dead?

Apu said, "They hardly look human."

These workers. Here and now. I said, "You surprise me, Apu. I mean, black . . ." I guess I nodded at him, all the dark tropical tan of him, before glancing back at the workers.

His lip seemed to curl for a moment, then he laughed, that same genuine-sounding chuckle that never changed. "These *hubshi*, Hans? Vwell." Another little titter. "*My* people were the ones who first called themselves *Aryans*, Hans, not *your* pathetic Hyperborean lot!"

He must have seen the surprise on my face.

"Look at *him*, Hans," pointing at a young Draka

officer standing with the mulatto overseer, overseer
who might be his half-brother for all he or we knew,
going over some paperwork. "*Look* at him. See? *Sahib
Log* must *earn* the right to their name."

Sahib Log's Hindi. I know that much from Kipling.
It means Master Race.

And the British adopted Nigger for the Hindoo,
who might well have been lighter than your average
Sicilian, long before it was given over to the Guinea
Men, whose own name, English pronunciation Portuguese spelling for native Ghana, became a pejorative
for Italian . . .

Home again, with another day's sunburn crackling
on my skin. Outside, I could hear dogs barking,
children playing, no more than a distant chatter and
clang, African sun staining the sky a vermilion-shaded
red, sun already set, light fading fast. Soon it'll be
quiet, children gone to bed, adults indoors, only the
Night Watch abroad.

Dinner was a lead-acid battery sitting in the pit
of my stomach, greasy fried Hamburger-sausage and
stale bread with *sauce mayonnaise* and a clumsy slice
of already-sprouted Bermuda onion . . . *Gott verdamm*
I've got to learn how to cook. Figure out where to
get some German-style food . . . nothing but curry
around here it seems . . . What if I'd run the other
way? Would I be sitting in some concrete bungalo
in Arizona, sick from a meal of greasy fried *tacos*
and . . .

I looked at the bottle of *kirschwasser* in my hand,
lacking even the will to pour it in a glass. Another
little swig? No. I put it on the floor, unfolded the
paper across my lap, and started picking through the
English. Newspapers are always the easiest read in
a foreign language, vocabulary-limited, English so
close to German, with so many loan words from a
French I'd studied in *gymnasium*.

African news, lots of sports, non-classified military-interest pieces, foreign affairs . . .

There was a big picture on one of the tech-piece pages, Willy Ley, looking every inch the little fat Jew, head of the America's new ballistic missile agency, greeting an exhausted-looking but still *richtig* Wernher von Braun, formerly with the *Wehrmacht*, broken arm supported at shoulder height . . .

I remembered Ley all right, from the *Verien für Raumschiffahrt* days. Remember how hard it was to convince the registry court that *raumschiffahrt* was a real word? We got a good laugh over that one, eh, Willy? Space-ship-flight. Yes, sir. Not just *raumfahrt*. That could be astral projection as well. Yes, sir. As in Anthroposophy. The *Götheanum* and . . .

I remembered Ley from those days, but not von Braun, who'd been some teenager hanging about, older than Krafft Ericke but . . . but he remembered me, when the time came for us all to go to Peenemunde. Those who hadn't already gone to America.

Behind them both in the grainy photo, I could see that so-called Hungarian, Edvard Teller. Rumor says he's talking about something called "the Super". I remember Apu seeming pale and quiet when we talked about it.

"That would be bad," said his musical voice. "That would be . . . the end it."

Our boss, affectless, said, "Unless we'uns get it first."

We'd had a guest that day, a skinny, bruised, haunted-looking Russian introduced around the office by a translator because his English was so poor. When we talked about the Super, this Sakharov's eyes seemed to deepen with fear, but he kept his mouth shut.

I wonder.

What if Hitler hadn't hated the Jews? What if they'd given *us* the bomb first?

Imagine that. Britain. Russia. America. Ours.
Maybe even these Draka. Where would I be sitting
now?

Imagining myself in a garden on the Moon.

After a while, I went to bed, lay in the darkness,
listening to soft breezes and phantom night-noises,
feeling my skin crawl and itch, feeling every wrinkle
in my sheets as a little princess-pea driving me
crazy . . .

Something. Something I need. Can't remember
though.

Everything from the past, memory, desire. Gone.

I got up after a while, went and peed in the
bathroom, a faint splatter down the hole, far enough
away I knew I wasn't missing and pissing on the floor.

Put on my robe and *zoris*, went out into the back
yard and stood looking up at the stars.

Alpha Centauri was just about the brightest thing
in the southern sky from here, Moon a slim crescent
waxing in the southeast. I looked toward the ecliptic.
Bright Jupiter over there. Which means Mars . . . yes.
Red dot, right where it ought to be.

Raumschiffahrt.

What would we have done, had we been allowed
to do it?

Newspaper story talked about the German-language
edition of Von Braun's pamphlet *Das Marsprojekt*,
now being reprinted in English.

I imagined the three-stage rocket, the *Wohnrahd*,
the moonship, the Mars fleet. Alpha Centauri like a
diamond in the sky, beckoning.

But then I remembered *Kristallnacht*. Broken-
glass-night. And the Jews went away, then Germany
went away, and here I am in Africa.

There was a smell of cooking from next door, the
smell of curry, dark figures on Apu's patio, his wife
and kids, being served whatever it is Anglo-Indians
eat. Chutney on milquetoast? Boiled cabbage and

mung beans? They were being served by a big fat
black woman who lived in their house six days a week.

Dark shape coming my way, coming over to the
low trellis fence where morning glories twined, waiting
to bloom.

Soft, musical words: "Can't sleep, Hans?"

"No, Apu."

"A glass of warm milk and sugar, perhaps . . ."

Well. How *Brit* of you, Apu. "Time. That's all it'll
take."

"I see."

Silence. I kept looking up at the stars and, finally,
whispered, "Ah, God. What foolish dreams we all have
dreamed!"

More silence, then Apu said, "You are too much
alone my friend. At least . . . get yourself a manser-
vant. Someone to cook, and press your clothes for
you."

I shrugged.

In a little while, Apu went inside to bed. After not
much longer, so did I. Morning came, and I went to
work as usual, glad for the deeds that were there to
do. The new motor was coming along fine, black serf
machinest craftsmen every bit as meticulous as any
German I could think of. And these new Russian
boys . . .

Their patience was . . . a surprise.

I started looking forward to the day we could test
fire the engine, and thinking about the . . . vehicle.

That's it then.

What dreams we all have dreamed.

At some times, in some places, when the season
is right, the flat blue sky seems tarnished and tawny,
golden dust mixed in with the blue, not a cloud in
sight, depthless yellow-blue suspended above the
world. This is the sky that says Africa to me, the
Africa of the explorers' books.

I wonder where Lowell Thomas is, right now? Somewhere safe in America, telling his tales of Count Luckner the Sea-Devil, no doubt.

Over jungle Africa, maybe this sky would look green, but here . . . not desert Africa but . . . dry. The Veldt. The Drakensberg. *Und so weiter.* Hard to remember the opal sea is less than a day's drive off, waves crashing on the shore, fishermen standing with their rods, children swimming, surfers on their boards . . .

Kommensie, Hans. Let's see you shoot the curl.

Funny when some of the Dutch-descended Draka try to talk schoolboy German with me, those rough accents of theirs . . . same accent I faced one day near Osedom, faced over a deadly, short-barreled gun: *Raus! Mit der hände hoch!*

And up went my cowardly hands: *Kamerad! Kamerad!* Balls shriveling away to nothing at all. And *Göring's got two, but very small* . . .

Funny. I thought they'd still be speaking Afrikaans in the cities of the South. A language I'd learn quickly, be more comfortable with. Lots of Dutch words in the English, *fon* for *von*, but the rest of it's gone.

One long, hard memory of being led away, shackled and bleeding with just a few other men, chosen men, stumbling through a haze of fear, confusion, Drak officer's machine pistol cracking, sharp and distinct, as he shot my friends, those lesser men, unnecessary men, right through the head, one by one by one . . .

"Okay, Hansel. Lemme know when y'all see what you want."

Billy Creech's hand on my shoulder, gesturing at the bustle of the common serf market all around. Maybe he was twenty-three years old, looking for all the world like some Antebellum American plantation overseer, with his tan hair, toothy grin . . . *redneck* is the word I'm thinking, learned from some novel I'd read between the wars, those Paris years . . .

The boss's words, once he finished snickering over what I proposed to do: "Go along with him, Billy. See this baby isn't robbed blind by those crooks."

Sometimes, you forget what the Domination *is*, forget where it's *been*, how all these people got to the here and now. Brilliant white cities, Archona, Virconium, *faux*-Classical architecture, gardens and boulevards and *this was the noblest Roman of them all*, like some Made-in-Hollywood fantasy world, as absurd in its way as Von Harbou's Germaniform *Atlantida*.

And Fritz Lang, they say, is Hollywood's rising star.

On a platform before me were a dozen tall, sleek black men, skin tone as of unfired sculptor's clay, more gray than brown, almost hairless, arms and legs thin but muscular, long, long penises dangling like dead mambas . . .

The man beside them, white djellaba-clad, with black beard a-bristle, black eyes already calculating a bargain. *Arab*, I thought. Zanzibar. Henry Stanley's famous newspaper accounts of Drakische Afrika. You forget who was here before, and what was going on, layered under the Draka, in and around their dream, those older dreams, straggling on into an unknown tomorrow.

Billy said, "Them boys're good workers, I hear, farmed up around the Suud these days. Course, they won't be cookin' anything *you'd* be willing t'eat."

I looked around, bewildered by sights, sounds, smells, dust and wind and tawny blue sky. Not what I was expecting. Not at all. This . . . *scene*. I . . . "Where are all the Europeans? I mean . . ."

Images of frightened, cowering Germans and French and Italians and Poles. Where are all the hundreds of millions now surrendered to the Domination? Where are my *friends*?

Billy said, "Well most of 'em's still *wild*. It'll be a few years 'fore you see too many hereabouts. Got to *tame* 'em first, see, but . . ." He took a long look around. "There." Pointing.

In the middle distance, all by himself on a platform, was a slim, handsome, dark-haired white man dressed up in diaphanous veil and thin silk kimono. Thin enough you could make out his body, slim and boyish. He was shading his face from the sun with a garish Chinese parasol, face made up with lipstick and rouge, steeply arched eyebrows neatly penciled in . . .

Billy snickered. "There's rich ole Draka will pay *powerful* good money for a pretty French queer. Exotic. Too exotic fo' the likes of us."

Exotic. And tame.

Billy said, "Must be something wrong with that 'un to be in a cheap market like this. Anyway, that's the sort of merchandise you always see first."

So. Milling crowds, eying the tame *merchandise*.

Arabs and Crackers, Bedwine Hindee and nasty little blond Dutchboys with their gaggles of property up for sale. Farm workers and household servants and whatever the Hell . . .

Voice, thick Draka Southron accent cut by something else, something undefined, spoken softly: "Girl, I done tol' you before, keep your legs *apart* 'f'n you don' want the switch later on! I want 'em to *see* yo' pretty little hole . . ."

Beyond the tall Nilotics, a little man with yellow skin and tight black peppercorn hair, dressed in bib overalls, nothing but rope sandals on his feet.

Billy said, "Hmh. Sometimes these here *Reservation* Hottentott get above themselves." Disdain. "Nothin' anybody'll ever *do* about it though. Museum piece, they say. 'Heritage of Africa.' Shee-it!" Underlined with a gob of spit in the dust.

I felt my mouth suddenly go dry.

The little yellow man saw me looking, and . . ."Ah, step right up, you *fine* Archona Gentlemen! Step right up and feast yo' *eyes* on a *prime* piece o' real estate!"

Billy said, "Cripes. Like one o' mah grandaddy's plantation-bred preacher-boys . . ."

The girl stood still, slim and long-waisted, tall, brown of skin, black of hair and eye, standing hipshot, with one knee drawn out to the side, foot arched up *en pointe* as instructed, so we could see . . .

A little rise of bone there, right there where it counts, rising beneath the taut skin of her abdomen . . . Dry medical voice in my head, *hypogastric region* . . . There was a slight matching protrusion around her mouth, lips parted slightly, pushed open by a faint glint of white teeth, black eyes looking right at me, into my eyes and . . .

Strangling, I took a breath, looking away and . . .

Billy snorted, a single-syllable laugh, and said, "Well, I *reckon* she can cook and press yo' suits, Hansel ole boy. And I *reckon* yo' account can bear the expense . . ."

"I . . . I . . ."

"Just give the man yo' account number, Hans. Have him package her up fo' delivery and we'll get on back to work."

When I looked at the girl again, there was nothing at all in her face, black eyes impenetrable bits of night sky set deep in her face. I turned to the little yellow man and said, "Wha . . . what's her name?"

The man shrugged, hardly glancing at her. "Don't know."

Don't know?

Billy said, "What difference does it make? You'll think of something, Hans. Let's go. You've got a guidance design review meeting in two hours, then this afternoon we've got the all-up shot."

Go.

That afternoon, the harsh sunlight over the veldt had a milky translucent quality that made the cloudless sky look almost white. We were under awnings, in the shade, but you could still feel its sting, stealthy on your skin.

In the distance, a mile or so away, the Test Article stood smoking on its pad, gentle curls of water vapor falling groundward, a fading wisp of cloud like a ghost-snake by the LOX overpressure vent.

Loudspeaker said, "Four minutes."

The Test Article looked like two long, thin A-4's stuck side-by side, each eighty feet tall, booster, my baby, a featureless silo beside the missile itself, with its broad white delta wings, cannards and twin vertical stabilizers. Ten thousand imperial gallons of alcohol and liquid oxygen aboard the booster, another ten thousand gallons of carefully refined and filtered kerosene aboard the missile.

From this angle, you couldn't really see the big pods of the twin ramjet engines, about to have their first all-up live-fire test. I felt confident, though. The Fiseler and Argus boys had done fine work, once they'd gotten properly organized under Dr. Kuznetsov. Who would've thought a Russian engineer, of all things . . .

"Three minutes. Oxygen system isolated." The vent wisp suddenly diappeared.

"Hans? Boss says you'll want to look at this." I turned away, unwilling. A thin, gray-faced man was holding out a folder full of papers.

"Thanks, Sergei." Korolyov was doing good job managing the engine team, but . . . you could tell his heart was damaged by the things that'd happened to him, before, during, after . . . They say Stalin had him in the *gulag*. What a fool. Stalin should have given him money and workers. Then Sergei Korolyov would have given him anti-aircraft missiles and rocket planes that might have done to the Nazis and Draka what . . .

Hell.

Dreams. All just dreams.

"Two minutes." Near the pad, a siren began to blow, and you could see tiny figures moving away, getting aboard their little steamers, raising clouds of dust as they drove toward us.

Sergei was looking over my shoulder as I opened the package. "See? What do you think of your friends now?"

The first sheet was a grainy telex photo, taken at a long slant angle across some stony gray desert country, low mountains in the background I recognized from mid-war newsreel footage. *Jornada del Muerte*. The Death's Journey Mountains.

Hanging against the pale sky, gray in the photo, undoubtedly bluer than this one, here and now, was a fat white rocket, two stages separated by a gridwork truss, rising on a long, transparent flame beaded with big shock diamonds.

"So," I said, just to myself. "So they went with the hypergolics after all." Aniline and nitric acid maybe? No. It'd have to be better than that.

Korolyov said, "Apparently. Chelomei has turned up in America." There was something else, in Russian, words I thought I knew. He leaned close, studying the photo. "Nitrogen tetroxide and unsymmetrical dimethyl hydrazine make a lovely clear violet flame."

I said, "Did you just say, 'lucky bastard' about your friend Chelomei?"

"One minute," said the loudspeaker.

He shrugged. "Not quite. If you look at the stat sheet, you'll see that thing could deliver Teller's 'Super' from a site in North America to anywhere on Domination territory."

I flipped the page. The next photo was of the rocket in the sky, bending in the middle, as its interstage truss gave way. The third page was a picture of a lovely explosion. I tried to imagine it as a purple flower in the sky. "They'd better try harder then, if he's to have any luck at all."

He said, "If the Draka don't win, the Americans will just give us jobs. Capitalists are like that."

In what Russian I could muster, I muttered, "*Tíshe. Durák!*" Shut up. You fool.

He shrugged, and . . .

The loudspeaker began, "Ten, nine, eight . . ."

"Ignition." The booster lit, black smoke and dull red fire fluttering around the base. After a few seconds, the dull thud and soft rumble.

"Turbine spin up." The fire brightened, blowing away the smoke, turning yellow, then white. Another delay, then that familiar, steady waterfall sound.

"Release."

The Test Article lifted off the pad, climbing on a clean yellow flame, turning so the missile would be on top as she headed out over the blue waters of the Indian Ocean.

Watching her go, shading his eyes against the afternoon sun, Sergei said, "What would it be like, if a man wanted to ride that thing, I wonder?"

My turn to shrug. "Well, now. A man's just not as heavy as an atom bomb, is he? If they let us do it, there will be . . . a lot of new work for the team."

Sergei smiled. "What was it you fellows used to say, Hans? *Arbeit macht frei?* Was that it?"

Unwilling, I remembered.

Before they got us sorted out, figured out who to cajole and who to kill, the Draka put us on work gangs, clearing away rubble, clearing streets, burning the sad debris of war, until, one day, I found myself with a rag tyed around my face, laboring through a fearsome stench, throwing dead Jews in a ditch, covering them with white lime and black dirt, while ritual-scarred Janissaries watched, laughing, joking with one another, uncaring, amused, relaxed black men with deadly black guns.

I remember I bent to pick up a skinny, naked, dead woman.

Skinny. I can't imagine how she got so thin, a skeleton covered with parchment skin. Everything about her sunken in but her mouth and pubis, all elbows and knees and hips.

I bent to pick her up, looking at that lovely tuft of shiny black hair, and wonder how, disembodied, dead, it still had the power to enchant me.

I remember how, suddenly, I wanted to . . .

No. Think about your rocket, Hans, rising into the sky.

Another part of me wanted to think about what was waiting for me at home.

And yet another did not.

As well try to turn back the tides of the sea.

Home, sunset staining the sky brick red, full dark rimming the eastern sky, beyond the mountains, out over the Hindoo Sea, *Drakische Mare Nostrum* soon enough, I went and stood by the mailbox, examining the day's worthless . . .

Apu crossed his lawn, dressed in loose, garish shorts, some wild maroon pattern print I understood was called Madras, a white linen shirt, sandals. "I saw it, Hans! What a sight that was!" Voice musical and full of enthusiasm.

I nooded, sorting the mail, trying not to think.

He said, "The range safety officer detonated her just after she cleared the coast. Ten thousand kilometers an hour, at full cruise! She would have been in Australia in no time all!"

I nodded again. What the hell are you doing outside? What are you waiting for? Hm?

He said, "My wife says you, ah . . . received a delivery today."

I felt my face burning, not looking up, not wanting to see whatever expression was on his face.

"Well," he said. "I won't be expecting to see you later on then!"

No? When I tried looking at him, his expression proved to be serious and gentle.

"Sometimes," he said, "I envy you, Hans." Then he turned and walked away, head down, hands in pockets, toward the veranda of his house, where I saw his wife sitting drinking a tall glass of tea. She waved.

When I opened the front door, the light was dim inside and . . . different. Something different here. As if I could smell something . . .

Abruptly, I remembered how, sometimes, I would become, oh, call it subliminally *aware* of my wife. She would come into a room where I was working, would just stand there, and no matter what I was doing, no matter how focused, no matter what she was wearing, however unflattering, I would suddenly imagine her naked, imagine her hips and thighs and belly . . .

We talked about it, the thought amusing her so, *really, Hans*, making her blush, and it turned out these things happened most often right around her fertile time, nature subverting all our attempts to control . . .

No sign of her in the Draka serf intake records. *Sorry, Hans*. Too bad, old man.

She stood, emerging from the shadows, apparently having been sitting on the bare floor between my battered divan and the cold ashes of the fireplace, which I'd been afraid to light for fear of burning the place down in my abstraction, my evenings full of dreams and regret.

"Massuh de Groot."

Her voice was soft. Throaty. Full.

"Uh." I stood there like an idiot. What does one say to a . . . serf? Nice little euphemism, that. Latin *servus*, meaning slave. In my family, we never even had servants.

She crossed the room, face shadowed, eyes glinting, uncertain, looking at me. Kneeled in some kind of ritual posture, making me feel even more ridiculous.

"Um. Your . . . name?"

She looked up at me, curious, eyes seeking, questioning, probing. What is it a serf needs to do, then? *Understand the wishes of her master. Anticipate.*

She said, "Khoikhoi called me—" something abrupt, with a couple of clicks embedded in it.

"Um. And your real name?"

"My Mammy say—" something musical, like Italian but obviously not. Malagasy?

"Um."

She stood, something odd in her face now. I felt myself strangling, unable to breathe. How am I going to manage this . . . this . . . Oh, you know.

She said, "Massuh, you want yo' dinnah now?"

All I could do was nod.

"Ah'll do my bes'. Yo' kitchen . . ." A slow shake of the head, an amused look. "Bes' I lights a fire too. Chase away them shaduhs . . ." Turning away then, and I thought, Talking like some American movie Negro. Where would they learn that?

What those movies were about, of course, was the world many of the Draka's ancestors had left behind, little Porgie helping Pocelain make the bed, nyuk-nyuk-nyuk . . .

I sat in my chair, helpless, watching her bend in a thin linen dress, looking at the shape of her, watching her move, suddenly half-starved and . . .

Later, suddenly later, I was in my room, sitting on the edge of the bed, that wonderful dinner a solid lump in my middle, a dish whose name I didn't know, made from ingredients I didn't know I'd had. When I asked, stuttering, she said what I thought was the name of the fat black woman who served Apu's family. "She a nice lady. Bonded servant. Almost free."

Whatever the Hell that means. Draka society was

mostly a closed book to me, so many things, so many differences. Not at all like the Germany I'd known, Germany no more. Maybe a bit like America the Movie, but only a little bit.

Suddenly, she was in the open doorway of my room, standing there, looking at me, face . . . unreadable.

"Yes."

"Where you wants me to sleep, Massuh? They's a spare room, but no . . ."

Right. No bed. Not even a pile of rags for her to sleep on. "I . . ."

She came into the room then, dark shadow in wan lamplight, eyes shining on mine. "Well. I sees." Then she unbuttoned the few top buttons of her shift, reached around to untie the back, pulled it off over her head and was naked.

Nakeder than any woman I had ever imagined before.

She stood, posed, something like a smile, a knowing smile on her face, watching me stare.

Look at me. Mouth hanging open. Sweat beading on my brow. What next, a rope of drool from my lips?

She reached down, hand passing slowly over her smooth belly, going between her legs, pausing there, drawing in my eyes. Then she took her hand to her face, covering her mouth and nose, drawing in a deep breath.

And said, "This a good time fo' me, Massuh. Hopes to make it a good time fo' you, as well."

Some time later, we stood out in a slit trench, my comrades and I, out in the dry Namib desert under a featureless morning sky, sky the neutral color of the primer coat on a brand new steamer, just before the factory lays on that familiar enamel gloss, with all its color and glow.

We stood, and we waited.

Nothing. A soft, dry wind. The soft murmur of

people talking, talking in whispers, as though . . . something were listening.

Apu put his hand on my shoulder, and said, "You seem . . . vwell. Relaxed."

Unbidden, the memory of her in the night, lying in the bed with my hands upon her, looking up at me, eyes . . . watching mine, looking into them, as if deep into my soul.

I remembered the way her breath had quickened later on, perfectly responsive, responses in sync with mine, as if . . .

I remember awakening from a dream, flinching out of it, running from a memory, three naked women standing by a ditch, pretty girls, Ukrainians I think, maybe Jews, maybe not.

The Three Graces. One so tall and brave. Another, smaller, almost like a child despite the pretty breasts and lovely pubic swatch, head down on the other's bosom, eyes closed. A third by her side, looking frightened and cold, but modest even now, one arm across her breasts, the other hand covering her vulva.

I remember the clatter of the bolt being drawn back, machine gun being cocked.

I remember, behind the women there was a ditch, already half full.

I can't remember why I was at Babi Yar that day, only that they invited me out to watch, as though to a picnic.

And when I awoke from the dream, gasping, covered with cold sweat, she said, "Theah now, Massuh. Jes' a dream, tha's all. You safe now. I's heah."

A voice with the power to make it all right again, lying under me, breath quickening, at just the right moment, clutching me close, crying out with joy.

I felt myself flush, avoiding Apu's smile.

Down the way, the boss said, "One minute, gentlemen. See to your goggles."

We were ten miles away, far behind the front lines,

where soldiers and experimental subjects waited. I remembered the boss saying, "This had best work, gentlemen, now that Teller . . ."

Korolyov, in a harsh whisper, "Teller's Super is too heavy for the Atlas. We've got time yet."

Over a loudspeaker, someone's voice began counting down. I pulled down my goggles and the world was blotted away, nothing but darkness under a brilliant African sun, the sound of my breathing, other people . . . almost as if we were holding our breaths, no more whispers now.

"Four . . . three . . . two . . ."

The world came back, colored gray and silver, the desert cast with stark, impossible shadows.

Beyond, the entire horizon seemed to lift away, a flat line rising, then an impossible sunrise, ball of light bloating from the edge of the world, falling skyward like a huge bubble of steam lifting from the bottom of the sea.

There was a brilliant corona, streamers of light, a visible shockwave, atmosphere constraining the event as best it could.

The ground slammed my feet, making me stagger.

Darkness closing in as the bomblight faded.

I pulled up my goggles then, gaping at a towering malignancy, fat column of black smoke reaching already into the stratosphere, spreading there because it could go no farther, coming toward us swiftly, like the front of an onrushing storm.

"That's bigger than yo' said, I think. Some of them boys up front . . ."

Five megatons, I thought. We calculated five megatons. This . . . ten? Fifteen? Somewhere, we've done something wrong.

Watching the pressure wave cross the desert toward us, raising a cloud of dust, Apu, in a voice hushed with wonder and sorrow, said, " 'I am become Death . . .' "

" '. . . the Destroyer of Worlds.' " replied Sakharov, lifting his goggles away, looking upward into face of his child, eyes like two pieces of dead, empty stone.

Then the hot wind struck and roared overhead, while we cowered together in the bottom of our ditch.

And, when I went home that night, dark, sweet Gretel was waiting for me just inside the door, wearing the new linen shift I'd bought her.

Ready and waiting, with a smile just for me.

Then the dreamer becomes the dream, as mourning became Electra, making her oh-so-pretty indeed.

Harry Turtledove has been called the master of alternate history. This is annoying.

Not because he isn't a master of that form, but because he's also a master of heroic fantasy, *humorous* fantasy—far more difficult to do well—space opera, idea-oriented hard science fiction, straight historical fiction, and an implausibly large range of other types of literature. For relaxation, he reads Byzantine Greek chronicles.

Harry is an unfairly tall man of frightening intellect and reassuring warmth, who lives with his wife Laura (also a writer) and his three intimidatingly bright daughters in Southern California. It's as if the IQs slated for legions of surfer dudes and val-gals had been suctioned out and concentrated in one hilariously scholarly household in the San Fernando valley, where the art of conversation still lives.

Harry's work includes the classic WORLDWAR series, which single-handedly resurrects the alien-invasion stories of yore and updates them, *The Guns of the South*, a meditation on the American Civil War with Afrikaners and AK-47s, and the grimly majestic alternate-history masterpiece which begins with *How Few Remain*, continues through *The Great War: American Front*, and most recently culminates in *Walk in Hell*.

Here he shows—through a protagonist many of us may somehow recognize—how even utter defeat can be a kind of victory.

THE LAST WORD

Harry Turtledove

Commodore Anson MacDonald strode into the underground refectory. "What's the latest?" he asked.

Nobody paid any attention to him. All eyes were riveted on the big, wall-mounted televisor. The news reader, her pretty face worn and haggard, her eyes red with tears that hadn't—quite—poured down her face, spoke like a machine: "—San Francisco now definitely known to be vaporized. The government did not escape. Along with the destruction of Manhattan and Washington, this confirms—"

Someone had a remote control. He aimed the little box at the televisor as if it were an assault rifle. And the infrared beam killed the screen, which went black. "That's that," somebody else said. "The Alliance for Democracy is washed up."

249

Across the room, someone said, "For God's sake, get me a beer."

MacDonald looked from one soldier to another. He was a lean, bald man in his mid-fifties, the graying hair he had left cropped close to the sides and back of his skull, a thin line of mustache—darker than the hair on his head—just above his upper lip. He felt very much a stranger here: he'd been rotated to the Nantahala Redoubt for a familiarization tour . . . just at the exact moment the Snakes chose to launch the Final War.

Even his uniform was wrong. He was a thirty-year Navy man, and proud of the deep blue, the blue of the tropical ocean at night, but it didn't fit here, not with everyone else in mottled woodland camouflage.

And the Navy-blue uniform wasn't the only thing that didn't fit in. Anson MacDonald felt as devastated as the news reader had sounded. The country he loved, the system he believed in, going down under the Domination of the Draka? What had that Englishman called the Snakes? *A boot in the face of mankind forever*—something like that, anyhow. He had every right to feel as if the world had just ended. For all practical purposes, it had.

But the men in the mottled uniforms seemed grimly content with their fate, with their country's fate. One of them, a fellow with captain's bars on his collar tabs, came up to MacDonald and said, "Take it easy, Commodore. They didn't put us in the Redoubt for when things were going fine. This is what we're here for: to give the Draka as much trouble as we can for as long as we can, even though the Alliance for Democracy has lost the war."

"Madness," MacDonald said. "I've always thought so. Defeatist madness."

"No, sir." The captain—the name tape above the right breast pocket of his uniform said FISCHER—shook his head. "Strategy. The Draka have won the phase of the game that just ended. Now we have to make sure they get as little joy from it as possible. We have to tie them down in endless cleanup operations, make sure they'll need to worry about us ten years from now, twenty years from now, maybe fifty years from now. We've got men and women in here, you know. We can raise up a whole new generation to give the Snakes grief."

"What's the point?" MacDonald asked bitterly. "The Afghans gave them grief after the Great War. The Finns gave them grief after the Eurasian War. The Afghans are Draka Janissaries these days; the Finns, poor bastards, are mostly dead. And those sons of bitches are going to turn the free men and women of the United States and the rest of the Alliance into serfs. Do you know what that is, Captain? It's the biggest rape in the history of the world."

"Yes, sir." Fischer had a long, skinny face that seemed stupid till you studied it for a little while. MacDonald had known a few men like that; what made them seem not quite in the real world wasn't stupidity but intense concentration. After a few seconds, Fischer returned to the here-and-now. "Sir, like it or not, you're here for the duration. Ever play a game of chess where you threw away your queen like a damn fool?"

Caught off guard, MacDonald let out a couple of syllables' worth of barking laughter. "Unfortunately, yes."

"Okay." When Fischer grinned, he looked years younger, almost like a kid. "You aren't going to win after that. But if you're feeling stubborn and you've got a halfway decent defense, you can go into a shell and make the other fellow work like a son of a bitch to finish you. That's what we're all about."

"But what's the point?" Anson MacDonald demanded. "The point was, we never should have lost our queen in the first place. Now that we have, we're still facing a lost game. We would have done better to put all this energy, all this manpower, all these resources, into first-strike capability. I always said so, to anyone who would listen. Not enough people did."

"And maybe we would have lost all those people, all those resources, on account of the Snakes' stinking virus," Captain Fischer said. "We're *still* dealing with that; the drugs only help so much. But that's not the point. The point is, this isn't chess. The rules are more elastic, when there are rules. And you've forgotten something else."

"What's that?" MacDonald barked—he didn't like getting a lecture from this whippersnapper. Captain Fischer spoke two quiet words. MacDonald stiffened to attention. "I am at your service, sir."

Janissary Sergeant Hans rubbed at the orange slave tattoo behind his left ear. It didn't itch, but he imagined it did. He held up a hand. The squad he led was glad to stop for a blow. They liked the look of the mountainous woods ahead no better than he did. Even if the leaves were off the trees, anything could be hiding in there. It probably was, too.

"Where's the map say we're at, Sarge?" asked a trooper named Usama.

Being a sergeant, Hans had been trained in such mysteries. He didn't even need to consult the map to answer, "That last little town we just went through was called Cheoah." His English was the slurred dialect of the Domination—not so very much different from what the folk here in the U.S. district of North Carolina spoke—with something guttural underneath, a reminder that both his grandfathers had fought for the *Reich* and the *Führer* against the Draka. They'd lost, and now he marched under the dragon that held chains and sword. He didn't worry about it. He just did what his officers told him, and handled the squad with a veteran's lack of fuss.

"Nothing left of that place no more, not after the gunships gave it the once-over." Usama was tall and lean and dark, with a long scimitar of a nose and a neat black beard. He carried a scope-sighted sniper's rifle on his back.

"No more town there, sure enough." Hans spat. He lit a cigarette. "But those bastards nailed Boris and Kemal. Shouldn't never have happened."

Everyone nodded. "Stinking civilians," somebody said. "What're they doin' with so many rifles?"

"It's like they're all Citizens," Hans said.

"My ass." That was Usama again. "*We* can lick these Yankees hand to hand. Real Citizens, they'd have 'em for breakfast."

"No, not Citizens like that." A thoroughly hard man, Hans admired the Draka not least because he knew they were harder. "But they've all got the right to carry weapons. Somethin' in their constitution— the . . . fifth amendment?" He shrugged. He couldn't precisely remember the briefing. "So we got to deal with more goddamn *francs-tireurs* than you can shake a stick at, on top of whatever real soldiers— holdouts—they've got left."

He scowled at the last sentence. The USA wasn't pacified. Hell, it wasn't even occupied. That was his job. It was a nasty one, too. He wondered what his chances were of getting old enough to retire and buy himself a tavern or something. He shrugged against the weight of body armor. Not so good, probably.

"That one old bastard got Boris right between the eyes." Usama spoke with grudging professional respect. "Had to be five, six hundred meters, too. Good shot."

Corporal Soshangane was a Zulu; his folk had been under the Draka yoke longer than almost any other. From what he'd told Hans, he was a sixth-generation Janissary, and he thought very much like his masters. "Damn fools," he said now, in accents that might almost have belonged to a von Shrakenberg. "Kill a coupla us, cost 'em that whole damn town."

"I don't think they reckon that way," Hans said. "This here's like it was in Europe fifty years ago, only more so. They ain't gonna go down easy."

"Long as they go down." Soshangane grinned, white teeth extra bright in his dark face. "Some o' the girls, they go down mighty nice."

"*Ja*," Hans said, a word that did duty for *yeah* in the English spoken between the Rhine and the Oder. He ground the cigarette out under his bootheel. "Come on—into the woods." He pointed north and south. "We aren't gonna let those bastards go in all by themselves, are we?" Nobody said no. You didn't let your buddies down. The Janissaries fought by few rules, but that was one of them.

Hans's boots scrunched in dead leaves. He cursed under his breath, in English and in the German he'd learned as a child. Nothing to be done about it. The leaves were everywhere, here and there drifted deep like snow. Hans's eyes flicked back and forth, up and down. He wished for eyes in the back of his head. His buddies were the eyes in the back of his head, but that didn't seem enough.

Back and forth, up and down. They didn't have woods like this in Germany—not anywhere in Europe that he knew of. This place looked as if he were the first man who'd ever set foot here. It would probably be glorious in spring, with the trees in full leaf, with the birds singing songs he'd never heard before, and with squirrels peering at him out of beady black eyes.

Everything was quiet now, except for the small sounds he and his men couldn't help making. The hair on the back of his neck kept wanting to prickle up. He couldn't have proved he was being watched, but he had that feeling. He'd learned to pay attention to it. If you didn't pay attention to such feelings, you ended up buying a plot, not a tavern.

Still, he was taken by surprise when automatic-weapons fire ripped into the squad *from behind*. He whirled and dove for cover, his Holbars T-7 already spitting death. Even as he thudded down onto the ground, he knew he was up for a court-martial. How the devil had he walked right past those Yankee bastards without even knowing they were there?

Then a grenade burst half a meter in front of his face, and such questions became academic.

Anson MacDonald felt uncomfortable in a uniform of green and brown camouflage splotches, even though the holdouts had supplied him with one with a star on each collar tab—brigadier general was the Army equivalent of commodore. *I'm not betraying Annapolis*, he told himself. *This is the only way I have left to hit back at the enemy. Oh, some of the Alliance submersibles are probably still out there, but I'd have just as easy a time getting to the asteroid belt as going aboard one of them. They're on their own now, same as I am. I hope they do a lot of damage before the Snakes finally sink 'em.*

"Did you spray yourself with insect repellent?" Captain Fischer asked as they emerged from the mouth of a cave.

"Of course I did." MacDonald knew he sounded offended. He couldn't help it. "I grew up in Missouri," he told the younger officer, frost still in his voice. "I knew about chiggers twenty years before you were a gleam in your old man's eye."

"All right, sir." Fischer remained unruffled. "Some people need a head start." *I've just been given the glove*, MacDonald thought, and chuckled under his breath. Fischer went on, "Now—can you see the cave we just came out of?"

After looking back, Commodore MacDonald had to shake his head. "No—and we can't have moved more than three or four meters."

"That's right." Fischer smiled. Again, the grin took years off him. "That rock overhang hides it unless you know exactly where to look—and even then it's not easy to spot. It's even harder in the summertime. The trees have their leaves, and the wild rhododendrons and such grow like madmen underneath 'em. If you can't see it, the Draka won't, either."

"Not until we come out and give 'em a hard time." Anson MacDonald grinned a grin of his own, a savage grin that made his teeth seem extraordinarily sharp. "Those Janissaries never knew what hit 'em." He looked to the east. It was after ten in the morning, but the sun still hadn't climbed over the edge of the valley near whose bottom they stood. "This country's even more rugged than I thought coming into the Redoubt."

"Nantahala's a Cherokee word, they tell me," Fischer answered. "Supposed to mean 'Land of the Noonday Sun.' A lot of the valleys hereabouts are so steep, noon's the only time the sun gets down into 'em at all. Add in all the caves and all the mineshafts—people went after mica and talc and emeralds, but they hardly ever made enough to pay their way—and you've got some nasty terrain to overrun."

"And we've tied a lot of the caves and the shafts together into a nice network," MacDonald said.

"No, sir," Fischer said, quietly but emphatically. "Not *a* network. A lot of different networks, all through this whole area. Sooner or later, we'll lose prisoners. We have to assume they won't all be able to suicide, and that means the Draka will start squeezing things out of them. We don't want the Redoubt unraveling when the first string comes loose, the way a cheap sweater would. If they want us, they'll have to come in and dig us out, and it'll cost 'em."

"I should hope so." Anson MacDonald looked around. "You could turn most of this to radioactive glass without bothering us much."

Fischer nodded. "That's the idea. We come out, give them hell in four different states, and then disappear again." He grimaced. "The only rough spot is, since we're up against the Snakes it's hard as hell on the civilian population."

But now Commodore MacDonald shook his head. "If the Draka want to kill hostages, that's their mistake. Better for Americans to die as free men than to live as slaves."

"Sir, do me a favor," Fischer said. "Take that to the Propaganda Section. One of our biggest worries is how to get our personnel to carry on with the Snakes holding a gun to the country's head."

MacDonald's face and voice were bleak. "The gun's already gone off. The Alliance is dead. The USA is dead. We're not fighting to win—you said so yourself. We're fighting to hurt the Draka and keep on hurting them. That's a different business. I presume everyone in the Redoubt is a volunteer?" He'd never asked before, but the answer seemed obvious.

And, sure enough, Captain Fischer said, "Yes, sir."

"All right, then." Anson MacDonald had never been a man to brook much nonsense from anyone. "I presume they knew what they were volunteering for, too. We've got no magic way to throw the Snakes back across the Atlantic. We can't very well start a new religion and go crusading against them. All we can do is give them grief."

"That's right," Fischer said. "That's the attitude. If I'm down to my king, I want the other fellow down to a king and a pawn, and I want to make him have to work like hell to promote that pawn."

"There you go, son." Suddenly, crazily, MacDonald felt years younger than he had any business being. Maybe Fischer felt the same, for he grinned again. They both slid down into the cave. Once they'd scrambled a little way back from the entrance, there was room to stand up. The air inside was cool and damp and smelled of dirt. From what Fischer said, it was always like that, winter and summer. Fischer reached up and touched a piece of the cave roof that looked no different from any other piece. A doorway opened. Till it did, MacDonald couldn't have told it from the rest of the back wall. He and Captain Fischer walked into the Redoubt. The door closed behind them.

In a tent outside Gastonia, North Carolina, two Draka officers studied a map that looked as if it had a bad case of the measles. "Wotan's prick, what're we gonna do about this place?" Moirarch Benedict Arnold asked. These past couple of generations, every male Citizen surnamed Arnold seemed to have that first name, a reminder of just what the Domination thought of the Yankees they'd been hating for two hundred years.

"I know what I'd like to do, Ben," answered his superior, Merarch Piet van Damm. His family had deeper roots in southern Africa than anyone this side of the Bushmen. When Arnold raised a questioning eyebrow, he went on, "I'd like to air-burst enough H-bombs over that country to turn it all to slag."

"Still wouldn't get rid of the holdouts," Arnold said mournfully. "From what the Security Directorate says, they're based underground. They've been gettin' ready for this for a *long* time, the sons of bitches."

Merarch van Damm chuckled. "And we ain't?" But the grin slid off his face. He was all business as he went on, "I don't care if it'd get rid of 'em or not. It'd take away their cover. That's triple-canopy forest there—underbrush up to your chest, then a second layer twice as high as a man, and then the big hardwoods and pines on top o' that. Blast it down to the ground an' we'd be able to spot those bastards when they came topside to do their mischief."

"Sounds good to me," Arnold said. "We've lost too

many men already—not just Janissaries, either, but Citizens, more'n we can afford. Damn the Yankees, they stashed some of their best down there. How do we go about gettin' authorization for it?"

"I tried," Piet van Damm answered. "We don't. Won't happen. Forget about it. Wish for the moon. Hell, we've *got* the moon."

"Who's got his head up his ass in the High Command?" Arnold asked. The two of them were old friends. Had they been anything else, the moirarch wouldn't have put his career on the line like that.

Before answering, van Damm walked out of the tent into the cold, nasty rain that drummed down outside. Benedict Arnold pulled up his head and followed. "Never can tell who might be listening," van Damm remarked. "Even out here, I won't name names. But the initials are *v.S.*"

Benedict Arnold stared. "The von Shrakenbergs? Jesus Christ, why?" He was horrified enough to swear by something stronger than the neopagan pantheon.

"As best I can make out, two reasons, maybe three," Merarch van Damm said. "Number one, they say both sides have already used too many atomic weapons."

"Something to that," Arnold admitted reluctantly.

"Something," van Damm said. "Not enough, if you ask me. Number two is kind of related to number one. Those Yankee bastards there are enough of a nuisance to keep our soldiers sharp for years to come. They won't get soft from lack of anything to do. Our grandfathers used the Finns the same way fifty years ago."

"Something to that, too," Moirarch Arnold said. This time, he raised the objection himself: "But not enough, like you said before. We needed to stay sharp after we licked the Nazis and the Reds—we still had the Alliance to worry about. But now it's whipped. The world is *ours*, sir."

"I know." His superior walked a little farther from the tent, as if to put more distance between himself and any possible listening devices. Arnold followed once more. After a dozen squelching steps, van Damm deigned to continue: "And there's a third reason, or I've heard there's a third reason." He moved on again.

So, perforce, did Benedict Arnold. "Well?" he asked at last.

"You didn't hear this from me," Merarch van Damm told him. "I don't care if the Security Directorate shoves burning pine slivers up under your fingernails, but you didn't hear this from me."

"I got you," Arnold said. If the SD boys ever started grilling him, burning pine slivers were the least he had to worry about in this electronic age, but van Damm had made his point.

"All right." The senior officer nodded heavily. "The third reason, from what I hear—and you don't need to know where I heard it—is that the von Shrakenbergs want that whole region kept as a game preserve for the days after we whip this continent into our kind of shape. It's one of the last stretches of this kind of forest left in eastern North America."

"A game preserve?" Benedict Arnold didn't say the words out loud. He couldn't. He just mouthed them. After a few seconds, he found his voice again: "The von Shrakenbergs are going to let us bleed for the sake of a *game preserve*?"

Piet van Damm chuckled. "Sounds like them, doesn't it? And it fits together with number two. After all, what are the Yankees these days but game? You ever read the story that Englishman wrote back before we were born?"

"Who hasn't?" Arnold said. "But a proper Draka wouldn't have let that bastard bushwhack him. You hunt the way you do everything else: to win. You don't win, there's no point to it."

"Of course not." Van Damm nodded. "But he wrote it for Englishmen and Americans, so naturally the Draka had to lose." One hand folded briefly into a fist. "Well, we didn't lose, and we're not going to lose. The world is ours, and we'll do whatever we damn well please with it."

Benedict Arnold started to say something, then checked himself. When he did speak, it was after some little thought: "You're right, sir. And on that scale of things, what's one game preserve more or less?" He came to attention, ignoring the rain with the ease of a man who'd known worse. "Service to the State!"

"Glory to the Race!" Piet van Damm finished the secular—the nearly secular—invocation. He peered west toward the Great Smoky Mountains, not that visibility was even a kilometer right this minute. "All the same, the sooner we stop hunting holdouts and start hunting boar, the happier I'll be."

Anson MacDonald sat down at a table and opened an MFR. The initials stood for Meal, Fully Ready. The troops, predictably, had come up with a rather different meaning for the acronym, one that Oedipus would have approved of. The MFRs were supposed to be able to sustain life indefinitely. *Maybe it only seems like forever*, MacDonald thought as he opened the foil-wrapped serving of what was alleged to be beef stew.

Captain Fischer sat down beside him. His MFR held chicken à la king—*chicken à la thing*, in the parlance of the soldiers of the Redoubt. He spooned up a mouthful, then grimaced. "Eating these bastards is about the only thing that tempts me to surrender to the Snakes," he said.

He meant it for a joke, but MacDonald frowned. "Do you suppose that might prove enough of a problem to lead to desertions?" he asked.

"I doubt it, sir." Fischer waved to the televisor screen, which was showing Draka programming these days: at the moment, instructions on the proper behavior for serfs in the presence of Janissaries or Draka Citizens themselves. That was fairly innocuous. But Fischer went on, "Remember last night?"

MacDonald grunted. "I'm not likely to forget it." The Snakes had broadcast what they called an object lesson: the execution of several men who'd presumed to shoot at one of their vehicles. It had taken a long time, and it hadn't been pretty.

"I hope that's not going to be a problem with the troops here," Fischer said in worried tones. "They've been briefed that they have to think of the civilian population of the USA as if it were already taken off the board."

"And so it is," Commodore MacDonald replied. "Say what you will about the Draka, they're the most efficient slavemakers this poor sorry world has ever seen." He dug into his MFR, then wished he hadn't.

"I know," Fischer said. "But some of those new slaves are family or sweethearts or friends to our men here. Watching what happens to them as they go under the yoke can't be good for morale."

"Not for ours, and not for that of the other bands of free men still running around loose," MacDonald agreed. "But it's a military reality, Captain. We have to deal with it as best we can."

"I know that, sir." Was Fischer showing exaggerated patience? MacDonald studied him. He probably was. Fischer went on, "And it's one more problem the goddamn Snakes don't have to worry about and we do."

Anson MacDonald frowned, partly because of the alleged meal in front of him, partly because he saved profanity and obscenity for special occasions, and disapproved of those who didn't. He said, "You know, Captain, in a way this is a judgment on us. Worse than we deserved, maybe, but a judgment all the same."

Fischer frowned. "I'm not sure I follow that, sir," he said stiffly.

"By which you mean you think I ought to go soak my head," MacDonald said.

The younger officer chuckled. "Now that you mention it, yes, sir."

"You don't tell a man to go soak his head when you don't understand him. You ask him what he means." MacDonald forced his deep voice, raspy from too many years of too many cigarettes, up the scale to imitate Fischer's: " 'What *do* you mean, sir?' "

Fischer snorted, then tried to pretend he hadn't. "Go on ahead without me. You seem to be doing that anyhow."

"It's not hard, Captain." MacDonald went over to a tap to pour hot water on the instant coffee from the MFR. It was lousy, but better than no coffee at all. "We were soft, and we've paid the price for being soft. Draka Citizens are A-Number-One bastards, but they've always known what's on the line for them. If they ever let up, even for a second, they were doomed. They had responsibility and discipline forced on them. We didn't. And so . . . we're in the Redoubt, and they're out there."

That got under Captain Fischer's skin. MacDonald had thought it would—he'd hoped it would, anyhow. Voice wooden with disapproval, Fischer said, "I don't think it's anywhere near so simple as that, sir."

"Probably not," Commodore MacDonald said cheerfully. "But are you going to tell me it's not one of the reasons they won and we lost?"

Fischer's lips skinned back from his teeth in what was anything but a grin. He hid from the Draka down here in the Redoubt, but he hesitated to admit the USA and the Alliance for Democracy had failed all over the Earth, all over the Solar System. He said,

"We did the best we could, sir. We hurt the Snakes bad, and we're going to hurt 'em worse."

"And can you imagine anything more useless and more expensive than the second best military in the world?" Anson MacDonald asked. Fischer turned a dull red. MacDonald jabbed a thumb at his own chest. "That includes me just as much as it does you, son. Remember Lenin saying that the capitalists would sell him the rope he'd use to hang them?"

"I've heard of Lenin," Fischer said, at which MacDonald rolled his eyes. But it had been a crowded century, and Lenin and Communism both lay on the ash-heap of history long before the younger officer came on the scene. As if to point that out, Fischer went on, "Anyway, it was the Draka who hanged the Russians."

"That's true, but the principle still holds," MacDonald said. "Right up till the end, we kept dealing with the enemy, selling him things he couldn't make for himself, treating him as if he were just another neighbor. You don't trade steaks to the lion next door; it just makes him hungry."

"Nobody wanted this war," Fischer said. "You don't win a chess game by kicking over the board."

"You do if you see the other fellow's about to promote a pawn," MacDonald said. "Nobody *here* wanted this war. The Draka? That's liable to be another story. We might have beaten then economically. Some of our most effective propaganda went into letting their serfs know what we had and they didn't and couldn't. So they kicked over the board— and we helped. By rights, they should have been stretched too thin to charge full speed ahead into electronics and space engineering and genetic engineering all at the same time. But we sold them half of what they needed. Even after they gobbled up India, we kept on selling to them. I can't think of anything in the universe that will kill you deader faster than stupidity."

"You . . . have strong views on these things," Fischer said after a brief pause for thought.

"So I do, and much good it's done me," Commodore MacDonald replied with lighthearted bitterness. "People kept telling me I'd have two stars, maybe three, by now if I could learn to keep my mouth shut. They were probably right, but . . ." He shrugged. "I've always been a loose cannon."

Captain Fischer's eyes said something like, *I never would have guessed*. But all he said aloud was, "Well, they're not going to court-martial you for it now."

"No, indeed." MacDonald laughed. "They can't even discharge me. They're stuck with me, is what they are."

By Fischer's expression, he felt stuck with Commodore MacDonald, too. Again, though, he kept his speech circumspect—more circumspect than MacDonald thought he would have been able to manage himself: "Yes, sir." Hard to go wrong with that.

"And speaking of which," MacDonald persisted, "as things stand right now, I'm just eating up food—to use the term loosely—that would do better going to a genuine fighting man. We can't really afford to keep noncombatants down here. When do I get my rifle and my Snake-hunting license?"

"You're, ah, not so young as you might be, sir," Fischer said.

"I know that. I get reminded every time I look in the mirror," MacDonald said. "One good reason for not looking in the mirror very often." That jerked a chuckle from Captain Fischer, even if it was the heartless chuckle of a man who didn't yet have to worry about such things—and who wasn't likely to get that old, anyhow. MacDonald pressed on: "I'm not asking to be a brigadier up there. But I know how to shoot. I've got marksman's medals on my record, even if they are from Annapolis and not West Point."

"There is one thing you have to take care of first, you know," Captain Fischer told him. "You have to go to the dentist."

Anson MacDonald winced. Somehow, going up against the Draka was easier to contemplate in cold blood. But, after a moment, he nodded. "The sacrifices I make for my country," he said. Fischer laughed again, though MacDonald hadn't altogether been joking. And the United States was already a sacrificial victim. That being so, how could he begrudge one more sacrifice? He couldn't, and he knew it.

"Idiots. Fools. Morons. Bureaucrats." Merarch Piet van Damm glowered at the orders the fax had just delivered. "But I repeat myself."

Moirarch Benedict Arnold nodded. "If they were going to send us into the mountains after those holdouts, why did they wait till springtime? Why didn't they do it three months ago?"

" 'More urgently prioritized tasks elsewhere,' " van Damm read, as if the words were scatological rather than insipid. He came to stiff attention. "*Ave, Imperator! Nos morituri te salutamus!*"

"Maybe it won't be as bad as that," Arnold said.

"You're right. Maybe it'll be worse. Matter of fact, you can bet your balls it'll be worse." Van Damm pointed west, toward the Great Smokies. "Pretty, aren't they—all nice and green?"

"Yes, sir," Moirarch Arnold agreed. "No country like that back in Africa. Hardly any like it anywhere in the Domination. I suppose the Urals come closest, but they aren't really what you'd call a good match, either."

His superior suggested that the powers that be use one of the Urals—or perhaps the whole range; van Damm was more irate than precise—as a suppository.

Before Benedict Arnold could do anything more than begin to contemplate that, van Damm went on, "Do you know what all that bloody green means?"

"Spring," Arnold said. "Some of the oddest birds you've ever seen, too," he added, for he was an enthusiastic amateur ornithologist. "I saw my first hummingbird the other day. Astonishing creatures— it's as if vertebrates were evolving to compete with bees and butterflies."

"Hummingbirds!" Piet van Damm clapped a hand to his forehead. "We're all going to get our nuts shot off, and the man's babbling about hummingbirds. Thor's hammer!—and don't I wish I could drop it on those mountains? What the green means is, all the trees and bushes in Wotan only knows how many square klicks are in new leaf. And do you know what *that* means, or are your brains still flitting like those hummingbirds?"

"No, sir." Moirarch Arnold, like any Citizen officer, quickly returned to the business at hand. "It means our airborne infrared and satellite reconnaissance views aren't going to be worth much."

"Give the man a cigar!" van Damm said sourly. "That's just what it means, and they want to commit more Citizen troops along with the Janissaries: have to set the proper example, you know."

"Oh, yes." Benedict Arnold nodded. Of necessity, the Domination fielded far more slave troops than Citizen formations. Never letting the Janissaries believe even for a moment that the tail might wag the dog was a cornerstone of Draka administration. Suppressing mutinies was feasible, but expensive. Making sure they didn't happen in the first place sometimes cost Citizen lives, but paid dividends in the long run.

"We *will* have some ghouloons," van Damm said, brightening for the first time. "They'll help in the tracking—but not enough, dammit, not enough."

"When do we go in?" Moirarch Arnold asked.

"Orders are to commence the operation at 0600 hours tomorrow and to continue until there are no more Yankee holdouts in the area," his superior answered. "We're allotted three weeks to root 'em all out."

"Three . . . weeks?" Arnold burst out laughing: it was either that or burst into tears, and he hadn't cried since he was a little boy. "What's the High Command been smoking? Whatever it is, I want some, too."

"Oh, yeah." Piet van Damm nodded. "But we've got our orders. And ours is but to do—or die." He turned soldierly again. "I'll see you at 0600. Let the games begin. Service to the State!"

"Glory to the Race!" Benedict Arnold finished the formula. Moirarch and merarch exchanged somber salutes.

Commodore Anson MacDonald didn't like the feel of the automatic rifle he held. He hadn't been lying about his marksman's medals. But he'd won them a long time ago, at a Naval Academy far, far away. Since then, he hadn't worried much about firearms light enough for one man to carry. The Navy was the gentlemanly service, the one that did its killing at ranges too far for the human eye to note the details of what it had done. Close-in fighting, the sort that involved assault rifles and entrenching tools with sharpened blades? That was why God made marines.

He hefted the Colt-Enfield again. It wasn't the weapon with which he'd trained, either. No long wooden stock here. No elegance. No beauty. No class. Just steel and plastic, as functional as a hacksaw and about as lovely. He shrugged. As a tool for killing people, it was first-rate.

Captain Fischer watched him with some amusement. "Well, sir, you wanted the chance. Now you've got it. The Snakes are coming in—and they're loaded for bear."

"Good!" MacDonald's doubts about the weapon he held vanished, swept away in a hot wind of fury and blood lust. "Now we make them pay."

"We've already started." Fischer's grin had a certain blithe ferocity to it, too. "You know about their ghouloons?"

"Oh, yes. Horrible things. A bad sign, too. If it hadn't been for their biotech, we *would* have licked them. Damned time-bomb virus." How were you supposed to fight a war while half your key personnel were having psychotic breakdowns?

"Dangerous things, too," Fischer said. "They started sending 'em into the woods to sniff out our doorways." The grin got wider. "But they missed a trick—no such thing as a gas mask for a ghouloon."

"That *is* a missed trick," agreed MacDonald, an avid, and highly skilled, bridge player. "Back in the Great War, they had masks for horses and even for runner dogs. I've seen the old photos. Well, too bad for the Snakes." He paused. "I presume they can't use the gas to find any of our tunnel entrances."

"Oh, no, sir." Fischer still wore that grin. "Canisters, carefully set out while none of our little friends was looking. Some of them are close to the cave mouths, some a long ways off: the Draka won't be able to draw any conclusions by where we turned the gas loose and where we didn't."

"Sounds like good tactics." Commodore MacDonald set a pot helmet on his head. It was of some fancy synthetic, lighter and stronger than steel. Unlike the steel helmets U.S. soldiers had worn in the Eurasian War, this one offered proper protection for the back of the neck, as Draka headgear always had. As a result, the soldiers universally called it a Snake hat. They sneered at it, but they wore it.

"You ready, sir?" Captain Fischer asked.

"Ready as I'll ever be," Anson MacDonald answered. His heart thuttered—part eagerness, part buck fever. The stars he wore for rank badges were a joke. He was just an overage grunt, ready to do or die—ready, in the end, to do *and* die—for the United States and against the nastiest tyranny the world had ever seen.

As he followed Fischer through winding corridors toward a cave mouth, he pondered the strangeness of the Draka. A lot of the Snakes he'd met had been perfectly charming, but they all kept that slight . . . carnivorous undertone, as if descended from hunting dogs rather than social apes.

Or maybe *tribal* was a better word for the undertone. As technology advanced, so had the recognition of who counted as a fellow human being. After a while, it wasn't just your family or your clan or your tribe or the folk who spoke your language or looked like you. For most people, *human* came to mean *walking on two legs and speaking any language at all*. Not among the Snakes, though. To them, anybody not Draka counted as fair game.

And now the whole world was their oyster.

Well, here's to grit, MacDonald thought. Along with Captain Fischer and six or eight other men half his age or less, he came out of the Redoubt and into a natural cave. When Fischer closed the door behind them, it seemed to disappear.

Inside the cave, it was as cool and damp as it had been back in the fall. Once MacDonald and his comrades left that cave and came out into the real world, though, he knew the season had changed. Even under the trees, it was warm and humid. And it would get worse when summer replaced spring. *Of course, by then there may be no trees left standing*, he thought.

Just pushing through the underbrush took work. It also made a frightening amount of noise. "Take it

slow and easy," Captain Fischer called from somewhere ahead—he'd vanished into the thick greenery.
"No Snakes anywhere close. We've got plenty of time
to get where we're going and set the ambush."

"Right, Captain." That wasn't Anson MacDonald.
It was one of the youngsters moving along with him.
His voice also came from in front of MacDonald, who
fought down worry. *Can I keep up? Can I nail some
of those bastards? Can I get some tiny bit of revenge
for my raped and murdered country?*

Sweat sprang out on his forehead. *I'm an old man.
I feel like an old man, by God, trying to get through
this brush*. He coughed. His eyes watered. He knew
it was just pollen in the air, but it made him worry
more, about his lungs this time. As a young officer
just out of Annapolis, he'd come down with TB. A
few decades earlier, before antibiotics, that would have
washed him out of the Navy. He wondered what he
would have done. Politics? He'd always had strong
views about everything. Engineering? He made a
decent engineer, but no more, and he always wanted
to be the best at whatever he did. Writing? He'd been
called on the carpet plenty of times for making his
reports and evaluations livelier than the wooden
official style. Reading that stuff bored him; writing
it bored him worse.

But, thanks to wonder drugs, it was moot. Even
though he worried about his lungs, they were as good
as any of those kids', or they would have been if he
hadn't kept on smoking in spite of everything.

Somewhere not far off, a mockingbird trilled—
except it wasn't a mockingbird. It was Captain Fischer,
whistling to let his men know they'd reached the slope
where they would meet the enemy.

MacDonald whistled back, fluttering his tongue
against the roof of his mouth. He was pretty good
at bird calls, but he didn't need to be note-perfect:
how many Draka knew what North American birds

really sounded like? You used whatever edge you could get.

He found his foxhole in the middle of a laurel thicket. Settling himself, he peered out toward a game track along which enemy soldiers were likely to come. They couldn't possibly see him, not when the undergrowth shadowed his position. His countrymen had had plenty of time to fortify these mountain valleys. They'd had to do most of it at night, of course, but they'd got it done.

He wondered how many soldiers had come up out of the Redoubt to challenge the Snakes here. He didn't know. Nobody'd told him. That made excellent military sense. If he didn't know, neither pharmaceuticals nor wires clipped to sensitive spots nor the impaling stake could rip the information out of him.

What had that Nazi general called the memoirs he'd written once he got to London? *Without Hope and Without Fear*, that was it. That was how Anson MacDonald felt now. He marveled that people had got so exercised about the Nazis and paid the Draka so little attention before the Eurasian War. Hitler's crowd talked the talk, but the Draka walked the walk.

But the Nazis did what they did to white people, to Europeans, MacDonald thought. *The Draka came down on niggers and ragheads and chinks, so it didn't seem to matter so much. One brutalized blond kid is worth a dozen with black skin and kinky hair.* That was how a lot of people had looked at it, anyhow. MacDonald didn't weep that the Nazis had gone down. But who would have thought they'd go down to something worse?

Somebody somewhere stepped on a dry twig—the oldest cliché in the book, but one of the hardest things to avoid just the same. Anson MacDonald stopped worrying about what had happened long ago and what might have been. None of that mattered any more, not compared to staying alive through the next few minutes.

An American screwing up . . . or a Snake? He had a round in the chamber of his assault rifle, and he peered along the sights down to the little stretch of path he could see. He had an earpiece to listen for Captain Fischer's orders, but Fischer was maintaining radio silence. The Draka would be listening.

And then he saw the bastards: lean, sun-browned white men in camouflage colors that didn't quite fit this forest. Ice and fire ran through him. *Not Janissaries*, he realized. *Those are Citizen troops. They've sent in the first team*. That only made him want to kill them all the more.

Gas masks gave them snouts, made them look like things rather than people. *They* are *things*, he thought as his finger tightened on the trigger. *And they'll make things out of us. But some of them will burn in hell before they do*.

He wanted to kill them all. If that meant gas, he didn't mind. If he'd had a nuclear bomb, he would have used it on Citizens—no point wasting it on Janissaries. He wondered why the Draka hadn't cratered these mountains with atomic weapons. *Their aristocrats probably want to keep them for a hunting park*, he thought. *Come on, you murdering slavemasters. I'll give you something to hunt*.

His finger twitched on the trigger again. He didn't open up. Someone else, someone who had a better notion of when the time was just right, would take care of that. But when the time came—and it could only be moments away—he would take a good many Snakes with him before he went.

Moirarch Benedict Arnold's head kept whipping back and forth, back and forth. In these woods, it didn't do him a hell of a lot of good. It wouldn't have done him much good even if he hadn't been peering out through the lenses of his gas mask. The Yankees could have stashed a couple of armored divisions within a klick of him, and he never would have known it till they started their engines.

The mask was bad enough. Full protective clothing . . . In this heat and humidity, he didn't even want to think about that. One big reason neither side used gas all that much was that the countermeasures you needed against it made any sort of fighting almost impossible.

But the Americans had been smart to take out the ghouloons that way. Right now, probably, someone was designing a mask they could wear. And somebody else was probably busy figuring out how to persuade them to wear it. In the long run, that would make them more useful to the Race. In the short run, somebody's career had probably just gone down in flames because he hadn't figured out they would need masks.

All through the woods, birds chirped and sang. Sweet sounds, but not sounds he was used to. He wouldn't have been surprised if some of those calls didn't spring from feathered throats. Easy to hide information there.

And he wouldn't have been surprised if some of those calls weren't the sound of a goose walking over his grave. The Yankees had shown they didn't want the Domination sending semianimal reconnaissance patrols into these woods. They wouldn't take kindly to soldiers marching through.

If somebody opened up on him right now, he'd dive behind . . . that rock. *Unless there's a Yankee behind it already*, he thought. The mask hid his chuckle. *If there is, I'll kill the bastard*. Hand to hand, the odds were with him; even American soldiers were soft and slow by Draka standards. But nobody dodged the bullet with his name on it.

Those folk who took their neopaganism seriously— a tiny minority, a century after the old Germanic gods

were reborn and then seen to be no real answer—
would have called him fey. He didn't look at it that
way. He wanted to live. It was just that his superiors
had set things up in such a way that his chances were
less than they would have been had those superiors
had any real idea what the devil they were doing.

No sooner had that thought crossed his mind than
small-arms fire started barking. A second later, after
two or three bullets cracked past his head, he was
behind that rock, with no company but a little liz-
ard with a blue belly that scurried off into the leaves
when he thudded down.

"Base, we are under attack!" he shouted into his
radio. "Map square Green 2. I say again, we are under
attack at Green 2. Do you copy?"

The only noise that came from the set was the one
bacon might have made frying in a pan. Benedict
Arnold cursed. The Yankees had always been too
stinking good with electronics. They were jamming
for all they were worth. No instant air support. No
friendly helicopter gunships rushing in to hose down
the enemy with Gatlings and rockets. No fighter-
bombers screaming down out of the sky to plaster the
Americans with napalm. If he and his men were going
to come out of this in one piece, they'd have to do
it themselves, for the time being, anyhow.

He squeezed off a short burst in the direction from
which the enemy fire seemed heaviest. A couple of
Citizens were down in spite of body armor, one
writhing with a leg wound, the other motionless, shot
through the head. Moirarch Arnold cursed again.
Dammit, the Race shouldn't be spending men like
this in a country it had already conquered.

One thing—everybody who heard the fighting
would move toward it. The Draka took care of their
own. They had to—nobody else would. He just hoped
the other units in these stinking woods weren't pinned
down like his men.

Well, if they had to fight the old-fashioned way for a while till they could beat the jamming, they bloody well would. "Forward by squads!" he yelled, hoping his voice would carry. "Leapfrog!"

What would the Yankees least expect? A movement straight toward them, unless he missed his guess. He didn't think so. He wanted to get at close quarters with them. At close quarters, he and his men had the edge.

He scrambled out from behind the rock and dashed toward a tree up the slope. The men from the squads not moving fired to make the enemy keep his head down. Bullets stitched the ground by his feet. Grenades burst not far away. Mortar bombs started raining down on the Draka. And one of his men stepped on a mine that tore him to red rags.

Arnold dove down behind the tree. Somewhere behind him, more Yankees opened up on his beleaguered men. He cursed every von Shrakenberg ever born. *Hunting preserve, my left ballock*, he thought. *The Americans couldn't have set a better ambush if they'd planned it for years.*

Of course, they *had* planned it for years. And now the Draka would pay the price. Arnold's grin behind the mask was savage. The Alliance for Democracy had already paid the price. In the long run, this was just small change. But a man who got killed in a fight that didn't mean much was every bit as dead as one who got killed any other way. Benedict Arnold didn't want to die. That, after all, was what enemies and serfs were for.

Ground combat was even more chaotic, even more frightening and frightful, than Anson MacDonald had thought it would be. On a ship, he was part of a smoothly functioning team. He didn't have that feeling here. On the contrary: he'd never felt more alone in his life. And every Draka in the world seemed to be trying to kill him and nobody else.

· He'd hit a couple of Snakes. He was sure of it. He wasn't sure he'd killed them. Their body armor was at least as good as his, and they could carry more than he and his countrymen did. The sons of bitches were just out-and-out strong.

They were quick, too. As Captain Fischer had predicted, the Draka came straight at the men who opened up on them. "Don't try to duke it out with a Snake," Fischer had warned. "You'll lose. We can't afford that. Shoot him or run away."

Fischer had told that to the twenty-year-olds who were supposed to be fast and strong. *What about me?* MacDonald wondered. But the answer seemed pretty obvious. *If you're dumb enough to volunteer for the Poor Bloody Infantry, you deserve whatever happens to you. And it will.*

I'm putting my body between my home and war's desolation. That sounded very fine and noble . . . till the bullets started flying. And war's desolation had already visited his home, and all the other homes in the Alliance for Democracy—and a good many homes in the Domination of the Draka, too.

So what am *I doing here?* The answer there wasn't subtle, either. No room for subtlety, not any more. *I'm going to kill a few Snakes before they kill me. All right—fair enough.*

A few tiny holes were left in the jamming that scrambled radio reception through the area above the Redoubt. "Fall back!" Captain Fischer called through the speaker in MacDonald's left ear. "They're putting a little more pressure on us than we thought they'd be able to."

That would do for an understatement till a bigger one came along. Enemy firing came from both sides of MacDonald now, not just from in front of him. In spite of everything, the Draka had got in among the Americans. Guessing what they'd do didn't necessarily mean you could stop them. Who was outflanking whom was now very much a matter of opinion. *They're good, damn them*, MacDonald thought as he scuttled back toward another foxhole. If the Snakes hadn't been so good, he would have been fighting on their home turf, not his.

His heart thudded in his chest as he scrambled through the thick undergrowth. He panted when he threw himself into the new hole in the ground and looked around for targets. *That'd be an embarrassing way to check out—dying of a coronary on the battlefield. You won't do it—you won't, you hear me?* He tried to give his body orders as if it were an able seaman. But if it decided to be insubordinate, what could he do about it? Not much.

Above the crackle and thunder of gunfire came another sound, a loud thuttering. It came literally from above: from over the forest canopy. MacDonald couldn't see the machines making the new racket, but he knew what they were. In spite of the jamming, the Draka had got helicopter gunships over the right part of the field.

They won't use them when their fellows are all mixed up with ours . . . will they? The Snakes would. They did. They seemed to take the view that getting rid of the holdouts was worth whatever it cost.

Gatlings overhead roared, a sound like giants ripping thick canvas. Snake gunners ripple-fired rocket pods under their helicopters. MacDonald had never imagined such punishment. The ground beneath him shuddered as the rockets slammed home. Blasts picked him up and flung him down. He tasted blood in his mouth. Those explosions had tried to tear his lungs right out of his body, and they'd damn near done it.

He knew he was screaming, but he couldn't hear a thing. Maybe the din all around was too loud. Maybe he was partly, or more than partly, deafened.

He felt all turned around. Where the devil was the closest cave mouth? He could use his compass to find out, he supposed, doing his best to think straight in the midst of hell. But what were the odds he'd get there? Thin. Very thin.

More rockets rained down. One of them burst close to his new hole—much too close, in fact. It picked him up and slammed him down, harder than he was designed to be slammed. He felt things snap that had no business snapping. Pain flared red, then black, as consciousness fled.

With the Yankees' damned jammers still going flat out, Benedict Arnold had no control over the air strikes flown to help the Domination's troopers. He wasn't at all sure they *were* helping; they were right on top of the Americans, sure enough, but that meant they were also right on top of his own men.

He wasn't ashamed to scream when rockets from the helicopter gunships plowed up the landscape right under his own boots. Anybody who said he'd been in combat without getting scared almost out of his sphincters was either a dangerous liar or an even more dangerous psychopath. It was necessary. That didn't make it fun, except talking about it afterwards over booze or kif.

Not far away, one of his men went down, head neatly severed by a chunk of rocket casing. Even through the gas mask, Arnold smelled blood and shit. *Friendly fire*, they called it, the lying bastards.

Another Citizen fell, this one shot in the face. The pounding hadn't settled the Yanks' hash, then. Moirarch Arnold cursed. He'd known it wouldn't, though it did help some.

And then, from a few hundred meters behind him, came a roar louder than any of the mortar rounds or rockets bursting. He cursed again: that couldn't be anything but a gunship going down in flames. Bad luck? Or did the Yankees have some of those nasty little shoulder-mounted AA missiles of theirs? He wouldn't have been a bit surprised. In their shoes, he would have made sure he stocked some.

Another gunship crashed, even more noisily than the first. "Missiles," he muttered. Even without the din all around, the mask would have muffled the word. Not all the helicopters were out of action, though. Gatling fire and rockets flagellated the forest.

Some of that came in much too close to him. He dove into the nearest hole he could find—and then started to dive right out again, because an American soldier, his camouflage uniform a medley of shades different from the Domination's, already occupied it. But the Yankee didn't go for the assault rifle by him— he was either dead or unconscious, Arnold realized. One of his legs bent at an unnatural angle.

An old man, Arnold thought. Then he saw the single stars the American wore; they were almost invisible against his uniform. Excitement coursed through him. *I've caught a big fish, if he's still breathing*.

He felt for a pulse, and felt like whooping. The Yankee had one. And he was coming to; he stirred and groaned and reached for the rifle. Benedict Arnold grabbed it before he could. And the moirarch shed his gas mask. If the American wasn't wearing one, he was damned if he would.

The Yankee's eyes came open. They held reason— reason and danger. *He might be an old man, but he's nobody to screw around with*, Arnold thought. If he looked away for even a second, this fellow would make him pay.

Well, don't look away, then. Field interrogation was an art form in its own right. He smiled. It could be fun, too. "Hello, Yank," he said.

❖   ❖   ❖

"Hello, Yank." The words told Anson MacDonald the worst. So did the greens of the other soldier's combat uniform—they were jungle greens, not those of the forest. And so did the barrel of the Holbars T-7 aimed at his head. That 4.45mm barrel looked wide as a tunnel.

MacDonald took inventory. Everything hurt—ribs and right leg worst. He could, after a fashion, bear it. If the Draka decided to give that leg a boot . . . Snakes were supposed to enjoy things like that, and they weren't exactly meeting over a tea party.

"My name is Anson MacDonald," he said. "My rank is commodore, U.S. Navy. My pay number . . ." He rattled it off. For close to forty years, it had been as much a part of him as his name.

How much good would any of this do? The Draka acknowledged the Geneva Convention only when they felt like it, and now there was nobody on the outside to pressure them to behave. The only rules left were the ones they felt like following.

For a moment, he'd succeeded in surprising this Snake. "Commodoah?" the fellow drawled. "You're a hell of a long way from the water, Navy man."

MacDonald started to shrug, then thought better of it. "I don't have to answer that," he said.

The Draka didn't reply, not in words. He just flicked out a booted foot and kicked MacDonald's right leg. MacDonald shrieked, then clamped down on it. "That there's just a taste," the Draka said mildly. "Don't waste my time, serf, not if you want to keep breathin'."

"Not likely," MacDonald said. "You'd never trust the likes of me as a serf, anyhow. You'll squeeze me and then you'll get rid of me. But I'll tell you this: when I go to hell, I'll have a couple of Draka sideboys along for escorts."

He wondered if that would get him killed in the next instant. But the Draka—a moirarch, MacDonald saw, gradually noticing finer details: *my luck to have one of their colonels get the drop on me while I was out*—just nodded. "All right, pal," he said. "We both know what's what, then. You better remember who's top and who's bottom, though."

Sex slang, MacDonald thought scornfully. But he nodded. "I'm not likely to forget."

"Right." The Draka had an easy, engaging smile. MacDonald might have liked him—had he not been one of the slaveowning sons of bitches who'd murdered the United States. "Now, Commodoah, suppose you tell me all about this holdout base of yours."

"Suppose I don't," MacDonald said.

That earned his broken leg another kick. He'd been sure it would. This time, he couldn't clamp down on his scream. Amid battlefield chaos, who noticed one more howl of anguish? Still smiling, the moirarch said, "You're hardly any sport, Yankee—too easy. But we're got all day, or as long as it takes."

Wrong, Anson MacDonald thought when he was capable of coherent thought again—which took some little while. Panting, he said, "I'll tell you something even more important first."

With a shake of the head, the Draka officer said, "No deal, pal. Tell me what I want to know."

"Afterwards."

"Who's top, Yank? You haven't got much in the way of a bargaining position."

Better than you think. MacDonald braced himself for another kick, not that bracing himself would do the slightest bit of good.

But the moirarch looked thoughtful. "Well, why not? Make it short, make it sweet—and then sing. You know how unhappy I'll be if you're lying or wasting my time. You know how unhappy you'll be, too."

"I have some idea," MacDonald said dryly. .

And that made the Snake laugh out loud. "I like

you, Yank, stick a stake up my ass if I don't. You're wasted on your side, you know that? Now sing."

"Oh, I will," MacDonald said. "How long to you think it'll take the Domination to clean things up here?"

"Fo'ty, fifty years," the Draka answered at once, and surprised MacDonald with his candor. "You Yankee bastards are a tough nut, maybe even tougher'n we reckoned. But so what? You're busted open now. We can do what we want with you—an' we will."

"No." Anson MacDonald shook his head. In spite of everything, this was what triumph felt like. "Because all the resources you spend here aren't going after what really matters."

"Nothin' really matters, not any more. This is mop-up time," the Draka moirarch said. "The Earth is ours. The Solar System is ours."

Baring his teeth in a fierce grin, MacDonald said, "And the *New America* is *ours*, by God." Those two words, *New America*, had kept him going after disaster engulfed the USA, engulfed the Alliance. "Alpha Centauri will be a going concern long before you Snake bastards can even start to try snuffing it out. *It's not over*, damn you. It's only starting. And I live for that, and so does everybody else in the Redoubt."

The Draka leaned forward. "The Redoubt, eh? So that's what you call it? Now you've made your speech, and you're going to tell me *all* about it . . . one way or another." Anticipation filled his voice.

MacDonald's smile got wider. "Goodbye," he said, and bit down hard. The false tooth the dentist had implanted cracked. The taste of bitter almonds filled his mouth, overwhelmingly strong, burning, burning— but not for long. The poison worked almost as fast as they'd promised. He nodded once before every-thing faded. He'd even got the last word.

Anne Marie Talbott lives in central Tennessee, has a master of arts in clinical psychology as well as an MBA; she also has an impish sense of humor, and several cats. I knew when I saw their pictures that this must be a writer. This story confirmed my intuition. It's her first professional sale, but not, I think, her last.

Many totalitarian movements of our century have used a "superman" ideology to inspire their followers. As a German joke used to go, the true Aryan superman would be as blond as Hitler, as tall as Goebbels, and as slim as Göring . . .

But past totalitarians didn't have genetic engineering. The Draka, eventually, do, and they literalize the metaphor of racial superiority. In doing so they lock themselves biologically into their self-chosen cultural role of predators-on-humans.

In *Drakon*, I imagined one of these engineered superbeings, designed to conquer and to personally dominate humans—through everything from strength to pheromones—loose in our world. Or at least something very like our timeline; one without an S.M. Stirling, who imagined the Draka.

Of course, once you've allowed travel from timeline to timeline, an interesting question arise: What if the travellers from the alternate history stumble across the reality of the writer who "sensed" them?

A WALK IN
THE PARK

Anne Marie Talbott

I amble along the riverwalk, binoculars ready for
any bird that'll sit still long enough for me to get a
bead on it. It's a bright, sunny day in early summer;
the humidity hasn't reached mythical proportions yet,
so it's not quite like being in a Tennessee Williams'
play. There are various couples, the ever-present roller
bladers, and some children bounding about. The
familiar smell of the river—slightly fishy, but not bad;
the scent of wildflowers threatens to overwhelm me.
The daffodils and other late spring, early summer
show-offs dance in the gentle breeze. It feels good:
I'm wearing new shorts and a rugby shirt, and my
favorite running shoes. I feel loose and relaxed; it's

a feeling I enjoy thoroughly as I proceed down the park path.

As I walk past one viewing area, I notice people turning to look at a couple who are resting against the railing. I look, too, and am stunned by their beauty. It's hard edged, athletic, and somehow fierce looking. Both the man and the woman are *something* to look at, and I immediately understand why people are making an effort not to stare. I'm doing the same thing. A small group is milling nearby, uncertain of their destination, but wanting somehow to be near these unusual folks. I feel drawn to them myself and wonder why. That puts me on the defensive; old habits die hard . . .

Finding a good spot to perch, I climb up onto a large limestone boulder on the side of the path, about twenty-five yards from the couple and the small crowd. I scan the trees listlessly now for birds, when what I really want to do is point the glasses at the couple and stare. I manage a few looks across them, and notice that they seem amused at something. The man, tall, lithe and muscular in slacks and a cotton short sleeved black shirt, deeply tanned, with bright red hair, leans over to his female companion and whispers briefly. She laughs, a husky sound that carries across the distance easily. It makes me shiver.

I notice that she's as tall and muscular as he is, and has dark mahogany red hair. It's cut short on the sides and top but has a long braid in the back; she's wearing khaki shorts and a white shirt that shimmers like silk from this distance. The crowd of people, not really formed enough to be called that—more of a collection of people who have been captivated by the couple's indefinable presence—hangs around, quietly. Children who've been wildly running down the paved pathways are entranced, apparently, by the two people. The kids become quiet, meek; they yell less than they had been.

Interesting, I think. *They look like people I've seen somewhere before, but I can't place them. Are they famous or something? They certainly have a* charismatic *effect on folks, that's for sure. And that's odd, too. I wonder how* . . . The peeping of a family of cardinals distracts me; I find the nest and watch the parent birds interacting for a moment or two. With my peripheral vision, I notice that the crowd is suddenly thinning out. People're taking their children and walking away, rather rapidly. That jerks my attention back to the couple by the cedar railing. They're not lounging anymore; standing more erect, they watch the people leave with a glint, seemingly, in their eyes. Of what, I'm uncertain, until I hear the man speak.

"Glad to cleyah them out afta 'while, Gwen! Didn' realize they'd be so easy . . ." His accent is deep South, with a hint of something . . . maybe a Germanic overlay. I've never heard anything like it in my entire life. His voice itself is as beautiful as he is handsome. *Maybe he's a singer or something,* I wonder to myself. *He's sure not from around here* . . .

"Yaz, they're quite . . . susceptible . . . to the pheromones, Dietrich," the woman answers, and leans back against the railing, chuckling. "Very susceptible, indeed. It can be amusing."

What? I say to myself. *What in the—*

The woman's head swivels toward me, and she fixes me with a level, green-eyed stare. *Hel-lo,* I wonder, *did I say that out loud? Who are these people?* She grins, then, showing even white teeth in a deeply tanned face. I feel like an antelope being stared at by a lioness, and it *doesn't* feel good. I decide that perhaps it's time to look for birds *elsewhere.* Climbing quickly down from the boulder, I walk farther down the trail. From the crowded condition it was in, it's now eerily empty, which doesn't reassure me any. I feel—what *do* I feel? A sense of growing concern; a muted fear begins to grow in my chest.

The pace I set is fairly rapid, but not a scurry or a jog. I look back, a quick glance over one shoulder, and see the couple is following me.

Oh, great, wonderful. The woman says something quietly to the man. They split, each taking a side of the walkway.

Where . . . where have I seen or heard of . . . no. The idea hits me like a cold rag in the face; *am I really going nuts? I must be—they can't be what I think they are. What I think they are doesn't really* exist.

A tiny, chill voice in the back of my mind asks, "Don't they, now?" *Hell,* I think, *one too many term papers to grade for this professor. I must be ready for a sabbatical. Maybe they're not really following me.*

To prove this to myself, I take the next turn-off in the trail, up to the Civil War memorial. *Surely they won't follow me here. They'll just go on down the trail, and jump in their car, and drive happily away . . . damn. They've turned in, too.* Now *what?*

My heart is beginning to race, and my palms are wet. *Haven't felt like this since rappelling.* Time seems to slow, become gelid, and things take on an unnatural brilliance and clarity. My stomach feels like a bucket of ice cubes has been dumped into it, and the chill spreads throughout my body. In a primal reaction to fear, my hair begins to bristle and stand up; I'm sure my heart is going to jump out of my rib cage at any moment. The binoculars seem to weigh more and more, and I wish I hadn't brought them. I hear a soft chuckle behind me, and a hand touches my shoulder. Startled, and really frightened now, I leap into the air a couple of feet, and turn. Or try to. The hand, hard as steel, holds me facing away from the person.

The logical, mild-mannered part of my brain is starting to become overwhelmed, and the more basic fight or flight reflexes are howling to take over. *Come on*, I say severely to myself, *there's no such thing as Draka. God! They're just characters . . . not real. Get over it, and tell whoever's holding your shoulder to let the hell go!*

I open my mouth to say just that, and nothing comes out. I'm spun around faster than I could possibly move myself, and find myself facing the redheaded woman. I look up into her aquiline, tanned face, and can't read what's in her eyes.

"Did she jus' subvocalize what I *think* . . ." says the red-haired man, coming up to us.

"Yaz, she most *certainly* did. An' I wondah *how* she knows . . ."replies the woman, and then says something in a language I don't understand.

Subvocalize . . . how could they possibly *have heard . . . they can't be . . .* yammers the logical portion of my mind, to a growing rush of fear hysteria. *Run, run, run,* says the rest of my mind, and I try to pull away. I might as well have tried to pull my shoulder out of a hydraulic press for all the good it does me.

"Hey, now, come on, lady—let me go! Please!" I manage to stutter. Her leaf-green eyes return to me, and I feel a sensation like heat flitting across my face. I blush, then blanch, as her grip tightens slightly.

"No, little 'un, you're not goin' anywhere raight now. Not until I know how and why you think we are *Draka*. That's not what I'd call *public knowledge* . . ."

The man's taken position behind me, and I desperately want to be able to see both of them, know what they're doing. I try once again to twist out of the woman's steel grip, and she shakes me. Just once, but enough to snap my teeth together and lift my feet off the ground.

"Answer me, wench. *How* do you know about the *Draka*?"

The man asks something in the guttural, slurred speech they've been using to each other, gesturing at me, then the river. She shakes her head, no.

"Not unless we *have* to, Dietrich. It could be messy—too many ferals about," she answers.

Ferals? my mind gibbers.

With her other hand, she cups my chin, raising my face to meet her eyes. Level, I come up to the middle of her upper arm; now with my head held in an immobilizing grip, I'm forced to maintain eye contact with her.

"One last time, while I'm *not* annoyed, girl. How do you know about the *Draka*?" Her tone of voice is hardening, as is her grip. She's incredibly strong, and I'm reminded of the strength mental patients often display when going berserk.

Oh, shit, I wonder, *what have I gotten myself into?*

"Ma'am, I . . . I . . . don't know—what do you mean—please, stop, that hurts. I don't know!" I burst out, fighting back the tears now, tears of fear and anger and pain.

"*No one* knows we're here, and you just *randomly* come up with the name *Draka* for us? I *don't* think so. Dietrich, let's take her to the car. This calls for further investigation, an' I don' want ferals comin' up on us while we do it."

She releases my chin, and looks over my head at the man. He says something in their language, a joke perhaps, and she laughs. The laugh itself is like a peal of a bronze bell; I could listen to that for days. But the fear and the weirdness of the situation overwhelm me, and all I can think about is getting away.

Once again, I try to break away from the grip holding me immobile, twisting and turning my shoulder to get loose. I plant my feet and yank backwards as hard as I can, and nothing happens. I'm not a waif; years of military and Tae Kwon Do training have left me fairly stocky and muscular. But trying to get away from this woman is obviously going to be difficult ... if possible, even ...

She snarls, slightly. The sound stops me dead in my tracks, and I look up at her, wide-eyed. I've *never* heard a human make a noise like that, not even in jest or while imitating a wild animal. Her wide eyes slash down into mine, and I can taste the harsh metallic taste of fear in my mouth. Still holding on to my shoulder with only one hand, she *slowly* lifts me off my feet.

"I can snap yoh neck and toss you in this river faster than shit, girl. Don't *annoy* me, if you want to survive. *Understan'?*" At the last word, she shakes me. I'm a couple of feet off the ground, and feel like a rag doll being shaken by an angry child. I nod, wordless.

At that, she drops me to the ground again. "Walk with us, an' don' try to do anythin' silly. Come on," she says, and I nod again.

Numbness is spreading though me; I feel trapped. Dietrich gives me a slight push, and the woman— *he calls her Gwen*, I remember—maintains her hold on my shoulder.

Dietrich takes the binoculars from my other hand, where they've hung, unnoticed, for the past few minutes. "Interestin'," he comments, looking first at them and then through them. "Archaic." His cool blue glance takes me in, and I feel an unaccustomed sense of being "sized up". Been a long time since some-one stared that way at me.

Gwen chuckles, softly, and runs her free hand through my hair. Been a long time since someone did that, too, and a damn long time since my knees felt this weak. I stumble as I walk between them, and glance up at Gwen's face. She looks down, an apprais-ing, evaluating look, and loosens her hand on my shoulder just a bit.

We walk down the trail, three abreast, until we

reach the next turn-off for parking. Dietrich walks ahead of us, now, after briefly saying something to Gwen in their language.

"Hey, ma'am, *really*, I mean, I was just *joking*, I mean, you remind me of characters I read about, a long time ago . . . it was just science fiction. I . . . I don't know *anything* you need to know—*please*, just let me go. Okay?" I plead, as he walks away from us.

Gwen shakes her head no and propels me up the incline to the parking lot. I know if I don't get away soon, I won't be getting away *at all*. I steel myself, hating to hurt her, but the fear that's taken up residence in my gut won't let me just "do nothing." *I'm a survivor, damn it*, I say to myself, and launch myself at her.

It may have taken her by surprise, briefly—a nanosecond or so—but after that, the fight is rather one-sided. My front kicks, side kicks, and fists just don't hit much, and what they do hit feels like steel. I begin to scream, opening my mouth only to end up gasping silently for breath as her fist sinks deep into my midsection. *Can't breathe, can't breathe* blasts through my mind, and I crouch, fighting for air. She sees some people coming down the slope toward us, their eyes alive with concern.

"Don't worry, folks, it's all right; she's just having a seizure. I can take care of everything, and the car's right up here. Thanks, thanks . . ." she says, brightly, a woman obviously in charge of an unfortunate situation. Her accent, deep Southern, aristocratic sounding, is flawless now. She picks me up in her arms, which feel like steel cables wrapped around me, and I'm held, immobile, gasping for breath.

She easily carries me up the hill, and the car's waiting, Dietrich at a side door. I notice a man in the front, a driver, as she slides me into the back seat.

"Oh, thank you—everything will be fine, I think,"

says Dietrich, to a man who's come up to see what's wrong. Gwen climbs in beside me, pushing me against the car's side.

"Not a word, wench, if you value your life—*silly girl*," she whispers, and then, in the bright, in-charge voice assures the concerned man. "Just a mild seizure—she's had them all her life. She'll be just fine. We'll get her home and put her to bed for a bit, I think. Thank you for your concern."

Dietrich climbs in next to her, and the car moves smoothly through the normal Saturday traffic, heading for the interstate. I'm trapped. *Oh, my God, I'm trapped* . . .

"May as well have some *fun* before we get to the House, eh, Dietrich?" Gwen murmurs, as she slides her hands down my chest, caressing, tugging off my rugby shirt . . .

He laughs, and says, "You can go first; I don't mind." Gwen's eyes seem to fill mine. My shorts rip like tissue paper under her hands. *Oh my God!* The last conscious thought running through my mind: *Draka? They can't be! Draka? They're not re—*

Markus Baur lives in Vienna, and works in the high-tech sector.

Herein is a tale of how high technology meets biotechnology, and leads to a case of curiosity endangering the observer.

HUNTING
THE SNARK

Markus Baur

Telephone conversation, 14.06.98 . . .

"Hello? . . . This is Mag. Kurt Gersen, I am with the Vienna Technical University—am I speaking to Mr. Prohaska?"

"Hello, Mr. Prohaska . . . did you receive my letter from last week? Yes . . . we are the Institute for Graphical Data Applications . . . what do we want? Well, we have designed a system for recognition and identification of humans that works off regular video cameras . . . and we would like to test it under proper field conditions in your mall. . . .

"It uses a neuronal network to recognize people . . . the

important thing is that it works also with bad quality video . . . and can recognize people even from behind and with only parts of them showing. . . .

"Yes—it obviously has security applications . . . later it could be used to allow access for cleared personnel or search for customers who are no longer welcome . . . what you would get out of it right now besides supporting us? . . .

"Well, we could give you visitor statistics . . . how many visitors . . . how many repeat visitors . . . how many men and women . . . that kind of thing . . . and we could arrange some kind of news release together . . . .

"Technically yes—but I do not think we would be allowed to do that at this point . . . the data abuse protection laws—you know . . . yes, we will have to follow those regulations properly. . . .

"Yes . . . we can come over to your place for a demonstration . . . this Friday would be okay with you? . . . Good—I will be there . . .

"Oh. Nothing much, Mr. Prohaska. Only electric power and access to your security video system . . . it is not very large . . . about a meter on every side and two meters high . . . well, it is still a prototype. . . .

"Thank you very much, Mr. Prohaska . . . I really appreciate your help and I thank you on behalf of the university. . . ."

```
subject: Houston, we have a
problem...
date: Mon., 27 Jul 1998 14:32:00
+0000
from: Franz Hinterreitner
<i989747@igdv.tuwien.ac.at>
to: kurt.gersen@igdv.tuwien.ac.at

Kurt-our system is acting
```

up. . . . it has troubles rec-
ognizing a man . . .

Even worse—it simply refuses to
recognize him as a human being.
I thought we were over that particular problem a year ago . . . and
this is the first time this happened (or did it happen to you .
too?)

Anyway . . . I pulled the video
tape and the system log for this
and will bring it to the lab
tomorrow—we should go over it
soonest. Please make time in your
schedule . . . this is important

Prohaska is making noises on
how much he likes the system and
how soon we could activate the
individual recognition part of the
system—I believe they have some
troubles with organized pickpock-
ets or shoplifters.

cu tomorrow . . .

fraaaaaanz

**Vienna Technical University,
institute for graphical data applications,
computerlab, 28.07.98:**

The lab has the usual heaps of hardware consist-
ing of repairs that have been waiting for days and
weeks and some prototypes in the process of being
rebuilt—again. The only tables not being cluttered
with parts, bits and pieces are those of the "pure"
programmers . . . they have stacks of printouts and
references perching on them instead.

The attention of the people present is focused on a large screen, showing a part of the shopping mall. The network marks every human it finds and recognizes with a bright outline, with a number hovering over each person.

"Kurt, did you turn those numbers off in the version that is running in the mall?"

"Oh yes . . . ," I answered, "Mr. Prohaska's interest in those features seemed to be very strong on our last meeting . . . it took a lot for him not to drool . . ."

"Okay . . . so far it is working well . . . it finds those people sitting down at the bar and on the benches . . . even those hiding behind the shrubbery," Franz points on the screen, " . . . and we had those cartoon costumes last week . . . it even managed to recognize some of those as human . . . Where is the problem?"

"Just wait a little . . . any second now," I sigh. "Here it is."

An apparently middle aged man appears on the screen—very good looking, athletic, above average height . . . walks gracefully through the field of view of the camera . . . his face well visible . . . but he does not receive one of those bright outlines, nor an identification number.

"I don't believe it . . . we had that running for almost a year . . . better than 99.999% reliability . . . hmm . . . let's try something—reduce the size of the picture and select only a few seconds . . . so that he is the only person on that video. Then we'll run it through again and look closely at the reaction of the network."

Franz and I start to work on the video. . . . Cutting and editing . . . half an hour later we have 6.3 seconds, showing only the mysterious stranger. . . . Franz unfolds his gangly frame and moves over to another workstation, where he plans to look at the internal reactions of the neuronal network in detail. . . . "Okay. I am ready—run it again."

Again the stranger walks over the screen, moving as if the whole mall belongs to him. Again the computer refuses to recognize him . . . .

"That's weird . . . ."

"What do the diagnostics say, Franz? . . . Not that we really will find out a lot—we still do not really know how the network trained itself to recognize humans.

Keyboard clicks . . . humming a mindless melody . . .

"Weeeeell . . . it finds a moving object . . . tags it as living . . . and then rejects it as human . . . basically it insists that that guy is a dog or another animal . . . not a human . . . that's really crazy!"

"What do you think, Franz—should we unfreeze the network and start another training cycle?"

"You know what happened the last time we tried that . . . reliability went down instead of up . . . I don't think that would be a smart idea."

"Yes—I believe so too . . . I think I will baby-sit it for a few days—just in case this happens again . . . can you give me that keycard for the mall? And we will have to insert some sort of warning that will go off when the system refuses to recognize a human, too."

"Karl . . . that will go off at every dog passing a camera!"

SCS mall, security office, 30.07.98:

A darkened square room, a little over ten meters on each side . . . one wall is covered with video monitors and recorders, showing scenes from the mall and the parking lot . . . the other one shines with readouts for fire alarms, power supplies, lift and

escalator status—the works. A console with lots of
buttons and phones faces the corner where those two
walls meet. Perhaps the architect was unconsciously
trying for a minuteman-launch bunker look . . . only
the guy sitting at the console does not look like a
steely eyed missile man.

The cabinet housing our system has been shoved
into the rear corner, a small table and a chair beside
it . . . cables snake over the ground to the monitor
wall . . .

"Ding, ding, ding . . ." the alert goes off in my head-
set. I mark the spot I am just reading with my finger
and look up at the monitor . . . another dog—a German shepherd this time. God, is this boring . . . but at
least I am catching up on my reading.

Conversation with the security guards has been
quickly exhausted—even more quickly than the norm
as they secretly fear that our computer might take
their jobs one day . . . which is patently untrue, as it
hardly can trundle out there and apprehend a pick-
pocket!

"Ding, ding, ding . . ." I look up—and put my book
away. This is what I have been waiting for the last
two days.

Crossing the main plaza of the mall is the stranger—
only this time our mysterious stranger is not alone. It's
him, all right—accompanied by three women. Two of
them have the bright outline and a number—the computer identifies them properly as humans. They both
look good and seem to talk to each other as they trail
the stranger and the third woman.

The third woman . . . has no outline, just like the
stranger. And she is a stunning beauty—as large as he
is, towering over the heads of the two other girls and
eclipsing them. Long red hair, very nice and muscular
figure, movements like a professional dancer . . . Actually
they both look similar to each other—brother and sister
perhaps?

They approach the bar area . . . and sit down at a table that has just been vacated. One of the other girls goes to get some drinks. I make sure that our computer is running well and that the video records this scene.

Vienna Technical University,
institute for graphical data applications,
computerlab, 30.07.98:

"Franz . . . it happened again . . . I have some nice video!"

"Really? While you were away lounging in front of the monitor and reading the newspaper, esteemed colleague, I have been doing some thinking on our problem. The network is so good, that this should not have happened at all—the chances for it are very low. Was it the same guy again?"

"Yes and no. It was him—but he was accompanied by a woman who also was not identified."

Franz raises his eyebrows at this information and comments dryly " . . . and hereby the chances go from low to ridiculously low!"

"Yes—I see what you mean. If it had been only one person . . . we could chalk it up as a singular bug—perhaps in his facial features or something. But with two different people—there has to be something fundamentally wrong . . . and we better find out what it is if we ever want to sell this thing."

Franz reaches out with his hand: "Please put the cassette in the recorder . . . let's see what we have."

We run the video over and over again . . . analyzing the reactions of the neuronal network to death and gaining nothing for our toils. At 2300 we give up in disgust; I take some printouts and a copy of the tape home with me.

❖   ❖   ❖

*The Gersen "residence," Vienna, 12th district,
31.07.98*

It is past one o'clock in the morning and I am
unable to sleep. I sit in my bed, the tape in the VCR,
running it over and over again . . . undistracted from
printouts and system status displays I start to notice
things.

How gorgeous both our strangers look . . . and how
similar. Both would have no real trouble getting a job
as a model—their muscles and the graceful way they
move would not be a hindrance either.

Other things are strange too—both move as if they
own the mall, like royalty, completely self-assured.
They never have to step out of the way of somebody,
instead they part the crowd like Moses the Red Sea—
people give them an awful lot of breathing space. And
that empty table at the bar they miraculously got
during rush hour—the previous customers left it as
if they got shooed away, but the strangers never said
a word to them.

The two girls in the group walk a few steps behind
the couple and carry some parcels—the strangers
carry none. Their attention is completely focused on
the pair and whenever one of the strangers looks at
or talks to them, they answer with a very bright
smile . . . like lovers. They pull out the chairs for the
couple; as one of the girls leaves the table to get some
drinks, she bobs her head—like a perfect waiter in
a really good restaurant acknowledging his customer's
orders.

One could think they would be personal attendants
or servants if they did not act like they were in love
half the time; the couple seems to expect this—at
least they do not look embarrassed when the girls do
things for them.

The whole group does not act as you would expect
it from some random shoppers in a mall. Perhaps I

am just overanalyzing a few minutes of video, reading too much into it, or it is one more statistical point to add to this weirdness—I simply do not know! Falling asleep finally, I dream weird dreams of a tall, muscular, beautiful woman with red hair who stalks me through the mall.

SCS mall, main plaza & security office, 31.08.98

I have just finished my dinner and return to the security office . . . walking through the mall and gazing into shop windows—passing over the main plaza to enter one of the service corridors.

On the other side of the main plaza a small group just leaves one of the tables by the bar and moves toward one of the exits of the mall. I know those people well—I have watched that video at least a hundred times!

I try to follow them, threading through the shoppers, and pass by the bar. On the table they just vacated I see a tray with four glasses. A sudden impulse makes me grab the tray and I carry it through the door to the service corridor, abandoning my pursuit . . .

The barkeeper yells after me, asking what I am doing with those glasses . . . I just flash the mall security keycard, which seems to shut him up. Standing in the corridor, tray in hand, I have the sudden crazy urge to ask loudly: "Where can I find the next cocktail party?" What shall I do now with these glasses?

Placing the tray on a stack of boxes I hurry out again and beg a few plastic packing bags from one of the stores. Using one bag as an improvised glove I place each glass in an individual bag and tie it closed. Carrying my treasures I enter the security office and start to look for the monitor that shows the parking lot in front of entrance 4.

"Can I rewind that tape a few minutes . . . or put a new one in?"

The guard only nods, sighs and reaches down to an open drawer, handing me a new cassette.

The Gersen "residence," Vienna, 12th district, telephone conversation, 31.07.98:

"Is this the Institute for Molecular Pathology . . . ? Could I speak to Ing. Katherina Mayer, please?

"Hello, Kati, how are you? That's good to hear . . . I have to ask a big favor from you . . . you are still working on those forensic things, aren't you?

"Well, I have here four glasses, from four different people . . . and I would need a DNA analysis on them . . . no, drinking glasses . . .

"Katherina, I know this is an imposition on you . . . especially after our breakup. But there is a truly weird thing going on here and I would not ask this if I did not think it important. If you wish, I will beg you to do it. . . .

"No—I am not in trouble! This is just something very strange that happened to us here at the university . . . and I have a hunch that this might be very important . . . no, really—I am not in trouble—legal or otherwise . . ."

"Can't you run it together with real tests . . . disguised as a calibration sample, run in parallel?"

"Really . . . ?! I am in debt to you for something large, Katherina . . . No, I handled the glasses carefully . . . Yes, I will be there . . ."

✧   ✧   ✧

Cafe Zainer, Landstrasser Hauptstrasse, Vienna
3rd district, 06.08.98

Sitting in the Cafe Zainer, eating apfelstrudel and sipping apple juice with soda water . . . Looking to the entrance to see if Katherina has already arrived. Around me people are doing the usual cafe house things . . . talking, reading the excellent collection of newspapers, playing a lethal game of chess, eating cakes and pastries . . . oh yes, and some are drinking coffee.

Katherina enters, looks around and sees me in a corner . . . she does not look happy—downright furious would be a better description. She obviously came directly from the lab—her short brown hair is still scrunched up and she is still wearing trousers and a plaid shirt with a small chemical stain on the breast pocket.

"Just what are you trying to do . . . where did you get those samples—from the ape house in Schoenbrunn Zoo? Can you guess what the control lab is asking me, you idiot?"

"What do you mean, please . . . ape house and control lab? Please start at the beginning—what is going on?"

"Okay. I slipped your samples into a large batch of tests we are doing for the police right now. All our samples are immediately divided in two—one half gets sent to another lab to check our results and both labs have to get the same results . . ."

"Yes, I heard about that . . . ."

"Okay . . . two of your samples are females, most probably one western caucasian and one oriental genome—do you need more information on them? I can get a little more out of the data if necessary. The two others are not human—at a first guess a male and a female ape of some kind. I will look that up more closely and god help you if I find out that you are playing practical jokes on me . . ."

"Katie, wait . . . you are telling me that two of those glasses were drunk by apes? That's not possible—simply impossible! Could it be contaminated samples or something? How sure are those results?"

"No . . . we do not work with monkey genes. At first I believed we just had a bad test result and threw the data out . . . but I received a call from the other lab and they had exactly the same results—and normally we get people into jail with those results, so they are good, reliable. Now the other lab is already asking a lot of awkward questions."

"And if somebody had carried ape genes on his hands? Or kissed a monkey just before . . . ?"

"Then I would see their human genes too. Can you tell me why those glasses were so clean?"

"Clean?"

"Yes . . . only traces of other genecomplexes on them . . . basically all we found was one individual set on each glass . . . and lots of plant genes from the drinks."

I try to remember the bar, thinking out loud: "Hmm. That is a self service fruit juice and soda bar. I believe the dirty glasses are stacked on large trays and put through a dishwasher; then they simply put the whole tray out for the customers to take their glass and fill by themselves. Nobody else touches them."

"Industrial dish washers . . . yes—could be . . . so tell me, what is going on, now?"

"Katherina—I do not know. But I will find out and you will be the first one to hear . . . that I promise to you. Wait—you said you are going to look those ape genes up—can you find out more about them?"

❖   ❖   ❖

The Gersen "residence," Vienna, 12th district, 06.08.98

Back home I have a message on the answering machine—it is Katherina: "I checked those genes more closely . . . they do not match any apes I have in the catalogue. Now it is your turn to provide some information to me . . . what are they?"

Not apes—not humans . . . I shake my head.

Looking at the video again . . . yes, one of the two trailing girls could be Chinese: round face, dark hair perhaps an epicanthic fold. I can't be sure as the quality of those security cameras is not that good. The other one could be English . . . or Swedish . . . at least she looks like a Northern European.

That leaves the couple . . . or brother and sister . . . and by elimination they are most likely to have carried the ape genes . . . but they look even less like apes than the girls do . . . everything—their looks, their movements— give a very unapelike impression. . . .

Who are they? What is going on?

No—Katherina asked the right question . . .

What are they . . . ?

Why is it that I have a strange feeling whenever I watch that video—it feels like a hunch that does not want to come clear . . . like I already know what is going on but cannot put it in words . . . the answer is right there, but I am unable to recognize it . . . or unwilling to recognize it. . . .

And I want to know—I must know!

I watch the video again . . . and again . . . and again . . . and then I remember the second video I have with me.

I watch them walking through the parking lot, the two girls opening the doors of a luxurious minivan (could be a Citroen Espace, I note to myself). They hold the doors open until the mysterious couple enters the back. Then the girls get in the front, and the van drives away. I lean forward, pushing tiredness from

my eyes, and see—yes—there are a few seconds
where I can see the license plate on the van. This
gives me something additional to check—tomorrow.

**Vehicle licensing center, Vienna, 19th district,
07.08.98**

"Ah . . . excuse me—could you tell me if it is possible to find out a car owner's address, if I have only
the license plate number?"

The man sitting behind the information desk looks
up and points at the bank of elevators, "Third level—
room 311 . . . they can direct you further."
About forty minutes later I have repeated my
request several times and have been sent through five
offices. But finally I am able to put a small computer
printout in my pocket.

```
>  license:  W-INGOLF2
>  vehicle:  Citroen Espace 2.2 TDI
>  color  :  white
>  date   :  16-12-1997 — license
number still valid
>  holder :  IngolfTech Austria
GmbH
>  Kaasgrabenstr. 23
>  A-1190 Wien
```

The Gersen "residence," Vienna 12th district,10.08.98

Fortunately the university library has a number of
good information retrieval experts (called librarians
in earlier times); they and the archive staff at one of

the news magazines have been very helpful, providing a stack of photocopies and printouts.

IngolfTech, I read in a copy of an *Economist* analyst's article, has appeared only a few years ago and is operating from some Caribbean island—in this short time they have already started to market a few, but very interesting, breakthroughs. Basically, they've been growing very rapidly. This analyst suggests that you buy any and all shares you can get your greedy fingers on, as soon as they go public with them, and he implies that that should happen soon.

He also gives a little background on the firm's history, the origins a little vague—it is rumored that the start-up money came from a Spanish treasure ship that sank in the Caribbean around 1600. The firm is owned by a Canadian citizen—self-made millionaire.

Oh, my God . . . I know that face—it is the red-headed woman on my videos! The photocopy of her picture is even more stunning than those low quality videos, and her name is Gwendolyn Ingolfsson.

I look through some of the other material I received from the library—mostly copies from technical and scientific magazines. My head starts to spin even faster—the things they have started to market are from very diverse fields: electronics, computers, bio-engineering—in one article there is a hint at a medical or cosmetic breakthrough coming soon . . . and although I am no expert in all of those fields—all that stuff seems to be very advanced, right out there on the bleeding edge.

During my studies, my thoughts and eyes return to the page containing that picture, thinking: "Who are you, lady? How did you manage all of this? From nothing to this in only a few years?"

And then . . . I remember the question Katie asked me only short time ago:

"What are they?"

SCS shopping mall, in the south of Vienna, parking lot, 12.08.98

I step out of the tramway station—there is a fast connection to the city that starts right in front of the university—and walk across the parking lot to the nearest entrance.

I am here to do a software upgrade of some parts of our system—carrying the program on a streamer tape in my briefcase, together with the inevitable books and other reading materials. In this case I've also got some of the copies I read yesterday as I want to go over them again.

Looking over the already half-full parking lot I see a white minivan sitting a few lanes over to the right—looks like a Citroen Espace . . . could it be?

I look at the license plate—W-INGOLF2.

They . . . are here.

Should I run into the security office, searching for them on the monitors? I might overlook them or they could leave while I am still on my way . . . no. There is only one safe way—I have to wait by the car.

Am I going mad? One cannot accost a stranger on a parking lot and ask *that* question: "What are you?"

But I have to know. . . .

I take out a newspaper to calm myself and lean on the side of the car, trying to immerse myself in the paper or I will surely run away. I glance toward the entrance every few seconds; my throat is dry—nerves.

Here they come—again there are four in the group. The strange couple and their two attendants. I put the newspaper away and keep my hands well visible—I do hope they do not shake too much . . . clearing my throat . . .

"Ah . . . excuse me . . . could I have a word with you?"

In the midst of the word he was trying to say,
In the midst of his laughter and glee,
He had softly and suddenly vanished away—
For the Snark was a Boojum, you see.

John Barnes is known for his SF novels and stories. *Kaleidescope Century*, *Finity*, and many more. He lives in Gunnison, Colorado, and teaches theatre at Western State College—and practices what he teaches. How he finds the energy to do all this mystifies *me*. It must be the extra oxygen in the lowland air. (I live at 7,200 feet, myself.)

John has also written a series of alternate-history, crosstime-travel romps featuring his hero Mark Strang, the art-historian turned gun for hire and interdimensional scourge of tyrants: *Washington's Dirigible*, *Caesar's Bicycle*, and *Patton's Spaceship*.

One of the great things about a multiverse of alternate timelines is that if anything possible happens, virtually everything will, somewhere.

So Mark Strang takes time off from the war against the Closers—sadistic descendants of the Carthaginians who rule a million timelines, all of them badly—to meet the gene-engineered Draka.

The Closers love to torment their helpless, hating slaves. To the Draka, that would seem crude; they consider making their subjects love them the ultimate domination. Mark Strang isn't enchanted with either approach, and shows it . . .

UPON THEIR
BACKS, TO
BITE 'EM

John Barnes

"Admit it, Mark, you're bored," Chrysamen said.

"I have no problem with *admitting* it." I poured myself another cup of coffee from the maker in our kitchen and took an absent-minded sip. "I just have problems with any possible way out of it, is all. Now, if you'll excuse me, our son is waiting patiently for his chance at checkmate, which I think he'll get in about ten moves."

"Six," Perry said from the other room.

I went back out into the living-dining room. Perry had moved the chessboard a little to the side. He was

reading some comic that had both Spider-Man and
The Incredible Hulk on the cover. His feet, gigantic in proportion to the skinny rest of him, were up
on the table, next to the chessboard. He looked the
picture of eleven-year-old contentment.

I gently lifted his feet to the side with one hand,
and set my coffee cup down on the table. Perry sat
upright, grumbling that there was no place around
here where a guy could get comfortable.

I remembered making the same grumble to my
own father, so I used his line. "If being comfortable
means destroying good furniture, then you're right.
There's no place here where you can get comfortable.
Better start saving to move out."

"Aw, Pop. That's Grandpa's line."

"Uh-huh. And that's your grandmother's table.
Which means, as I don't really have to tell you, Perry,
that it means a lot to Grandpa Strang." I looked at
my son intently for half a minute; then he shrugged
and nodded. My mother, Perry's grandmother, was
murdered in front of Dad and me, years before Perry
was born, just before I went into my present line of
work. Dad's as recovered as he's going to get, but he'll
never be over it. If Perry had scratched the table that
Mother had once found at a yard sale and spent those
summer hours refinishing, Dad would never have said
a hard word to either of us about it—but all the same,
it would have been an addition to the heap of pain
inside him, and neither Perry nor I could shrug that
off.

Salvaging a little pride, Perry said, "Anyway, I
wasn't going to scratch the table or hurt it, Pop. And
besides, it will be out of danger in no time—I've got
mate in six."

"I'm afraid he's right, Mark," a familiar voice said
behind and above me; I felt the friendly hand on my
shoulder even as I was saying "Walks!"

"Yep."

I turned around and stood up to greet him with a hug. Walks in His Shadow Caldwell is about six foot two, with what I think is an exceptionally handsome face—high-ridged nose, cheekbones wide and high, dark eyes, skin a copper-beige color. At least he was handsome by the standards of America in the early 2000s. I had no idea what they thought of him a few thousand timelines over, where he came from—a timeline where the assassination of Andrew Jackson prevented the Trail of Tears, the German Fever devastated the North, and Napoleon *fils* cut off European emigration for more than forty years. I'd been there once, on a training trip; the USA of 1960 had less than a hundred million people, and they were about one-third Native, one-third Euro, and one-third African in ancestry. Pretty country, but empty.

Walks was an old friend, but still, it was hardly usual for him to turn up in my house on July third. Nobody crosses timelines other than by necessity, because every crossing is detectable and could give away the position of both the starting and the ending timeline to the bad guys. ATN protocol restricts crossings to emergencies; ATN is the outfit that Walks, Chrysamen, and I all work for. Just think of us as "the good guys."

Chrysamen came out with a tray of iced tea—oddly, one of the few common tastes between Walks's timeline and mine. One of the iced teas was in a paper cup, which she handed to Perry and said, "Perry, if it actually is certain that you have mate in six moves, maybe you can spare your father total humiliation and let us get on with the adult business by, er—"

"Leaving," Perry finished for her, getting up, taking a gulp that half-emptied the glass, and starting for the door. He stopped, turned, and said, "Hey, could I have gotten mate in *four?*"

Walks beamed. "Great question, but no. See, you'd

have to expose yourself to check to do it." As he
talked, his hands played over the chessboard, showing things to Perry much too fast for me to follow.
"That would happen in any of the three ways that
were otherwise possible, so no, there's not a legal way
to do it. That leaves two more moves you always have
to go through—either an exchange for his white
bishop, so that your king can move, or a jump around
the problem with this knight. Either way, six moves
is your minimum."

I did my best to pretend I had any idea what Walks
was showing him. Perry seemed to get it at once,
however, thanked "Mr. Walks," and was out the door
just fast enough so that I couldn't tell him not to slam
the screen door.

After we'd all jumped at the bang, and settled back
down, I said, "Kids," and Walks said "Bless'em," and
the ever-practical Chrysamen said, "All right, so what's
the proposed job?"

Walks chuckled. "Well, it's a job for Mark, rather
than for you two as a team. So if you want to decline
it because you wouldn't be working together, I'll
certainly understand that. In fact, to sweeten the deal
a little, Mark, we've authorized a short-term exchange
for this mission, so you'll be gone only about a half
day here, but it might be as much as six months over
in the timeline we'd be going to. I told Lao and
Malecela and the other brass that giving you a short
time exchange would be more likely to get you to take
the job."

"Well, you might be right," I said, "if you would
just tell me what the job is."

"Be my bodyguard on a diplomatic mission. If you
don't mind being flattered a little bit, I requested you
specifically, because I needed a senior crux op with
clearance for all kinds of security, and with some
bodyguarding experience—and it needed to be someone I was sure I could trust, because for this job,

especially, I wanted someone with a proven record of saving my life, which each of you had."

"Then why not both of us as a team? That's how we usually work, and we can get somebody to look after Perry on ten minutes' notice—"

Walks shook his head and said, "This is not *just* diplomatic bodyguarding. This isn't even just *dangerous* diplomatic bodyguarding. We're going to go put our heads in the lion's mouth—and the lion says that it only wants two of us. Now, if you'll take the deal, Mark, we'll just open a gate into your bedroom and get going. I'm sorry to sound impatient but I'd like to start. You'll be back for supper—if you're back at all."

That last reference was what told me that this job was *really* dangerous, not just the usual dangers of being a crux op. Usually crux ops don't talk about dying, and one reason is because when we do, we get maudlin about it, generally while drunk or right after sex. I suppose that's the way life gets in an excessively romantic job.

I'd have thought, many years ago, that I had become a realist, probably too much of a realist. Most of my family had been killed in what appeared to be a pointless political murder. I'd gone through a deep depression and come out the other end as a professional bodyguard, dedicated to keeping assholes away from nice people, which not at all incidentally gave me an excuse to occasionally beat up people that needed beating up. I spent much of my time keeping scum at bay. I thought I was facing the real world, which was gritty and "realist."

Then I'd fallen through into the *real* real world, which is even grittier—but desperately romantic. More than a million timelines held down by the Closers, a whole culture devoted to the joyful practice of slavery. More timelines in a loose alliance called ATN, facing them—about even with the Closers when I started, but we have twice as many timelines now, and in those millions of timelines, every bizarre thing you could think of has happened. Buck Rogers science, storybook settings, desperate quests, mad tyrants, unspeakable crimes, ineffable beauty, all of your childhood heroes—I'd been on one mission with George Washington and Leonardo da Vinci as co-agents, but that's a long and different story . . . well. I learned, a couple of decades ago, that although I'd seen most of the dark corners of my own world, I'd only been living in a bad black and white polaroid of that big bold technicolor reality.

ATN was still mostly secret in our timeline; the public was being prepared for the news, but it would probably be a generation or so until we were ready to be open about it. It was scheduled for the presidency-to-come, twenty years or so in the future, of my ward Porter Brunreich. (That was the U.S. Presidency . . . that young lady doesn't settle for half measures.)

Meanwhile, I continued in my occupation as bodyguard for Porter and as part-time crux op. Seven hundred years in the future, time travel remains expensive, even for civilizations that can move whole planets around, and so most of the action involves small numbers of scouts, pioneers, agents, and liaisons; every so often one of those temporal explorers, agents, or diplomats goes missing, in circumstances that might be due to enemy action. When that happens, a crux op goes into the last known time and place location for the missing person, and the crux op is bound by just three rules:

Rule One: Find the missing person, or the body.
Rule Two: Make sure the original mission gets completed.
Rule Three: No other rules apply.

❖   ❖   ❖

We went back into the bedroom suite, where Chrys and I have a space that is always kept empty so that a gate can be projected there from ATN headquarters at Hyper Athens (a space station that will never exist in our timeline, but is just a few centuries forward and several possibilities to the side). Chrysamen grabbed me for just an instant, gave me a long, deep kiss, and said, "Come back."

Privately, Chrys and I call that Rule Zero.

A moment later in subjective time, Walks and I were standing in the receiving area at ATN, shaking hands with a whole committee of people. Walks in His Shadow was one of the most valued people ATN has because he'd done so many different things. He'd been spectacularly effective as a time scout, on the mission that had turned the tide of the war and promised to let us eventually rid all the timelines of Closers. He'd worked as a crux op himself. He'd held a bunch of command and staff jobs in everything from pre-imperial Roman legions to a 23rd-century LithuPolish Pentaku, and fought in everything from one-on-one epée quarrels to commanding a regiment of capsuleers in one of the Irish Empire's invasions of Mars. His multiply rebuilt body housed a mind with at least two centuries of adult experience—and much of that was in contact and diplomacy.

So if the Senate of Citizens had chosen him to make our first contact with this new family of timelines on this mission, it could be no ordinary mission.

As soon as we arrived, Walks immediately went off for a last-minute briefing. Ariadne Lao, an old friend and my usual boss, took me to a discreet little cafe that we both liked, to do the high level briefing and not incidentally to get reacquainted with the moussaka. "This place is still secure," she explained, as we sat down, near a window tuned to the outside, where we could watch the big, gleaming Earth roll by on one side, and the twinkles of dozens of spacecraft on the other, as Hyper Athens slowly tumbled.

"All right," I said. "Then tell me everything."

"We wish we knew more, obviously," she said, "but here's the basics. We've run into a civilization— to use the term *very* loosely—that has *just* found the technique of crossing timelines, within the last thirty years, and begun to explore outwards from its home timeline. A timeline fairly close to both yours and Plenipotentiary Caldwell's native timelines—" it took me a moment to realize my built-in translator chip had translated Walks's title from Lao's always-polite speech.

"Basically, in this new family of timelines, there's an enormous and frightening great power that never occurred in either your timeline or Walks's." She looked down at her notes; she was from the timeline where ATN had originated, and from her standpoint the whole settlement of North America from Europe was an aberration. "The difference was that after the American Revolution, the Loyalists went to South Africa instead of Canada, and in the fullness of time, grew up to be the nation that conquered the world, enslaved everybody, and bioengineered themselves into a new species. They call themselves Draka, which derives, distantly, from Drake having explored that part of the world."

I shuddered. "So in their timeline, unmodified human beings are slaves?"

"Extinct. We think. We know that there's a lot they're not telling us. As far as we can tell, there might be a hundred human-derived species in those timelines. All created entirely for the amusement and convenience of the *drakenses*."

"Plural of *drakensis*?"

"Right. Anyway, some of them might look like us— the Draka themselves do, superficially—but they're all designed, and the worlds they're designed for are mostly empty, with just a few masters in them."

I sighed. "They sound more like natural allies of the Closers, but I suppose if we can use them as allies, we'll have to."

"You know the basic principle. Any timeline that doesn't try to control other timelines is okay, even if their major civilization bakes babies for breakfast." She sighed. "Not that I'm happy about that principle just at the moment. Mark, this is one of those cases where I really wonder if any end can justify the means. Unofficially, yes, the Draka are quite unattractive, but officially, they have potential to help us shorten the war, and that's not something we can afford to pass up the chance at.

"Now, this next thing is a note of some importance. One aspect of their extraordinarily well-advanced genetic engineering is that they have have modified themselves to have voluntary control of their pheremones. They can make themselves smell like friends, or like dangerous predators, or whatever. They are quite capable, for example, of causing a non-resistant human to fall madly into sexual infatuation with them, at will. That is, at Draka will. The ordinary human doesn't have much in the way of a will, once the Draka get done with him.

"This is one reason why Plenipotentiary Caldwell is going in with a bodyguard. Part of your job is to watch each other. We *think* we can give you a shot of nanos that will protect you against Draka control. But if it should fail—if one of you falls under the sway of a Drakon—then the job of the other one is to get you both out of there, right then, before the Draka can gain any more information about ATN, and most especially before you both end up as puppets. Is that clear?"

"Does Walks know that's my job? Dragging him out of there if needed?"

"He thinks hiring you was his idea. And it was. But we already had it in mind, and we contrived a few situations that would reinforce the idea for him, to which, I must say, he responded beautifully. So yes, it was his idea, but it was ours before it was his."

"These Draka aren't the only people that practice mind control, are they?"

Lao didn't answer, but she seemed annoyed, and she's a good boss and an old friend I don't want to offend, so I dropped that line of conversation and we got down to business; she gave me the basic reports to have down cold before we left. ATN are good people, but when it comes to talking about means and ends, they can get as touchy as anybody.

The next day, while I was going over the material, and finding more and more things not to like about the Draka, Ariadne dropped by the guest apartment where I was staying. She apologized for having been abrupt with me the day before, and said it had a great deal to do with how much the ATN leadership had already been arguing about whether to open any kind of relations with the Draka at all; several of the citizen-senators described the Draka as "Super-Closers" and suggested that we should simply shove a planet-wrecking bomb through the gate and be done with them. "So they've thrashed through all the conflicts, and argued and screamed and so on for a long time, and now they've hit on a policy," she said, "which may or may not work, but if it doesn't work, all the ones who didn't favor it will be able to jump on our organization and blame us for it. So I'm afraid that for these last few days I've been hypersensitive."

"That's understandable," I said, pouring tea for both of us. "But I can't believe you went to the bother of coming in person just to apologize."

"Well, no, I didn't. I came to bring you a new toy for your expedition—you'll be the first crux op to carry one, ever. It hasn't been used by any agent in any real emergency, but the field tests have been very successful, and it's rated as fully ready to go."

"Unh-hunh. I hope the mission doesn't depend on it," I said. I have any normal person's horror of using experimental equipment in dangerous situations; heck, besides all the next-millenium hardware that ATN gives me, I always try to pack along a Model 1911A "Army automatic," because I know I can trust it.

She laughed. "No, absolutely not. It just gives you another option." She handed me something that looked a little like a modern concussion grenade—an aluminum egg with a pin in it. "They made your version of the gadget look like a grenade exactly so you'd be nervous about pulling the pin, because it's strictly for desperate situations," she said. "What it is, is a gate generator that forms the gate around you. If you pull the pin, the energy source inside—which stores about a gigajoule, so it's a big one—powers up a gate that encloses anything within three meters of the object. It does a very high speed search for oxygen and dry land, so that it won't dump you someplace you can't survive. Then it kicks you and whatever's with you through the gate, and sends out an amplified shockwave in probability space so that we can find you easily."

"Where exactly does it send me?"

"The first timeline that its search finds, in which you can survive, that's a minimum distance from where you were. Think of it as like the parachutes in your crude airplanes; it doesn't deliver you anywhere in particular, but sometimes where you are is so dangerous that anywhere else is worth trying."

I sighed. "Yeah, I've been places like that. So it's nondirectional, just a bailout device?"

"That's right," she said. "No time for rethinking, either—the gate forms the instant the pin is pulled."

"If it's all the same to ATN, I think I'll tape that

pin down," I said. "How much force does it take to pull it?"

"Two newtons. You can do it with one finger."

"Then I'm definitely taping it down."

Walks and I bounced through nine timelines in ninety seconds on our way to the Draka timeline where negotiations were to happen. That's a routine precaution; by putting the bounces close together, their signals overlap in a way that—the physicists tell me—can't be decomposed to find individual timelines. This way the Draka wouldn't be in any position to come looking for us, should negotiations go sour—which I was privately hoping they'd do, after what I'd read of them. ATN already has some pretty grim member timelines—some descended from Nazi and Communist world-states that liberalized, and a stomach-turning one that resulted from the Confederacy conquering the world before it was overthrown by theocrats. I didn't like those timelines much, though some very good agents came from them. There are people that you just don't want on your side, when you come right down to it, and I'd never seen anything that fit that description better than the Draka.

The blur of colors and the whirl of suns in the sky went away, and we stood on a platform in what would have been in South Africa in my timeline or Nouvelle Provence in Walks's. We were facing two remarkably beautiful redheads, who could easily have been sisters.

"Hello," the slightly taller one said, "I am Chief Negotiator Sabrina de Koenigen, and this is my assistant, Ailantha Rossignol."

The translator in my head made her words clear while another part of my mind recognized it as English of a sort—maybe about as close to my English as Flemish would be in my own world. It sounded like the thickest Southern drawl I'd ever heard, but the rhythm was different, somehow.

Walks stepped forward and bowed slightly. "I am Plenipotentiary Walks in His Shadow Caldwell, and this is my assistant, Mark Strang."

There were the usual interminable pleasantries about whether or not we were comfortable (how can you get uncomfortable on a less-than-two-minute trip?), and then about settling us into guest quarters. They played the game of pretending that they needed a couple of hours to be ready for us, and we sat in there quietly, assuming that our rooms were bugged, that listening devices were always trained on us, and that therefore we were to have no communication with each other that we couldn't have in front of Draka Security. We had some inconsequential discussion, figured out the sanitary facilities, and unpacked our one bag each.

The Draka hadn't really seemed to care that I would be armed; apparently if the situations were reversed, they would have expected and demanded it. Besides, what could Walks and I possibly do with just my hand weapons, no matter how potent? Even with an atom bomb in my suitcase, I could have done very little harm to a whole planet of them. Any act of violence I did would have gained us little and would only have put them on alert that our intentions weren't friendly.

Presumably, after enough listening, they were satisfied that we wouldn't blurt out everything as soon as it looked like we were alone. Then Rossignol came by to get us. She was good looking enough, with deep blue eyes and an athletic build, but I realized after we had walked a hundred meters or so that the antipheromone nanos in my bloodstream were doing their job; I was aware that her smell was saying "Trust me Love Me Do What I Say" into my nose—overlaid with occasional bits of "Wanna Fuck?"—but I didn't feel any need to do anything about any of it, except to pretend to be vaguely interested.

The basic procedure for the negotiations was that de Koenigen and Walks would slowly exchange information with each other, while Rossignol and I sat in opposite corners of the room, took notes, and watched each other for treachery. After three hours of polite exchanges—things like "I am authorized to tell you that we maintain a solar system with a very low population and we are not accepting settlers at this time" from de Koenigen, or "I have been instructed to tell you that we have a policy of strict noninterference by every member timeline in every other member timeline's affairs" from Walks—de Koenigen suggested that we have dinner and just get acquainted informally. Given that I was already bored out of my mind, and Rossignol looked like she desperately wanted to go to sleep, there were two votes in the room for it immediately, and Walks assented as well.

The place where we ate, was "famous not only in Archona but throughout the Domination," we were informed. Knowing the Draka background, I was moderately—and very privately—amused that much of the meal, which they assured me was traditional with them, dating back to their earliest days, was what I would call "soul food."

You can get a lot of intelligence out of casual conversation, especially when investigating another timeline, and that was what they were trying on us. I knew that when we told them that Walks and I were not from the same timelines, this information would be squirreled away somewhere: *Inter-timeline travel is routine for them.* When I mentioned the death of my first wife, my mother, and my brother, in an act of violence, a note would record *Strang's world has endemic terrorism or violent crime.* They were drawing conclusions about sizes of families, social customs, economics, and all the rest, just as quickly as they could ask us questions.

We were playing the same game, and the more I heard, the more I realized that being a serf for the Draka—specifically being a *servus*, their genetically-controlled utility workers—was probably indistinguishable from being a slave of the Closers. The only difference was that the servus were bred to like it and need it; the Closers, who were a whole culture of brutal sadists, often as rough on each other and their own children as they were on their slaves, preferred to own and torment something that was able to hate them, I guess because it enhanced the experience. I wasn't sure whether I found the pragmatic Draka or the sadistic Closers less attractive.

I think I managed dinner with them rather well. I did have to work to hold a bite of fried chicken down when, right after I swallowed, Rossignol began talking about the teenage girl she had picked to implant with a cloned egg, creating a little Rossignol inside her bed partner.

I was careful to keep thinking "Rossignol" even though, by that time, we were all on a first-name basis; I was willing to call her "Ailantha" at her request, to be polite, but if it came down to it, I'd rather have to kill "Rossignol," or better yet, "That nasty Drakon bitch."

Both de Koenigen and Rossignol must have been putting out pheromones for all they were worth, because I could feel it whispering in my bloodstream. The wine they kept ordering—and filling our glasses with—didn't seem to bother my nanos one bit, though. So though I was feeling the booze a little, drinking it faster than the artificial scrubber built into my kidney could deal with, the signal getting to me was a faint whispering in the back of my mind—"I Love You I've Always Wanted Someone Like You Adore Me Trust Me Wanna Fuck?" I played along,

mildly; I kind of thought Walks was overdoing it, and
by the end of dinner he'd let de Koenigen rest a hand
on his arm for quite a while.

We staggered back to our quarters—one thing you
can say for totalitarian states, the streets are safe at
any hour—and sacked out. By the time we got back
to our own door, of course, the alcohol was gone from
our systems, but we kept right on playing drunk—
or at least I was playing. I was starting to wonder if
maybe there was something wrong in Walks's scrubber, or if he was just a too-thorough actor.

Stretched out on my bunk in the dark, I practiced
my old habit of privately thanking whoever or whatever beings might rule the multiple universes; I
thanked them for my chance at a second life in a
wider world, and for people to love and take care of
like Porter, and for good friends and comrades like
Walks, and of course for Chrysamen. I always finished
with her. Then I set my mind to drift off to sleep.

I was mildly disturbed by a little noise from Walks,
in the next room; it took me a second to realize that
I hadn't heard that sound since the days when I'd
lived in the frat house. He was masturbating like a
crazy monkey, but trying to be quiet about it.

Well, maybe his pheromone screen wasn't as good
as mine, or perhaps he had a major thing for red-
headed lady wrestlers. It was, so to speak, no skin
off mine.

The next morning, I'd have sworn that Walks had
an actual hangover, which seemed all the stranger—
that shouldn't happen to anyone with a scrubber.
Maybe his wasn't working—and that led to the equally
horrifying thought that perhaps all of his biochemi-
cal defenses were malfunctioning. I had no way to
ask him; not only did we have to assume that audio
was bugged, but there was no way even to write a
note to him, or to tap his shoulder in Morse code,

or do any other trick to avoid surveillance. We had
no way of knowing what their surveillance capabili-
ties might be; for all I knew there could be a camera in the lamp I wrote under, or a monitoring system
in any hard surface I might write on, or any number of subtle listening devices anywhere in the rooms.
Certainly if Draka representatives had come to ATN,
we'd have bugged them in all of those ways, and half
a dozen more as well.

It hadn't seemed like such a serious problem in
the abstract, back at Hyper Athens, when we'd dis-
cussed and reviewed procedure, and noted that we
could not and must not have any communication
about any covert matter until we were out of the
Draka timeline. But now . . . was Walks all right? I'd
never seen him having visible problems before. Was
this part of a ruse? If so, how should I react?

My dread only got worse when, halfway through
the morning, de Koenigen suggested a long break
to take a walk through a park. To judge by the
sheen of sweat on Walks's forehead, my friend's
pheromone resistance was failing just as badly as his
alcohol scrubbers had. Someone had screwed up
royally on the whole mission; as soon as Walks and
I got back to our quarters, I'd have to officially pull
out my emergency orders, and request a recall. I
was tempted to do that now, but I couldn't risk
embarrassing our envoy in front of the other side,
and besides, as yet, Walks in His Shadow hadn't
quite done anything that could make me certain he'd
actually lost control.

Still, I was also worried by how fast he agreed to
the walk, and by the smile he gave de Koenigen.

Somehow or other the walk through the park would
first require going back to our guest quarters, and
when we got there, Walks went in, and Sabrina de
Koenigen went in after him, and just like that, I was
separated from him—Rossignol stepped in between

the door and me and said "I think they badly want to be alone."

Her pheromones were now sending "Obey me" and "Get hard" at about equal intensities.

I didn't quite have an excuse to pick a fight with her, and frankly didn't like my chances if I did—a Drakon is as strong as an ape or a bear, and I'd get taken apart, while achieving nothing for the cause. I didn't have any way to argue with her about them wanting to be alone; in fact, Walks was making a number of strange noises that made me think that he'd probably rather not be rescued for a few minutes, anyway. Softly, Rossignol said, "You know that all the damage is done already. We can tell you have some kind of resistance system, Mark, and that Mister Caldwell has one that doesn't work. You can't get to him because if you try, I'll kill you. And he won't want to get away from Sabrina for another hour at least. So we're going to learn what we're going to learn. Now, you and I can stand here and face each other at this doorway, or we can go somewhere comfortable and sit. Which will it be?"

"Let's keep the faceoff going," I said.

"You know perfectly well that I won't tire as fast as you will," Rossignol said, smiling. "And incidentally, even out here in public, we have some privacy. No one will be coming by. Want to see what it's like with one of us? Are you sure you want Caldwell to have all the stories?" I couldn't entirely tell if she was only teasing, or if she was just looking for something to do during a dull watch.

Meanwhile, inside, I heard Walks howling with pleasure. I did my best to ignore it.

I thought about agreeing to have sex, and then pulling out the .45 and shooting her. My guess was that with her strength and reflexes, she could probably take the gun away from me, use me, and kill me, faster than I could draw the gun.

"You're right, it wouldn't work," Rossignol said evenly.

I admit I gaped at her.

"We don't read minds," she said, "but you obviously thought of something for a moment and then gave up on it. The way your body moves. The way you smell. It's not hard to tell."

"Why are you doing this?" I asked. "Assaulting and interrogating an envoy is a good way to start a war. Do you *want* to fight a million timelines?"

"Well, the million may be exaggerated," she said, "or it may not, but I'm willing to agree there are more of you than there are of us. Part of the sport, you might say. A bigger challenge. And after all, mostly you came here to get to know us. Well, you're finding out. We don't bargain with feral humans, any more than you bargain with cattle. The real question is just how soon you'll be serfs. That son you mentioned at dinner last night will have a tattoo on his neck one day."

I kept my voice low and even, but I stared at her with complete disgust. "A tattoo on his neck?" I asked. "Is that how you mark serfs?"

Her pheromones were now sending a bunch of signals intended to rile me up; she must be under orders to get me into some kind of a fight or something, I thought. Perhaps I needed to be killed while attacking her.

But the thought of Perry with a neck tattoo . . . I ran my hand over my own throat, trying to imagine that, and kept an eye on her while I did.

"Oh, he'll wear it," she said. "You'll see the tattoo on any captured serf. But not where you're touching yourself." With a cruel little smile, she turned her head to show me. "The serf tattoo extends across here—"

She drew a line with her finger, and as she drew it, I pulled the .45, thrust it forward, and fired three times into her neck.

Later on I found out that they all have what amounts to a Kevlar underskin; the rounds penetrated only because it was at point blank range, and without much force. Chances are she survived with the mother of all headaches and some bed rest. But the impact of the heavy rounds was enough to throw her backward against the doorframe, and to daze and disorient her. I kicked her hard to knock her to the ground and pressed my thumb against the door's reader plate. There was some mercy in the universe; it popped open, and I rolled inside.

De Koenigen came at me, hands reaching to break my neck, and I put the rest of the clip into her face. I wasn't as close to her as I had been to Rossignol, so I don't think it had much more effect on her than being whacked hard with a broom handle in the face would on me—it stunned and stalled her, but I don't think she was really hurt.

Still, she took a step back. I dove forward, onto the bed, and had just an instant to realize that Walks was tied out in a naked spread-eagle, and that he had pretty obviously been having a very good time. I landed on top of him, reached into my pocket, and pulled the pin on the new escape device. The world turned a weird noncolor, and we were out of there.

The landing was a bit rough; whatever hunting the device did apparently didn't care about a two-foot drop in a bed whose legs had been severed at uneven lengths. We were outdoors in bright sunlight, probably the same place and time of day as before, but if the gadget had worked correctly, we were out of Draka territory.

Or at least we would have different Draka to cope with.

I pulled out my knife and cut his bonds. Walks, still naked, sat up and drew a deep breath, sobbing.

"Can you move?" I asked, "Because—"

There was a loud thunder and a brief darkness. I looked up to see an aircraft belly slide over us, perhaps a hundred feet overhead, and the shape and insignia told me instantly.

"Uh, because I think we're on the runway of a Closer airport," I said.

That got his attention. We ran for the nearest building, and barefoot and naked though he was, he got there ahead of me. There was an open doorway and we rushed into that; there was still no evidence that we'd been seen, but surely there must be alarms sounding in the terminal and a gang of armed men on their way. "Inventory," Walks said, gasping. "Oh, god, her pheromones are still all over me; I've never been so horny in my life. Inventory, Mark, what do we have?"

"You've got nothing," I said. "I've got the .45 and a NIF. If I spray it around now, we can probably knock off the whole airport around us, but that's going to cause attention."

"You got any better plans?" he asked.

"Nope."

The NIF—Neural Induction Flechette—is a weapon that shoots little needles that take over the nervous system. They're self-guiding and will go looking for human beings to hit; you can select any effect from mild itching to immediate cardiac shutdown. In this case, I just stepped out the door, drew mine—it looked a bit like a cordless drill with a keyboard—set it to hit everywhere that wasn't us for a kilometer around, and fired it up into the air. To maximize the effect, I set them to kill—quickly and painlessly, but all the same, anybody who wasn't in an airtight room would be dropping dead.

I slipped back into the building and listened to the explosions and crashes outside—presumably driverless vehicles plowing into things, and aircraft with dead pilots crashing. Walks was frantically rubbing himself with oily rags he'd found. "Oh, god, I can't believe it, I really can't," he said. "None of my protection worked at all. And they grabbed our personal computers, and . . . um, well, I told her everything she asked. We're absolutely screwed, Mark."

"Well, almost absolutely," Chrysamen said. She stepped out of the shadows. "And at least Walks is dressed for it. I'm here to bring you guys home."

She pressed the button on a hand-held gate call, and abruptly there were bursts of no-color alternated with colors and lights; we ran through another deception set, and there we were, back at Hyper Athens, two days older and much the worse for the wear.

By tradition, in my family, we have a little review of the past year every Fourth of July. My father is just about the most patriotic person I know, and the Fourth is always our biggest holiday, by far. After we watch the Frick Park fireworks, and the various children are sent off to bed, Dad and I, my sister Carrie, and of course since she married into the family, Chrysamen as well, all gather in Dad's study, to talk a bit about what's happened in the last year, and what we hope will happen, and so forth. Sometimes it's been about dangers, and sometimes about opportunities, and most years, more often than not, it's just been a pleasant, satisfactory review of all the things that have gone right with our lives.

This time, though, I had a story to tell. Thanks to the short-term exchange they had granted me, so that I didn't have to be away from my timeline on a day-per-day basis, though I had experienced being away for about six weeks, including all the debriefing time at Hyper Athens, I had gotten back home only an hour after I'd left, on the third. Now I'd had a good night's sleep and a soothing family holiday, and was feeling rested and ready to talk. So I did, with

Chrysamen filling in many parts, because, of course, she knew much more of the story.

We talked for a long time, in the warm glow of Dad's study; in the lamplight, the sharp angles made the old pockmarks from the long-ago bullet holes more visible, and I tended to get lost in looking at them, and thinking, even after all these years and even with my very rewarding family life, how life might have been different if we'd seen the attacks coming.

"So that was really all it was," Dad said. "The old standard way of planting disinformation—have it carried by someone who believes it and will try to guard it. Neither Walks nor Mark knew that they were doing anything other than what they were ordered to do—but Ariadne Lao set Mark up with that escape device, so that when things got desperate enough, he'd 'accidentally' bounce right over to a major Closer military base. That must have caused some excitement."

"It did," I said, and described the situation of popping onto a runway with Walks naked, and then of massacring the population around the airport. "Anyway, the one thing that Lao didn't lie about," I said, "was about the amplification of the timeline-crossing shock wave. The Closers got a real good fix on that Draka timeline, I'm sure. And the Draka— if their physics is up to it—know where the Closers are, as well. I should have figured that that escape device couldn't possibly work the way they were describing it, anyway. Why have something that has to look for a safe place to set you down? Why not just design it to always take you somewhere safe?"

Dad nodded. "Because that's the basic technique for planting disinformation. Don't let anything that actually is important sound like it is. Lao gave you a plausible explanation for something you weren't supposed to need, and with so much else going on, you didn't worry about the fine details." He sighed and took a sip of brandy. "Anyway, as a guy who once followed the activities of a few espionage outfits, I have to admire this as a sheer piece of trade craft. How much of it did you know about, Chrys?"

"All of it, once Mark was already on his way," she said. "Always assuming they're not running some scam on me, as well. Ariadne Lao came and saw me ten minutes after Mark left. They sent Mark and Walks in there, deliberately vulnerable, and knowing full well that the Draka were apt to just grab them and try to extract intelligence information. They knew that Mark would get both of them out—they hoped, leaving the documents and a lot of hints behind—and that the device would take them *very* noticeably through Closer territory. The whole operation was one big setup to insure that the Closers and the Draka were going to find each other, and not in a friendly way . . . . "

My sister Carrie sat up a little straighter in her wheelchair. "But don't you have to worry about them allying with each other?"

Dad chuckled. "I suppose it's possible, but consider who's involved. Totalitarian states with a long record of treachery. Both eager to find whole timelines to enslave. The Closers were just hit with an unprovoked attack that apparently originated among the Draka; the Draka know that we're now hostile, and they think that Mark and Walks in His Shadow escaped into the Closer timeline. So my guess is that whichever side crosses over first will go in shooting."

Chrys beamed at him. "Not bad," she said. "But it's more than that. How will the Closers react to a threat like the Draka? They do know their limitations—they know that a slave society like theirs tends to stagnation. But they also know that when you're dealing with a secrecy-minded aggressive bunch of totalitarians, you need to be even more paranoid and secretive than they are. So they'll liberalize a few timelines, hoping that in those timelines they'll get some basic research done. And they'll tighten up in others, to make them better defended. Now you've got a crackdown in one part of the Closer domain, and a loosening up elsewhere . . ."

"Cultural drift and conflict, maybe leading to civil war?" Dad asked.

"Maybe. At least a lot of internal tension. Look, the Closers have been dependent on ATN for new technology for a long time, and essentially their whole system of a million timelines has been a parasite on the ATN system. A very costly, dangerous parasite. Well, we're giving them one of their own. The Draka probably only had a dozen timelines at the point where we introduced them, and they already seem to be stagnant, so we're giving them the chance to loot the Closers—after all, better them than us. Now either the Closers will wipe out the Draka menace, or—more likely—the Draka will bleed the Closers for centuries. Good for us, no matter how you look at it."

"Well, not quite good for everybody," I said, leaning back and taking another sip of brandy. "It's not really much fun to think of yourself as easily fooled—and to fool them, ATN had to fool both Walks in His Shadow and me. And then too, there's another little problem . . . Walks is married, you know, back in his timeline. I don't think his wife knows what he does for a living, but I bet she can spot guilt as well as any other woman. And Walks is pretty guilty about it all."

"Oh, I have faith in a trained agent," Chrys said, sitting on the arm of my chair. "He'll manage to lie well enough so that she doesn't have to know anything was amiss."

"I don't know." I put an arm around her and said, "If it had been me in his situation, could I have lied well enough to keep the secret from you?"

She shrugged. "But it wasn't. You never know what might have been, now, do you?"

Severna Park is the author of several SF novels, including *Speaking Dreams* and most recently *The Annunciate*, bold works which take the tropes of classic space opera and use them for profound meditations on power, sexuality, and the nature of human relations. Plus a cracking good story, of course!

In this little fable, Ms. Park shows the underside of the Domination, and how the plain fact and sanity of one timeline can become the paranoid fantasy of another.

THE PEACEABLE KINGDOM

Severna Park

What made Doctor Hamilton Guye's office different from the rest of the cardboard cubicles in the Police Psychiatric division were the paintings, his own paintings, hung on the walls. There were the small ones with the wide-eyed animals lying down together in a peaceful clump; lions, zebras, gazelles, all together by a silvery waterhole. Those were the ones he showed to his patients, like Rorschach ink blots, letting hardened criminals and first-time offenders wander through the fiction of a perfect world, while he waited to hear their impressions. The small ones were quick works—impressions of a peaceable kingdom, but his masterpiece—the one he used to calm himself while the murderers and rapists and robbers and lunatics hunched in the heavy wooden chair across the desk from him, was the big painting of Paradise on the opposite wall.

His patients sat with their backs to it, facing the white haze of Baltimore summers and the gray misery of Baltimore winters, while Hamilton only had to look over their shoulders to see golden rays of sun lying over lush jungle. Leopards, languid on high branches; elephants, quiet and hidden in the shade of vast palms. Lemurs and giraffes; eland and white herons. Here, the dark viridian green of ferns in the undergrowth. There, the bright vermilion where sun cut through the upper branches. While the rest of the department went to Tully's bar, down on St. Paul Street, Hamilton stayed focused, day after day, year after year, on his own inner visions.

One July afternoon, a police lieutenant brought him a prisoner. The prisoner was a young man, white, about thirty, with stiff black hair and flashing black eyes. He was shackled in a leather belt, with hands and feet chained. He had the look of an angry crow, thought Hamilton, and wondered how that kind of bird might fit in the upper right corner of the painting he was working on at home.

"Sit down," he said to the prisoner, who dropped into the wooden chair, facing the window.

The police lieutenant handed Hamilton a blue Psych Eval Request folder. "He's nuts," said the lieutenant. "Thought you should know." He glanced around the office, which only had enough wall space between the paintings for a bulletin board and a small table with a coffee pot. "You do all this stuff yourself?"

"Oh yes," said Hamilton.

The prisoner slumped in the chair, manacled hands between his knees. He didn't look at the paintings, or the torpid view out the window. Just the floor.

"We picked this joker up last night," said the lieutenant. "He was trying to break into a gun shop."

Hamilton opened the folder.

Name: Malik Rau.
Age: Unknown
Address: Unknown
Delusional, confrontational and violent. No
known prior convictions or arrests. No
known medical history.

"Thought he was a crackhead," said the cop. "He
was yelling his head off, trying to jump us. One guy,
five cops." He grinned and patted his nine millime-
ter. "Good joke, huh?"

"Good joke," said Hamilton.

"They did a blood test on him downstairs," said
the cop. "But there wasn't any crack in his system.
So we decided he wasn't a crackhead. Just nuts. So
now he's your problem."

"I guess he is," said Hamilton.

The lieutenant turned to go. "When you get done
with him, send the chains back downstairs, okay?"

"No problem."

The cop left and closed the door. Hamilton got up,
made himself a cup of coffee and sat down again. The
prisoner didn't move.

"Mister Rau," said Hamilton. "Would you like a cup
of coffee?"

"No," said Rau. He didn't say it like a Baltimore
native. He said *noh,* like a foreigner.

"Can you tell me where you live?" said Hamilton.

"No," said Rau.

"Can you tell me how old you are?"

"No."

"Can you tell me why you were trying to rob the
gun store?"

Rau just stared at the floor.

Ten minutes, thought Hamilton, and then he can
come up with some answers in the cellblock downstairs.
He let his eyes stray to the painting of Paradise on the
far wall of the office. There was a dark area at the

bottom left, which he had been thinking needed a dab of cerulean blue. Maybe he'd bring paint in tomorrow and fix it during lunch. He turned his attention back to the matter at hand.

"Mister Rau," he said. "I'd like to ask you some questions. Would that be all right?"

Rau shrugged.

Hamilton picked up a small framed painting from the top of his desk. This was one inspired by Rousseau; a man sleeping peacefully on the ground, approached by a lion. The colors were pure and fanciful. The man was deep in a dream. The lion looked curious, not hungry.

"Can you tell me what this picture is about?" said Hamilton.

Rau frowned and held the painting clumsily in both hands. His chains jingled as they moved.

"This is an innocent man who is oblivious to the dangers around him," he said.

Hamilton listened to the soft accent, unable to place it. Not British. Not quite Jamaican. Almost one of those west African dialect-accents, but this man was distinctly Caucasian. He looked almost Greek.

"Have you ever seen a lion?" said Hamilton.

"Yes," said Rau. "Many."

"In the zoo?" said Hamilton.

"No," said Rau. "I've slept out in the dirt like this, and they would come to see if they could eat you. But I never let them get this close."

Hamilton smiled. This was going to be a much easier evaluation than he had expected. Rau was projecting himself into the painting. His sense of reality was skewed in an almost textbook manner. "Where was this?"

"At home," said Rau. "Where the Draka are."

"The Draka?" said Hamilton. "Is that a kind of animal?"

"No," said Rau, and his face seemed to close. He

put the picture down and put his hands in his lap and didn't say another word. Finally Hamilton called the Psych department officers and had him taken to the holding cells on the first floor.

The next day, they brought Rau up in handcuffs, not shackles.

"Have you had anything to eat?" said Hamilton.

Rau nodded.

"Would you like some coffee?"

Rau gave the pot a longing look and Hamilton poured him a cup. "Would you like anything in it?" asked Hamilton.

"No," said Rau and took the cup in both hands like a child.

"I'd like to show you some more paintings," said Hamilton. "Would that be all right?"

"Yes," said Rau.

Hamilton took a painting down from the wall. This one was larger than the one inspired by Rousseau, although it had a few of the same elements. In this one, the sleeping man was surrounded by big cats—leopards, lions, cheetahs and a white tiger which Hamilton had painted in gleaming opaline. To Hamilton, the cats looked protective, but he had painted them so their teeth showed. He held the canvas where Rau could see it. "What do you think?" he said.

"I think you are an excellent painter," said Rau.

"Thank you," said Hamilton, "but what I meant was, what does the painting say to you?"

Rau hunched over the hot coffee and took a long time to answer. His eyes darted back and forth across the canvas as though searching for an escape for the sleeping man. "Why don't they kill him?" he whispered finally. "Is it because they want him to wake up and see them before they tear him to pieces?"

"Who?" said Hamilton.

"The cats of course," said Rau. "They will descend on him."

"Perhaps they're protecting him," said Hamilton, but Rau let out a bark of a laugh.

"The Draka only protect themselves," he said and then his eyes went wide. He shot to his feet, spilling the coffee all over the desk. "Are you with them?" he shouted. "Are you with them!"

Hamilton called security and they took Rau away, still screaming. Hamilton prescribed a tranquilizer, called in maintenance to clean up his office and went home early.

At home in his crowded apartment, he put on Chopin and the air conditioning and opened his paint box. The work on his easel was only halfway done. The preliminary sketch, done in broad strokes of burnt sienna over primed white canvas, showed a garden of Eden with a dove in one upper corner and a Rau-like crow in the other. Below, gazelle and wolves drank together from a sparkling fountain. Trees dotted the horizon and tiny wild roses filled the foreground. Rabbits and squirrels capered in the undergrowth. Hamilton stood pensively in front of the half-finished painting thinking that there needed to be more predators. He brushed in a hawk, circling, but the wings were wrong, making it look more like a vulture. He needed a picture to look at and put the brush down to search for his Peterson's *Field Guide to North American Birds*. In the section between "Smaller Wading Birds" and "Birds of Prey," his doorbell rang.

Through the peephole, he saw a tall, fair-skinned woman with a knot of red hair. She was wearing a suit and carrying a briefcase. The fisheye distortion of the peephole made her look odd—long-nosed, like a heron.

"Yes?" said Hamilton.

"I'm with the tenants' association," said the woman. "There's a meeting this weekend to discuss the rent increase."

"Rent increase?" said Hamilton.

"Twenty-five percent," said the woman. "Haven't you been reading the fliers in your mailbox?"

He couldn't recall a flier in his mailbox. He opened the door and the woman smiled, showing perfect white teeth. She stepped through the door without an invitation. Her perfume—or some indefinable odor—filled the air around him, subtle and predacious. She shut the door with her heel, dropped the briefcase and her false manner.

"Rau," she said in a low voice, which resonated in the spaces between his belly and scrotum. "Where is *Rau?*"

"R-r-rau?"

"We want him," she said. "He knows we're here. You'll bring him to us."

"Uh-us?" he echoed. She was taller, wilder. Her eyes were all pupil, focused on his tender organs. His heart hammered in his chest. His palms turned cold and wet. He felt like he would fall to the floor in a dead faint, and that she would stand over him until he woke up and agreed, or if he refused, she would smile with those teeth and tear him to shreds. He was the rabbit staring into the eyes of the lion. He was the bird on the edge of flight. He wanted to scream, but her presence overwhelmed any panicky sound he might make.

"Tomorrow," she said, "you'll bring him to the warehouse at 411 Center Street at three PM. You'll come alone. You'll drop him off and you'll leave. You understand?"

"Yes," he whispered.

"Very good. Remember the time. Remember the address."

"Yes," he whispered.

She picked up her briefcase, opened the door and left.

As her footsteps vanished down the carpeted hallway, he pushed the door shut, ever so quietly, and stood behind his deadbolts, breathing so hard he thought he might pass out. He went into the kitchen and opened the drawer where he kept the knives and his service revolver. He took out the gun, put it back and took out a cleaver instead. He went back to the room where the painting was, and slashed at it, breathless and silent until the false vision of the peaceful kingdom was nothing but a stained rag hanging in a wooden frame.

First thing in the morning, he went down to see Rau in the lockup and took him to a soundproof interrogation room.

Rau took a long look at him. "They came to see you."

"Yes."

"They know you have me in here."

"Yes."

"They want me back."

Hamilton nodded, dry-mouthed at the memory. He hadn't slept at all, and his body felt thick and heavy, lagging behind his racing mind. "I have to take you to them," he said. "I can't explain why. I'm sorry, but I have to."

Rau sat down at the battered interrogation table, which was stained with coffee and scattered with donut sugar. "They're different than us. They have different chemicals in their bodies. Pheromones. They affect you like a strong emotion you can't explain."

Hamilton nodded and sank into the other chair.

"When they talk, you can't argue," said Rau. "Did you feel that, too?"

"Yes."

"When do you have to do it?" he said.

"Three. This afternoon."

Rau put his palms flat on the dirty table. "I have friends who can help you. I was getting weapons for them when I was arrested. It's very important that I not go back with the Draka. We've been working a long time to fight them and now we're almost ready."

"How?" whispered Hamilton. "How can you fight that . . . that kind of *feeling*?"

"From a distance," said Rau. "With scopes and rifles. You understand? You have to help us now, because you understand."

He didn't understand. He could barely make himself talk about it. To think about the woman in his apartment made Hamilton want to break into helpless sobs. *Draka*. Was that the word that described this hollow terror?

"What do I have to do?" he said.

"First," said Rau, "you have to get me out of here."

That wasn't the difficult part. Rau's psychiatric evaluation made it easy for Hamilton to initiate a transfer to Behavioral/Criminal department at Shepherd-Pratt. Because of the urgency of Rau's condition, Hamilton's supervisor Okay'd immediate transport. When the prison van showed up at the station, Rau, shackled climbed in. Hamilton told the driver he had a phone call, and when the driver was out of sight, he got behind the wheel and slowly drove away. It was ten-thirty in the morning.

"Where to?" he said to Rau.

"Turn left," said Rau. "I'll tell you where to go."

They ended up on the west side of town, deep in the baking, ungentrified ruins of the old city. Treeless, lawnless brick rowhouses loomed on either side of the narrow street. Most of the windows were boarded. Those that weren't were dark, ominous, and

framed with broken glass. Now and then a stray dog
would trot across the littered street. Ravens topped
the high walls like gargoyles. There wasn't a human
being in sight.

Rau leaned forward, still chained in the back of
the van, separated from Hamilton by a layer of wire
mesh. "It's this block. The house with the blue door."

The house was just as deserted-looking as its
neighbors with boards over everything but the blue
door. The only difference was that instead of being
flanked on either side by other buildings, one side
faced an alley.

"Pull in there," said Rau.

There could be nothing more noticeable than a
police van in an area like this. Hamilton peered
around before he backed into the alley, which ended
fifty feet from the street in a pile of trash and scraggly
trees. This was heroin territory; crack-factory frontier. It was the part of police work he had avoided
for years by dealing with its denizens in his own
environment instead of plunging into theirs. The
Draka had scared him—surprised him—but the hidden inhabitants of this neighborhood were a known
and terrifying quantity.

"Are you sure we're in the right place?" he said.

"Positive." Rau shifted impatiently in his chains.
"Hurry up. We don't have much time."

The blue door was unlocked, which made Hamilton's
heart pound even harder. He'd brought his service
revolver, and clenched it in his sweaty hand. Rau
pushed the door open and let it swing inward. Except
for the spill of dull light through the front door, the
inside of the rowhouse was dark.

Rau said something in a language Hamilton didn't
recognize and a tall man with the same hair and
similar features as Rau stepped out of the shadows.
He was holding a gun that was almost as long as

his body, festooned with scopes and gadgets, like something out of a *Terminator* movie. He swung the gun up in an easy motion and aimed it right at Hamilton.

"No," said Rau in his soft accent. "This is a friend."

"Scan him," said the man with the gun, and two more men appeared silently from the darkness. They were as alike to each other as brothers, but it wasn't a family resemblance so much as a racial similarity. White men with Mediterranean features and West African accents. Hamilton tried hard to place the combination and simply couldn't. One of the men pointed a palm-sized device, about the same size and shape as a cell phone, in Hamilton's direction. He examined the tiny screen and gave his companions a quick nod. The three of them relaxed. The gun went down. Rau closed the door and lights came on.

Normally, rowhouses like this opened up into a small living room and dining room with a door at the far end for the kitchen. This one had been gutted to the plaster walls. In the middle of the former living space was a vehicle parked as though it was in a garage. At first glance, it looked like an ultra heavy-duty SUV, but on closer examination, Hamilton could see that it was armored. The front wheels were sheathed tires of some kind, and the back of the vehicle hunkered on distinctly tank-like treads. The front windshield was only a slit, and the tube-shaped sidelines were open in front, perforated along the tops, like machine-gun barrels. The cap on the back of the truck extended over the cab, where openings like air scoops lay on the roof over the slit windshield. Sharp metal cones peeked out of the openings and those were missiles, Hamilton realized. Whatever it was—tank, or truck, or the latest from Detroit—it was outfitted for war.

"You're going to fight the Draka with this?" he said.

At the word, *Draka,* the three men stiffened. Rau put

a finger over his lips. "Come upstairs," he whispered.
"I have to explain our situation to them."

Upstairs, the accommodations were Spartan and
temporary. There was a card table with half a dozen
folding chairs. Blankets and mattresses covered the
floor. It would have been a stopping place for the
homeless except for the guns in racks along the walls.

Rau and his companions spoke in low, urgent
voices while Hamilton sat in a chair and looked
around the room at the collection of firepower. Hand
guns, rifles, automatics and semiautomatics. Some
looked like Vietnam vintage, some he didn't recognize. The guns covered the walls like a museum
exhibit. He counted the folding chairs, counted the
men and counted the number of guns. He speculated
at the number of passengers the tank/truck downstairs
could hold, and came up with a sum total of utter
fear.

What did these men expect? That the Draka—that
woman in her heels and briefcase and frightening
attitude—would stride toward them through a hail of
bullets untouched? Did they imagine throwing down
gun after gun as they ran through boxes of ammunition until all they had left to blow her away were
the missiles from the top of the truck? How many
Draka were there? An image formed in Hamilton's
mind of an army of them, so many that an arsenal
like this would barely dent their ranks.

"What are they?" he blurted in the dim room.
"Where do they come from?"

The men, who had been talking in low voices,
stopped and turned to stare at him.

"They're a breed of human," said Rau. "*Homo
drakensis*. They're the future of this planet if we don't
stop them."

"The future?" echoed Hamilton.

"They're not from this time," said Rau, softly, as

though he was afraid of invoking evil spirits. "They've traveled here to find us, and we've traveled here to stop them from ever starting their Final Society."

"Traveled?" said Hamilton. "From . . . where?"

"From when," said Rau. "Not where. We're here to change the future. That's all you need to know."

Three o'clock came marching toward Hamilton with dogged determination, too slow and still too fast. At two-fifty-five, he was sitting in the police van in front of the warehouse at 411 Center Street, letting the engine idle as traffic rumbled past. Rau's voice was a tinny whisper through the clip in his ear.

"Can you see anything?" said Rau.

Hamilton shook his head, just a little. The warehouse was ordinary. The sign on the door said *MODERN PLASTICS.* There was no more hint of an infestation of Draka than there had been a suggestion of a tank housed behind the blue door on the west side of town. And where was the tank? He eyed the rearview mirror, but all he could see was a battered Chevy Nova parked behind him and the dirty glass front of an abandoned car dealership on the opposite side of the street. Rau's compatriots had made him leave first, but as he'd turned the corner, heading away from the blue door, there had been an unmistakable *thoom* of collapsing masonry, and he suspected that they had driven their tank right through the front wall.

He eyed the warehouse, dry in the mouth, hands sweaty on the steering wheel. What would the Draka woman do when she discovered that he hadn't brought Rau? He thought of his benevolent tiger painted in opaline shades and could only picture its gleaming teeth.

Three o'clock. His watch beeped twice.

"Get out of the van," said Rau.

"I can't," he whispered.

"Get out," snapped Rau. *If you don't, I guarantee they'll come and kill you."*

Hamilton took a breath and obeyed, almost too numb to feel his feet on the asphalt.

"Go to the door and knock twice," said Rau. *"When they ask, tell them I'm still in the van."*

Hamilton made his way to the door. The sidewalk glittered with shards of broken glass. Scraps of old newspaper lay limp in the heat. He came to the door and stopped. He raised his hand to knock in the worn place beside the sign, *Modern Plastics*, but the door opened before he touched it.

The Draka woman stood in a rush of cool air from inside. Her perfume. Her pheromones. Her breath of domination swirled around him. Hamilton steadied himself against the side of the building.

"Where's Rau?" she said.

"In the v-v-v-van."

She made a motion to someone behind her and a tall, elegant looking man stepped past her onto the heat of the sidewalk. His emanations were nothing compared to hers. His body language was docile, and he almost scampered to do what she told him. He was like Rau, Hamilton realized. He was a flunky, or worse, a slave.

The elegant man got to the van and peered through the window. Rau's tinny voice snapped in Hamilton's ear.

"Two steps back. NOW!"

Hamilton leaped backwards, eager to put as much distance between him and the Draka as possible. The elegant man turned to tell his mistress that there was no one in the van and at the same moment, the dirty plate glass window in the abandoned car dealership across the street shattered.

The tank erupted from the building in a cloud of glass and dust and smoke from the missile batteries over the cab. The missile arced over Center Street and

Hamilton had time to throw himself to the littered sidewalk. Traffic screeched to a halt as one of the missiles hit *Modern Plastics*. Hamilton curled away from the heat and noise of impact. Broken glass and mortar showered around him. The tank roared across the street and he looked over his shoulder long enough to see the police van tilt and crumple under its treads. The Draka was nowhere in sight. The tank fired again at point-blank range. *Modern Plastics* collapsed, roof-first, in a cloud of dirt and drywall plaster. Hamilton picked himself up, fighting the urge to run for his life. The dust fell in a gritty rain, and in the ruins of the building, he expected to see nothing but bent girders and torn bodies.

Instead, he could see some kind of metallic shielding flush with the ground and just visible through broken masonry and debris. It was immense, like the side of a barn. As Hamilton watched, it moved as though it was about to open. Wind blew grit across the broken sidewalk and Hamilton smelled the Draka—angry, present and very much alive. The hair on the back of his neck rose up. The tank's door swung open and Rau leaned out.

"Get in!" he yelled. "Hurry up!"

"You've killed them!" Hamilton shouted back, even though he knew it wasn't true.

"Get *in!*" shrieked Rau, and as he did, the metallic shielding in the ruins bulged upwards and parted.

Every instinct told Hamilton to run. His legs shook. His mouth was dry. His feet would have dashed off by themselves if they could. But as he stood there, frozen with the breath of awful terror that drifted up from the rising metal, he knew he could never outrun what was about to emerge. The instinct to flee would mean certain death. He ran for the tank and crawled in behind Rau, clumsy and awkward with fear. He glanced into the red-lit interior, expecting to see Rau's companions but the back of the tank was deserted except for an immense plastic container.

"Where the hell're your friends?" he shouted.

Rau was tensed over a joystick instead of a steering wheel. His right hand rested on a control panel blinking with red and green lights. He didn't take his eyes off the metal door, which had opened to an angle of about twenty-five degrees. Broken bricks slid off as it rose. Plaster dust and fractured floorboards surrounded it like a giant nest.

"Where *are* they?" demanded Hamilton.

"They're right behind us," said Rau in a low, hard voice and he indicated the passenger seat with a jerk of his head. "Sit." Hamilton obeyed, and Rau snared his hand with wire-hard fingers. He pressed Hamilton's thumb next to the biggest of the red-lit buttons on the control panel. "This is yours," he said without taking his eyes off the destruction in front of them. "When I tell you to push that, you *push.*"

"What is it?" said Hamilton.

Rau cocked his head toward the back of the tank where the plastic container hunkered in the dark. Hamilton knew without asking that it was a bomb. A big bomb. Probably big enough to blow Baltimore off the eastern seaboard.

"I can't—" he started to say, but the metal door in front of them was rising, opening onto a black space below the ground, an emanating darkness that clenched in his throat, in his gut. There were Draka down there—he could *feel* them—and all the punks and murderers and rapists in the world were angels in comparison. He held his thumb over the button, shaking harder than he'd ever shaken in his life. Rau touched a button and the tank shoved backwards as a missile shot away from the roof. The missile plunged through the metal door, leaving a ragged hole. A cloud of smoke blew out—but it was a thin cloud—as though the space below was big enough to absorb the rest of the smoke and the explosion. Rau made an adjustment and fired again. This time the metal door burst apart, leaving a smoky view of a wide, cratered ramp leading into an immense cavern. Rau punched the accelerator and the tank bolted forward.

Hamilton expected an army to meet them as the tank banged and jounced over what had been *Modern Plastics*, and held on to the edge of the hard seat with one hand as the tank bounded down the ramp. Rau snapped on a glaring halogen floodlight and the infested space beneath the block—the street—the *city*—leaped up in stark contrasts of black and white.

Like Hieronymus Bosch demons, the Draka minions swarmed below. Their weapons sliced blue swaths through the weird-lit dark as armies of them ran heedlessly into the rain of bullets from the tank and fell like cut wheat. The *budda-budda* of automatic weapons vibrated through the cab and bullets pinged off the windshield. Voices blared through a tiny loudspeaker while Rau shouted back in his own language. Hamilton turned in time to see one of Rau's compatriots gun down a horde of black-clad lackeys before being mowed down himself in a spray of blood and brain. They had to be lackeys, Hamilton told himself, because the overwhelming, doomish presence of the Draka was too faint.

The tank surged up a small incline, looming over the Draka slaves, plowing them down as though they were no more substantial than shadows. Their mouths opened in bellows of agony as they succumbed to bullets or the front wheels of the tank, but their shouts were drowned out inside of the tank by the noise of the engine and the rasping static of the radio. Even when Rau's second companion screamed into his microphone and the speaker went dead, Hamilton couldn't hear anything from outside, only the rumble within.

The tank lurched to the left. Abruptly there were

no more soldiers—nothing but a graded dirt roadway that led to some blurrily lit point in the near distance.

"Can you see that?!" shouted Rau. "Can you *see?*"

"What?" Was he supposed to press the button now? But Rau grabbed his wrist.

"Look!"

Now he could see it. In the distance, maybe a mile away, was a tower. It rose above everything else in a cocoon of gantries, harshly lit, like a rocket ready for a night launch.

"What is it?" Hamilton heard himself whisper, but Rau answered as if he'd spoken in a normal voice.

"It's a molehole," he said. "It's the tunnel between their world and yours." He let go of Hamilton's wrist and gunned the tank, faster and faster down the dark road.

For a minute, the road looked like a straight shot to the tower, but as they rumbled along, Hamilton could see silhouettes of entrenched defenses—cannon, he thought, and long, angular shadows of weapons he didn't recognize. *The future,* he thought. *Is this what it's going to look like?* He glanced at the bomb in the back of the tank and realized finally that Rau had volunteered him on a suicide mission, and the future, for him at least, would only be the length of time it took to get to the end of this dark and foreign road.

Rau took a sharp breath. "Can you smell them?" He hissed and stabbed a button on his console. Hamilton sniffed, but his heart was racing and he was breathing too fast to smell much of anything. A whiff of ozone caught him by surprise, deadening the pheromonic fears in his gut and he realized that the odor masked what he'd been aware of on a subconscious level.

Draka.

He stared out the window as the tank jerked and roared over the uneven terrain. They were out there—

maybe dozens if not hundreds of them—waiting behind batteries of guns, or ready to step forward with their tiger teeth and overwhelming smiles.

Draka.

"How many do you think there are?" he said.

"They never send more than two or three on missions like this," said Hamilton. "Their slaves do all the work. That's why we even have a chance."

"Were you a slave?" said Hamilton.

"I was *servus* since I was born," hissed Rau. "Not anymore." He stabbed the ozone button again and again until the stink filled Hamilton's nose and mouth.

How did you get away? Hamilton wanted to know, but he didn't get a chance to ask. Rau gunned the engine and the tank bolted forward. Blades of blue light swung down like swords from overhead artillery. They traced across the hood of the tank and Rau swerved. The tank blundered as explosions ripped the road, blue flashes muffled by the engine and Rau's furious bellow. He dodged recklessly around sudden gaping holes and the tank banged and groaned as he manhandled it through spews of dirt. Hamilton kept his finger poised over the red bomb-button, his hand so stiff, it was cramping. He made a fist and held it over the button, keeping his eyes on the harsh lights of the distant gantry, which loomed over them now, so close and tall, he could no longer see the top of it through the windshield.

A barricade rose in front of them, lined across the top with men and artillery. Bright blue light washed across the hood and touched the windshield. The intensity half-blinded Hamilton and he threw his arm up to cover his eyes. The tank blundered and coughed and Hamilton felt the front end buckle as a tire blew despite its sheathing. Rau let out an animal cry and punched the accelerator to the floor. The high but-tressed wall of Draka slaves and unrecognizable guns towered over them. Hamilton braced himself and the

tank slammed against the wall. Rau hunched over his
joystick, teeth clenched, forcing the engine, his face
stained by red and green lights. The treads spun. The
metal body groaned. For a moment, everything seemed
suspended in the darkness, an impending disaster at
pause for a single, fragile second. Then Rau jabbed
a button on the control panel and launched the last
missile at point-blank range.

The wall of men and artillery vanished in a blinding
burst of light and heat. It resonated through the tank,
through the ground, and into the roots of Hamilton's
teeth. It made hot images inside his eyelids and when
he could see again, Rau was driving, gunning the tank
through twisted metal and ruined weaponry and barely
recognizable bodies, heading for the gantried tower.

Now we've had it, thought Hamilton. "Where are
they?" he said, and peered into the lights for some
trace of even bigger guns, with all available Draka
closing ranks to kill them once and for all.

"Can't you smell them?" hissed Rau.

Hamilton breathed deep, but he could not. The
ozone stink in the cab overwhelmed everything. He
glanced at Rau, whose face was bathed in sweat. He
was gripping the joystick with both hands holding it
with grim determination, as though it was burning his
palms. The light from the molehole tower bathed his
face in garish shades of black and white, but his eyes
were huge and his pupils wide, despite the glare. To
Hamilton's amazement, Rau let the tank roll to a stop.

"What're you doing?" whispered Hamilton.

Rau gave him a wild, harried look. "You can't smell
them."

"No—how can *you?*"

"I'm bred for them," said Rau. "You're not." He
shoved himself out of the driver's seat and grabbed
Hamilton, pulling him toward the joystick. "You have
to drive. You understand? You *have* to."

"But I don't know—I mean where the hell are we

going?" Hamilton slid behind the joystick. The seat felt hot and damp with sweat. He found the accelerator with his foot. The tank jerked and roared when he touched it, as responsive as an expensive sports car.

Rau pointed to a dark opening in the tower's floodlit exterior. "There," he said in a dull voice. "We're going in there." He made a fist and held it over the bomb-button. The fist shook like a leaf in a strong wind. "Go," whispered Rau. *"Go!"*

Hamilton drove. The tank leaped forward as he leaned over the joystick. The deflated front tire made it difficult to steer but not impossible. He leaned against the pull and aimed the tank at the opening, which, he could see now was as big as the side of a barn. He had time to wonder if the tank was out of bullets as well as missiles before they surged into the bowels of the tower.

Dirt road turned to smooth pavement. The tank's lurching gait evened out into a bumpy ride. Hamilton craned his neck to see out the gritty windshield. Ahead and above them, some Frankensteinian mechanism rose through the interior of the tower, cupped in a curve of white walls which rose like a second sky. The machinery wound upwards like a twisted ladder from the bottom of this immense well. A molehole? Aptly named, thought Hamilton, and glanced ahead to see the Draka.

Three of them, all in black, standing between the tank and the molehole machinery.

Two women and a man. Five hundred meters away, Hamilton felt as though he could see every feature, every hair on their heads, every wrinkle of bad intent around their mouths. He could see how beautiful they were, how gentle they could be. He could almost smell . . . .

"Drive!" yelped Rau. "Just drive!"

Hamilton shoved the accelerator to the floor and

the tank lurched forward, bumbling on its deflated wheel, faster and faster. The scent of flowers filled the cab, and he heard Rau take a gasping breath. With only a few hundred meters between them and the tank, the Draka, dead ahead, didn't budge.

What in heaven's name are you doing? said a kindly, concerned voice inside Hamilton's head, and the flower scent turned thicker.

Was that how they really sounded? thought Hamilton in surprise. How could he run down a being so gentle?

"Drive!" cried Rau, and huddled in his seat, fists pressed against his face, knees against his chin. "Drive!"

Hamilton looked down at his foot where it pressed the pedal to the floor. The smell in the cab changed ever so slightly to ferns and damp woodlands and he thought of the painting he'd torn to pieces at home after *she* had set foot in his apartment. He thought of the delicate flowers he'd spent hours feathering with the brush, and the lion lying peacefully in the shade. He thought of *her* and how she'd showed him the true face of his painted predators.

He looked up.

The Draka still hadn't moved. Beside him, Rau let out a sob of real anguish. The space between the tank and the smiling, black-clad tigers closed with dreamlike slowness. He could see their eyes now, brown and placid, so harmless when you saw them up close.

Stop, said the voice in his head.

"Stop," croaked Rau in the passenger seat. *"Stop!"* he shouted, and as the tank bore down on the immovable Draka, he screamed it, *"STOP!"* Hamilton pressed hard on the pedal and squeezed his eyes shut.

Did they leap aside, or was the clattering unevenness under the front tires made when he'd run them over, three at once? Hamilton had no idea, and there were no rearview mirrors to check the damage, but the voice in his mind vanished, and the smell of flowers in the cab abruptly seemed stale. He looked at Rau, and was amazed to see tears streaming down his face.

"Did I kill them?" demanded Hamilton, but Rau didn't say anything, just pointed to a red rectangle, directly under the climbing ladder of machinery and in the very center of the tower's floor.

"Hurry," he panted. "Before they realize what's happening."

Did the floor shake? Did the air seem to tremble? Hamilton aimed the tank for the red rectangle, even though he couldn't quite focus on it. A side effect of the Drakan pheromone attack, he thought and blinked hard to clear his vision, but the rectangle quivered before him like a mirage.

"What the hell?" he said and glanced at Rau for an explanation, but Rau was tapping buttons on the control panel. The quivering air thickened and Hamilton felt his stomach lurch. The tower itself seemed to vibrate. "What the hell's happening?" demanded Hamilton. He hit the brakes, but the tank rumbled forward without hesitation.

Rau reached behind him to make some adjustment to the bomb. Hamilton heard the casing snap, like a suitcase opening. "Now," Rau said in an almost reverent whisper, "you'll get a chance to see their world."

The front wheels of the tank touched the edge of the rectangle and Hamilton realized it wasn't a part of the floor at all. It was a hole. A *deep* hole. A deep *red* hole that plunged straight down to a distance he couldn't even judge.

The tank tipped forward. Hamilton let out a yell. Rau punched the red bomb-button and the top of the tank flew open. As the bomb ejected, Hamilton felt a weird surge of relief that they would fall away safely from the explosion and that this wasn't a suicide mission at all, but Rau's words echoed in his head— *their* world—and his heart contracted with terror.

He felt it when the bomb went off. Not a blast or a noise or even a feeling of being pushed from behind. He just *knew*, and as they fell through the expanse of red space, he could sense the tower collapsing, the disintegrating tangle of machinery—maybe even the parts of Baltimore above the Drakan burrows falling like some unlikely and unexplainable earthquake. He squinted at the thinning scarlet outside, and realized they were no longer underground. The were airborne, high in dense clouds.

"The molehole," said Rau. "It's falling in behind us."

"The bomb destroyed it?" said Hamilton. "But where are we now?"

"We're following the distortion in space and time—the hole—to its destination," said Rau, and he took a ragged breath. "You've saved your planet," he said. "You should be proud."

Hamilton peered out the window. Now he could see a wide sweep of grassy plains below them, and snowcapped mountains. The tank was descending, but not in an uncontrolled way. A shadow crossed his face and he glanced up to see stubby wings extending from behind the cab. He looked down again. Pristine rivers cut the side of a mountain. He could see a waterfall arcing down a green cliffside, limned with rainbows.

"This is *their* world?" he whispered.

Rau nodded wearily.

The tank-plane—whatever it was—swept lower over another wide savannah, and Hamilton could see animals. Horses, he thought, and marveled at the size of the wild herd as it galloped through lush grass. Then he thought he saw riders, but that wasn't right either. The bodies of the men and women and cavorting children emerged from where the horse's necks should have been. The riders and the horses were one being. *Centaurs* he thought in utter astonishment and stared until the herd was well behind them and his neck hurt from twisting at such an awkward angle.

"I just saw *centaurs*," he said to Rau, who just nodded, like this was nothing worth commenting on.

The tank swooped lower. They flew over a large watering hole filled with hippos, surrounded by zebras, punctuated at a distance by content-looking lions. The surreality and at the same time, the familiarity of the scene struck Hamilton like a blow to the chest. It could have been one of his paintings, spread out below in flesh and fur, water and mud.

He wanted to ask Rau where these creatures had come from, and how African animals and mythical beasts could coexist, or exist at all on what was supposed to be an alien planet as far as he knew, but the tank rushed over a pine forest, descended into a valley, and that was when Rau sat up straight. He broke into a relieved grin and pointed at the column of rising smoke in the distance.

"Look," he said. "The Samothracians are here."

In the valley, the remains of a village burned and smoked. Hamilton had a clear view of the human bodies scattered on the cobbled walks, blood draining down the hill in dark rivulets. The largest of the burning buildings was a tower, just like the one buried in the bowels of Baltimore, and it had crumbled to half its height. Gleaming winged vehicles, about the size of a small airplane swooped around the tower and cruised just above the ground, strafing survivors with startling blue bolts of light.

"What's going on?" he said. "The Draka did this?"

Rau shook his head. "This was a *servus* village. They were the molehole engineers. They're loyalists. They couldn't be spared. They would have fixed everything we destroyed."

He tapped the controls and the tank descended on its stubby wings, angling lower over the decimated houses and dead bodies. Hamilton could see children, limp on the ground like they were sleeping. There was a dead dog. Here was a roofless house with a garden in back. Someone had painted a mural on the back wall of the yard and Hamilton got a glimpse of it as the tank angled for a landing.

A black lion and a lamb with a curly white coat lay together in a bed of red roses, watching each other warily with the unmistakable expressions of predator and prey. Even from a distance Hamilton thought the work had the look of ironic parody. He glanced into the distance where the centaurs and lions and gazelles frolicked beyond the hills, then back to the blackened remains of the town below.

Not a peaceable kingdom in sight. Not now. Not ever.

The following excerpt is from

THE INDEPENDENT COMMAND

by James Doohan & S.M. Stirling

available in hardcover from Baen Books
November 2000

PROLOGUE

Excarix entered the presence of his queen with terror thrumming in his thorax. Like all queens Syaris was easily twice as large as he was, her pedipalps capable of severing his head from his body in one neat snip, her temperament such that this was an all too likely conclusion to any interview. Therefore the abject fear instinctive in a male of his species when approaching the most puissant female of the clan was greatly increased.

Over time he had, perforce, learned to ignore his feelings. But a private audience, like this one, arranged for a male of no consequence, like himself, strengthened his terror almost to the point of pain.

Yet no sign of his turmoil was apparent. He moved with solemn dignity, holding his pedipalps in a position of worshipful subservience.

Syaris seemed unaware of him as she idly stroked

a writhing, silk wrapped bundle suspended from the ceiling. That she was not hungry was apparent to Excarix by scent. But not to the bound prey that mewled in terror as she tapped its cocoon to make it spin.

As he drew near to her desire grew in him and added its own rhythms to the disturbance within.

So beautiful, he thought as the power of her phero-mones began to work on him.

It was not merely the influence of her scent that made him find her ravishing. By the standards of his species the young queen was indeed very lovely. The exquisite shape of her head at the end of her unusually long and graceful neck, the subtle shadings of her gleaming, reddish-brown body, the slender length of her legs, the charming placement of her eyes—especially the anterior dorsal pair, the "gates of the soul" as the poets put it—all this made her a bewitching sight.

At this point he would have found it very difficult to withdraw from her presence, even if he were actively threatened.

She wants me, he realized in dawning joy, and felt distant surprise. For he knew that she had been trained by her mother queen to have great control over the passion inducing secretions. The release of these particular pheromones implied permission to approach the queen and receive one of the highest honors a male could achieve.

The simple privilege of mating with a female so beautiful was worth aspiring to. But to deposit his seed with the *queen*! He had plans and hopes, of course he did, but there was no reason at this juncture for her to anticipate and agree to them. Even in his own somewhat arrogant estimation he had not earned such an honor.

And yet ... by his own unmistakable reaction she was deliberately arousing him.

Excarix struggled to maintain his impassive appearance even as her scent caused his throat sac to swell with sperm. He struggled to resist the urge to stroke her slender body and to spin silk around her delicate limbs.

Excarix stopped at a respectful distance from the queen and lowered his fore-body submissively.

After a few more spins of her bundled prey she turned her gleaming eyes upon him.

"Yes?" she asked in a voice both musical and indifferent.

Excarix rose to a speaking position.

"It has begun, my queen," he said, noting with dismay the lustful depth of his voice.

The queen's chelicerae adopted a position of pleased amusement.

"Our forces are . . ." he said, his voice trailing off helplessly. He struggled to maintain his focus, to dispense his message with appropriate dignity.

"Come closer," Syaris purred. "I would see you better."

He approached, embarrassed to hear his breath hissing audibly. Inhibition slipped away like illusion. Without her permission he reached forward and stroked the delicate down on one of her legs.

She made a pleased, sighing sound. "Closer," she invited.

With a nimble leap Excarix found himself upon her back, stroking her abdomen with all of his limbs. All thought of restraint was forgotten as his spinneret whipped back and forth, spinning strands of silk to bind her to him.

"Bold," she cooed and fell onto her side, allowing him freer access to her larger body.

Disbelief prompted him to caution and he rose over her, slowly, so as not to startle. Carefully, carefully Excarix stroked her tender underside, moving ever closer to the dainty hairs of her genital opening, just below the juncture of her last pair of legs. Syaris hissed her pleasure and with this encouragement he moved forward. Using the very points of his clawed hand he traced the outline of the inviting, forbidden zone. Boldly he reached out and sank the sharp tip of one claw into the tender inner flesh.

The queen's legs thrashed helplessly, then began to stroke his back as she encouraged him with a wordless murmuring. He continued to stroke and tickle her as he gathered a droplet of his sperm in his chelicerae. She opened to him and he leaned forward, intoxicated by her scent.

Excarix struck the wall with great force. For a stunned moment he feared that he might have cracked his chitin. Then she was upon him, his slender neck held in her powerful pincers.

"Ambitious!" she sneered, her chelicerae still showing pleased amusement. "But as yet you've done nothing to make you worthy of such an honor, have you, Third Minister?"

"I . . . I apologize for offending your majesty," Excarix stammered. "I misunderstood."

"Y-esss, you did misunderstand, Third Minister." She straightened, lifting the smaller male by his neck. "You were being invited to give me pleasure. And you gave me precious little of it before you made a grab for what you wanted, didn't you?"

"I was foolish, Majesty, I am truly sorry to have offended you."

"You have done worse than offend me, worm." She dropped him in contempt. "You have disappointed me."

She slashed him several times with her tailwhip, each strike depositing a healthy dose of acid on his chitin. The humiliation was worse than the pain.

"Leave me," she said, turning her back on him. "I don't want to see you again until you are whole."

Excarix slunk from the room, smoke writhing

around the holes in his carapace. It would be months before he would be allowed into her glorious presence again. And he had not delivered his message.

CHAPTER ONE

Commander Peter Ernst Raeder gazed contentedly at the scenery flashing by, sipped his perfectly chilled champagne, stretched out his long legs and crossed them at the ankles.

The mag-lev train on which he was a passenger was an antique, a feature of travel on Come By Chance, and the most luxurious method of travel he'd ever sampled. The extra cost of first-class private accommodations was well worth the money. The seats were wide and comfy, the leg room ample, the windows enormous and the company . . . Raeder glanced at Lieutenant Commander Sarah James and caught her watching him instead of the lush mountains they traveled through.

He smiled, she smiled; warm, fuzzy, blissful, idiot happiness infused the air. Raeder could care less about anything just now but the rightness of things as they currently stood between him and Sarah James of the rich russet hair, the smooth lips, the . . .

They clinked glasses and gave each other the conspiratorial grins of people in love. The glorious

forest-meadow-mountain vistas of Come By Chance
came in a poor second to the limitless horizons they
saw in each other's eyes. The scent of pine and spring
flowers went by unnoticed.

Suddenly Peter began to chuckle.

"What?" Sarah asked.

"Oh, it's just that this," he gestured around him
with his glass, ended by tipping it in her direction,
"is a switch."

Sarah gave him a look of smiling confusion.

"A switch from what?" Her eyes betrayed the flash
of thought, *Us?*

"I'm not under suspicion, on suspension or awaiting
trial." He leaned in closer. "Or alone." Her lips
twitched in acknowledgement. "In fact," Peter continued, leaning back with a slightly smug smile tugging at his lips, "everything is going incredibly
smoo—"

There was a jerk, and the ear-torturing, inhuman
screech of metal scraping against metal with phenom-
enal force. Raeder and Sarah were shaken and tossed
like dice in a box, flung back and forth against each
other and the sides of the compartment. The bellow
of ripping steel struck the ear like a blow; so loud
that Raeder couldn't hear his own voice when he
shouted Sarah's name. . . .

Things are back to normal, he thought. *All screwed
up.. And here I thought the gods had relented.*

Memory scrolled through his mind. He hoped it
wasn't the end-of-life flashback you were supposed
to get; at least it wasn't his whole life. Just the start
of his latest planetside leave. . . .

Raeder gripped his carryall a little tighter and
squared his jaw. He exited the tiny shuttle to find
himself at a landing area so small it barely existed,
just a circle of cerement large enough to hold the
shuttle and a few antennae. He walked towards the

security shack, which was no more than a roofed cubicle for the soldier on duty, and handed over his ID and Dr. Pianca's invitation. With a wordless salute the soldier took them and began inputting a query.

It had been a brief and uneventful trip from Marjorie Base, on Come By Chance's lone moon, to Camp Seta, Star Command's hospital/convalescent center on CBC itself. Raeder would have welcomed a delay somewhere along the line, but wheels had turned with miraculous smoothness and here he was in incredibly short order. Luckily, he was completely superfluous on the *Invincible* while the dockyard crews worked her back up—a fact that they'd made abundantly plain.

The guard in the security shack handed back Peter's documents with another salute and Raeder walked out into the open. The warm, moist air held a delicate scent of spices and flowers, making it a pleasure just to breathe.

Peter gazed about himself. The camp was set in a verdant valley cupped between craggy, snow-capped mountains, under a clear sky full of wings—most too far away to show that they were scaly leather instead of feathers—and it had an aura of serenity about it. The buildings were sleek and modern with large windows and colorful native woods bright against the white stucco architecture. Each ward-complex had its own unique fountain and brightly flowered courtyard. The foothills beyond were lush with tropical vegetation; many of the trees were a species of giant bromeliad and the colors varied from a green so deep it was almost black to hot pink, deep red, rusty orange and good old Earth green. Beyond the buildings, just visible between two low, green hills, the hint of a lake sparkled, fed by a waterfall that leapt from stone to stone down a tall, narrow cliff in a glittering white cascade.

As though resisting the charm of this place a vague

anxiety stirred within him concerning duties left unfinished on the severely damaged *Invincible. Belay that,* he ordered himself. *You've left Main Deck in very competent hands.* Now what did he do about his anxiety in regard to this visit?

Sarah James' doctor, Regina Pianca, had called and invited him to visit her. "She says she misses your sparring matches," the doctor explained with a smile.

The physical or the verbal ones? Raeder had wondered.

But just the idea of visiting Camp Seta, universally known in the service as Camp Stick 'Em Together Again, gave him the collywobbles.

Spent too much time getting repaired at one of these myself, he thought.

Which was true, but unreasonable in this case. He wouldn't be visiting Sarah in the burn ward, covered with pink, regenerating goo. He wouldn't see her in the reconstruction section, struggling to master a new electronic limb. He'd be visiting her in the psych unit.

Well . . . maybe that's what really has me scared. The doctor hadn't gone into detail regarding Sarah's problems. But the fact that her physician was making the invitation seemed ominous to Raeder.

When she'd shipped out for Camp Seta Sarah was holding herself together by sheer willpower. The Mollies hadn't had her in their hands long, but it had been more than long enough to torture her.

Raeder remembered the last time he'd seen her—she'd smiled at him, her voice had been controlled, her hand steady as she saluted the captain. But her eyes had told a different story; wide and shocked and wild. It made him glad that Star Command policy was to send anybody recovered from Mollie captivity for psych evaluation.

He looked forward to seeing her; he dreaded seeing her.

Dr. Pianca had told him that they'd taken Camp

Seta over from a very exclusive spa. "No sense in trying to keep it open with the wartime travel restrictions in place," she'd said. "The environment is wonderful for the patients, and the Commonwealth is paying the owners a pretty good rent."

Raeder noticed that each building was so positioned that it would be difficult, if not impossible, to see into another's windows.

Leave it to rich people to insure their privacy, he thought.

"Commander Raeder?"

Peter turned to find a young medic at his elbow.

"Warren Bourget," he said and held out his hand. "Welcome to Camp Seta."

Civilian, Raeder thought.

"Where's Doctor Pianca?" Peter asked, shaking Bourget's hand.

"Unfortunately she's been delayed by an emergency, Commander. I'll show you to your quarters and give you an escorted tour, if you'd like, while you're waiting."

Raeder struggled against imagining the type of emergency a psych specialist would have.

"When do I get to see Lieutenant Commander James?"

"Ah, well, Dr. Pianca would prefer to brief you before you actually see the patient," Bourget said with a smile.

Raeder's features hardened.

"Why, is there a problem?"

"No, no, Commander. I should more properly have said, *debrief* you, sir. Then, when you've spoken to the lieutenant commander, the doctor will want to interview you again. It's standard procedure, nothing more, I assure you."

Raeder gave him a look. Then smiled and nodded.

"If you'll show me to my quarters," he said affably, "I'll just unpack and then maybe wander around for awhile. Then I'll check back to my quarters to see if you've left me a message. How's that sound?"

Bourget hesitated.

"Very well, Commander, that sounds fine. I'd just like to caution you that Doctor Pianca would like to speak to you before you see her patient."

"I'll bear that in mind," Raeder murmured.

The preceding excerpt is from
The Independent Command,
available in hardcover from
Baen Books, November 2000.

Got questions? We've got answers at

BAEN'S BAR!

Here's what some of our members have to say:

"Ever wanted to get involved in a newsgroup but were frightened off by rude know-it-alls? Stop by Baen's Bar. Our know-it-alls are the friendly, helpful type—and some write the hottest SF around."
>   —**Melody L** *melodyl@ccnmail.com*

"Baen's Bar . . . where you just might find people who understand what you are talking about!"
>   —**Tom Perry** *perry@airswitch.net*

"Lots of gentle teasing and numerous puns, mixed with various recipes for food and fun."
>   —**Ginger Tansey** *makautz@prodigy.net*

"Join the fun at Baen's Bar, where you can discuss the latest in books, Treecat Sign Language, ramifications of cloning, how military uniforms have changed, help an author do research, fuss about differences between American and European measurements—and top it off with being able to talk to the people who write and publish what you love."
>   —**Sun Shadow** *sun2shadow@hotmail.com*

"Thanks for a lovely first year at the Bar, where the only thing that's been intoxicating is conversation."
>   —**Al Jorgensen** *awjorgen@wolf.co.net*
